EMMA BABBINGTON is a London-born, Sydney-based journalist and is currently news editor for Australia's bestselling weekly magazine, *Woman's Day*, where she heads up the real life and crime section.

The Neighbours

EMMA BABBINGTON

H Q

ONE PLACE. MANY STORIES

HQ
An imprint of HarperCollins*Publishers* Ltd
1 London Bridge Street
London SE1 9GF

www.harpercollins.co.uk

HarperCollins*Publishers*
Macken House, 39/40 Mayor Street Upper,
Dublin 1 D01 C9W8
This edition 2025

1

First published in Great Britain by HQ,
an imprint of HarperCollins*Publishers* Ltd 2025

ISBN: 9780008764463

Printed and bound in the UK using 100% Renewable
Electricity by CPI Group (UK) Ltd

MIX
Paper | Supporting
responsible forestry
FSC
www.fsc.org
FSC™ C007454

To Dad aka Mike aka Papa

Before

MEREDITH

January 1989

That summer, Meredith watched their house every night. She watched their comings and goings, the dinner parties they threw, the evenings spent watching telly with the windows thrown wide open and the real and canned laughter drifting across the road to where she stood, underneath the fig tree.

And throughout those warm Sydney evenings, she learnt the family inside was everything hers wasn't. They had an abundance of friends, enjoyed light entertainment and game shows on the TV, never ate with dinner on their knees in front of it and rarely, if ever, before 8.30 at night. They were, Meredith concluded just a few days into her observations, a sophisticated family but also a boisterous one full of love and laughter and fun.

She was wildly envious.

They were also quite obviously theatrical. Meredith felt as though she was watching a performance as the parents frequently gesticulated as they spoke, the father often standing up, pacing or stabbing at the air when he was in the midst of an impassioned exchange.

The mother, meanwhile, was exotic and beautiful in a way that transfixed Meredith. She had a way of throwing her head back when she was laughing and lightly touching her sternum which appeared sophisticated and almost balletic. Meredith studied how the mother would position herself by the window when she smoked a cigarette but appeared not to notice, or care, when the smoke billowed back inside. She seemed so free and without everyday concerns.

Then Meredith would watch the daughter and try to imagine herself in the girl's place.

As she stood under the fig's knotty branches that spread out across the road and were filled with feasting bats during these summer nights, Meredith would picture herself sitting in the girl's spot at the dining table. She would imagine what it would be like when the father placed a hand on her own shoulder and gave it a gentle squeeze, or the mother smiled fondly in her direction or beckoned her over for a kiss before she disappeared upstairs to her cosy bedroom. It would be lovely.

And as she stood there, sometimes for up to an hour, sometimes for just a few brief minutes, Meredith would breathe in the sweet scent of rotting figs scattered on the pavement below while the noisy squawks above filled her ears, and would will herself to cross the road.

All she needed was to summon the courage to knock on the front door. To lift the shiny brass knocker and tap, tap, tap, until one of them opened it and, smiling, stepped to the side and gestured her in.

Because once she managed that simple action, Meredith was almost certain the family would welcome her into the fold and into their lives with open, loving arms.

Then they would listen to what she had to say and surely make it all better.

Chapter 1

LIV

Thursday, 30 January 2025

Liv watches the immovable dog. Sophie is doing her usual trick of lying diagonally, almost splayed out in the open doorway, so half her body's inside the house, the rest on the veranda. Liv gives her belly a gentle nudge with her bare foot, but the Labrador's head sinks to the ground and her eyes slowly close. It is time for her morning walk, but Sophie is old and tired and it seems she has already done her business so now has no impetus to rouse herself and go out into the already scalding hot day.

'Come on. Time for a walk,' Liv says, but she doesn't sound convincing to even her own ears. And the dog appears to be asleep and, really, Liv can't blame her.

It is one of those unbearably muggy Sydney summer mornings when the air feels heavier with moisture than oxygen. Tropical downpours on and off during the night have done nothing to lower the heat, and Liv's work clothes – shorts and a synthetic T-shirt, suitable for the physio clinic – already feel hot and scratchy and are sticking to her damp skin.

A door creaks at the end of the long, dimly lit corridor of the single-storey terrace and Liv turns to see Gracie emerge from her room, wrestling with her tote bag, pushing her laptop inside and not looking up as she heads towards Liv and the door.

'Sorry,' she says. 'I took her out for a pee earlier.'

Liv wants to remind Gracie that they'd all agreed not to do that unless they had time to take the dog for a proper walk but something about her daughter's stiff body language stops her.

'Did you go for a run?' Liv asks, although she knows her daughter did thanks to her still-pink cheeks. Gracie may be tall and dark-haired like Andy but she has inherited Liv's fair skin tone which means it takes ages to calm down after exertion.

'Yeah,' Gracie says as she pulls on her Converse.

'Wasn't too wet?' The rain had woken Liv at 1 a.m. and her first thought had been: *I hope Gracie doesn't go for a run in the morning, she could slip.* 'I don't know how you run in this heat.'

'It's fine.' Gracie ties her laces, her bag slipping briefly to the ground and it's not until she straightens up, readjusting herself, that Liv gets a full view of her daughter's face and sees eyes that are puffy and bloodshot.

'You okay? Bad night's sleep?'

But Gracie has already climbed over the dog, has her AirPods in and is almost gone.

'I'm fine,' she repeats and is down the front steps before Liv can tell her to wait. 'See you later.'

She moves swiftly down the path and then in a metaphorical puff of smoke, Gracie is gone and Liv is left with that familiar feeling of unresolved concern that will remain in place until she next sees her daughter or, as is more likely, Liv texts to check the nineteen-year-old is okay and gets, at the very most, a 'heart' reaction in response.

Liv stands in place for a few moments, then, before she can think better of it, slips into her Birkenstocks and climbs over Sophie. She picks her way down the path until she is standing on the pavement, squinting against the sun to see her daughter's retreating figure as it rounds the corner. But she is too late.

Liv is turning to go back inside when she sees the police car. Two police cars, in fact, parked up opposite, outside her neighbours Sandra and Richard Wellington's house. A uniformed officer stands by their gate.

The Wellingtons' house is the largest, smartest and, even in a suburb where there is almost constant building and redeveloping and landscaping, the most frequently renovated property on their street. Its paint-fresh creamy-white facade gleams in the sun. Two blooming potted frangipani trees sit on either side of the front stone steps like sentries, as if greeting the suited man who has just exited the front door. The man is grave-faced as he talks briefly with the uniformed officer and then turns to go back inside. Alarmed at what might be going on, Liv keeps watching as the uniformed officer slides a phone from his pocket and turns away from the road with it clamped to his ear.

'What's going on?'

The words echo her own internal dialogue as Liv realises her husband's standing next to her. Andy is finally dressed, in shorts and T-shirt, but still bleary-eyed and unshaven, a slice of half-eaten toast in hand and a reluctant Sophie trailing behind him.

'Was there a break-in?'

'Don't know,' she replies. 'Looks more serious than that.'

The uniformed officer is back to his position at their neighbours' gate, his face giving nothing away.

'Shall I ask him?' Andy says, taking a step towards the road, where steam is rising as the heat burns off the rain from earlier.

'God, no. Anyway, they won't tell you.'

Undeterred, Andy looks along the street for someone else who might be able to explain what's going on. A neighbour three doors down, whose name Liv doesn't know because he and his wife moved in only before Christmas, is corralling his young children into an enormous black car. Andy walks over to him before Liv can tell him not to.

She watches as the man's arm drops and the small yellow backpack he's holding is quickly snatched by a girl of about four or five who scampers into the backseat, lower lip set in triumph. It's clear the man doesn't know and probably hasn't even registered whatever is happening on the other side of the road and Andy quickly moves on.

Bill Anderson is next and Liv knows he'll have an opinion. Their older neighbour is busy tending to his front garden, watering his beloved plants before the real heat of the day sets in. He and Andy speak for a few moments, there is a bit of nodding and back and forth then Andy returns to Liv, visibly shaken.

'They found a body,' he says, his voice low. 'At the park. Down at the Gully.'

Liv inhales sharply. 'Who?'

'No idea, but there's a massive operation going on down there,' Bill says. Forensics, crime scene investigators, the lot. He reckons it's got something to do with this.'

They look back at Sandra and Richard's house and Liv feels a flutter of panic in the pit of her stomach and her mind begins to race with possibilities. Has something happened to their neighbours? Gracie runs at the park. Was she there this morning? Is that why she is upset? Did she see something?

Liv is reaching for her phone when Sandra and Richard's front door opens again and this time a uniformed policewoman steps onto the veranda, followed by the same man as before, another uniformed policeman and then, Sandra, her tiny form dressed in loose linen trousers and a white shirt.

Their neighbour's expression is a blank mask but Liv can see something is very wrong.

Sandra walks stiffly, almost robotically down the stairs and through the front garden and then at the gate she appears to hesitate a moment, glancing back towards the house. She says something to the female officer who nods and then in turn speaks

6

to her uniformed colleague. There is a bit of back and forth but Sandra doesn't move. There appears to be some kind of impasse that's stopping her from leaving the boundary of her house and then Liv realises what's going on and automatically takes a step into the road.

'Sandra,' she calls out. Her neighbour looks over, momentarily confused as her gaze searches for the voice and finally looks at Liv. 'I'll check on the animals,' Liv says, her voice ringing out across the narrow residential road. 'I've still got your keys.'

Sandra gives a tight nod then lets herself be guided into the black unmarked police car. She settles into the back seat and it is only then Liv sees the woman's expression change, clear, brittle grief flooding her features. Sandra's bony hand reaches to her brow and her shoulders hunch slightly as she dips her head and begins to sob.

'Oh Sandra,' Liv mutters, her own eyes welling up at the sight of her neighbour's pain.

Bill has travelled down the pavement and is now standing a few metres away from Liv and Andy. He rocks on his heels as he waits for the police cars to drive away.

'It's being reported,' he begins when the vehicles have rounded the corner, 'that the body found in the Gully is a man in his late fifties. It's being treated as a suspicious death.'

Chapter 2

LIV

Thursday, 30 January 2025

Bill waits an appropriate few moments and then turns and heads back towards his house. Liv and Andy stand there for a few moments in stunned silence.

'So, Richard's ... dead?'

'It might not be him,' Liv says automatically. 'It might be a mistake. It might not have anything to do with this.' She motions to across the street.

'Yeah, maybe,' Andy says, although both of them know this is unlikely.

Sophie is lying in a scrap of shade from the branches of the neighbour's magnolia tree, her eyes once again closed. Watching her, Liv is suddenly aware of the scalding sun on her own face and the sweat pooling in various regions of her body. She takes a step into the shadow of the tree and as she does so, her gaze does a brief sweep of their road. Their normal, suburban Sydney cul-de-sac. A higgle-piggle of different style housing, like most streets in this city. Their side of the road is mostly original one-storey terraces, some renovated with second levels tacked on. Opposite, on the slightly larger blocks, the houses have grander facades, swimming pools and room for generous extensions out the back.

This is a lovely street. A safe street. Not the kind of place, or neighbourhood, where residents die violent deaths, although she knows this is a ridiculous assumption. People are killed in every neighbourhood, so-called good ones as well as bad. Dull middle-class suburbs, filled with bankers, lawyers and doctors, like Richard, aren't immune.

Liv's mind whirrs, trying to find an explanation for what might have happened if it is indeed Richard who's been found dead.

'It could have been a mugging. But at the Gully?' Andy makes a face at the thought. 'Who gets mugged there?'

Liv remembers why her phone is in her hand and she brings up Gracie's number, thumb hovering over the call button momentarily before switching to messages.

Did you run at the Gully this morning? Something's happened there – the police are involved. Did you see anything? x

Could there have been a murderer down there this morning, lurking in the shadows of their local park when Gracie was there running? Liv pictures an attacker lying in wait, her daughter jogging past them.

Had whoever is responsible stood on this street, perhaps on this very spot, watching Richard and waiting for him? Following him down to the park? Liv feels a wash of nausea, not helped by the almost sickly sweet scent of the murraya hedging that lines their front wall. The little white blooms have opened up overnight thanks to the heat and rain.

'It must have been something else,' Andy says. 'Someone Richard knew. He mixed with some pretty dodgy characters.'

Liv sees it in Andy's eyes, an almost hopeful expression she understands.

Because they go to the idyllic Middle Harbour park on an almost daily basis. The Gully park is an extension of their home. Gracie runs there, Liv goes there for her walks and they take Sophie there all the time. It's been the location of dozens of picnics, birthday parties, coffees with friends. It cannot be somewhere that is now off-limits. That is possibly dangerous. And a crime scene.

Liv stares at her phone, willing a response to come through from Gracie. But of course there is nothing because Gracie is notoriously hopeless at checking her messages or replying to them.

'Maybe it was a hit. Like, a planned murder. A disgruntled patient? A pissed-off husband or heartbroken mistress?'

Liv only half hears what Andy is saying. She is still picturing the park and its manicured oval and easy walkways, the communal barbecues that stand near the water's edge and the picnic tables nearby. In her thoughts she is moving across the grassy park, past the oval and along the path that leads into the Gully bushland and creek.

The bushland that is surprisingly wild and rugged considering its proximity to the city, where she goes only occasionally when she's on her own because she always feels as though it's possibly not quite safe. The pathway that winds its way past the creek and then up into a steep climb, flanked by thick trees and shrubs and rock faces and sharp drops until suddenly, you step foot back onto concrete and are back in the modern world of netball and tennis courts and the swimming centre that is in the midst of a rebuild.

Liv imagines a person being killed there. Somewhere beside the slightly dank, muddy Gully water or amid the thick forest of towering gumtrees. All while she and Andy readied themselves for this day, had their coffee, their showers, their yoghurt and granola.

'What was the name of the guy who sued Richard? Martin something.' He snaps his fingers. 'Martin Finch.'

Liv knows the name. It's been all over the papers, how this man took Richard to court after his wife died from post-surgical complications. How he lost, kept issuing threats and how Richard took out a restraining order against him.

'Maybe he's been stalking Richard all this time, waiting to pounce.'

Liv blanches. 'Can we leave the speculation for later? When we actually know something?'

He reaches out to take her hand, drawing her to his side. 'Sorry,' he says into her head.

The other neighbours who had been standing on the street have retreated back to their homes. As her cheek rests against Andy's shoulder, Liv's gaze travels to the end of their cul-de-sac, towards the tall, conspicuous building by the small reserve.

A person steps from the entrance onto the pavement, begins heading towards them and then abruptly stops mid-stride. The figure doesn't move for a moment, as if considering something, and then turns and walks in the other direction.

Liv knows, despite the distance, that it is Meredith Edwards. She recognises the woman's statuesque, narrow frame; the short cap of brown hair, the dark trousers and blouse that is Meredith's daily uniform at the nearby hospital where she also works.

The figure retreats down the stairs beside the reserve that leads to the street below theirs. Liv knows that Meredith will then take a left up the gradually sloping hill towards the main road where she will catch the bus to work. It is the long way around and the only reason to go that way is to avoid passing their end of the cul-de-sac.

Liv thinks about the night a few months back when she and Andy returned from a late-night stroll with Sophie. They'd heard the soft tinkle of female laughter across the road and turned to see the back of a man standing a few doors down from his own house against a neighbour's front wall, legs splayed, his body pressed against a woman with dark hair and bare legs. The man shifted slightly and the women's head rested against his chest and Liv had seen it was Richard but couldn't make out his companion.

Rumours about the plastic surgeon's many affairs are always circulating on the hospital campus where Liv is an exercise physiologist at the on-site physio clinic. And in December, the gossip mill was abuzz with rumours about something going on between Meredith and Richard after how she'd behaved at the Christmas party.

Liv has no idea if Meredith was the woman Richard was kissing that night. She only knows that whoever it was certainly wasn't his wife, Sandra.

'I'll take Soph for a quick walk,' Andy says. 'Do you need to check on Sandra's menagerie? Maybe by the time we're done there'll be more news.'

Checking to see if Gracie has messaged back, Liv lets herself back into the house then texts Robyn, the receptionist at work, to say that she'll be half an hour late but that her first appointment isn't until eleven.

As she rummages for Sandra and Richard's house keys in the kitchen drawer that contains all manner of ephemera, she wonders if Meredith's heard the news. If she hasn't, she'll undoubtedly find out as soon as she sets foot in work. The onetime star surgeon of Northern hospital being found dead in suspicious circumstances? The news will have spread like wildfire.

Liv finally sees what she's looking for: a wooden owl keychain with a brass key attached to it sitting in between a random assortment of metal skewers, steak knives and chopsticks.

Will the police get in touch with Meredith when they find out about the affair? Will someone tell them what happened at the party?

Will Meredith be a suspect?

As she crosses the road, the blazing sun prickling at her skin, Liv thinks: *I hope Meredith has a good alibi for this morning.*

Chapter 3

LIV

Thursday, 30 January 2025

Liv goes into Sandra and Richard's garden, crossing the wide deck, travelling past the shimmering swimming pool and along the stone path to the double garage. Steam is rising from the pavers, the sudden downpour from earlier drying out in the heat.

The garage is where Sandra keeps the enclosures for the abandoned pets and injured native creatures she nurses as part of her duties volunteering for the local wildlife rescue organisation. Liv eyes the various cages warily. She feels momentary dread that she might have to do something complicated like bottle-feed a baby possum or hand-feed an injured bird. But a quick survey of the cages tells Liv that she's got lucky. Sandra appears to only be looking after two rescue kittens and their mum, a tiny scrap of a tabby cat who eyes her suspiciously from the far corner of her cage, her offspring snuggled up next to her, fast asleep.

Liv fills their food and water bowl, checks the litter tray at the other end of the large cage which appears empty of anything that needs cleaning up. Then she peers into the other cages one more time in case there's something hiding in the shadows. Satisfied there aren't any, she returns to the house, going inside and seeing that Sandra and Richard's dogs, two elderly Cavaliers are still fast asleep on the sofa and don't seem in need of anything.

Liv's phone buzzes with a message.

Body confirmed as Richard, Andy's text reads, linking to a news report.

BREAKING NEWS: TV DOCTOR DEAD
A man found dead at a park in Sydney's north this morning can be revealed as well-known plastic surgeon and Morning! *presenter Richard Wellington. His body was found by a dog walker earlier today and it's been reported police are treating the death as suspicious. While the 59-year-old's cause of death is yet to be formally confirmed, sources tell the* Daily News *the medic was found with head wounds at a park near his home at around 7.30.*

Liv blinks. She surveys the room and takes in the signs of Richard everywhere: his bike helmet on one of the kitchen stools, a sun-faded baseball cap on the table by the landline telephone, a neat pile of what looks like medical journals on the dresser.

The wall by the door is covered with framed photographs and Liv goes over to them. The largest one is of Richard standing next to an attractive blonde woman and a handsome grey-haired man. The main presenters of *Morning!*, the TV show where Richard was the resident medical expert.

Liv occasionally puts on the bland breakfast show for company as she eats her own breakfast or packs her lunch and always gets the same jolt of surprise to see her neighbour there on the sofa alongside the main hosts, explaining how viewers can slow down the signs of ageing or lower their cholesterol. Richard hadn't been on the show recently, of course. A few months back, Sandra confided that the court case with Martin Finch had made the channel executives wary. Presumably it wasn't a good look to give airtime to a man being accused of killing a patient. Even if unproven.

Liv studies the next photo and that's when the tears well in her eyes. It's from Richard and Sandra's wedding in the Nineties. Sandra's hair is longer than she wears it now and not quite as blonde, her face softer without the cosmetic enhancements that presumably came as a perk of being married to a plastic surgeon. She looks young and happy and relaxed, and so does Richard, whose face is in profile and shows him grinning widely, pre-veneers, like someone who can't quite believe their luck.

Poor Richard, thinks Liv. Despite being an awful vain peacock of a man, no one deserves to die like this.

As she walks to the bus stop five minutes later, Liv checks her phone and the tracking app which shares the whole family's locations. Gracie has hers switched off which could mean she is saving her data, has run out of data or doesn't want her parents to know where she is. It is likely the former. Liv can see, however, that Andy is, as she expected, down at the Gully park, presumably trying to find out more about what's going on. She feels a wave of both irritation and fondness for her predictably nosy husband.

Are you at the park? she texts Andy and the reply comes back immediately: No, why?

I can see you're there, she replies.

Sophie wanted to see her mates! he eventually messages back.

Be careful xx, she messages and he replies with a thumbs-up emoji. Then she quickly types, Have you heard from Gracie?

No.

Liv taps out another message to her daughter.

Did you see the news? Pls call me x

That day, new rumours spread across the hospital campus on an almost hourly basis.

Richard was tied up and dumped in the water, so it had to be some kind of mob hit.

A paramedic from the hospital was there just after his body was found and no, he definitely didn't drown, he'd been hit on the head but someone also tried to weigh him down so he wouldn't float.

No, that wasn't true either, he was found half in and half out of water, but only his feet were submerged, according to someone who works with someone who is friends with the lead detective on the case.

As always the whole hospital campus is a fevered hot bed of gossip and misinformation.

'They reckon he had a bleed on the brain, caused by the impact of whatever hit him,' Andy says when Liv calls him on her lunch break. 'So maybe he was bludgeoned and then slipped into the water or he was pushed? They're waiting for the pathologist to confirm, Stan says.'

Stan is a retired policeman who claims to still have contacts at the local station, but up until now Andy has always been doubtful of his credentials. He once told Liv he thought Stan had just worked in the IT department.

'Last night's rain's making it hard though for forensics. The whole place is a mud bath.'

'If he was in the water does that mean all the evidence has been washed away?' Liv says, careful to keep her voice low.

She is sitting on a bench outside the clinic, aware that if anyone overhears, her musings will be taken as fact. News has already spread that she lives on the same road as Richard and everywhere she goes, people keep giving her second glances or just come right out and ask her what she thinks is going on.

'No idea,' he says through chews Liv can hear echoing down the line. 'Stan reckons the wound site might have fibres in it or they might find something under his fingernails if there was a struggle.'

Liv rewraps her uneaten sandwich, her appetite gone.

'Must be fascinating work, being a forensic pathologist,' Andy continues. 'Seeing what a corpse tells you about a person's last moments alive.'

'Andy, can you not? A man's died. We don't even know if Sandra witnessed it. She might have been with him and only just escaped. Can you imagine how traumatised she must be?'

There's a pause. 'I know, sorry. But look, he was our neighbour. Our friend. I think it's normal to be interested.'

'He wasn't our friend.'

'You know what I mean. Neighbour, sort of friend.'

'Sandra's my friend.'

'Richard was a dickhead but he wasn't all bad.'

'We'll have to agree to disagree on that one,' she says.

Liv has enjoyed the occasional daydream about Richard coming to an unpleasant and untimely end. Every morning, in fact, when he revved his mid-life-crisis Maserati at 7 a.m. And every time he shot a creepy, appreciative glance in Gracie's direction.

'The police have put up tarpaulin in case there's another downpour, so they can work the scene.'

'Are you still down there?'

'I brought my lunch down, just to see what was going on. Stan, Phil and Con are here too.'

Since taking voluntary redundancy from his position as in-house counsel at an insurance company, hanging out with Stan, Phil and Con at the local café first thing appears to be the only absolute in Andy's daily routine. Andy takes along his laptop and makes noises about job applications and future projects, but as far as Liv can gather, he spends his hour or so there gossiping with the other far older, retired men.

'What's everyone saying at the hospital?'

Picking up her lunchbox, Liv stands and heads back to the clinic entrance.

'Just the usual gossip. No one thinks it was a random attack and unsurprisingly no one seems that devastated. Have you heard from Gracie?' She passes through the automatic doors and heads towards the clinic's back room where they store their personal possessions.

'No, but I think she's got classes all morning.'

'Let me know if you hear from her. She'll be freaked out when she finds out what's happened.'

'She'll be fine.'

Liv closes her locker door and fastens the padlock back into place.

'Someone on our street's just been killed,' Liv says as she walks along the corridor. 'Where Gracie goes running every day. At the same time as when she goes running every day. Of course she's not going to be fine. Nothing about this is fine.' There is a tight coiled pressure of emotion rising in her throat. 'God's sake, Andy, there's a murderer on the loose in our neighbourhood.'

Chapter 4

MEREDITH

November 2024

There was no hiding Liv's dismay when she first crossed paths with Meredith on the corner of what was now both their streets.

It wasn't the first time they'd seen each other. That moment had come a few weeks before when Liv appeared on Meredith's ward to pick up an elderly patient's paperwork and, stunned, greeted her with, 'Meredith Edwards? Oh my god!'

They'd had their awkward reunion next to the nurses' station, spending a stilted five minutes catching up on the vague outlines of each other's lives since last seeing each other nearly three decades earlier and swapping numbers.

'Old friend?' one of the senior nurses asked as Meredith stood there afterwards, watching Liv walk down the corridor.

'School friend.' Then Meredith gave a slight shake of her head as if dislodging that thought. 'Family friend really.'

But as the two women stood on the corner of their shared street, Liv in shorts and a T-shirt, an elderly Labrador by her side and a takeaway coffee in her hand, Meredith in her workout gear on her way to a Pilates class, there was none of the polite surprise Liv had shown Meredith at the hospital.

'So, where's your new place?' Liv had asked. Her expression was guarded. Suspicious.

'The Malabar block. At the end?'

'Oh, how lovely,' Liv said, making it sound anything but that. 'You must have a great view of the water.'

'That was the main reason I took it.'

Liv stared at Meredith for a moment and the unsaid thought hovered between them: *Why of all the streets in North Sydney are you living on mine?*

She glanced down at her dog who was now lying panting at her feet, and then back to Meredith, a quizzical smile in place across her face. 'Such a small world. You living on this street.'

'Yes,' Meredith agreed. And it really was.

As Liv made to leave, giving the lead a tug so the Labrador reluctantly got to its feet, Meredith remembered to ask, 'So, what house number are you?'

There was a moment's hesitation, then Liv gestured vaguely. 'We're just down on the left.' Then understanding she couldn't really dodge this question added, 'Number 32.'

'Number 32,' Meredith repeated, giving Liv an easy, friendly smile she hoped would reassure her old school friend that she wouldn't be making any impromptu visits. 'Great.'

'And, yeah, if you ever need anything, just knock. Day or night.' She paused. 'We'll have you over some time and officially welcome you to the neighbourhood.'

They said their goodbyes with Meredith knowing full well this official welcome would never eventuate. Except, to her surprise, the promised invitation came via text message a few weeks later.

Come to ours for a BBQ! Saturday 16 November, after four. Bring a bottle or just yourselves. Everyone welcome! Andy and Liv – number 32 x

That Saturday in November was muggy and overcast but the perfect day for a lazy afternoon barbecue. The gathered neighbours all brought platters of food despite the instructions not to and there was an endless supply of char-cooked sausages and burgers wrapped in white bread.

Andy had finally passed his barbecue duties to another neighbour but was still wearing his 'The Grillfather' apron as he stood on the grass, bottle of beer in hand.

'So,' Andy said in a way that made Meredith grin at his wide-open, friendly face. 'Is it really true you were Liv's babysitter?'

Meredith nodded. 'Sort of.'

'I don't get it. You're only a bit older than her, aren't you?'

'I think there's what … eighteen months between us?'

'That's right,' Liv said.

'So Liv's parents got Meredith to keep an eye on Liv when she was a teenager because she was really, really naughty and they didn't trust her to be alone,' Andy explained to the semicircle of guests gathered around him.

'I wasn't that naughty. Just averagely so.'

'That's patently untrue,' Andy said, playing to his audience. 'I knew you at twenty-two and you were pretty wild then so I can imagine you were totally out of control as a teenager.'

Liv finally smiled. 'Don't give Gracie any ideas.'

'I think we've safely passed that stage,' Andy said. 'So go on, tell us about your out-of-control adolescence.'

Liv rolled her eyes. 'It wasn't like that. Okay, to explain – Mum and Dad went out a lot and often to overnight events or ones that ran on until the early hours, and they always organised for babysitters to stay over. Meredith lived nearby and she was very responsible and sensible for her age.' She glanced at Meredith, a small smile on her lips. 'Weren't you?'

'I think that translates to me being very boring and uncool,' Meredith only half-joked and the gathered group made appreciative noises.

'Pete and Ang knew Liv would trash the place if left to her own devices,' Andy interjected.

'I honestly wasn't that bad. Anyway, now, all these years later we've found ourselves working at the same hospital and living on the same street.' Liv's smile was more watery now. 'Such a crazy coincidence.'

'So crazy,' Meredith agreed.

'Well, cheers to weird coincidences and new neighbours,' Andy said, raising his beer in toast. Everyone raised their drinks too.

They were a nice couple, Meredith decided, despite it being obvious that Liv was wary of her. Thanks to Andy they were one of those 'fun couples' everyone wanted to be friends with and who always put on a good show. Performers who knew their lines and made everyone feel welcome.

By mid-afternoon Meredith had drunk and eaten far too much and decided she wanted to fall asleep on her sofa in front of an old movie. She extricated herself from the small group she was sitting with outside, found Andy and said her thank-yous and goodbyes and went in search of Liv.

Someone said they'd seen her out the front so Meredith walked along the open side passage to avoid the large group of chattering, laughing women in the open-plan kitchen. She wasn't there, so Meredith crossed the front garden and re-entered the house through the front door.

She froze as the conversation in the kitchen travelled along the hallway.

'She just had this really intense manner. The way she looked at everyone and watched us? I'd feel it in the back of my neck during assembly and when I'd turn, she'd be *there*, a few rows away.' Liv paused. 'Just staring at me.'

'Creepy,' said a woman's voice.

'Well, a bit odd maybe.'

Meredith felt her insides turn liquid.

'Teenage girls are all a bit crazy,' another woman said. 'It's the hormones and being at single-sex schools. Don't you remember how you'd get fixated on another girl, especially the popular ones? They were like celebrities.'

'Oh, I wasn't popular, at all. And I think she was just a bit lonely. The summer before I started at St Mary's, she'd write me these sweet notes and stand outside my house watching me.'

'Watching you? Why?'

'I have no idea.'

'You didn't ask her?'

'No.'

'Or tell your parents?'

'God, no.' A pause. 'She was just a lonely kid. I don't think she had any friends.'

'And then she became your babysitter?'

'Yes.'

'And now this woman's just moved in down the street from you?' said another voice, sharp and knowing.

Liv laughed easily. 'Look, I'm sure that's a coincidence. Loads of people from the hospital live around here. Half the street's doctors. It's an easy commute to Northern.'

'Well, if you start finding dead animals on your doorstep it might be time to move,' the sharp voice said. 'Remember that movie?'

'Oh god, *Single White Female*?' said the other woman. 'I loved that film.'

'*Fatal Attraction*,' said the sharp voice. 'Glenn Close.'

Their laughs ricocheted down the corridor as Meredith stepped quickly towards the front door. She didn't pause or break stride until she was at the end of the street by her building.

Chapter 5

LIV

Thursday, 30 January 2025

The evening of Richard's death, Liv and Andy eat dinner alone. Gracie has ignored all Liv's texts and has instead messaged Andy to say she's staying at her best friend Kristina's and to confirm that she's heard the news. She has also promised not to go anywhere near the Gully park for the foreseeable future.

'Have you spoken to Sandra yet?' Andy asks as he reaches for the sweating bottle of white wine.

'I texted earlier to say how sorry I was and that I'd checked on the animals, but she didn't reply.'

'Do you reckon she's back home?'

'No idea. She must be. Maybe I should check again? In case the animals need feeding?'

Andy makes a face as he gets up and begins to clear the table. 'She must be back by now, surely? Maybe she went in the back way. She wouldn't want to deal with all the cameras out the front.'

The TV crews and photographers started camping outside as soon as the news broke. Liv assumes they'll be there until they get a reaction shot. They're probably hopeful Sandra will go outside and give a tearful statement, which she knows will never happen.

Andy pauses with Liv's plate in mid-air. 'Have you considered the possibility that Sandra was somehow involved?'

Liv gives him a sharp look.

'Don't make jokes,' she says, as she stands and begins clearing the rest of the dishes from the table. 'The poor woman's just lost her husband of nearly thirty years. Even if he was a pig.'

'It's just as likely to be her as some random stranger,' he says as they head inside. 'More likely maybe. And you've got to admit, she'll probably be a lot happier now he's gone. So there's your motive.'

Liv opens the dishwasher and begins slotting plates inside. 'Sandra had nothing to do with it.'

'All I'm saying is Richard was not the best husband. Think about it. All those affairs, all those gossip stories in the papers? Remember that thing last Easter? Maybe she finally had enough.' He is reaching for his phone and front door keys from the bowl on the kitchen counter. 'I'll take Sophie out and see if Sandra's lights are on.'

Liv rolls her eyes. He just wants to see what's going on outside with the camera crews.

'Don't get photographed or give anyone a comment,' she calls out when he's halfway down the corridor.

As Liv tips leftovers into plastic tubs, she thinks about the time Andy is referring to. They'd never socialised much with Richard and Sandra apart from the odd neighbourhood get-together, but last year they'd been invited over to their house at Easter with some other neighbours. The weather had been warm and they'd eaten at the enormous outdoor dining table on the deck. Someone had spilt red wine across the putty-coloured linen tablecloth and Liv sprang up to get a cloth and some salt. Just as she was about to step inside, she saw Richard and Sandra in the kitchen, Richard was facing away from Liv but was positioned close to his wife,

25

almost looming over her. Liv knew instantly that something was very wrong about both their body language. Then Sandra began nodding very rapidly, repeating 'yes, yes, of course'. Then she saw Liv and her expression slid to one of panic. Liv quickly stepped back onto the deck before Richard noticed her too.

An hour or so later, while the men remained outside on the deck and Richard held court, smoking a disgusting-smelling cigar, Sandra showed her female guests the abandoned pregnant Staffy she was looking after in their huge garage. Richard's booming voice had carried across the garden – 'Sandra, Sandra' – until his wife finally responded with a polite 'Yes, darling?'

'I was just telling everyone about the little friend you've got in there.' He'd given a low chuckle. 'Why don't you get it out and everyone can see her huge belly.' At that he'd motioned to his own and puffed out his cheeks. 'You've got to see her. She looks like a bloody whale.' He called out again to Sandra. 'Come on, get her out.'

Sandra had emerged from the garage and she'd forced a smile.

'She needs to rest, darling. She's giving birth any moment now,' she added, a little too brightly, smoothing her short blonde hair against her neck.

'Come on, don't be a spoil sport,' Richard said, a slight edge to his voice, then to one of the other neighbours, 'She's a sweet thing but my god, the size of her. She must have ten pups inside. Come on, go and get her.'

'Richard, no,' Sandra said. 'She can barely move. Besides, she's too heavy to carry.' Richard held his wife's gaze a moment and then gave slight shake of his head, his expression hardening. 'Hormonal bitches,' he said as he took a long puff on the cigar and then exhaled. 'That's why owners need to get their females spayed.'

'You know Richard started coming to Paco's a few months back,' Andy says later when they are sprawled on the sofa watching TV and he has reported that there has been no change outside.

'After I told him how good the coffee was since Paco got that new supplier.'

'Yeah, I remember you said.'

'So, just before Christmas, all the staff were wearing bits of tinsel on their uniforms? I think Gracie had some around her neck and waist.'

There's something in Andy's tone that makes Liv look over to him, instantly wary.

'So one morning I'm having my coffee and I'm kind of tucked around the corner but when I hear Richard's voice giving his order I lean over to say hi.' He pauses. 'He's standing over by the counter and Gracie's there too and as she passes him, Richard kind of pulls at a bit of the tinsel around her waist and calls her a grumpy little Christmas elf or something. She says something, is clearly pissed off and then Richard says she looks cute when she's angry.'

Andy still has his gaze determinedly fixed on the TV.

'So anyway, I was going to get up and say something but then he took a call and got his coffee and left. I asked Gracie if she wanted me to have a word, but she said no, she could handle it.' He exhales. 'Then two days later, Paco tells me Richard's been banned. Wouldn't say why, Gracie wouldn't either but one of the other guys said that he'd overstepped the mark with Lucy, the blonde waitress? Apparently he'd slapped her on the bum.'

'Fuck's sake. Why didn't you tell me any of this?'

'I would have if it was Gracie. If it was Gracie, I'd have fucking decked him.' Andy lifts the TV remote and pauses the programme they're watching. 'I didn't want you to worry and she only just got the job. She didn't want you to know.'

Liv knows what that means. They thought she'd overreact.

'Look, I know it's wrong to speak ill of the dead,' Andy continues, 'but Richard was not a good guy and I'm not, you know, devastated that we won't have to deal with him and his bullshit anymore.'

He finally looks at her, as if for reassurance, and for a few moments, neither of them speaks, then Liv finds his hand on the sofa and gives it a soft squeeze.

'I feel the same.'

'But it makes me nervous, you know? The possibility that there might be someone out there who was watching Richard. Watching the street maybe.' His frown deepens. 'Let's just be extra vigilant. Keep the doors and windows locked. Check the side door every night. At least until the police figure out who did this.'

'And we should tell Gracie not to walk home alone. Tell her you'll pick her up, no matter what time it is?'

'I'll text her now,' Andy says, reaching for his phone on the coffee table.

'But don't scare her,' Liv adds quickly. 'We don't want her freaking out and getting anxious.'

'Yeah, course.' He stares at the phone in his hand, confused, and Liv reaches for it.

'Don't worry – I'll make it sound like you,' she says, tapping in Andy's passcode.

Liv stands by the bedroom window as she brushes her teeth before bed, her gaze travelling from Sandra and Richard's house in front of her to the dark spaces in between the houses on either side. Then she looks at her own front garden. A low brick fence and gate, a small patch of bedding filled with shrubs and a frangipani that has barely grown since she planted it three years ago. Nowhere for an intruder to hide in wait, thank goodness.

Then Liv looks down at the geometric tiles on the narrow, covered veranda attached to the front of their house and immediately notices what isn't there but should be.

With the toothbrush still in her mouth, she goes outside to double-check. The roar of humming cicadas is almost deafening. Gracie usually leaves her running shoes on the veranda to air or dry, especially when it's been wet but there is no sign of them here tonight.

Liv stands there a moment, the warm night air and scent of murraya mixing with the peppermint from the toothpaste. She crouches down and checks the trainers haven't been shoved under the small bench but there is nothing there either.

After going back inside and double-checking the lock, Liv goes into Gracie's bedroom and searches for a bit, finding the shoes under the bed.

Her heart gives a little flutter when she feels how sodden they are and how they are caked with mud. Were they submerged in water or just damp from the rain? She stares at them for a moment, confused.

Why hadn't her daughter left them outside to dry like always?

Chapter 6

LIV

Friday, 31 January 2025

The outside broadcast vans are still in place when Liv takes Sophie out for her early morning walk. Even Channel Two, which has the logo of its main news programme and Richard's former show *Morning!* emblazoned on its side, Liv sees, feeling a frisson of distaste. His former colleagues have probably already reported on his passing in between segments on the best budget-friendly back-to-school tips.

Liv wonders if she should check whether Sandra needs her to take out the dogs but decides her neighbour's garden is probably big enough for them to run around in. Besides if she knocks on Sandra's front door, she could end up on the news too. So, instead, Liv ducks her head and walks quickly towards the end of the cul-de-sac and the small grassy clearing there, which is Sophie's favoured spot for her morning toileting.

Liv reads from her phone as she walks. In just twenty-four hours, Richard's death has become the main news story across every online outlet. This morning, several are now openly speculating about who might be responsible. *The Post*'s online headline is *MURDERED BY THE MAFIA?*

But then, apparently unable to decide which one of the many suspects might be responsible, and mindful of being sued, it goes on to mention everyone from Richard's good friend, a 'notorious' nightclub identity to disgruntled ex-girlfriends who they suggest might be contacted by police investigating the death. It reports how Martin Finch, who was subject to an Apprehended Personal Violence Order that meant he was restricted from contact with Richard, will also be interviewed by investigators.

There is no mention of Meredith Edwards, Liv is relieved to see as she pulls at Sophie's lead and guides her past a ginger cat who is sitting on a low garden wall, eyeing the dog with suspicion.

Another piece rehashes what happened between Martin and Richard and how Martin's wife died a few days after having a breast augmentation performed by Richard. How Martin sued Richard, lost the case and then made serious threats to the surgeon's life. The report explains how he sent Richard dozens of emails and letters saying he was going to 'get' him then adding that the outlet was in no way suggesting Martin Finch is under suspicion or has anything to do with Richard's death. Although they clearly are.

Liv is at the end of the street and stepping onto the grass when she finally looks up from her phone and sees Meredith by a bench, stretching. Her heart sinks and she hesitates a moment, trying to work out if she can get away with quickly going down the stone steps that lead to the street below or whether she should just turn on her heels and hope Meredith hasn't seen her. But then in a beat it is too late to do either. The other woman lifts a hand in greeting and Liv forces a polite smile.

'Hi, Meredith!' she says in a faux-jaunty tone. 'Been for a run? Goodness, I don't know how you do it in this heat.'

'A run-walk,' the other woman says in her usual solemn tone. 'Well, mostly walk. I got out later than usual.'

Meredith glows with good health and Liv feels lumpy and short

31

compared to her. The other woman is wearing a black cap and matching running shorts and a baggy sleeveless vest and has one long brown leg resting on the back of the bench as she stretches out her calf, careful to keep her muddy shoe from touching the bench. She looks as though she could run a marathon without breaking sweat.

'Personally, I can't wait for winter,' Liv says, unclipping Sophie's lead and watching as she crosses the lawn to her favoured wee spot. 'So how are you doing? It's shocking what's happened. I honestly can't believe it. At the Gully park of all places.'

'Yes, it's awful,' Meredith agrees, lifting her other leg into a stretch.

Liv waits for something more from the other woman, but apparently this is it. Meredith doesn't even look particularly fazed.

'What do you think happened?'

'No idea,' Meredith says. 'A mugging? Although I assumed this was a pretty safe neighbourhood.'

'Oh, it is, absolutely,' Liv says. 'Nothing like this has ever happened in the time we've lived here. And the idea of someone being attacked at random or it being a mugging gone wrong … I don't know. It's just terrible.'

Liv waits for a response and finally Meredith nods.

'I think it was the man who took him to court. Apparently he'd made some serious threats against Richard and I think that makes more sense than it being some random maniac on the loose.'

Meredith looks up sharply.

'I was actually at the park yesterday morning,' she says after a beat. 'I don't know if I was there when it happened. I mean, I didn't see anything. But I was there first thing.'

'God. That's terrifying.'

'I'm actually going to the police station later to give a statement.' She pauses. 'There were police at the park today, asking everyone about their movements. They want people who were there when it happened to give statements. Just so everyone can be accounted for or discounted, I suppose.' Her gaze travels across the grass to where Sophie is sniffing around the edges of the stone wall that encloses the reserve. 'How's Gracie doing? Is she okay?'

Liv blinks twice.

'Gracie? I think so. Why wouldn't she be?'

She pictures her daughter yesterday morning. Her puffy eyes. How it looked as though she had been crying.

'After what happened to Richard? I mean, she's at the park most mornings, isn't she? Having a run?' Meredith shifts slightly and Liv feels a loosening in her stomach. 'I just mean, if she was there, she should probably let the police know. It's good to be transparent about these things. Helps the investigation.'

Liv stares at the other woman. 'Well, she doesn't go down there every day,' she says finally.

Meredith nods slowly. 'Of course, but if she was there, Detective Inspector James Mitchell at North Sydney is the person she needs to talk to. I already forwarded her his number but she hasn't got back to me.'

Liv frowns. How does Meredith of all people have Gracie's number?

'It won't be anything detailed,' the other woman says. 'Just a brief where and when and how long she was there.'

Liv nods vaguely, not really taking in what the other woman is saying. All she knows is that it feels as though there are layers to what this woman is saying and not saying and Liv feels suddenly wrong-footed and unsettled. Just as Meredith always made her feel since they first met as children four decades ago.

'So, sorry, are you saying you did see Gracie at the park then? I'm a bit confused.'

Sophie appears between them and immediately flops down on the grass.

Meredith hesitates before responding. 'I thought I maybe caught a glimpse of her from the other side of the oval, but I might be wrong,' she says, giving a quick smile. 'I don't usually put my contacts in until after my run so I'm pretty short-sighted.'

Liv gets a sudden flash of Meredith years back, when her dark, heavy-lidded eyes were covered by thick glasses. Buggy Mole, they'd called her.

'You must be very upset about Richard – I heard you were really good friends,' Liv says, feeling only a small pang of regret when she sees Meredith's reaction.

'We weren't. At all. I know there's been … gossip, but I barely knew him. We were colleagues and in different departments – our paths crossed very occasionally.' Meredith pauses, seeming to gather herself slightly. 'But it's always awful when someone dies, isn't it? Especially in circumstances like this.'

At home Liv goes to Gracie's room and takes the running shoes from under the bed to put into the laundry. She inserts them in an old pillowcase which she ties up at the end, adds the detergent, a splash of vinegar and then as an afterthought, some stain remover, and sets the dial to a hygiene wash. When the cycle finishes, fifty minutes later, Liv takes the dripping bundle outside into the sunshine.

She finds an old newspaper from the recycling, stuffs the insides of the shoes and props them up against the wall, in the sun to dry. All traces of mud have gone and they look almost brand new again.

Chapter 7

LIV

Friday, 31 January 2025

It is more than thirty-two hours since Richard died when Gracie finally texts at four on the family chat, saying that she's going to be late but giving no other details about what late might mean.

Liv's thumb hovers over the reply box.

This is one of the main things about having an older child who is no longer a child that Liv finds challenging. Of course Gracie should be out with friends on a Friday night or staying over with anyone she wants to, and not feel she always has to tell her parents if and when she's home for dinner. But at times like this when Gracie gives her nothing, no explanations, no excuses, no response, Liv feels both frustration and a creeping sense of worry.

By late afternoon Liv can't hold off any longer and messages Gracie again:

Were you at the park on Thursday morning – when Richard was attacked? Please can you let me know.

But Gracie doesn't text back.

There aren't any available parking spaces when Liv returns from work; the TV vans have filled them all. Most have their engines running, whoever's inside presumably remaining cool in the air-conditioning while just a few, most male, camera operators mill around in small groups on the pavement outside Richard and Sandra's, talking among themselves, checking their phones and yawning, their cameras resting on the pavement next to them.

Richard's death has been relegated to being the third or fourth item on the home pages of most news outlets thanks to a school bus crash in Brisbane. But as soon as Sandra steps outside or a development is announced, it'll be back to the top slot again.

Liv can sense impatience among the waiting and watching journalists and wonders how many more notes will have been pushed under her front door from reporters trying to cajole her and presumably her other neighbours into giving an interview. There had been five in their letterbox this morning and a further four on their doormat. The majority offered a fee and she had put them all straight into the recycling.

Liv parks up on a side road and when she enters her street, she walks quickly to her front door before any of them can accost her. As it is, there are just two notes stuffed under the door when she pushes it open. The house is quiet and Liv can tell there is no one home except Sophie.

She bolts the door firmly behind her. Since Richard's death Liv really doesn't feel safe within the walls of her home and while she supposes this is to be expected and will eventually dissipate, it means she finds herself constantly checking and rechecking that the doors and windows are locked. Andy is even worse. He spent an hour that morning trying to find the side gate key which had gone missing years before.

When she's changed out of her work clothes, Liv pours herself a large glass of wine and leans against the kitchen counter with phone in hand to compose a message to Sandra.

Everything she writes sounds trite and pointless, so in the end she keeps it simple:

Sandra, we are so sorry for what's happened. Please reach out if we can do anything. All our love x

A message from Andy comes through seconds later, saying he will be back soon and that he's on his way back from her parents' house.

While Liv worries about Andy not working, one very positive outcome of him being unemployed is how often he's now able to visit Liv's parents. He's always helping Angela and Pete with shopping or small DIY jobs; occasionally joins her dad for a round of golf, which she knows he loathes; or ferries them to medical appointments. Liv is especially grateful that this means he's able to keep an eye on them which is becoming increasingly necessary with her father's early-stage Alzheimer's and her mother's mild dementia. 'The double fuck whammy', they call it between themselves.

Liv puts her phone down, takes a slug of wine and with her glass still in hand, opens the fridge, chewing on her lip as she surveys its contents.

Friday night has traditionally always been takeaway night but now Andy cooks most days, not only because they're on a budget, but because it's another pursuit he's taken to with surprising enthusiasm since becoming unemployed.

She lifts foil off the top of a glass bowl and sees there is some chicken marinating within it and replaces it, closing the fridge, thankful her husband has thought ahead, as he always does.

Whatever happens, Liv knows she can depend on Andy. If she has a niggling worry, Andy will reassure her. He remembers to pay bills she's forgotten about; book restaurants when she's happy to wing it; will keep them stocked up with tins of tomatoes and loo rolls, messages friends they haven't seen for months to suggest dinners.

And when he comes home, Liv knows Andy will reassure her about Gracie and the news vans and the possible killer on the loose. He will tell her everything is going to be okay and she will, mostly, believe him.

Liv follows Andy into the kitchen and watches as he takes a beer from the fridge while she settles on one of the stools on the other side of the stone counter that divides the living and cooking areas. She has told him about her conversation with Meredith and now he is digesting it, turning over the various possibilities before he responds.

'Gracie would have already said something if she was there,' he says finally. 'Don't worry about it.'

'But she was upset yesterday morning before she left. It looked like she'd been crying.'

'Do you think she might have seen something at the park? Richard being attacked?' Andy takes the chicken from the fridge.

'Not necessarily. Maybe? I don't know. I'm probably over-thinking it as usual.' Andy slides the large wooden chopping board towards her.

'She'd have told us if she saw something.'

'She hasn't been here to tell us,' Liv points out.

'She'd have texted. Something like this? She'd be totally freaked out.'

Liv begins to chop a cucumber.

'Well, if she was there, she needs to speak to the police and give a statement. And you need to take her. She needs someone with her. Representing her. You'll keep her calm and obviously you know about the law.'

Andy gives a small shake of his head as he bends for a frying pan in the cupboard below him.

'Stop catastrophising,' he says softly. 'She's not involved.' Then he straightens up and places the pan on the stove. 'So,' he says. 'How was your day?'

Liv looks at her husband, mystified that he can move so swiftly from the topic of their daughter and her possibly witnessing a murder.

'Fine,' she says. 'Yours?'

He is pouring oil into the pan. 'Your mum was pretty distressed.'

'What happened?'

A shrug. 'I'm not sure but she wanted to go to the shops and it became this whole … thing.' The oil is already spitting and Andy tips the chicken into the pan and begins stirring.

'Couldn't Dad take her?'

Incredibly Pete still has his licence although Liv thinks it's probably just a matter of weeks before they should insist he gives it up.

'He'd forgotten it was Friday. And when he told her he was busy she got angry. Furious actually. Shouted at both of us. Threw a book at Pete.'

This doesn't surprise Liv. Angela has always been and always will be a drama queen.

'Why couldn't you take her to the shops?'

There's a hesitation before Andy replies. 'We were busy. Pete and me. Sorting out some of his stuff.'

'What stuff?'

Andy pokes at the chicken. 'I don't know. Just … stuff.'

'You played golf.' Liv can see it on his face. Andy gives a guilty shrug. 'You know you can't leave Mum on her own. She gets confused.'

'Yeah, I know, I know. But your dad's been asking me every day this week to go with him. We haven't been for ages.'

Angela had boiled two saucepans dry the other week and set off the smoke alarm another few times. Somehow her parents muddled along quite well when they were together, but apart things tended to go wrong. Quickly.

Andy leaves the chicken and goes over to the fridge and pulls out a second beer.

'I'm sorry. I know it's not ideal,' he says after twisting it open and taking a swig. 'Pete needed some Friday fun.'

'Did you and dad have a good time at least?'

'Yeah, great. Lots of fun.'

'Did you stay for drinks at the clubhouse?'

Her dad enjoys drinks at the clubhouse.

'Yeah, course.' Andy returns to the chicken, clearing his throat. 'Your dad loves happy hour there.' He clears his throat a second time.

There it is. Andy's tell.

A very obvious one to her, especially after more than two decades of marriage but one he doesn't appear to be aware he has. And which is too useful to tell him about.

'Anyone I know there?' she asks, watching him closely.

He frowns. 'Don't think so.' He clears his throat again and Liv stares at him, confused. Why on earth he would lie about something as innocuous as golfing with her dad?

'So you had a nice leisurely game of golf while my poor abandoned mother was left home alone.' She smiles as he finally looks across at her, giving a sheepish shrug. 'You'll never hear the end of that one.'

He gives a tight laugh. 'I know. I'm a terrible son-in-law.'

Then he clears his throat for the fourth time.

Chapter 8

LIV

Saturday, 1 February 2025

Gracie finally came home soon after Liv went to sleep the night before. Now it is Saturday morning and Liv feels relief that Gracie is once again within touching distance. But now her worry has been replaced with trepidation.

Gracie drops a banana into the blender, then adds some frozen berries, yoghurt and milk into the mix. Liv, who is making herself some toast, flinches at the screaming roar as the blender pulverises its contents.

'Are you in a rush to get to work?' Liv asks when the noise finally stops.

'My shift got cancelled. I'm on tomorrow. Why?' Her tone is defensive.

'No reason.' Liv takes a bite of toast. 'I just wanted to ask you about Thursday.'

Gracie's hand, which is now holding the glass containing the purple smoothie, pauses midway to her mouth.

'Why?' she repeats.

'I spoke to Meredith yesterday and she seems to think you might have been at the park around the same time as when Richard died.'

Gracie takes a sip of her smoothie.

'The police are apparently asking people who were at the Gully park to go to the North Sydney station and report their movements. I guess they want to know who was there and when, to build up a picture of possible eyewitnesses. Work out who might have seen something. Or someone.'

Gracie nods but doesn't say anything. Just takes another sip of her drink.

'So, were you there?'

The question hangs in the air, unanswered.

'I didn't see anything,' Gracie says finally. She turns towards the sink and begins rinsing her glass. 'I don't know anything.'

'So you were there?'

A shrug. 'I run there every morning.'

'Okay. Well, we better get you to the station, then. You'll need to tell them.'

'What's the point?' Gracie says with an edge to her voice.

Liv knows Gracie doesn't mean this, that she understands police procedures and investigations and how they work.

'Well, they have to rule you out.'

'I didn't see anything.'

'That's okay. Tell them that. You'll just have to say when you were there, what you were doing and when you left. If you saw anyone who looked suspicious or out of place. Nothing major. Nothing scary.'

But when Gracie turns from the sink, Liv sees she is more distressed than angry. In fact, she looks to be on the verge of tears.

'Hey, it'll be okay.' Liv's voice is soft and she reaches for her daughter's hand. 'You don't need to worry, I promise. Dad can go with you. I can too if you like. Maybe we can explain you need someone with you, even though you're over eighteen.'

Gracie nods stiffly.

'We could take you over to the station later today if you like,' Liv says as Gracie heads back to her room. 'We haven't got any plans today.'

'Maybe,' her daughter says, her voice now flat. 'I'll let you know,' she adds before Liv hears the click of her daughter's bedroom door shutting.

Gracie spends the morning in her room. When she emerges at lunchtime for food, Liv watches her move around the kitchen making a sandwich, and steels herself from asking if she's called the police station.

Early afternoon, she and Andy go and do the weekly shop and agree that Andy will ask Gracie again, and offer to take her when they get home. He doesn't seem to think that it being a Saturday afternoon is a problem.

'The police are a 24/7 operation,' he says with a shrug when Liv mentions this during their drive home.

But when they get back, the house is empty, save for Sophie. Gracie has left a note on the kitchen counter: *Back late x*

That night, Liv tries to stay awake until Gracie returns. She texts her daughter at ten to remind her to take an Uber on the family account if she wants. She checks Gracie's location and sees she is in Haymarket, probably getting dumplings, hers and Kristina's favourite late-night pit stop.

It's 3.38 when Liv wakes with a start.

She automatically reaches out to feel for Andy but his side of the bed is empty. She sits up, heart thumping, pulling out her earplugs. 'What's wrong?'

'It's okay. It's Gracie. Think she's sleep-talking,' Andy replies from the foot of the bed, his voice thick with sleep. 'I'll check on her.'

But Liv is already pushing off the sheet and is halfway up to standing. 'I'll go. You go back to sleep.'

Liv pads down the dark corridor to Gracie's room and finds her daughter sitting upright in her bed, drenched in sweat, breathing quickly and whimpering.

'It's me. It's okay, sweetheart.'

Liv sits down on the edge of Gracie's bed and reaches for her, finding an arm, slick with sweat, in the darkness.

'It's just a bad dream. Come on, back to sleep now. Lie down, darling.'

Her daughter makes an unintelligible noise. Gracie has always been a profligate sleepwalker and sleep talker. When she was little it would take just a mis-timed door slam or a raised voice in another room to rouse her from sleep and propel her out of her room. She'd charge into the living room, babbling nonsense until they guided her back to bed and sat with her, stroking her arm gently until she fell into a presumably deeper sleep again. She still does it on occasion, but usually only when she's stressed or anxious about something.

'Back to sleep, now,' Liv says softly. She gently nudges Gracie until she sinks back down onto the mattress then reaches for the remote on her side table and switches on the overhead fan.

It takes a minute or so but Gracie's breathing gradually becomes steady and drawn out.

The next morning Liv wakes as the first signs of morning light start to appear around the edges of the blinds. She finds Gracie sitting on the sofa in the living room, in her running gear, her bare knees tucked into her chest, her head burrowed into them.

She sits next to her daughter and places her hand on the small of Gracie's back.

'What's wrong, sweetheart? What's happened?'

But Gracie doesn't reply and after a while her soundless crying begins to ebb and she reaches for a handful of tissues from the box on the coffee table and wipes at her eyes.

'Is this about going to the police? Or what happened to

Richard?'

Gracie blows her nose and then there is a long silence before she finally nods. 'Both,' she says.

Liv hesitates. 'Did you see something at the park?'

Gracie sniffs.

'Richard?'

A nod as Gracie pats her face with a fresh tissue.

'Before or after he was attacked?'

There's another long pause. 'Before,' Gracie says, her voice raspy.

'Did you talk to him?'

Gracie buries her head back into her knees.

'Did something happen?'

Another nod.

'Can you tell me what?'

There is another excruciating silence. Liv's mind scrambles and slows at the same time and it is as though she is watching them both from above, like she is suspended in the air. Her limbs feel hollow with fear.

This is it. Right now, this is it, she thinks.

'I don't know how to say it,' Gracie says finally, looking at her mum with tear-filled eyes. 'I don't think I can even say the words.'

Chapter 9

MEREDITH

November 2024

Meredith looked out across the reserve which, like the rest of the street, stood high above trees and houses that sloped down towards Middle Harbour, and wondered if she'd made a terrible mistake.

What was the point of any of this, of relocating her whole life and moving back to Sydney, if Liv was going to be like this? Wasn't even going to give her a chance? Was just going to assume she was the same kid she'd been all those years ago.

'No, Sophie, stop it!'

The voice broke into her reverie and she turned to see a young woman standing next to a familiar Labrador who was squatting and relieving itself on the grass. She was tall and athletic, wearing tan shorts and a white vest, her feet slipped into Converse that were left untied. There was a small black tattoo on the inside of her forearm, but Meredith couldn't make out what it was.

'No more, Soph, please, I can't deal.'

The dog moved away from the mess it had made, making a

feeble attempt at scratching the ground to cover it as the young woman bent over to scoop it up. When she'd finished she turned towards Meredith, holding out the plastic bag at arm's length with a disgusted expression on her face and deposited it in the council bin.

'She ate a whole wheel of brie earlier,' she said apologetically, seeing Meredith only as she closed the top of the bin. 'So gross.'

Meredith smiled. 'My dog did that once. With a whole block of cheddar.'

'They're so stupid.' The girl reached down and gave the dog an affectionate scratch. 'So stupid but so lovable, aren't you? Yes you are, yes you are.' She buried her face in the Labrador and Meredith saw then that the tattoo was a simple outline of a dancing nude, arms aloft and one leg slightly bent as though the figure, a woman, was leaping through the air.

'That's Labs for you.'

'Total pigs. But I forgive her every time.'

'You're Gracie, right, Liv and Andy's daughter?' She quickly added, 'I'm Meredith. I was just at yours for the barbecue.'

Her face lit up. 'Oh, right.'

'I live just there,' Meredith said, gesturing to the building behind her. 'But I knew your mum when she was younger.'

'Oh you're the old babysitter! Sorry, not old, but you're the reason for the barbecue, right?'

Meredith nodded. 'Both are true.'

Gracie gave an easy laugh and Meredith liked that the young woman didn't rush to tell her she was wrong.

'Your mum told me you were a runner, is that right?' Meredith asked. Liv hadn't but Meredith had spotted the muddy running shoes by the front door. 'I think your mum mentioned you were training for a race?'

Meredith had seen a flyer stuck to the fridge door advertising an Easter trail run up the coast and didn't imagine it was Liv or Andy's thing.

'Trying to. I've done a half marathon but this is a forty km trail run so a bit different.'

'Do you happen to know if there are any local parkruns nearby?'

Gracie thought for a moment. 'I think there might be one at North Sydney Oval but I haven't been.'

'Great, thanks. I'll look into it.' She made a move as if readying to leave. 'Oh, and are there any good spots for beginners around here? Anywhere shady and flat?'

'The park's good. The Gully park?' Gracie gestured towards the water and Meredith saw it again, that tattoo. It was like an outline of an art deco statue. 'Not loads of shade but if you get there early it's okay.'

'Thanks, I've heard about it but haven't been yet.'

'There's a big oval if you just want to go round and round or you can go into the actual Gully for a trail run. And it's by the water so you get a bit of a breeze. I go around six most mornings, if you're ever up that early.'

Meredith smiled. 'Sounds perfect. I might see you there.' Then as an afterthought, she said in a way she hoped sounded casual. 'I love that tattoo by the way. Really unusual.'

Gracie smiled. 'Thanks.' She made a face. 'Mum and Dad hate it, obviously.'

Meredith laughed. 'Obviously.'

When Meredith got home she dug out her old running trainers from the back of the wardrobe. They smelt faintly of mould so she took them outside onto the balcony to air them in the late afternoon sun.

Then she made herself a cup of peppermint tea and sat outside drinking it, enjoying the warm, uncurling happiness as it spread through her. Despite Liv's conversation to her friends at the barbecue and their unkind words, it had been a good afternoon in the end.

Thanks to Gracie, Meredith had found a way in.

Chapter 10

LIV

Sunday, 2 February 2025

Liv watches Andy who is sitting on the armchair in the corner of the living room. He has not said anything since she told him what happened to their daughter on Thursday morning, but she can see his rage, his grief, bubbling under the surface. He is taut with it.

Every so often, he shakes his head and his expression hardens. She knows he is imagining Gracie that morning. Her fear. What Richard did to her. Then the horror of discovering the man who assaulted her had been killed, possibly just minutes after Gracie broke free from him.

'Gracie had nothing to do with what happened to Richard afterwards,' Liv says, her voice clipped and precise. 'She wasn't there. She didn't see what happened to him. She got out of there as quickly as possible.'

The door to the garden is open and the sounds of their neighbour's morning activities, a young family with three children under five, lifts and travels over their fence. A toddler squealing; the low hum of an adult in response. The loud, insistent shout of an older child from somewhere within their house, then a slammed door.

'So what I'm saying is, I can't see any reason for her to mention any of this to the police. She can say she saw Richard briefly on the oval, said hi and then kept going. No more than that.'

Liv waits for Andy to respond, to agree, to nod and say, yes, of course, because Gracie has already been through so much; has dealt with so much and has come out the other side. Doing anything to jeopardise her hard-fought recovery is too risky. Would actually be a madness in itself.

But he doesn't agree.

'No,' Andy says when he finally speaks. 'Absolutely not. Gracie has to tell them exactly what happened.'

Liv stares at her husband, confused.

'What?' she says finally.

'They'll find out soon enough and, besides, she won't be able to keep her story straight or lie convincingly. She's traumatised enough by what's happened. She needs to be honest from the outset or she could get in serious trouble.'

Liv feels a stabbing fury in her gut. 'Are you completely insane? No! We can't put her through that. She had nothing to do with that man's death but the police won't believe that. Richard attacked her. Assaulted her. *Sexually* assaulted her. That's a motive. Even if they decide it was self-defence, they'll still think she's responsible.'

Andy looks down at his hands. A slight shake of his head as if he's holding himself back.

'She has to tell the truth. And when she explains what happened, everything that happened and she tells them the way she told you, they'll believe her.' His voice has a firmness that unsettles her. 'It'll be obvious she's not lying. Like it's obvious to us she's not the one who killed Richard.'

Liv blinks.

'And what if they don't believe her?'

She can hear it in her voice. The desperation. The fear.

'What if they break her down?' she says. 'What if she falls apart when she's being interrogated, has a panic attack or goes mute? They won't understand that. They won't understand how Gracie isn't like most nineteen-year-olds. They'll assume it's an admission of guilt, even if we explain why.'

'No, they won't. They're not that insensitive.' Andy shakes his head. 'They're not going to be looking to pin this on just anyone. They'll be looking for the actual killer.'

And that's when Liv understands how her husband is absolute in his belief.

It hasn't even crossed his mind that Gracie might have had something to do with what happened the other morning.

She sits down on the edge of the sofa, her fingers digging into the heavy fabric. While Andy immediately believes their daughter is telling them everything, she, conversely, has imagined all kinds of other scenarios since learning Gracie was at the Gully on Thursday morning. Of course she has. Because if she were Gracie and some man assaulted her, she'd have felt no hesitation in killing him.

'Don't you think the police will be delighted to wrap this case up as quickly as they can?' she says, trying hard to keep her voice calmer now, knowing that she has to convince him with logic not high emotion. 'Why would they bother looking any further when Gracie tells them she was there, in the Gully, presumably around the same time, just footsteps from the location of his death? And then that she'd been assaulted by him just before his death. She'll be the perfect suspect. And even better, she probably won't defend herself. She'll get so overwhelmed she'll shut down.'

Andy is leaning back against the armchair, his head tilted so he is staring up at the ceiling, the nape of it cradled in his hands. Liv can see he is considering her words.

'But if they find out she's lying …' he says eventually.

'They won't.'

A long exhalation. 'What if they do?'

'We'll deal with that if it happens. By then the police might have tracked down the real killer. We can say Gracie was traumatised, that she blacked out the assault. We can explain about her past issues, they'll be lenient. Surely.'

She sees the cogs of Andy's thoughts as they turn over and around and she wills him to agree with her. They sit there, in silence, for a while longer, until she notices his body begins to sag a little. Until his face loses some of its anger. Until he shifts, sitting upright so he's looking directly across at her.

'Okay,' he says finally. 'I think it's the wrong thing to do but okay.'

Andy drives and Gracie sits in the front passenger seat, picking at her fingers and jiggling her leg.

'Try not to speak too quickly and you'll be great,' Andy says. 'If you feel nervous, just say you are, say how you've never spoken to the police before or done anything like this. They'll be sympathetic. They'll understand.'

Gracie nods but she looks queasy. Her hair is lank against her face and a fresh collection of spots has broken out on her forehead. She looks far younger than her nineteen years. Her hand traces at the small tattoo on her left forearm, her dancing girl, inked the day after she turned eighteen, to Liv's horror.

'We'll be in the waiting area. It'll all be over and done with before you know it,' Andy adds.

'You're doing the right thing, sweetheart,' Liv says, attempting to keep her tone soothing and low. 'This had nothing to do with you or what he did. You don't need to get involved.'

Liv repeats this to herself like a mantra as they park up on a nearby side road and then walk to the station. When they get inside, Andy takes the lead, crossing past rows of seating to speak to the young, uniformed officer at the front desk.

He explains how Gracie has an appointment, and the officer taps on the computer, nods and then, a little brusquely for Liv's tastes, motions for Gracie to follow him through the double doors on the far side of the room. Gracie glances back just briefly before the doors swing shut behind her and Liv forces what she hopes is a reassuring smile.

Liv and Andy sit down on the bank of chairs near the window and wait, variously distracting themselves with their phones or just staring at the double doors, willing them to open.

Other people come and go; an older man who sits a few chairs from them until he's called to the front desk and then after some back and forth, leaves, looking disgruntled. A young woman pushing a pram sits by the separate bank of chairs, jiggling the pram constantly until a young, stony-faced man appears from behind the double doors and after some filling out of forms at the front desk, they leave together. The man reaches out to take over pushing the pram as they step out onto the street.

She and Andy are in another world, Liv realises. A place she never imagined she'd see. That she hadn't really even thought about until today.

Half an hour later, Gracie finally emerges looking flushed but relieved it's over, a young female uniformed officer holding the door open. She gives a small nod towards her parents before the policewoman gives a businesslike acknowledgement and 'thanks for coming in' and then it is all over.

'They were nice' is all Gracie will say until she is inside the safety of the car.

Once they are on the road Gracie tells her parents how she had to go over the timings of her run and show them on a map the route she ran through the Gully and confirm that, no, she hadn't seen Richard at all while she was there. Keeping as close to the truth as possible, they had decided eventually, was the best course of action.

'I told them about the other people I'd seen in the park, just described them and said what dogs they had, that kind of thing. But it was pretty quiet so there wasn't much to tell.'

'Do you think they believed you?' Liv asks when Gracie is finished.

A shrug. 'Think so.'

'Did they say what happens next?'

'They said they'd be in touch if they needed anything else clarified.' She pulls a business card from her pocket. 'The main guy came in at the end and gave me this.'

Liv takes the card from Gracie's outstretched hand.

'He said to call him if I remembered anything else.'

Detective Inspector James Mitchell, Homicide squad, North Shore Area Command.

'Did you tell them you saw Meredith there?'

Gracie nods, but she's on her phone, already absorbed. Soothing herself by scrolling through TikToks.

'What did you say? Exactly.'

Gracie glances up, her face a blank. 'Nothing.'

'Did you say you spoke to her?'

'I just told them I saw her when I came out of the Gully when I'd finished my run, we spoke briefly to say hello and then I left and went home.'

'Did they ask what Meredith did when you left?'

Gracie blinks. 'What do you mean?'

'Did they ask what direction she was going in when you left, like towards the Gully or away from it?'

Gracie looks confused. 'No, because she was just running around the oval.'

'You saw her doing that? Running around the oval after you left?'

There is a micro-second's hesitation and then Gracie lets out an irritated, 'Yes, I said so, didn't I? She was just running. Like me.'

Liv and Andy exchange a look. Gracie has reverted back to stroppy teenager mode, which is a good sign.

Chapter 11

LIV

Sunday, 2 February 2025

'Just someone I knew growing up' was how Liv described Meredith to Andy months back, when she'd seen the other woman for the first time at the hospital. When she'd felt her stomach dropping in horror at coming face to face with the grown-up version of the girl she'd last seen nearly thirty years before. Same short brown hair, same blunt fringe. Same intense, hooded dark eyes that seemed to look straight through her and had always made her feel slightly unnerved when she was younger. And now.

'School friends?'

'Not exactly.'

'You didn't like her?'

Liv had hesitated. 'It wasn't that.'

She'd tried to summon the words to explain. 'Meredith Edwards was that weird kid at school. Weird when she was a kid, weird when she was a teenager.' A grimace. 'Sort of a bit weird now?'

Andy had raised his eyebrows.

'Just a bit … different? A bit socially awkward? Serious. Too grown-up for her age probably. I don't know. She'd had a tough childhood. Maybe that made her grow up quickly.'

'What happened?'

'Her mum died when she was little, her dad raised her and he was … Well, he was also weird. So my parents told me. They were both just a bit eccentric. Clearly both very, very clever. He was a doctor and taught at Sydney University, she was in all the accelerated classes. I suppose she just always stood out at school because she was so different to the rest of us. And you know what teenagers are like, especially at girls' schools. Bitchy pack animals. So she was a bit of a target.' Liv shifted, uncomfortable now, under Andy's gaze. 'You know what kids are like, you follow the crowd and if the crowd says someone's an outsider then you kind of follow along.'

'Well,' Andy said eventually. 'I think weird is good.'

Liv smiled. She had known this would be Andy's response.

'Why don't we try and make up for what happened at school by being nice neighbours now and inviting her for a barbecue? Introduce her to everyone.'

Liv looked at him with dismay. 'Really?'

'It'll be your chance to show Meredith how much nicer you are now,' he said.

Andy is a natural-born, one-man welcome party. He prides himself on making newcomers to their road feel welcome and bringing disparate people together. He also loves any excuse for an afternoon beer and a burnt sausage.

So, a month after Meredith moved onto their street, reappearing in Liv's life for the first time since 1993, there she was, standing in their garden, smiling politely and conversing with the other guests in that solemn, slightly humourless way that Liv saw now, with adult eyes, was probably simple social awkwardness.

It is now two and a half months on from that November afternoon. Liv fills a glass with chilled water, picks up her phone and takes it out into the garden where she positions herself in the only scrap of shade on the deck and searches for Meredith on Facebook and Instagram but eventually has to make do with her LinkedIn profile.

Orthopaedic Surgeon, Northern Public Hospital.

October 2024 – present.

Then a rundown of her other positions below the note *Meredith hasn't posted yet.*

Liv turns over the idea she's had, examining and considering it. Trying to work out whether it's a terrible or genius idea, although above all else it is clearly an immoral one.

But this idea, if carried out, could be exactly what is needed: insurance for Gracie.

It would prompt the police to look in Meredith's direction and dig a little deeper. They would find out about the relationship, or whatever it was, between Meredith and Richard. They would undoubtedly question why Meredith hadn't mentioned it.

Then it wouldn't be long before they discovered what happened at the Christmas party. The public fight everyone at the hospital has been gossiping about since then. Meredith's alleged attack on Richard.

It would be the perfect way to ensure the police quickly forgot about Gracie's presence at the park on Thursday morning and turned their attention to a much more likely suspect.

Later that night, Liv places the business card next to her laptop. She sets up a new anonymous email account and then in case it is somehow traced back to her, sets up two more connected to each other. Then, under her new account, Concerned_witness@ gmail.com, she emails Detective Inspector James Mitchell and explains a little about Meredith Edwards's connection to Richard, both professionally and personally.

There were rumours that Meredith and the victim of the recent killing at the Gully park not only knew each other

57

but had been intimately acquainted. Their relationship ended badly and witnesses can confirm Meredith physically attacked Richard at a hospital function the month before.

While it's likely Meredith had nothing to do with what happened to Richard Wellington, I believe this is a line of enquiry that should be looked into.

Liv's heart is pounding and her hands shaky when she finishes. She sits back and re-reads the email and then stares at the screen, feeling queasy.

Is she really doing this?

Her finger hovers over the send button but she can't do it. Not yet, not now.

Instead, she saves the email in drafts and logs out of the account, clears her browsing history and snaps the laptop lid shut. Then she goes over to the fridge, pours herself a large glass of wine and joins Andy on the sofa where they watch an episode of *Grand Designs*.

That night Gracie has another nightmare that wakes Liv and Andy. As Liv soothes and hugs her panicked, hyperventilating daughter – this is a first, Gracie has never had a panic attack in the middle of the night, let alone in her sleep – Liv feels the decision is made for her.

As soon as Gracie settles, Liv goes into the kitchen and brings her laptop to life.

She checks the message, reading it twice, wondering if she is crazy to imagine no one will be able to trace it back to her, then lets out a long exhale, whispers an apology to the gods and presses send.

Chapter 12

MEREDITH

November 2024

After the barbecue, Meredith had messaged Liv to thank her for the lovely afternoon, but hadn't explained her abrupt departure and Liv hadn't asked. Meredith assumed Liv would just think she was still as strange as she had been growing up. As socially inept as she'd been as a teenager. But aware that she needed to continue her attempt at befriending Liv, Meredith had texted a week later to ask if she had time for coffee some time and Liv had replied enthusiastically.

But the tentative date came and went; then Liv messaged back with effusive and over-the-top apologies for not getting in touch and suggested a morning the following weekend. Meredith was away so suggested another time before work but then Liv cancelled at the last minute, apologising again and explaining she had to travel across the city to take her mother to a last-minute medical appointment.

Meredith understood by then that they would never have coffee and that, if she didn't draw a line under their attempt, this planning and cancelling dance would play out for eternity or when one of them dropped dead. So Meredith stopped messaging and instead decided to concentrate her efforts on Gracie. At least for now, she would be Meredith's way in.

Since meeting Gracie that afternoon at the reserve, Meredith had been dragging herself out of bed before six at least three times a week and going down to the park so that she could see the girl. Meredith downloaded a couch-to-5km app and would spend thirty miserable minutes inching her way around the perimeter of the oval, keeping alert for Gracie's movements, ready to stop the moment she'd finished her workout and headed for the clearing by the water for her cool-down and stretches.

Meredith soon realised Gracie ran for at least an hour most mornings, beginning around 6 a.m. Meredith adjusted her arrival accordingly, usually arriving after 6.30 so they finished around the same time. After a week or so of waves and hellos across the grass, by the end of November, Meredith started joining Gracie for these stretches, under the auspices of asking for advice on how to avoid shin splints.

By week two of Meredith's running programme, and the turning point for her actually beginning to enjoy it and the accompanying endorphin rush, they'd swapped numbers and followed each other on Instagram. They started sending each other reels on training tips or running-related posts then moved on to funny Labrador ones involving food.

Then one evening, Meredith messaged Gracie to ask if she knew of any good local tattoo artists.

You getting one?! came Gracie's response.

Thinking about it. Maybe a Xmas pressie to myself?

She replied back immediately: I was thinking about getting a second one. There's a new place on Pac highway @happyink-sydney – want to take a look with me?

Love to, Meredith replied immediately.

Smiling at the screen she clicked on the Instagram handle

Gracie had sent through and began scrolling through its feed, looking at the different designs it offered, from delicate line drawings to more detailed coloured graphics. Meredith hadn't ever considered getting a tattoo but now she thought, why not? Something small and hidden away might be nice. It might be a good way to mark this significant new chapter in her life.

While it was no coincidence that Meredith ended up living on the same cul-de-sac as Liv, it was pure serendipity that Dr Richard Wellington also turned out to be her neighbour.

Meredith had a vague memory of hearing that Richard operated out of Northern Private on the far side of the campus it shared with the public hospital of the same name and also had a regular slot on a television programme. His name occasionally came up among her new colleagues and from what they said she immediately understood the kind of man he was. She had come across dozens of surgeons like him during her career and it sounded like he ticked all the boxes: arrogant, tunnel-visioned, rude, slightly sociopathic, but also talented and knowledgeable.

Then Meredith heard about the legal case brought against him. Although it had ended some months before, everyone still appeared full of opinions and theories about what had happened and why. She learnt how Richard had refused to follow his legal team's advice and come to a financial settlement with the man who'd brought it against him. How despite all the evidence apparently being against him, he'd won the case.

Meredith finally met the apparently infamous medic at a lunch put on by one of the hospital's charity partners in mid-November. A selection of senior staff members had been asked to attend and she drew the short straw to represent Orthopaedics.

It had been a long morning and she was already tired and headed straight to the fruit platter to get a sugar fix. She was onto her third slice of watermelon when Richard appeared, reaching for a sausage roll.

'Shouldn't really,' he muttered, flashing a smile. 'What the hell, eh?'

He took a bite of the pastry as his eyes lingered on the space above Meredith's chest where she'd affixed her name tag.

'Dr Meredith Edwards,' he said, drawing out the syllables of her name. 'Orthopaedics, eh?'

'Hi,' she said, politely. He didn't have a name tag on and Meredith decided not to flatter him by admitting she knew who he was.

'I think I know you,' he said. 'Susan was singing your praises the other day at panel.'

Meredith flushed at the thought of the Director of Orthopaedics discussing her. It was always hard to gauge whether she was pleased with Meredith's work although she never said anything to suggest she wasn't, but being new to the team and pathetically desperate for approval meant these things mattered.

'You've not been here long, have you?'

'Just a few months.'

'You settling into life at Northern? Everyone welcoming you in, making you feel wanted? You've got a solid team with Susan at the helm.'

'Yes, she's wonderful.'

A pause longer than necessary, then he nodded. 'Yes, she is rather.'

Meredith's smile wavered. As well as being a talented medic, her boss was also conventionally very attractive.

'Where were you before then?' he asked, his tone suddenly back to businesslike and clipped.

'John Hunter in Newcastle.'

He looked predictably surprised.

'Well, this is a big change for you then. Little mouse in the big city and all that. I must take you out. Show you our beautiful city.'

'Oh, I'm from Sydney originally,' Meredith replied and then understood immediately that this was the wrong thing to say.

'But thanks anyway.'

His brow furrowed. 'Have our paths crossed before? You do look very familiar.'

'I don't think so,' Meredith said.

'USyd?' he pressed and when Meredith feigned confusion, he clarified, 'University. Did you go to Sydney University?' as if he were talking to a particularly dense child.

'Oh yes, I did.'

He looked pleased at that of course, because he was a predictable old snob.

'Year?'

'I graduated in 2003.'

He reached across the table for a sushi roll and popped it into his mouth. As he chewed, she saw it: that click of recognition.

'Any relation to Stephen Edwards?' he asked as Meredith knew he would. As everyone of his generation always did.

She smiled. 'My father.'

Richard gave a nod of satisfaction, pleased he'd figured out the great mystery of her provenance and was now able to slot Meredith neatly into whatever pigeon-hole he had reserved for the offspring of well-known medics.

'He was head of clinical when I was at Sydney. I think we were his last rotation.'

'Oh really?' Meredith's interest was finally piqued.

'It was such a shame what happened to your old dad. We were all so very sorry to say farewell to him.'

Then his expression suddenly transformed and he was grinning and raising a hand in greeting to someone across the room.

'It's been lovely to meet you, Dr Edwards,' he said, returning to Meredith, all obsequious charm again. 'Welcome to Northern and I do hope our paths cross again,' and then with another flash of his cosmetically enhanced smile, he turned and was gone.

Chapter 13

LIV

Monday, 3 February 2025

Sunday has been the day Liv visits her parents for as long as she can remember. No matter what else is going on in her life, she finds a way to see them, even if it's just a flying visit.

But yesterday, amid all the worry surrounding Richard's death and Gracie's police statement, she completely forgot. She is only reminded now when she misses a call from their landline, halfway through her workday. When she calls back it rings and rings. She tries both her parents' mobiles but they go straight to voicemail so she calls Andy to check whether he's at their house or has heard from them, but his phone is switched off.

Liv leaves work early and drives straight over the bridge in awful rush-hour traffic, trying to suppress the mild worry she is feeling. She finds her mum in the back sunroom, sleeping in the overstuffed chair by the window, her eyes closed, her hair freshly blown dry, her make-up – of course – impeccable. She is wearing a long, sleeveless dark green silk dress because Angela isn't the kind of woman who would ever consider donning shorts and

T-shirt, not even in 32-degree heat.

Leaving her mother to nap, Liv sees the light is on in the courtyard studio where her father spends most of his time, the faint tinkle of jazz music coming from behind the closed door. She looks through the tiny window to the side of the door and sees he is at his desk, sifting through paperwork.

The concern she'd felt now appeased, Liv goes upstairs to her old bedroom to try and find the items she hopes will still be packed away in the wardrobe, untouched in, what would it be, thirty years?

Her childhood bedroom has been redecorated since she moved out decades before, the old floral Eighties wallpaper taken down and a soft white paint in its place. A double bed has replaced her old wrought-iron single one, but everything else is just the same. The white side table, art-nouveau-style lamp on it and all Liv's old books spanning from babyhood to her teenage years on the shelf by the window; the same framed watercolours on the wall and floor-to-ceiling cupboard on the other side. It even smells of the same lavender potpourri her mother used to keep in a bowl on her chest of drawers.

Liv opens the cupboard door and feels a wave of relief when she sees it is still stacked with boxes. Of course it is. Her parents are terrible hoarders and never seem to throw anything away, and for that Liv is now grateful.

She finds the bundle of letters and notes, contained in a large manila envelope, tucked in among her high school books and old board games. There are dozens of letters although she knows that she would have received many more throughout her teenage years that she hasn't kept – and sent just as many to her friends in response. Life before mobile phones.

Picking out one at random, Liv smiles when she sees it is from her old best friend Caro. Her eyes skim the page, reading this glimpse from year nine or maybe ten, something about Caro freaking out over what a girl called Sarah had done in biology.

Something about wanting to go to the beach at the weekend amid a complaint about her stupid parents dragging her up the coast to her grandparents'.

Liv finishes reading the note then tucks it back into the pale pink envelope it's been living in for the past thirty-odd years. The last thing she heard, Caro inherited and moved into that complained-about beachside house up the coast and was living what sounded like an idyllic existence there after divorcing her husband and giving up her career in finance. She'd also retrained as a yoga teacher.

Liv sifts through the other letters until she finds one with Meredith's familiar handwriting. She had perfect cursive, presumably the result of spending careful hours doing the prescribed handwriting exercises Liv had always rushed through.

As Liv opens the envelope, she can still recall the excited bubble she'd felt when she'd first received a letter from Meredith. It had been sitting on the dining table, separated out from the other correspondence, the pile for her mum, the pile for her dad, the boring pile for bills. And there it was: a small sky-blue envelope for her, Miss Olivia Elliot.

She had only met Meredith the previous weekend at their school fair. They'd got talking next to the ice-cream stand, when her mother had turned and seen Meredith's smiling face and responded with a 'Oh, hello,' and Meredith had greeted her back and said, 'I think you know me,' and Angela had looked a little taken aback and said that yes, she did, from when she was at the primary school they were standing in.

'I'm Meredith Edwards,' the odd girl said to Liv and then turned back to Angela. 'I believe you know my father, too.'

Her mother hesitated a moment and then said, 'Yes, I do, you're quite right.'

'Thought so,' said the girl.

Meredith had followed Liv to the over-tens line for the bouncy castle and begun talking to her as if they were old friends. Liv didn't mind, she quite liked having the attention of a clearly older girl. And soon Meredith was quizzing Liv on what year she was in and then when she discovered Liv was going to St Mary's, her school, after the summer holidays, telling her all about it.

Liv never did find out how Meredith got her home address, but four days later, the first letter arrived, and the following, another. And now both of them are in her hand, hidden away for decades in one small envelope with a picture of a Beatrix Potter mouse on the right-hand corner.

24 November 1988
Dear Olivia/Liv – what do you like best? People seem to call you both.

It was very lovely to meet you on Saturday. I hope you had a nice time at the fete. I did very much. My favourite stall was the tombola and I won a game where you have to put little black balls into this cat's eyes but it's really hard because every time you get one in, the other one comes away from the right position. Did you have a go of that one?

I didn't get to stay for the costume parade but Corrine Masterson looked so good as Bo Peep – did you see? The costume was very well done.

Hopefully you'll write back to me. I would really love a pen pal over the summer holidays and because we only live around the corner from each other we wouldn't even have to use stamps – I'm going to put this through your front door.

I thought I could tell you more about St Mary's, where to go and what teachers are the best and worst, etc. I've got lots of good information as I'm about to go into year 7 and have been there since year 3.

I hope you write back. My address is at the top of this letter.
Yours faithfully,
Meredith Sandrine Edwards

25 November 1988

Dear Liv/ Olivia,

What do you want to be when you grow up? For a while I thought I might want to be a ballerina or even an actress but now I think I want to follow in my father's footsteps and be a doctor of some kind.

Will you be an actress like your mother? Is it strange that she's so famous and well known and everything? Do people stop and ask for autographs when you're out?

I actually didn't know about your mother's job until I read something in my father's newspaper a few weeks ago. It was an interview with her. She mentioned you. Did you see it? She said you were the apple of your father's eye and they both adored being parents but being away from you when they were working was difficult. Is it? What do you do when they are working? When my father's working I just stay at home on my own but when I was smaller we had babysitters and a housekeeper. I think I preferred that. It's a bit quiet and lonely when I'm on my own. Luckily my father doesn't go out now.

Yours faithfully,

Meredith Sandrine Edwards

PS My address is at the top of this letter.

Liv folds the two letters and returns them to the envelope and then in turn, puts it back in the large manila one containing all the others. She searches for Meredith's other ones but when she can't find them begins pulling out the boxes, one by one, from the wardrobe.

They must be here. She has a distinct memory of shoving them all into an old shoe box along with other knick-knacks and note-books she no longer wanted but couldn't bring herself to throw out. But after sifting through every last box she admits defeat.

Her eyes itchy from the dust, Liv repacks the wardrobe and when everything, apart from the original manila envelope, is back inside, closes the doors and goes over to the small window that looks out onto the street.

The summer holidays after Liv left her little school across the road and was waiting to start at St Mary's, where she'd be going into grade five, had been a long and particularly boring one. She and her parents had gone away for a week up the coast to the usual beachside house they rented from a family friend, but, apart from that, both her parents had been working on a new project that summer. While they went to what seemed like endless meetings and lunches, Liv was looked after by a series of babysitters even though she was ten now. Meredith continued to write Liv notes after that first one and Liv would reply back quickly, the excitement of having a pen pal peppering the endless and dull days of summer.

But while Liv knew she only had to ask once and Meredith would readily agree to come to Liv's house or invite Liv to hers, something stopped her. Despite a friendship being there for the taking – Liv knew it was with absolute certainty – she just couldn't bring herself to take that next step. In person Meredith was just a bit too different and even at that age Liv was very aware that different was wrong.

It was one evening after she and her parents returned from their week away at the beach house that Liv saw Meredith outside their house, looking in, for the first time.

She was helping her mum clear the dining table when a shadowy figure across the road caught her eye. The figure moved slightly, the streetlight catching at them and Liv had given a start. Her mum had noticed and asked what it was but Liv said that it was nothing, just a possum.

As Angela cleared the last plates, Liv looked again, just surreptitiously in her peripheral vision and saw that yes, it was definitely Meredith. She could tell by the girl's particular gait and the outline of her short bobbed hair.

Liv thought it coincidental. She knew Meredith lived just a

few streets away so it seemed perfectly acceptable that she should pass by Liv's house on occasion. But then it happened again the next night, a little later this time, when Liv was readying herself for bed and choosing a book to read from the small shelf under her window.

This time the other girl was motionless, standing on the opposite side of the street, in the shadow of the big fig tree. Like the night before, she was facing their house and this time she'd brought a dog with her. The dog was lying on the ground, in a position that suggested he hadn't stopped for a quick sniff or pee, but had possibly been there for some time.

Liv took a quick step backwards into the dim of her room, hoping Meredith hadn't seen her. A few minutes later, when she found herself unable to concentrate on the book she was reading, Liv got out of bed and sidled up to her window, careful to ensure she remained hidden as she took another peek outside. Sure enough, Meredith was still there.

It happened again the following night and the one after that and in the end, for the remainder of the summer. Liv became so used to seeing Meredith there that she found it more surprising when, by February and the start of the new school year, the other girl stopped coming.

Liv sits on her bed and tips out all the letters and sees there is one more note from Meredith among the collection that she missed the first time around. She quickly opens it and sees that it is another one of the early ones and begins to read.

15 January, 1989
Dear Liv,

I hope you are very well. How are your family? I am good. My dog Liston ate a whole packet of chocolate biscuits yesterday and I had to take him to the vet and they gave him something to make him vomit. He's in a very bad mood now and doesn't want to go for a walk, but on the good side of *things, he just wants to lie on my bed.*

I've been quite bored these holidays. I miss school. Dad's been a bit unwell so we haven't been doing much because he's had to rest.

What do you do in the holidays? Are you excited to start at St Mary's? Have you got your uniform and everything? I like preparing for the new school year. My favourite thing is buying new stationery and pens and things and then organising everything in a new pencil case.

I've been writing a story about a girl who is able to swap lives just by tapping on her wardrobe three times and then going inside. It's inspired by The Lion, the Witch and the Wardrobe. Have you read it? It's very good.

In my story, Alice (that's the girl's name) likes to swap lives with people she already knows. So one day she swaps with her friend from school, another day the lady who has three sausage dogs she sees walking in the park, then a teacher and then her mum. Well, that is my plan. I've only got up to the day where she swaps with her friend from school but that's already six pages, both sides so it's quite long.

I'd like to swap lives. Would you? If you did, who would you swap with?

I know you've been busy but you've only written to me four times and I've written to you a lot. I love getting letters. Things are very boring here in my house as my father is still unwell and can't go out. Please write soon!

Yours sincerely,
Meredith Sandrine Edwards x

Chapter 14

LIV

Monday, 3 February 2025

Liv steps into the courtyard and across the cobbled stones to the shed which was long ago stripped of gardening tools and old bikes to be reimagined as her father's study. The jazz music is still playing but Pete isn't there and she feels a twinge of concern that he might have gone wandering. Then she looks towards the French windows that lead from the southern end of the courtyard into the living room and there she sees the top of his head leaning against the high-back armchair. His still-thick silver hair is a fluffy nest against the maroon velvet wingback.

She returns to the study and sees it is set up for filming. It is a pretty amateur arrangement, as far as Liv can tell, although she suspects that's all you need these days with smartphones and ring lights. Two small portable lights face the old leather armchair that has been her father's favourite as long as Liv can remember. A tripod sits in front of it with a smaller empty holder that is just big enough for an iPhone and Liv smiles at the thought of her father still hard at work on some kind of project, dedicated to his craft after all these years.

She goes over to the desk in the corner and begins sifting through the various papers spread out across it as if she might find the rest of Meredith's old letters among them. The whole studio is in chaos and this desk is at the epicentre of the mess.

There are bills, old newspaper clippings and various scribbles on notepaper that don't make any sense to her. A stack of photos rests at the edge of the table; large A4, mostly black-and-white prints from her father's various productions over the years. There are stills of actors who she recognises from her father's films and backstage shots of the auteur himself in his trademark untucked white shirt and chinos. A few are of her mum looking elegant and beautiful, the same high cheekbones and knowing smile despite the different hairstyles and fashion spanning the many decades of her work as an actress and her father's muse.

'As you can see, your father's latest project is very messy.'

Liv turns to see Angela standing in the doorway. She greets her mum with the usual two kisses – one on each cheek, European style.

'What's he up to?'

Her mother gives a dismissive wave. 'Telling the story of his illustrious career and life apparently,' she says. 'As if anyone would be interested. Come on, let's go into the kitchen.'

Liv follows her mum out of the studio and across the courtyard, watching her mother's gait closely, ever watchful of changes or signifiers of decline or the after-effects of the mini-strokes.

Angela settles onto a kitchen chair at the small round table. She picks the one on the far side by the bookshelf stacked with cookbooks and a tiny old TV that no longer works and Liv knows the drill. She makes the tea, Angela receives it.

'Did you bring me any of those delicious biscuits?'

'Oh sorry, I didn't.' Liv throws Angela a regretful look and opens one of the cupboards, reaching for the biscuit tin which she opens to see is, predictably, empty. 'Next time, promise.'

When they are both seated at the table, tea and a small bowl of almonds and raisins set in front of them in place of biscuits, Liv asks her mother if she remembers Meredith.

'She used to babysit me,' Liv says. 'I think you knew her dad?'

'Of course, Marianne and Scott's daughter. She's a principal now on the South Coast. Was always good with unruly children, even at that age.' She smiles. 'She was good with you.'

Liv doesn't take the bait.

'No, not Helen. Meredith. Meredith Edwards. She lived over by the park? She was younger than Helen. Tall, with dark hair. In a bob with a fringe. Was quite intense and serious. Her dad was a doctor.'

But Angela looks blank.

'She went across the road then switched to St Mary's in year three,' Liv says. 'She only babysat when Helen wasn't available. Probably because she wasn't much older than me, I don't know. She was really clever. Maybe you thought some of that would rub off on me?'

Liv waits for the memory to lodge into place but there is not even the slightest suggestion that Angela knows who she is talking about.

'We were pen pals too, before she started babysitting. That summer before I started at St Mary's?'

Angela sips her tea with that familiar expression that tells companions she is both bored and getting irritated. Liv could keep her interest by telling her about her neighbour's death – her mum doesn't read or listen to the news so will not have heard what's happened. But Liv knows this will likely spin her mother into overdramatic worrying so she changes tack.

'Actually I'm looking for all my old letters, do you have any idea where they might be? My old teenage ones. Do you know if you'd have put any of my old things in storage or would they be in Dad's studio?'

Her mother shrugs. 'Everything's in your wardrobe where you

left it. I haven't touched a thing.'

'I've looked there but I think I've got an old shoe box some-where with more stuff in it. Does that ring a bell?'

'I don't know, darling, maybe. But it could be anywhere. Your father has us living in chaos. Complete chaos.' She picks out a raisin from the bowl and deposits it into her mouth. 'You know your father is being especially tiresome about this new project,' Angela says in her grandest, most actressy voice. 'All he's doing is drivelling on about all his boring films. I honestly don't know why he's bothering.'

'So what's he doing? Recording his memories?'

'He says it's a documentary.' Angela purses her lips. 'I call it droning on and on about the same thing on a loop.' She gives a defensive tilt of her chin. 'Well, I'm not saying anything we're not all thinking.'

'I think it's nice he's recording his memories,' Liv says, careful to keep her tone light. 'Maybe you should think about recording yours too?'

Angela's eyes immediately and predictably light up.

'You were just as famous as Dad. More so, maybe.'

'I suppose I've never really talked to anyone in depth about my time in London and on *Greener Grass*. I mean I did interviews at the time of course, but it would be nice to look back on that time and … reflect.'

Liv picks up her tea. 'I know I'd love to hear more about all your movies back in the Seventies and Eighties. You've told me some of your stories but not all of them.'

Liv is lying. She's heard them all on multiple occasions.

'Well, there's a lot to tell, darling.' A trace of a pout settles on her mum's lips. 'Not that anyone ever asks.'

'Oh Mum, don't say that. You should use the set-up in the studio Dad's organised. There's a tripod, the lights are there. You can ask Dad to show you how to use the phone to record yourself.'

Angela scoffs. 'Your father? He hasn't got a clue.'

'Well, he must do – there's a great set-up in his studio and you could just record yourself on your phone.'

'I could ask Andy to help.'

'He could show you how to use your phone to record yourself.'

'I think he could do a bit more than that,' Angela says. 'God knows he's had enough practise recording all of Pete's nonsense.'

'Andy's been helping Dad?'

'Of course.' Angela's gaze travels across the courtyard towards the studio. 'They've been up to all sorts in that studio together, darling.'

Liv frowns. 'All sorts?'

'All sorts,' Angela repeats with a satisfied smile, clearly delighted to know something Liv does not.

Chapter 15

MEREDITH

November 2024

A few days after meeting Richard at the charity function, Meredith had checked and found confirmation that he had been among the cohort that were taught by her father during what became his last year teaching. But she didn't have any way to know if Richard was one of the students who'd all but ended his career.

Richard had begun emailing Meredith a few days after the event. The notes were professional at first: he'd come across a scholarly article about something he thought she might be interested in or had she ever read something by so and so, naming a surgeon who specialised in her area. Of course she had, Meredith wanted to respond, but didn't. Instead she wrote back benign but hopefully discouraging responses such as 'Thanks!' or 'Yes, interesting.'

Then came the text messages.

How about a coffee? Feel I should offer you an official welcome some time.

Meredith had no idea who sent that first text and deleted it immediately, assuming it was sent wrongly to her. Then two nights later she received another message just as she was about to turn off her phone and head to bed.

Let's get together soon. Dinner? R.

She'd stared at the message for ages trying to figure out who R could be. Eventually, she searched for the number in her emails and sure enough, there it was, in Richard Wellington's email signature underneath his full medical title.

She had been preoccupied with discovering which of the students it was that ended her father's career for a while. Now, she couldn't dislodge the thought that perhaps Richard had been one of them, or if not, perhaps he could point her in the right direction. So, as she considered his message, Meredith decided she had nothing to lose.

She texted back the next day, so as not to appear too keen.

When were you thinking?

Predictably he suggested an expensive harbourside restaurant, with views across the water towards the Harbour Bridge and Opera House. She knew this went a step further than a friendly colleague welcoming a newcomer into the fold but Meredith also knew that if she had any chance of finding out his role in her father's downfall, she would have to play along. While keeping at a safe distance.

Things didn't get off to the right start when they finally met on a Wednesday evening towards the end of November. When Richard ordered a bottle of wine and Meredith explained she wasn't drinking that night, he was momentarily irritated but accepted it. When she told the waiter she'd prefer the fish rather than the beef ragu Richard recommended, he'd sat back in his chair and regarded her with amused annoyance.

'I see, you're one of them,' he said, wryly.

'What's that?'

'One of those women who won't allow a man to take the lead on anything.'

Meredith forced a smile because that was the only way she knew how to deal with men like Richard Wellington and she'd come across a thousand of his kind.

'You're not a lesbian, are you?' he said in a low tone, leaning across the table.

'Because I like to eat fish?'

He burst into a peal of appreciative laughter.

The ice was broken and when Meredith asked him about balancing his clinical and TV work, he beamed and she knew they were off and running.

For the next hour and a half, Richard talked about himself. He talked about his illustrious career and what it was like to be both famous in the medical and real world, he told Meredith stories about famous patients – 'naming no names,' he said smirking, then named them – and boasted he'd operated on royalty across the globe. He gossiped about the presenters he worked with, famous faces who'd been on the TV show, an apparently well-publicised scandal involving a weather man Meredith had never heard of.

By the time their desserts arrived, he had polished off a gin and tonic, a bottle of wine and was on his second brandy and Meredith decided it was time to address the real reason for her being there.

'I'd love to hear your memories of my dad,' she asked him after taking a bite of the chocolate torte. She disliked heavy chocolate desserts but, predictably, Richard had suggested it, and she decided to let him have this one. 'Was he a good teacher?'

Richard cradled his brandy as he considered the question.

'Professor Stephen Edwards,' he said, his voice thick with alcohol. 'Well, he clearly had a brilliant mind, was an incredibly skilled practitioner and, from what I remember, was a competent teacher, although

I suspect his heart wasn't really in it by the time I got to him.' He paused. 'I think everyone agreed, didn't they?' Meredith looked at him quizzically. 'That he was better off in research than teaching.'

Meredith did agree and explained how research had been her father's life's passion and that he'd returned to it in the early Nineties, continuing his research into pain management techniques for cancer patients and advising on a joint initiative between the University of Sydney and St Vincent's Hospital.

Richard looked surprised at this. 'He held on to his research position?'

'Absolutely. The university didn't want to lose him.'

'I don't remember seeing anything he published after he left his teaching post.'

Meredith hesitated. 'Dad was never quite well enough after everything that happened, to publish again. He contributed to some of his colleagues' work.'

Richard shifted his position, his gaze no longer meeting Meredith's as he picked up his spoon and scraped it around the edge of his already empty plate.

Meredith worked quickly to lift the dark mood that was threatening to settle over them.

'I haven't met any of Dad's students for a long time and to find out that you're one of them, of all people …' She hoped her smile was convincing. 'Well, he'd be thrilled, honestly. Just thrilled.'

That did the trick. His chest visibly puffed out as he reached for his glass.

'And I'm sure he'd be very proud of you.' He held it up, his eyes clearly struggling to focus on Meredith's, and said, 'Let's look to the future, to you being at Northern, to your brilliant career and to new friendships. Our friendship.'

Meredith held up her glass of Acqua Panna and plastered on another smile, understanding in that moment that if she wanted to know more about her father then this would be the cost. A friendship with Richard Wellington.

Chapter 16

LIV
Monday, 3 February 2025

The road is finally clear of news vans and reporters and Liv slides easily into her usual spot outside their house. She presses the car horn lightly, two times as is her usual signal to Andy, and a moment later he appears to help with the boxes Liv's brought back from her parents.

'Mum says you've been helping Dad with some kind of filming project,' she says as they take a box each, full of paperwork and notebooks that Liv has smuggled from her parent's house in the hope that they might contain the old Meredith letters.

He doesn't reply immediately, instead reaching inside one of the boxes as if checking something. 'Oh yeah. Well, we play golf and then we work on your dad's project.'

'But what do you do?'

There's a moment of hesitation. 'Filming,' he says finally. 'Filming him. Editing, digitising old cine-films, organising the stills we're going to use.'

'We're?'

He holds the front door open, not meeting Liv's eyes. 'It's a collaborative project.'

She looks at him confused. 'So it's going to be what … an actual documentary?'

'Hope so.'

'Dad thinks people might be interested in watching it?'

'Liv, your dad's one of the most respected filmmakers in the country.'

Liv lets out a laugh. 'Really?'

'He was part of Australia's new wave. A trailblazer back in the Seventies and Eighties.' A pause. 'We've already got some interest from the ABC.'

Liv stares at her husband as he passes her to return to the car to retrieve the other bags. As she watches him close the car door, her gaze lands on Richard's red Maserati, still parked up in the opposite driveway behind an electric gate. Liv wonders how Sandra managed to get Richard to agree to park his $400,000 car in the open air so that she could house all her rescue animals in their garage. Maybe he wasn't as selfish as she imagined.

'We're shooting footage with Max Robertson and David Shepherd next week,' Andy is saying as he steps back onto the veranda. 'Which is great because I really want to pay homage to that whole era of filmmakers, not just your dad.'

She looks at him, baffled.

'What?' he asks, part-defensive, part-amused.

'I don't understand why you didn't tell me any of this before,' she says. 'It's like you've been keeping it a secret.'

'It's not a secret,' Andy replies. 'I just didn't think you'd be interested.'

She looks at him, stung, then she sees Andy's expression change. He raises his hand in a wave and smiles politely at something or someone in the distance. Liv turns and sees he is waving at Sandra, who has come out of her house and turning towards the main road. She doesn't acknowledge either of them or raise a hand in greeting and Liv wonders if she thinks they're the neighbours who've been giving quotes to journalists.

'Poor woman,' Andy says as they make their way inside. 'Have you spoken to her?'

'I sent a few messages.'

'She probably just needs to grieve in peace.'

Sandra has replied only once to Liv's various messages since Thursday. A brisk 'as well as can be expected' and nothing more since then.

'You know it wasn't that I was trying to keep it from you,' Andy says when he's sat down at the dining table, in front of his laptop. 'I didn't want to say anything because … I don't know. I suppose I thought you'd think it was all one big vanity project and take the piss out of it.'

Liv frowns even though she suspects this is exactly what she would have done.

'And at first I didn't imagine we would produce anything that good. I presumed the shots I did would look terrible and the lighting would be all wrong and your dad would get muddled and end up repeating the same things over and over.'

'Does he?'

'A bit but not much. It's actually been wonderful listening to him talk about his career and remember all these events that happened years ago. He's really clear on it all. He remembers everything.'

Liv feels her eyes prickling.

'At first I just helped him set up the phone and lights and he pretty much did the rest. I'd occasionally prompt him or ask questions but then after a bit I started helping him with the research, because he does get in a bit of a muddle with that. I've been getting back in touch with his old colleagues, setting up interviews.' He nods, a smile forming. 'And we've got some great footage. It's actually looking really good.'

He sees her expression and gives a little self-deprecating shrug.

'We found some boxes of old cine-films from storage which I've sent off to be digitised. Behind-the-scenes stuff from *The Ballad of Angels* and *Mystery Moon* as well as family movies.' He smiles. 'I think once we put it all together, the interviews, the old footage, the behind-the-scenes stuff and link it with the interviews and clips from his movies, it could be good. Really good.'

Andy's eyes are sparkling with enthusiasm and Liv feels suddenly caught off guard. When was the last time he'd seemed so enthused by anything?

'So is this project going to take quite a bit of time to finish? Sounds like it's a massive task.'

He looks wary. 'Is this your way of asking if it's interfering with me looking for a new job?'

She shrugs. 'Little bit?'

'Look, I've got six months of salary. We're okay. The mortgage is being paid, we're being careful with our spending. There's no rush.'

Liv knows Andy knows that they're rapidly burning through his redundancy settlement even though, yes, they're being careful with their spending. No more takeaways, no more Airbnb weekends away, no clothes shopping unless vital. But it's not easy. Her salary is pitiful compared to Andy's.

But she also knows Andy hated every minute of his former job and looking at him now, listening to him talk about this project, she can see how much happier he is.

'I'm sick of law, Liv, you know that,' Andy says as if reading her mind. 'I don't want to go back to it. I don't want to spend the rest of my life doing something I hate. And doing this project with your dad made me realise how amazing it must feel to do something you love doing. Your dad loved his work. *Really* loved it.' A pause. 'I want that too.'

'But this isn't a job,' she says softly.

'It might be. It could lead to something. And even if it doesn't, doing this has made me realise that I want to do something I love, next. I want the rest of my working life filled with something that matters and makes me happy.'

'So what will you do?'

'I want to go back to university. Not university actually, film school.' He swallows. 'I want to go to film school and learn to direct.'

Liv stares at her husband, almost too surprised at first to react, and then, despite knowing it is definitely not the reaction Andy is hoping for, or she should give, she begins to laugh.

Chapter 17

LIV

Tuesday, 4 February 2025

Sandra looks as though she has aged a decade when Liv visits her on Tuesday morning before work. Her usually blow-dried hair is lank and unwashed; her face, which Liv isn't sure she's ever seen make-up free before, is grey with exhaustion and etched with grief.

'Oh Sandra,' Liv says, unable to embrace her because of the casserole dish she is holding in front of her. 'I'm so sorry.'

Sandra gives a wan smile and steps aside to let Liv in.

'Sorry I haven't been in touch. Everything's been a bit of a blur.'

'Oh god, don't be silly. Have you had anyone with you? Family? A friend?'

Liv follows Sandra down the hall and into the large open-plan space at the back of the house.

'Oh no, I prefer to be on my own.'

Liv puts the lasagne in the fridge where she suspects it will sit untouched until she returns for the dish.

'And I'm sorry about all this.' Sandra gestures, frowning, to the dining table, which is covered with scattered paperwork and notepads and unopened and opened envelopes. 'I'm trying to get everything organised for the solicitor but I don't really know where to start.' She sits down and begins sifting through a pile of paper. 'There's so much to get through and every time I think I'm getting somewhere I forget what I'm up to.'

Liv sits down opposite. 'Can I help?'

'No, no, I'm okay. I just can't think straight at the moment. My doctor's given me these awful drugs which help me sleep but make me foggy and useless all day.'

'Can you leave all this for a bit? Come back to it in a few weeks?'

Sandra blinks as if she hadn't thought of this and then something else crosses her features.

'Oh Liv, I'm so sorry about all the news vans. It's so awful and intrusive. Will you tell everyone how sorry I am? Richard would be mortified.'

Liv thinks that Richard would actually be quite delighted by the attention but says, 'Don't worry about that. We're all just concerned about how you've been coping with them. It must be very upsetting having them on your doorstep.'

'They just keep putting notes under the door, asking for an interview. Alistair, Richard's agent, thinks I should make a statement to get them off my back. I think he wants me to go outside and burst into tears in front of the cameras or something.' She frowns as she studies a piece of paper and then passes it to Liv. 'This one's from Richard's old producer. She keeps calling and leaving messages.'

Liv reads the note, which is typed on a letterhead emblazoned with the *Morning!* logo.

Dearest Sandra,

My god, I am so shocked by darling Richard's death. Everyone on the show is so very, very sorry for your loss. We are all utterly devastated and if there is anything we can do to support you or indeed help bring Richard's killer to justice, please reach out. We are here to help in any way we can and with that in mind we want to invite you to appear on Morning! *whenever you feel strong enough.*

Liv puts down the note.

'Ironic that she'd been ignoring all of Richard's calls before this happened,' Sandra says.

'Do the police have any leads?'

'I don't know. They're building a timeline apparently. Working out who was there and who might have seen something.'

Liv has decided it's better to have it all out in the open so says what she came here to tell Sandra.

'I wanted you to know that Gracie was there, at the park on Thursday. Doing her run. She's given a statement to police. Not that she saw anything, or anyone out of the ordinary,' she adds quickly.

Sandra looks at Liv. There is a slightly frozen expression on her face and then, just as quickly, it's gone.

'The poor girl,' she says. 'Is she okay? She's not too … spooked by something like this happening so close to home?'

'She's fine. Devastated and shocked like all of us.'

Sandra suddenly gets up from her seat, her chair making a scraping noise as she pushes it back.

'God, I'm so sorry, would you like a glass of water? Tea? No, you're more of a coffee person, aren't you?' She goes over to the kitchen. 'I'll make us some coffee.'

'Sandra, they will catch who did this,' Liv says, watching the other woman with concern. 'The police will figure it out.'

But Sandra doesn't react. She is too busy flitting about the kitchen, taking glasses and mugs from cupboards and pulling out teabags and coffee.

'Don't worry about me, really. I'm fine. I had a coffee earlier.'

'But you'll have another, won't you?'

Sandra is standing in front of the enormous stainless-steel

coffee machine on the counter. Liv remembers her saying once that it had cost over two grand. One of Richard's silly toys, she called it. Sandra fiddles around for a few moments, pressing buttons and turning knobs.

'I have no idea how to make this thing work,' she says finally, looking across at Liv who is already getting up.

'Sit down. I'll make some plunger. And maybe some food. Have you eaten today?'

Her neighbour looks at Liv blankly.

'Yesterday?'

Sandra doesn't answer.

'Okay, go sit down. That's an order. I'll make you some food.'

Before Sandra can protest, Liv has guided her back to the chair and then returns to the kitchen. As she cooks some scrambled eggs, and makes coffee, she checks on Sandra intermittently, who is now back at the dining table, gazing at the various pieces of paper surrounding her, still looking perplexed by all of it. At one point while she is stirring the scrambled eggs, Liv sees Sandra wiping her face and then pressing her fingertips against her eyelids as if that will stem the flow of tears and Liv looks away quickly, leaving Sandra to her private grief.

A few moments later Liv puts a plate of food in front of Sandra. As she moves the paperwork around her away so it's safe from any dropped food or spilt coffee, Liv's eyes are drawn to words written in Sandra's looping writing, on an open notepad.

Gracie – Meredith / Martin Finch? Possible?

Liv freezes.

She reads the words again, checking.

'What's this?' she asks Sandra, careful to keep her voice steady. 'Why is Gracie's name written down?'

Liv tilts the page so Sandra can see what she is looking at. Did Sandra already know Gracie was at the park on Thursday morning?

There's a moment's silence as Sandra stares at the piece of paper and Liv can feel her own pulse loud in her ears.

'Oh, I think that's just notes I made while I was talking to Detective Mitchell yesterday. He was giving me a list of people at the park.' She gives a weak smile. 'My memory's so terrible at the moment. I can't remember what anyone tells me from one hour to the next so I'm writing everything down.'

Liv watches Sandra for a moment, seeing how the other woman closes the notebook firmly and places it on a pile of loose paper in the middle of the table, then puts a pen on top.

'I read in the papers that Martin Finch seems like the most likely suspect.'

'Well, I think the police are keeping an open mind,' Sandra says, turning her attention to the scrambled eggs.

'What do you think?'

'I don't know. I mean, he's a chronic alcoholic. I just can't see him managing it, physically, I mean.'

'But he sent Richard threatening messages, didn't he? He had a restraining order against him? And a motive after losing the court case.'

Sandra picks up a piece of toast, seems to consider it and then places it back on the plate.

'I think the police have probably questioned him already and I suppose they must have ruled him out if he hasn't been arrested.'

'I read somewhere that his bank took his home, just before Christmas. And he's estranged from his children.' Liv hesitates. 'People who have nothing left to lose are often the most dangerous.'

Sandra doesn't react. She is now staring at the eggs as if confused as to how they ended up there.

'So are the police being good at keeping you informed of what they're doing?' Liv says, briskly changing the subject. 'Have you got a liaison person to talk to?'

'There's a woman who keeps leaving messages. Elise? Elena? I think she said she's coming over today. Or tomorrow?' Another nervous smile. 'See? I'm forgetting everything. Useless.'

'No, you're not.' Liv looks at her neighbour, feeling a wave of sympathy for her. 'You're grieving and in shock. It's no wonder you can't remember things.'

Sandra rests her fork back on the plate and folds the paper towel in half and places it on top of the remaining eggs. She has only had two, perhaps three, mouthfuls at the most.

'I just want this to be done with,' she says. 'I want to bury my husband and for the police to leave me alone.'

'But you want to find out who did this, don't you? There might be a killer on the loose.'

Sandra gives a tight smile, her gaze travelling to the wall opposite where the wedding photo of her and Richard hangs.

'I just want this all to be over,' she says.

Chapter 18

LIV

Tuesday, 4 February 2025

The messages on her work WhatsApp group start gathering pace later that morning.

I heard Meredith Edward's going to be suspended. Pete in paeds said. He reckons she's been told to hand in her pass, etc.
What? Why?
Someone saw her go into the police station.
OMG has she been charged????
I heard she's going to be arrested before the end of the day :(
Who says?
Where did you hear that?
Just people talking around and about.
Bloody hospital gossip. She clearly didn't kill Richard Wellington!
Yeah, but what about the thing at the party? She pretty much assaulted him.

I was there, no one was assaulted.

RW is a creep. Correction, was a creep – more likely he assaulted her.

As Liv reads the messages, the guilt settles over her like a shroud. Is this all her doing? Surely the police don't think Meredith's the actual murderer, do they?

She goes back and forth over whether to message Meredith and ask outright, to see if she's okay and the rumours are true.

She makes it to lunchtime and then texts her.

Hi Meredith, this is Liv. I've heard some worrying rumours on the hospital gossip mill – is everything okay? Please let me know if I can do anything.

She feels duplicitous given her own actions have possibly led to this, but she reminds herself, over and over, she is doing this to protect her daughter. Just in case.

But Meredith does not message back.

'The police would have been told what happened at that hospital party between Meredith and Richard,' Andy says that evening when Liv tells him about the rumours, leaving out her role in this possible development. 'Loads of people would have seen it happen and maybe the hospital wants to distance itself from her while the investigation's going on.'

'I don't even know if any of it's true. It takes a lot to suspend a member of staff. It's more likely they'd have made out they want to support her by taking away the stress of having to go to work while everything's going on and encouraged her to take some leave.'

Liv goes over to the bathroom sink and begins taking off her make-up.

'The police can't seriously think she had anything to do with what happened to Richard? There must be other more likely suspects.' Then Andy frowns. 'Is it terrible that I'm relieved the attention's on Meredith and not Gracie?'

She smiles. 'Course not. Our priority is Gracie, not Meredith. How does she seem to you?'

'Okay.' Then he looks less certain. 'Why?'

'She seems anxious. You don't see it?'

He regards her with that familiar blank expression that tells Liv that he's feeling guilty and also defensive for not noticing.

'Let's just keep a close eye on her. She's been through a lot.'

'Course. I always do.'

'It is possible Meredith might have actually killed him,' Liv says when she's applying moisturiser to her clean face.

'Seriously?'

'It's possible.' She turns to face Andy. 'Maybe there was stuff going on between Richard and Meredith that no one knew about.'

'You think they were together? Romantically?'

'I have no idea, but exes getting revenge, intimate partner violence, you read about it every day.'

Andy gives a firm shake of his head. 'No way.' A pause. 'She's not the type.'

'What are you saying? Intelligent people don't kill? Well, that's patently untrue.'

'No, I mean she's not the type Richard would go for. She's way too intelligent. Way too normal.' He looks uncomfortable. 'Oh, come on, his type was always more ... clichéd, wasn't it? Younger, blonder, more ... cosmetically enhanced.'

'Well who's to say she was the perpetrator? Maybe she was defending herself; maybe Richard assaulted her and she lashed out in self-defence. He might have done to her what he did to Gracie, and Meredith did what she had to to get away from him.'

But Andy looks doubtful. 'He was hit on the back of the head so it wasn't a defensive move.'

Liv goes over to her chest of drawers and pulls out a fresh

T-shirt to wear.

'He could have turned quickly, say if he heard someone, and whoever hit him might have thumped him in that moment because they felt it was their only chance.'

As Liv pictures this in her mind's eye it recalibrates and shifts. Her imagination adds in another person. A more familiar figure. She has been picturing this over and over for the past twenty-four hours.

'There's another possibility,' she says quietly when she has swapped her T-shirt and put the old one in the dirty washing basket. 'What if Gracie was somehow involved in Richard's death?'

'What?' He looks at her, almost amused at the suggestion. 'Gracie? No chance.'

'What if she was assaulted, like she told us, and Meredith was there and saw and hit Richard on the head to stop him? What if all this stuff about the mafia and Martin Finch is rubbish and has nothing to do with anything? What if Meredith and Gracie were there when it happened and one of them hit him?'

His expression becomes more serious. 'Don't be crazy. Absolutely not.'

'How can you be so sure?'

'There's just no way. Gracie had nothing to do with this. She would have said something. She would have told us.'

Liv studies her husband a moment, wondering how he can be quite so naive. 'Are you absolutely sure about that?'

12 November 1989

Dear Liv,

I am writing to say that I hope you're not worried about Saturday night. I know you probably think it's a bit strange, me coming to 'babysit' you and I hope you know it's not really that. I'm just keeping you company because you're too old for a real babysitter but probably a bit young to be left on your own. I think it's because everyone always says I'm mature for my age.

Anyway, I thought it was very nice of your mum to ask me. I suppose she knows she can trust me because we are sort of family friends. My father told me that he's known your father since 1966 when they were both at the same university which is what Mrs Callivar would call a Very Big Coincidence.

Is there anything you would like to do? I thought we could have supper then play some board games and maybe play charades. Do you like charades? I feel like you would as you come from a Theatrical Family.

On Saturday should I bring some food or will there be some? I don't think we should have too much 'junk food' because your parents probably would think I'm a Bad Influence. But maybe I could get some chocolate biscuits?

Please let me know.

Yours faithfully, Meredith

Chapter 19

MEREDITH

November 2024

After her dinner with Richard Wellington, Meredith became consumed in her attempt to discover everything she could about the group of medical students whose actions led to the end of her father's on-site academic career. Who were the young medics who had ruined his life and what had become of them?

She knew the bare bones already: her father, Stephen, had always struggled to interact effectively with the young people he was meant to teach. In 1988 he had become increasingly frustrated with one particular group of students he'd decided weren't working consistently hard enough to merit being at one of the country's most prestigious medical schools.

When they performed poorly in their mid-year exams, they'd been told by the higher-ups that they were putting their enrolment at risk unless they did exceptionally in their resits. Which they apparently had done. However, Stephen suspected they'd cheated on these resits and when the students heard about this, buoyed by their success however it had been achieved, played a childish prank. All Meredith knew was that it had something to do with dumping horse manure on his desk or near his office.

All this happened to coincide with her father's depression making an unwelcome reappearance. Now under the strain of various professional pressures, as well as still struggling to cope with grief after losing his wife, Meredith's mother, just a few years before, he made a terrible professional misstep.

In October, when the Australian academic year was almost over, Meredith's father attempted to confront several of the students about their prank. When they denied having anything to do with it, he went to their college residence, forced his way into one of their rooms and when he was caught by some other students, apparently looking through personal effects, all hell broke out.

There were raised voices, the student whose room it was arrived, then there was pushing and shoving and threats to call the police. A senior residential warden arrived to find Stephen rounded in on by a large group of braying students. When he was pulled from the throng, one he had been raging at had a bloody nose. Stephen denied being the culprit but no one believed him.

Meredith had been told all of this when she began her medical degree at the same university years later, by one of Stephen's closest friends and old colleagues, Benita. She had told Meredith what happened over coffee in her first week as an undergraduate, presumably concerned that rumours might reach her somehow and deciding it was better that she knew what happened. She never said whether she thought it likely Meredith's father had thrown the punch which led to the bloody nose. To Meredith it seemed preposterous. Her father was slight and not at all physically inclined. It was far likelier that the student had fallen awkwardly or been hit by someone else's fist.

Meredith never forgot the intonation of Benita's voice when she described what happened next.

'A witch hunt. An awful, shameful witch hunt.'

The injured student and his family went to the police and then issued the university with a lawsuit, she explained. Stephen was suspended and then cautioned by the police; subject to an internal university investigation and removed from the teaching roster, although his long-held position at the university gave him some protection.

'What happened to the students?' Meredith asked immediately, mostly anxious at that stage about crossing paths with them one day.

Benita had raised her eyebrows. 'I don't think you need to worry about that.'

'Did they become medics?'

She nodded.

'Where?'

'I don't think that's important.'

'Had they cheated?'

Benita let out a long exhalation. 'Probably.'

Meredith never told her father what she'd discovered; she couldn't bear to see the shame on his face or upset him by bringing up something that had obviously been so traumatic. Besides, it had been agreed upon between her and Benita that she would remain silent. Benita was only telling her all of this because she knew Stephen never would and Meredith deserved to know given she was now studying at the same university.

Now Meredith wondered if it would all be there somewhere, in a yellowing folder in a dusty filing cabinet somewhere on campus. If she really pushed for it, she might be allowed access to her father's old professional file which would perhaps include a log of his supposed crimes. If it still existed.

She had already spent hours sifting through piles of her father's papers which she retrieved from storage soon after he died the previous year. Now she pulled them out again and checked his notebooks where he'd kept meticulous records of all his appointments and activities and then when that didn't bring up anything of use, she spent hours searching online for clues. Nothing had come up. Just obituaries from when he'd died and the occasional mention of his name in old research projects or in the alumni sections of the university's website.

If it happened today, Meredith knew there would have been an instant deluge on social media and online news outlets. Newspaper columnists and TikTokers would have given their opinions on her father's cancelling. Thank goodness, she thought more than once, that this had all occurred before the advent of the smartphone.

But now Meredith had one clue: Richard Wellington had been one of her father's students in 1988. Was it possible he was the ringleader of those cheating students? Had he, among others, led to her father's almost breakdown, from which he never really recovered?

She pictured Richard as a student. Arrogant, self-satisfied even then, she imagined. A young man who was lazy and cut corners and cheated.

Would he have been someone who would bully others, even a teacher?

She was determined to find out.

Chapter 20

LIV

Wednesday, 5 February 2025

It doesn't surprise Liv that Andy is steadfast in his belief that Gracie had nothing to do with Richard's death. He has always seen the absolute best in Gracie no matter what.

Even when she was little and had done something naughty and was obviously lying when she said she wasn't, he would study her with an amused scepticism, she'd give him a besotted smile and he would laugh and forgive her anything. As she grew up and the issues she faced grew increasingly complex, Andy struggled far more than Liv to accept and understand Gracie's suffering.

Neither of them could bear to watch their daughter crumble as anxiety took hold in her second year of secondary school when she was the victim of an online bullying campaign by a former friend. Liv could see that for Andy it was like a living grief. While Liv was ever pragmatic, looking for practical ways to help their daughter; booking appointments with recommended psychologists, exploring other therapies, Andy became almost paralysed by his inability to cope with what Gracie was going through. And his way of dealing with it was to pretend it wasn't happening. Just like now.

Liv knows while he buries his head in the sand, it will be up to her to figure out exactly how this will go. It will be up to her to police Gracie's behaviour and moods; watching for any changes or signs that she is struggling under the pressure. And it will be up to Liv to keep Gracie protected. She will do all she can to find out what really happened to Richard and if the worst comes to the worst and she discovers Gracie was involved, she will try and ensure someone else takes the blame. At any cost. At all, in fact.

The morning after her terrible realisation, Liv asks Gracie if she wants to make an appointment to see her psychologist. But the suggestion is, predictably, met with an eye roll.

'It's not like I can actually tell her what Richard did to me, can I? She might have to give evidence against me at a later date or something.'

Liv feels a jolt of adrenaline course through her at this.

'Why would she give evidence?'

Is the Pandora's box they are sitting on top of, forcing shut, about to be opened?

But Gracie simply opens the fridge and takes out the sliced bread.

'Mum, I'm fine. I don't want to talk to anyone.' A pause. 'And can you just stop?'

'Stop what?'

'Talking about everything? Therapising me. Worrying. Looking at me like I'm about to crack.'

'I'm worried.'

'You're being hypervigilant! I thought we talked about that and you weren't going to do it anymore?'

'Sorry, sorry, I know. I'll stop.' She goes over to Gracie, squeezing her shoulders and then kissing her on the cheek. 'Old habits die hard.'

Gracie tilts her head a little to lean into Liv's and they remain there a moment. Liv feels a pang of relief that her daughter is in a forgiving mood.

'I'm fine,' Gracie murmurs. 'You don't need to worry so much. It's really annoying.'

Liv is grateful for Gracie's reassurance, but as she sips her coffee and scrolls on her phone she can't help surreptitiously watching as she makes breakfast. She observes how Gracie carefully spreads two slices of bread with peanut butter, then puts the bread and jar away when she would usually leave them out. She notices how Gracie wipes down the kitchen surface so not a crumb remains in sight. Then, after eating she wipes down the kitchen surface twice despite using a plate.

The tell-tale signs have been there for a day or two. Every time she goes into Gracie's bedroom, Liv notices it is a little neater, a little more organised than before.

Gracie is also spending more time in bed than usual, endlessly scrolling or watching her favourite shows, which is what her daughter has always done when she's feeling overwhelmed or upset or exhausted. She doesn't have the stereotypical OCD people think is all hand-washing and light-switch-turning-on-and-off. When Gracie is upset and anxious she retreats into the safety of everything that is familiar. She becomes preoccupied with ensuring the space she is within remains highly controlled. The piles of books in her room become tidier; her towels are placed almost geometrically neatly on the heated rail; when she is not lying in it her bed is all hospital corners and carefully placed cushions.

'So what are your plans today? You going into uni?'

Liv knows Wednesdays are usually a busy day for Gracie, who has signed up for extra classes over the summer period when many students are on holiday. There are several lectures and a seminar to attend, all of which Gracie generally prefers to do in person rather than online.

'I'm here today.'

'Have you been for a run?'

'Not today, no,' she says in a clipped voice, irritation flaring again, then turns away, leaving a frisson of dark, agitated energy in her wake.

'Let me know if you want to come out for a walk with me and Sophie. We can get a snack after,' Liv calls out, down the hall. 'Oh, and will you be here for dinner? I was thinking I could make that Thai beef salad you like.' There's no response so Liv calls out again. 'Gracie? What do you want for dinner? Will you be in?'

A moment later, Gracie pushes open her bedroom door, her eyes flashing with anger.

'Can you please stop?'

'What?' Liv asks, confused.

'All the questions, all the checking, all the do-you-want-dinner?'

Gracie glares at her.

'And stop looking like that. Stop doing the manipulative hurt thing. You're really stressing me out!' Her voice is high pitched and bordering on shouting. 'We're all on edge, we're all terrified there's some, I don't know, some psycho serial killer on the loose and you need to just … just bloody chill out and stop doing … all this. Stop asking me if I'm okay, stop checking in on me. Stop offering me food!'

Her face is red with emotion, and then she lets out a strangled noise of frustration and turns to go back into her room.

This time she slams her door with such force that Liv jumps.

That evening the three of them eat dinner in front of a new reality show with the air-conditioning blasting. The door to the garden is closed and the blinds have been down all day with the heat peaking at 36 degrees in the late afternoon. Liv feels foggy with the fatigue which always sets in after these endless days of high heat and humidity and the charged atmosphere that seems to have infused the house.

Gracie eats while scrolling on her phone, sitting at the dining table, her face thunderous. Andy gives Liv a questioning look but Liv just shrugs. Surely he can figure out that they've had an argument.

'Forgot to tell you, it's confirmed that Meredith's been suspended from work,' Liv tells Andy during an ad break.

She hadn't forgot to tell him, but she wanted to recount this in front of Gracie to watch her reaction. But Gracie's attention remains fixed on her phone.

'That seems unfair. She's not been charged.'

'No, but that interaction with Richard at the Christmas party apparently had the board concerned and then with the investigation happening they probably don't want her treating patients.' A pause. 'Better to be safe if they find out she was involved.'

'There's no way she was involved,' Andy says, looking mystified. 'They should be supporting her not pushing her out.'

'Everyone's saying they were having some kind of relationship and she couldn't deal with him ending things,' Liv says.

'That's rubbish,' Gracie says, suddenly looking up. 'Richard was harassing her, not the other way round. She's the victim here. He was practically stalking her.'

'How do you know that?'

Gracie holds his gaze a beat then replies, 'She told me.'

'I didn't know you were friends.'

'Since when do you talk?' Liv asks simultaneously.

Gracie shrugs, then returns to her phone. 'At the park sometimes. She runs there in the mornings.'

'And you what … just started talking one day?' Liv knows this can't be true. Gracie would no sooner start a random conversation with a stranger than an actual neighbour she knows.

'Oh right, you met at the barbecue,' Andy says, returning to Gracie for confirmation. 'Was that it?'

Gracie shrugs, her expression back to being stony. She is acting like a child but Liv knows this is because she is feeling the pressure.

'So, what, do you message each other when you're going for a run, then?'

Gracie ignores her.

'Do you plan when you meet up?' Liv presses. When Gracie doesn't respond, she says, 'Gracie. I'm asking you a question.'

'I don't know. Why are you even asking? It's not actually any of your business.'

'And she's talked to you about Richard?' Andy asks.

Gracie lets out an irritated sigh as she stands up and takes her plate over to the kitchen. 'Not really. We don't really talk about much. I sometimes give her advice on running and stretches, nutrition, that kind of stuff. She mentioned Richard a couple of times because we saw him down at the park.'

Liv gives an internal eyeroll at how Gracie is playing the I'll-only-talk-like-an-adult-to-Dad game.

'What did she say about him?' Andy asks.

She shrugs. 'That he was a creep.'

'What else?' Liv presses.

Gracie narrows her eyes at Liv. 'Why are you asking me so many questions?'

'I just want to know what you know and what Meredith said,' Liv replies. 'A man's died in suspicious circumstances, you were both at the park when it happened and now we've found out you're both friends. We're your parents. I think we have a right to be interested.'

Gracie rolls her eyes and directs her response to Andy. 'She told me he was always saying suggestive, gross stuff to her. Texting her. Asking her on dates. She wasn't interested. She wouldn't have gone near him in a million years.'

'No? Why not?' Andy looks surprised.

Gracie makes a face. 'God no. He's married. Gross. And not that it matters but I'm pretty sure she's gay.'

'Really?'

'Yes, really,' Gracie says, her voice heavy with sarcasm.

'Has she told you what happened at the Christmas party?' Liv asks. 'Apparently she pushed him over.'

'More likely she pushed him away.' Gracie turns to open the freezer. 'The police are idiots if they think she had something to do with anything. Just because she wasn't interested in him and was harassed by him, she didn't kill him.' Standing with an ice-cream tub in her hand she looks across at Liv. 'You know that, right?'

Liv doesn't reply.

'And even though he assaulted me, that doesn't mean I killed him either.' Gracie pulls off the lid of the ice cream. 'I mean, maybe he just had like a medical episode, have you ever considered that?'

'What medical episode would have caused him to be bludgeoned on the back of the head?'

Gracie gives a slight shake of her head as if she can't be bothered to explain.

'Just don't take everything Meredith says at face value,' Liv says as her daughter takes a bowl from the cupboard and fills it with ice cream. 'And steer clear of her while this investigation is going on.'

But Gracie doesn't respond. Instead she puts away the ice cream, carefully wipes down the surface and tears off a strip of kitchen towel to take with her.

This time she doesn't slam her bedroom door shut.

Chapter 21

LIV
Thursday, 6 February 2025

On Thursday morning, a week after Richard's death, several news-papers renew their concern that Martin Finch has possibly got away with murder because police haven't charged him yet. To get around being sued for defamation, they word their reports in a way that doesn't actually come out and accuse Martin of being the killer but just heavily hints that he has somehow evaded justice.

The *Daily News* makes their views even clearer. Their lead story that morning screams: KILLER IN PLAIN SIGHT?

There is a second piece in the *Daily News* where they boast about uncovering more details about Richard's last movements, repeating verbatim from his personal social media posts that he'd taken up running as his new year's resolution and would go out most mornings.

They report how the 'tragic TV doctor' had been just a few weeks into this new running regime when he was 'brutally slain', writing how Richard would usually run the perimeter of the park oval, 'less than a kilometre from his multi-million-dollar luxury

Sydney home'. There were details about how he had recently bought himself some $350 trail-running shoes so he could attempt occasional runs along the uneven Gully path and had ambitions to complete the True Grit NSW 10k trail run in March.

They also republished the many running selfies posted by Richard on his social media. Trail-running or walking is great for balance and coordination at any age! he posted two days before his death alongside a sweaty, grinning selfie.

Liv reads another newspaper's more in-depth report about Martin and it does a good job of convincing her that he must be the person who killed Richard. She already knows much of it already: the claims made against Richard by Martin Finch regarding how his wife, Maria, one of Richard's private patients had died soon after breast reconstruction surgery. How questions had been raised over Richard's possible negligence during and after the operation. The case had been well publicised and gone on for months. Journalists and TV crews had also camped outside Richard and Sandra's house for weeks then.

'A telly doc being accused of bad practice and causing the possible death of a patient? A patient who just recovered from breast cancer? Bloody newsroom gold,' Andy had said matter of factly when the first news vans had rocked up outside their house.

And as more details were uncovered, the public drank up the lurid details. How Richard had been out the night before the operation, champagne flute in hand, at a red tie event for Channel Two; how Maria had endured three years of gruelling breast cancer treatment and having finally completed all the chemo and radiation, how family and friends banded together to pay for her to have the reconstruction done privately so she wouldn't have to wait years in the public system.

Unsurprisingly Richard's public reputation had yet to recover from the stain of the lawsuit when he died, but his private practice was apparently as busy as ever. He no longer performed any surgeries at the public hospital but apparently unbowed he'd still roam the corridors there, making his presence known, making sure to stop and chat to the consultants and charm the heads of departments. He was ruthless but charming, both characteristics Liv had witnessed.

Martin's reputation was probably more tarnished by what happened than Richard's, Liv realises now. She reads reports on her phone that raise questions about his motives in taking Richard to court in the first place. It's clear he was counting on a huge payout. One newspaper had uncovered the multiple drink-driving charges levelled against Martin over the years; how his small building company had gone bankrupt the year before, how he and Maria had to sell their house and move into a small apartment above a relative's shop, how he'd left her briefly and had a relationship with a much younger women and then returned to Maria.

Just before Christmas, Maria's sister, Donna, gave an interview to one of the weekly women's magazines where she talked about Maria's gruelling cancer battle and once she was in recovery, her excitement at having new breasts in time for her fiftieth birthday. Donna spoke tearfully about the family's devastation when Maria died so unexpectedly soon after the operation, and their grief at watching Martin unravel afterwards.

Donna made it clear without being explicit that there had been continued marital difficulties between Martin and Maria, and hinted that it was Martin's struggle with alcohol and gambling that had caused the couple's financial problems. And that in turn, she believed Maria's cancer had likely been caused by years of stress and worry.

The day after the magazine hit the shelves, Martin Finch had been arrested for assaulting his nephew outside Donna's home. Liv puts down her phone, her brain whirring as she considers all of this.

She pictures Martin lying in wait in the bushes for Richard to pass. Maybe he'd watched Richard run that route before. Maybe he was secure in the knowledge that no one would see him but also, given his behaviour in the past, probably didn't care too much if they did. Martin Finch is clearly a man with little left to lose.

Liv wonders if he could have somehow got in and out of the Gully where Richard's body was found, without being seen. Apart from the usual trail that runs in a loop back down to the main path, the only other way to get in is along the old fire trail. The fire trail is just a narrow, cleared path to the foot of the Gully, put in place in case of a bushfire so firefighters can travel by foot into the thick of it. Its opening at the top of the steep, wooded slope is almost impossible to spot and it's mostly longtime residents or older state emergency service volunteers who know it's there, nestled in between two apartment blocks, just across the road from the steps which lead directly up to the reserve at the end of Liv's cul-de-sac.

Liv has only been down it a couple of times. It's a narrow, difficult path and you'd have to be careful not to trip up, but it is certainly possible to travel along it almost directly to the spot where Richard had died. And no one at the park would even know you'd been and gone.

But how would Martin Finch have known it was there? A bit of googling tells Liv that all his past businesses and family are firmly rooted in the south. The trail isn't marked on maps, old ones or Google. Maybe he had inside knowledge? Could he have been an SES volunteer?

Liv googles 'Martin Finch SES' but nothing comes up. She tries a few other permutations to see whether he is involved in any volunteer firefighting but there is nothing. Then she has an idea and tries 'Martin Finch bushcare gully' and gives a small noise of satisfaction when there it is, on the second page. His name is included within a PDF document of attendees for the Warada community garden visit of 2011.

Liv reads the document and learns how members of the Warada community garden, which had included Maria and Martin Finch, visited in 2011 to learn about propagating native plants. Included in the day's events had been a tour of the Gully's less-travelled parts where bushcare volunteers had been stripping out introduced weeds to protect natural and native regeneration efforts.

Liv googles again and discovers it was Maria who was the community garden member. Martin, she sees, as she scrolls back and back through its Facebook page, appeared to have once been the garden's unofficial driver, using his large work van to transport plants, sacks of soil and fertiliser and, occasionally, people around the city.

There is a photo of him, looking far happier and healthier than in recent ones, standing next to a beaming Maria and other gardeners, surrounded by bags of soil. It is captioned 'Delivery time! Thanks, Martin!'

Liv considers all she knows: that Martin Finch had a motive, the means and an escape route into and out of the Gully.

She wonders if the police know about the fire trail and Martin's membership of the community garden. She wonders if Martin could have made good on his promise and caused Richard's death.

Chapter 22

LIV

Thursday, 6 February 2025

By lunch it's been confirmed that Meredith has been suspended from her position at Northern pending an investigation into what happened at the Christmas party and her alleged attack on Richard Wellington. Liv feels an unpleasant shroud of guilt settle over her, yet there is still that small niggle. That sense that it wouldn't be out of the realm of possibilities for Meredith to have had something to do with Richard's death despite Martin Finch also being a likely suspect.

As she drives over to her parents to make the most of a two-hour gap in between seeing patients, Liv trawls her memories. She thinks about all the times the other girls at school were unkind to Meredith, barely disguising their distaste at the girl they'd cruelly nicknamed Buggy Mole due to Meredith's heavy eyes and small dark mole on her cheek. What bitches they'd been.

Amazingly Meredith always appeared oblivious to the bullies. She would walk around school with a book in her hand, sit alone in the playground at lunch and recess, or disappear to the library.

Liv never saw her look upset or bothered by being targeted or not having any friends.

On Liv's first day at St Mary's, Meredith had found her at lunchtime with the other year fives and said hello and asked her how it was all going. Liv had replied that it was good or something benign and then the bell had gone and they'd all dispersed. As Liv walked back to her new classroom, one of the other year fives she'd sat with at lunch had commented that her older sister was in Meredith's class and had told her she was 'super strange'. Liv had got the message loud and clear and had made sure not to acknowledge Meredith again after that. Meredith soon got the message too and didn't attempt to communicate with Liv at school from then on.

As Liv sits in traffic on the Harbour Bridge, the Opera House resplendent in the distance as always, she remembers one lunchtime when she was in year eight and Meredith year nine and the main core of bullies, also year nines, rounded in on Meredith in a hidden corner of the playground. One of them apparently managed to wrangle Meredith's skirt off her and Kath Willis, one of the ringleaders who happened to be the school's star netball shooter, threw it up into the high branches of a nearby tree.

Liv heard later that when they were done with her, Meredith had simply sat down against the wall, pulling her legs against her chest, saying nothing and not asking or calling for help. Her face had been a blank mask. 'Buggy Mole was like a robot,' a friend had told her later. 'Like she hadn't even noticed or had any feelings or even cared. Such a weirdo.'

That evening Liv had written a note to Meredith, saying that she hoped Meredith was okay and, to her shame, suggesting she try looking less weird and then maybe the bullies would leave her alone. She even has a mortifying memory of suggesting Meredith did something to her hair so she looked cool. Liv cringes at the memory. But the following week, Meredith had come to school without her usual thick glasses on. She'd got contact lenses, Liv assumed, and had privately applauded the decision. Not standing out in the crowd had been Liv's main objective since starting at St Mary's; having such extroverted parents in the public eye made her acutely aware of how, conversely, she had to fly under the radar to survive adolescence. Now Liv feels sick at how awful she was. How awful everyone was to Meredith, who clearly didn't give a damn about fitting in.

She thinks of Gracie and how the bullies had tortured her online with spiteful jibes and mean comments via various social media channels. Liv and Andy had gone to the school to demand action was taken but they explained it was out of their remit. None of the comments had been made during school hours. Liv understands now that she was just the same as those mean girls. She'd followed the pack and had been as bad as the ringleaders.

'Do you remember a girl called Meredith Edwards?' Liv asks her dad when they are settled in the corner of his favourite café, their lunch in front of them. Angela has her physio session at home for the next hour giving Liv time to take Pete out and get him on his own. 'She lived opposite the park, just around the corner. Her dad was a doctor, she occasionally babysat me? Went to St Mary's?'

Pete takes a sip of his coffee, which leaves behind a thin line of foam on his top lip.

'You and Mum knew her parents. Or maybe just her dad? Her mum died when she was little.'

She watches Pete's expression for some sign that he is listening or registering what she was saying.

'Tall girl. Short dark hair. Very serious and very clever.'

Her father stabs at a piece of wilted spinach on his plate.

'Why all these questions?' he says, frowning. 'Can't I just eat my food?'

Pete has always been good-natured and a kind, witty man, but Alzheimer's is quickly stripping these characteristics away. Andy had mentioned the other day how angry her dad had been at not being able to make the fan work in his study. Pete hadn't seen that it wasn't plugged in – his clogged brain no longer able to make that connection – and he'd had what sounded like a tantrum at not being able to figure it out. Liv can't imagine how frustrating and confusing times like this must be for her dad.

'I used to see Meredith standing outside our house, on the corner with her dog, watching us.' Liv tries again. 'I think she wanted to be my friend. Do you remember she used to write me letters?'

But Pete's attention is diverted to a table by the window where a woman with a baby strapped to her chest is trying to stop her toddler from spilling the contents of a large glass of juice.

Pete's forehead wrinkles into a frown. 'Why is she giving him that enormous drink?' he says loudly. 'I guarantee he'll spill it.'

Liv looks over at the exhausted-looking woman, who shoots her an irritated glance at hearing Pete's comment. Her brief lapse in concentration gives the little boy just enough time to sip his juice and then spill it as he tries to return it to the table. He lets out a yelp of anguish as the orange liquid spreads across the table and onto his lap.

Pete shakes his head. 'I knew that would happen.'

Liv grabs a handful of napkins and rises to help the woman clean up but the waitress gets there before her.

'She shouldn't give him that big glass,' her father says as she sits down again.

'Dad, stop, she's doing her best.'

When the woman finally leaves a few moments later, ushering her now-crying toddler from the café, Liv catches her eye and mouths an awkward 'I'm sorry' but the woman gives her a filthy look.

Liv picks up on the conversation again when they are making their slow way back to her parent's house. She loops her arm through Pete's and he pats at her hand, acknowledging it.

'Dad, do you remember my old babysitter Meredith?' she

116

begins. 'She was only eighteen months older than me so I'm not sure why you chose her.'

'That egg was overdone,' he says quietly. 'I can't stand an overdone poached egg.'

'Dad,' Liv tries again. 'Do you remember Meredith and her family – how did you know them?'

He stops walking suddenly. 'Meredith?'

'Yes, Meredith.' Liv feels a pang of hope that her father's memory has cracked open. 'Meredith Edwards. My old babysitter.'

'Meredith,' he repeats.

'They lived near the park. Her dad was a doctor,' she prompts.

'I thought we agreed we weren't going to mention her anymore.'

'Why wouldn't you mention her, Dad?'

He gives her a sideways look and lets out a surprised laugh. 'After everything she did?'

'What did Meredith do, Dad?'

But he doesn't reply and instead begins to walk again. They head down the main street and then take the turn before the church which is attached to Liv's old primary school. She tries again when they get to her parent's street.

'Dad, can you tell me what Meredith did?'

He shakes his head. 'You need to ask your mother,' he says. 'I'm staying well out of it.'

They have arrived at the front gate and Liv holds it open for her dad to shuffle through.

'I do remember Meredith always cooked your mother and I an exceptionally good steak when we were invited over for barbecues.' Pete gives a cheery smile. 'Not really very surprising considering how well her restaurant did.'

Liv wants to cry in frustration but instead she forces a smile. 'Really? That's nice, Dad,' she says. 'I know you love a barbecue. Just like Andy.'

Chapter 23

MEREDITH

December 2024

Meredith's own public shaming took place at a pre-Christmas gathering that also marked the opening of a new section of the Orthopaedic floor. She was standing in a small group, making polite conversation and sipping at a glass of mineral water, when she saw Richard enter the large room with another surgeon, deep in conversation. Her heart sank. She didn't have the stamina to deal with him today. To fend off his leering manner and pointed conversation which seemed to always circle back to the same thing: when was she going to go out for dinner with him again? Which translated to: when was she going to fully succumb to his charms?

By 7.10 Meredith had successfully avoided Richard and was heading towards the exit, looking forward to a takeaway and some easy TV. She was almost at the double doors when his familiar boom called her name.

Heart sinking for the second time that night, Meredith turned and forced a smile. 'Hi, Richard,' she said. 'How are you?'

'Leaving so soon?' he asked, a trace of a frown across his smooth, tight forehead. 'Come and have another drink. I want to introduce you to some people.'

'Actually, I've got some work to finish up,' she lied. 'Another time.'

'Come on.' He took a step closer. 'You can't climb the greasy pole if you don't know who's at the top. You're at an important stage in your career. It's time to start thinking beyond the clinical.'

Meredith let him guide her back to the drinks table, his hand in the small of her back. There he asked for two glasses of champagne, waving away her protests. 'Don't deny your colleagues the pleasure of toasting your first Christmas at Northern, Meredith.'

As the waiter turned to reach for a fresh bottle, he leant a little way towards her, again not so close that anyone would think there was anything untoward about his actions, but close enough that she could smell the tang of the alcohol on his breath. The woody undertones of his cologne. Her stomach shifted unpleasantly.

'You're too uptight, Meredith,' he said quietly. 'Loosen up a bit. You might enjoy yourself. 'Tis the season and all that.' Then another surgeon approached, smiling widely, arm outstretched to shake Richard's.

'Lachlan, have you met Dr Meredith Edwards yet? The new star of Orthopaedics, working with Susan.' He leant closer and spoke in sotto voce. 'Great bedside manner.'

The other man gave a roar of laughter and patted his friend on the back approvingly.

The next half an hour was filled with more introductions, other old leering medics, sweaty handshakes and the constant topping up of her champagne glass despite her not wanting to drink at all that night.

'I need to go,' she finally said when there was a gap in the introductions.

'Meredith, Meredith, Meredith,' Richard said in a sing-song tone. 'Please relax and enjoy yourself. And please do stop this playing-hard-to-get silliness,' he said in a quieter tone. 'We're too old for it.'

His gaze met Meredith's and this time she averted her own.

'I don't want to be a killjoy,' she said in a similarly low tone. 'But I assume you're hoping something might happen between us?' She watched his expression, which remained one of bemused indulgence. 'You should probably know, I'm not interested in any kind of personal relationship.' She gave a quick smile. 'I'm gay, Richard. I date women.'

Meredith saw his obvious surprise, then a flash of something else cross his face – anger, embarrassment? – and she felt a pang of regret for being honest. Would he hold this against her? Undoubtedly.

'Well, you certainly kept that quiet, didn't you?' he finally said, his voice clipped.

'I can assure you it's no secret.' She smiled. 'But it's lovely to see you and thank you for introducing me to so many people. I really should go. I've got a busy week.'

Richard exhaled slowly.

'You know you're very like your father,' he said finally. 'He also took himself far too seriously. Couldn't take a joke, which ended up being a bit of a mistake in the end.'

A wash of saliva filled Meredith's mouth.

'He'd have done so much better if he'd just played the game,' Richard said in an almost languorous tone. 'So I feel it's my duty to tell you the same: play the game, Meredith. It's lots of fun up here.'

It took a few moments before Meredith was able to respond.

'What do you know about my father not being able to take a joke?' she finally managed.

A self-satisfied smile hovered on Richard's lips as he studied Meredith.

'I think you're right.' He tutted, reaching for the half-empty champagne flute Meredith was holding. 'You've probably had enough Christmas cheer for the night, wouldn't you say, Meredith?'

Meredith looked at him in confusion.

'I said, you've probably had enough to drink.'

She was suddenly very aware that Richard's voice was far louder than it had been up until that point. A few people nearby were even glancing across in their direction.

'In fact I think the champagne's gone straight to your head, Dr Edwards,' he said and Meredith felt the heat rising in her cheeks as if what he was saying had reminded her body of the effect alcohol always had on her.

'I'm absolutely fine. I only had a few glasses.'

'I think it was more than that. I'll get you some water.' Richard gestured to a travelling waiter. 'Would you mind getting my colleague a glass of water?' he called across to the blond man. 'She's had one too many champagnes.'

'I'm fine,' Meredith hissed. 'Please, stop.'

'A big glass. Thanks,' Richard added and the waiter nodded.

Meredith didn't wait for the water, or for permission from Richard to leave. She didn't say goodbye. She simply crossed the room, aware her face was burning as she weaved past the other attendees and headed for the exit and beyond that, the lift.

She needed to get out of there. She needed to breathe fresh air and be away from the hermetically sealed, institutional smell of the hospital and Richard Wellington and his stupid smirking face.

But a firm hand gripped her shoulder as she was about to step towards the already closing lift.

'She'll get the next one,' Richard instructed the people inside who were making no attempt to hold it open for Meredith.

'Please leave me alone,' Meredith said, shrugging his hand off her. 'I want to go home if that's quite okay.'

He let out an amused laugh. 'Oh Meredith, I was just playing,' he said. 'But I remembered I needed to ask you something.'

She stabbed at the lift button, willing it to hurry up.

'Hey, don't ignore me,' he said, in a toe-curling attempt at a baby voice.

Meredith swivelled towards Richard. 'What do you want?' she said. 'Why are you here?'

His eyes were bloodshot and puffy and she could see that if anyone had indulged in too much champagne that night, it was Richard Wellington.

'I wanted to ask you.' He took a step closer. 'I wanted to ask if you had a lovely lady waiting for you at home?' He gave a snigger, his lips wet with spittle. 'And if you did, I wanted to ask if you wanted me to come home with you and fuck you both?'

His hand reached out to grab at her but this time Meredith didn't hesitate: she shoved Richard Wellington with both hands and watched as he staggered back, his face puce with surprise.

It was pure coincidence and bad luck that one of the hospital's most senior board members appeared just a few feet behind Richard as he stumbled back trying to regain his footing.

'What on earth?' the man said, moving forward and reaching out to steady Richard.

Meredith stood frozen in place, taking in the thunderous, outraged expression on Richard's face and the confused one on the board member.

'God's sake,' Richard said, his voice dripping with outrage. 'You can't go around pushing people when you don't get your own way. What's wrong with you, woman?'

Meredith looked from Richard to the board member and then to the three other men accompanying him who were variously watching her with distaste and embarrassment. She felt a rising swell of shame and outrage that she knew wasn't warranted.

'I didn't do anything,' she finally said. 'You just—'

'I told you to stop drinking!' Richard interrupted. 'I told you to behave yourself! My god.' He glanced at the other medics. 'I'm so sorry, Gerry.' The man nodded. 'Andrew. Mark. Jeffrey. Apologies. Meredith had a tough day. Champagne on an empty stomach is never a good idea.' He made a face and the others gave polite smiles and nods, as if understanding immediately. 'Ah, Dr Mei.'

The female consultant, who had been hovering behind the men since they appeared, glanced up from her phone. 'Would you mind seeing Dr Edwards into a taxi downstairs?'

The other woman nodded and then looked down at her phone again. Meredith knew her only from her reputation: she was the first female neurosurgeon to join the hospital ten years before.

There was a ping and the lift door opened and Dr Mei stepped inside, putting her hand out to stop the doors from closing until Meredith had joined her.

'Get some rest, see you tomorrow, Dr Edwards,' he said in a cheerful manner and then turned away to join the other men, immediately patting one on the back and striking up a conversation about a patient.

Meredith knew that no one would believe her if she explained what had really happened. Everyone would trust Richard's version of events: that she'd got drunk, that she'd been inappropriate, that she'd shoved one of the hospital's most senior surgeons.

It wasn't even a question. He'd got away with killing a patient, hadn't he?

She looked over at Dr Mei, who was regarding her impassively, finally looking up from her phone.

Neither of them spoke until they were out in the open air and then Dr Mei finally turned to Meredith.

'Don't bother with an official complaint, he'll win. Don't bother to deny it, he'll figure out a way to make things worse for you. Work hard, do what you always do, keep your head down, he'll get bored and move on to someone else.' The other woman regarded Meredith grimly. 'And don't ever drink the shitty champagne.'

Chapter 24

LIV

Friday, 7 February 2025

Andy calls Liv when she is in the middle of giving her group exercise class on Friday morning. She phones him back as soon as the last person has waved their goodbyes and thanks to her.

'Is Gracie okay?' are her first words.

'She's fine. Still moody. Snapped at me because I didn't leave enough yoghurt for her breakfast. Swore at Sophie because she chewed her Crocs.'

'Do you think she's anxious or just stressed out?'

'Stressed.'

'Because the neighbour who assaulted her got murdered and his killer's still on the loose or because she's worried about uni or something else she hasn't told us about?' Liv says, attempting to keep her tone light.

'The first.'

Liv lets out a dry laugh. 'Okay, great. So why are you calling during work?'

Andy's voice turns more serious. 'Martin Finch's been

interviewed but Stan says they won't, or can't, charge him because he's got a solid alibi.'

Liv walks into the small staff kitchen. 'Which is what?'

There's a pause on the end of the line. 'He was in hospital, as an in-patient. At Northern.'

'What?'

'Apparently he turned up there the day before, intent on jumping off the roof of the hospital car park. Can you believe it? He wanted to, I don't know, protest what happened to his wife. What Richard did … or he thought he did. And I guess end his life. Poor bastard.'

Liv leans back against the kitchen counter.

'He never got as far as the car park roof. According to Stan, he got into a fight with a security guard and after a bit of shouting and screaming he was restrained. Then he started saying how he was there to throw himself off the roof so he was taken inside and held for observation.'

'Jesus. Poor man.'

'He was in for a couple of nights but somehow got discharged the day after Richard died.'

'So he couldn't have killed him?'

'Don't think so. He was held in the secure psychiatric unit.'

'Landley Clinic.' Liv thinks for a moment. 'It is possible he got out for an hour or so, killed Richard then went back?'

'Isn't security pretty tight?'

She hesitates. 'Off the record, I've heard breaches happen all the time, especially since the cutbacks.'

'Well, this is what Stan told me. But I'm sure the police have made sure and checked the security footage.'

'As if that always works,' Liv says. 'If it's anything like the rest of the hospital, it was probably broken.'

Liv stands in front of the freestanding, squat building. Most patients in Landley are there under an involuntary hold; it is a short-stay solution for people who've attempted suicide or had a psychotic incident and need a temporary stopgap before being shunted along the system and usually into another part of the mostly substandard and underfunded psychiatric care system.

Liv steps closer, scanning for CCTV cameras. She looks through the double doors and sees one like they have at the physio clinic above the reception desk.

Liv goes inside. There's no one manning the front desk so she walks through the reception area lined with chairs. On the far side of the entrance is a large window that looks out into a small walled garden, separated from reception by thick glass. A man in a pair of shorts and a grubby T-shirt is sitting on a bench smoking, his back to Liv. Smoking is banned everywhere on hospital grounds but Liv supposes of all places for the powers to be to turn a blind eye, it would be here. Liv can't see any way into the courtyard from the reception area and the walls on the far side appear too high to climb over, unless you dragged one of the benches over and stood on the back to give yourself a leg up. Difficult but not impossible.

It would have been impossible for Martin Finch to have walked from the hospital to the Gully and back without his absence being noticed on the ward. But, it might have been doable if he drove. Would he have brought his car here the day he attempted his rooftop protest? Again, possible. He could have parked up a few streets away where there is unlimited parking although it's unlikely the hospital would have let him keep his car keys. They surely aren't that negligent.

But still all this circles in Liv's thoughts and the next morning, she decides to see if the timings work.

She tells herself she is doing it for Gracie. That she has to do everything she can to ensure the real killer is found so that Gracie doesn't become a suspect if anyone discovers Richard assaulted her just before he was killed. Any parent would do this.

So the next morning she wakes early and slips out of the house

126

around six, driving to the hospital, parking up where Martin might have left his car the week before. There she walks to Landley Clinic, sets her timer and begins walking briskly back to her car. From there she drives back the way she came but instead of taking the first left after the shops, takes the second and parks about halfway down near the fire trail.

It is a warm morning and sweat prickles in the small of her back. She is wearing a loose long-sleeved top and leggings to protect herself against the mosquitoes that will feast on her otherwise. She stands at the entrance of the fire trail, taking a moment to consider whether this is a stupid or even potentially dangerous idea.

A man was killed within these woods just nine days ago and his killer is still at large. It is very possible the attack was random and could happen again. Is Liv really going to enter the area where it happened, this early in the morning and without anyone with her?

She goes briefly back and forth; weighing up the pros and cons. She knows she should be sensible and wait for Andy and go later in the day, but she is impatient to test her theory. She needs to know if Martin Finch could have killed Richard in the short timeframe he would have been able to escape the hospital unnoticed.

If she's honest, she also needs another reason to feel assured Gracie had nothing to do with Richard's death.

Liv taps a quick message to Andy sharing her location, even though he'll still be fast asleep, and checks her location tracking app is working. Then she takes a deep breath and steps into the woods.

The temperature drops instantly. It is cool and smells of rotting eucalyptus leaves and damp earth. She puts on her phone's torch but the narrow beam of light does little to illuminate any kind of usable path or even whether there is an actual path along here anymore. The bush has reclaimed whatever clearing there once was and Liv has to move slowly, picking her way down the hill, going sideways to avoid fallen branches and thick shrubs and foliage crossing her path every few steps. She even has to climb over a small tree which probably fell in a recent storm. But she presses on, following the downward trajectory and after around ten minutes gets to the bottom of the slope and then follows a more visible path to a small clearing and the regular path she has taken dozens of times over the years, that leads in one direction to the Gully trail, in the other to the harbourside park.

She checks the timer. Just over twenty-three minutes.

Then she keeps moving, travelling into the thick of the forest and down the path that goes alongside the waterway to the spot where Richard died. It feels more exposed here and Liv feels a sudden prickle of fear. That swiftly morphs to a more visceral anger but towards Richard rather than the person who killed him.

How dare her former neighbour turn this place into a scary one? How dare he assault Gracie in this beautiful, tranquil spot which has always been a place they treasured. Where Sophie stops to sniff and roll around in possum poo, where Gracie used to pretend she was an explorer when she was little, where they have been on numerous family walks over the years, where they've taken friends from other neighbourhoods and said, Look, look at this place, look at this incredible hidden bushland which is wild and untouched, right in the middle of the city. How fucking dare he.

Liv switches off her phone torch and her surroundings are immediately bathed in a blue, silvery hue. She turns in a slow circle. The birds are busy around her; kookaburras and whip birds making their own distinct noises among the cicada symphony while the sun starts to break through the tree canopy. Then she begins to walk again, moving to the area where Richard was found. It is a small clearing off the main path and Liv only knows this is the spot because there is still some police tape cordoning it off.

As she looks around she wonders how long the killer lay in wait; had they watched Richard's interaction with Gracie and then waited until she'd left before striking?

Or if Gracie and Meredith were involved somehow, where had they stood? Had they watched Richard die in the water?

Liv shivers, then ducks under the tape and carefully picks her way to the slope that leads down to the faintly sulphuric-smelling creek. The ground here is hard; the mud that had presumably been too slick and wet for the forensic examination now dry. She studies the bushes and trees around her. They're sparse; definitely not thick enough to do a very good job of hiding a person. She goes down the stone steps a little farther along which lead down to the water's edge. The steeper banks on this stretch, which is almost completely hidden from the sunlight, are still muddy and look slippery. Someone could easily slide down them if already feeling dizzy from being hit on the head. And the conditions would have been even more treacherous after the big downpour that occurred the night before Richard died.

Liv tries to picture the scene, replaying various versions of the attack. In one, Richard lunges at Gracie. Gracie at that point would be on the path, turned towards the clearing. She pushes him away, perhaps he stumbles and then in the melee she grabs at a rock and brings it down on the back of his head as he tries to reach for her again.

But if that's what happened, why hasn't Gracie told her and Andy the truth?

Richard assaulted Gracie, could have done something far worse given the chance. Lashing out at him to save herself in those circumstances would be justifiable and the police would surely see that.

Liv checks her phone and sees that thirty-six minutes have now elapsed since she left the hospital. It would take at least another half an hour for the return journey, likely longer going uphill through the trail. Would an hour and ten minutes be enough time to leave the clinic, come here, kill Richard and return?

Liv isn't sure but it might just be in the realm of possibilities.

And if that's the case then surely the police should be investigating Martin Finch a little more closely.

As she walks back along the open path past the oval towards the main road having decided to take the less spooky route back to the car, Liv thinks about all the problems at the hospital. How the staff are all overstretched and underpaid at her clinic, let alone in the other departments. How it is very likely they would not want to jeopardise their own jobs by reporting a patient going missing under their watch.

Martin Finch might very well have come here and killed Richard Wellington. He might have taken longer than an hour and a bit to do it. A hospital staff member might have realised this and decided not to mention it to anyone because they knew they'd lose their job if they did. And because they are burnt out, underpaid and overstretched they decided to remain silent. Does this mean Martin Finch has got away with murder?

Liv stands by the rocks that lead down to the water and looks out across the bay. The sun is now high above the water and its reflection shimmers against the glassy surface of the harbour. For the first time in a few days she feels the worry of the past week loosen slightly. All this hypervigilance and trying to work out Gracie's role in Richard's death might be drawing to an end. The killer was likely Martin Finch and the police will surely realise this and arrest him?

A few minutes later, as Liv walks up the steep road towards her car, she composes in her head the email she will send to DI Mitchell from the anonymous Gmail account. She will tell him about Martin Finch's visit with his wife's community garden group and how he knew about the forgotten fire trail. She will explain how there have been several security breaches at Landley before and that it would have been easy for Martin to have left for a while without anyone noticing. She will point out that the hospital CCTV is notoriously unreliable.

Even if some of this is dismissed after further investigation, it will at least put Martin Finch back onto the police's radar. While Liv and Andy work out other ways to protect their daughter.

7 June 1991
Dear Liv,

How are you? I know you're upset and don't want to talk to me. I know you don't want me to come over and stay on Saturday night but your mum has asked me three times over the past two months and I've said no each time but this time I said yes because she seemed totally desperate.

You can ignore me, I'll just stay in the spare room. But it would be very nice if you could try to be polite. You're being very immature.

Yours, Meredith

9 June 1991
Dear Liv,

I wanted to write and say what you did yesterday at lunch was really, really unfair and hurtful. I don't appreciate being made a laughing stock in front of your year group. It's unkind and childish.

I'll see you on Saturday afternoon. Please don't bolt the front door otherwise I'll go next door and ask Mrs Goldstein to call your parents.

Yours, Meredith

Chapter 25

MEREDITH

December 2024

The hospital gossip filtered back to Meredith over the coming days. She'd overheard a couple of the nurses repeating the rumours: they'd had a lover's tiff; she was obsessed with Richard; he had been trying to let her down gently; she had drunk too much and lashed out when he'd told her he wasn't romantically interested in her. Some were more outlandish than others: she had threatened to put in an official complaint against him at the hospital if he didn't agree to her demands, which were, variously, to be with her, leave his wife for her, promote her to the board or pay her off.

Meredith knew her best course of action was to ignore it all, as she'd always done with bullies. It would blow over. Besides she had just one more day of work before she was on leave and by the time she returned, people would have moved on to something else.

Christmas and New Year came and went and Meredith tried to decompress and enjoy herself with old friends up the coast, back in Newcastle. When everyone asked about her new life in

Sydney, she told some people it was wonderful and to other, closer friends, she admitted it was a bit of a challenge and that she'd been wondering if uprooting the life she'd made for herself was a huge mistake. They made all the right noises to reassure her, saying it would take time but she'd get there. Meredith would settle in and make friends, get used to the change and her old colleagues reminded her the move was good for her career.

But still, late at night, Meredith found herself composing and then deleting emails to her old department head, asking if there was any chance of her returning to her former position at John Hunter hospital.

Meredith didn't see Desi on that trip and hadn't let her know she'd be in town. She didn't know if any of their friends had said something or maybe they decided it was better if they didn't. Either way, their paths didn't cross, accidentally or on purpose, although Meredith later found out that she'd been in Thailand with a new girlfriend.

Instead Meredith filled her days with trips to the beach and lazy barbecues and sleeping in at the little Airbnb she had rented, and returned to Sydney on New Year's Day feeling, if not renewed, then at least fortified.

She would embrace a fresh start to coincide with the new year. She would give it six months before she even considered re-evaluating. And in that time she'd do all she could to learn the truth about Richard Wellington's possible role in what happened to her father. She would also do all she could to navigate her way into Liv, Gracie and Andy's world.

It was a complicated, challenging duo of resolutions but two that could either make or break her new life. But as ever, Meredith had determination on her side.

The morning after Meredith returned to Sydney, a day before she had to go back to work, she saw Richard's wife Sandra at the reserve on her way back from the supermarket. And everything changed again.

The older woman was sitting on the bench as her dogs sniffed around the edges of the shrubs that lined the low stone wall circling it. She wasn't engrossed in her phone or reading a book, but rather was just staring into space. Meredith paused in front of her building and after placing her grocery bags in the shade so the contents wouldn't spoil, crossed the pavement to the grass, deciding she would introduce herself.

When Meredith greeted her, she looked confused but still smiled politely.

'Sorry, I didn't mean to interrupt your peace,' Meredith said, feeling suddenly awkward about intruding on the woman's quiet moment. 'But I wanted to introduce myself. I'm Meredith Edwards. I moved onto the street' – she motioned to her building – 'in October.'

Sandra clearly still had no idea who Meredith was or why she was saying hello, but she nodded encouragingly and said, 'Oh of course, welcome. How are you? Lovely to meet you.'

'I know your husband,' Meredith explained, then seeing the other woman stiffen slightly, quickly added, 'I'm at Northern. In Orthopaedics. I just moved down from John Hunter in Newcastle.'

'Oh, lovely,' the woman said, looking relieved. 'Well, welcome to the Northern family. Was this your first Sydney Christmas?'

'Well, I'm from Sydney originally, so no,' Meredith said. 'And I went back to Newcastle for Christmas, to see friends.'

Sandra nodded, pretending to be interested. Meredith looked across the grass to where Sandra's dogs were lying in the shade of the bench.

'Your dogs are lovely,' Meredith said, for want of anything else to say. It worked; the other woman visibly and immediately relaxed.

'They're horribly spoilt but I adore them, my boys,' Sandra said fondly, looking towards the now sleeping dogs. 'Although it's a struggle to get them to go far in this heat.'

'Mine is hopeless in the heat, too. But loves the beach.' She smiled. 'I miss him so much.'

'Oh. You had to leave yours in Newcastle? How awful.'

'He's not really mine. My ex and I – well, she got him originally so she got to keep him.'

'I'm so sorry. That must be very hard.' She was looking at Meredith with genuine sympathy. 'Well, if you're in need of some doggy company, you'd be very welcome to borrow these two.'

Meredith was touched by the other woman's kindness and thanked her.

'I work with a rescue charity,' Sandra said. 'We always have animals who need fostering or adopting. Not just dogs, but cats, lizards, rabbits, you name it.' She smiled. 'Something to think about? Perhaps when you're feeling completely settled.'

Meredith tried to picture herself in her new apartment with a different dog but she could only picture Hugo and his big slobbery Staffy grin so she said instead, 'I've always thought it might be nice to have a cat,' although she had never really thought about it much.

'We always have cats who need homes and I'm fostering kittens at the moment if you can handle all that energy and naughtiness.' She stood and the dogs roused themselves from the ground as the offer hung in the air. Sandra took a phone from her pocket, tapped in the passcode then passed it to Meredith. 'Pop your number in. Maybe you'd like to come and have a look at them sometime?'

Meredith put in her number and then added her name as 'Potential Cat Lady' and after calling herself so she'd have Sandra's number, passed it back. Meredith had a hunch that Sandra wouldn't mention meeting her to Richard but it wouldn't hurt to try and hide where she lived from him for a little longer. The other woman acknowledged the joke with a smile.

'How long have you helped rescues?'

Sandra began clipping the double lead to her dogs. 'A few years now. I always wanted to be a vet when I was a child but I wasn't clever enough.' She smiled. 'This more than makes up for it. All of the fun, none of the gore.'

'So what does being a foster involve?'

'Round-the-clock care if necessary. Lots of gentle love and feeding. Tending to their wound sites if they have any. Really it's just helping them get strong enough to be adopted or return to the wild if they're natives.'

Her eyes were shining as she spoke.

'Which are your favourites?' Meredith asked as they began walking towards the pavement.

'Oh the baby possums, definitely. I got one last month. Dear little thing. I called him Poky.' She laughed. 'Poky the possum. He'd lost his mum and was probably only a week old. We tried to find her but I think she probably got hit by a car.'

'Was he okay? Did he survive?'

'Not only that but he thrived. He was beautifully plumped up when he was ready to be returned to the wild. But it's hard to say goodbye, especially when you've fed them and watched them grow. A bit like farewelling your child when they leave home.' A faint trace of a frown crossed her features. 'Not that I'd know.'

Meredith smiled at the other woman. 'Me neither,' she said and then, more brightly, 'Well, I think I'd rather have a possum than a child.'

'God, me too.'

The two women laughed and Meredith felt a wave of happiness wash over her.

Had she made another friend?

Chapter 26

LIV
Monday, 10 February 2025

On Monday morning Liv overhears Robyn, the receptionist at the clinic, talking about Richard's death and something about a new investigative podcast about it. Later that day when she and Robyn are alone in the kitchen, Liv asks her what the podcast is saying. Robyn, who until last winter worked in admin over at the main hospital, launches into an enthusiastic explanation of how the podcast thinks that there's a cover-up and dark forces, possibly the mafia, are responsible for Richard's death.

'He had friends in very high places,' she stage-whispers. 'I've heard some things over the years.'

'Does it mention Martin Finch? I'm surprised he's not the main suspect.'

'I think that's in episode two next week,' Robyn says. 'But he seems fishy too.'

Liv moves a little closer to Robyn and lowers her voice as she tells Robyn that she's heard Martin has been ruled out by police because of his watertight alibi.

'I don't know why this hasn't got out but he was actually in Landley at the time,' she says, watching as Robyn's eyes widen at this gold nugget of gossip.

Liv tells Robyn how Martin Finch had arrived at Northern on the eve of Richard's death, how he'd threatened to kill himself and then assaulted one of the security guards before being processed into Landley under an involuntary hold. She can't believe the hospital grapevine hasn't got hold of this news already.

'So that's why the police think there's no chance he could have got himself out the next morning and gone and murdered Richard,' she says, letting Robyn join the remaining dots herself.

'Well, that's bullshit,' Robyn says a beat later. 'Everyone knows security over there is a massive issue. The whole place is dangerously understaffed.'

Liv frowns. 'So you think he could have got out and then back in again without anyone noticing?'

Robyn makes a scoffing noise. 'More likely they knew but made sure they kept it under wraps so no one got in trouble.'

'Would they have normally?'

'Course, they'd have got a formal warning.'

They are standing in the staff kitchenette just off the reception area and Robyn goes over to her computer beside the front desk. There is just one person waiting, sitting on the bank of chairs opposite, absorbed in his phone with earbuds in. Robyn sits down and begins tapping on the keyboard.

'I kept an old email from an incident report log three months ago,' Robyn says, frowning as she scans the screen, using her mouse to scroll down through her email inbox. 'Give me a mo.'

It doesn't surprise Liv that Robyn has a record somewhere. She's an active member of the union that looks after ancillary hospital workers and is always trying to convince Liv and her other colleagues to join up.

'Here you go,' she says, a note of satisfaction as she opens an email and beckons for Liv to read it over her shoulder. Liv scans the email as Robyn explains.

'There was an incident report log three months ago with Landley which the union had to help with. There was a patient who had issues post-surgery. Diabetic but also some serious mental health issues. He had a foot amputation but didn't have a good outcome, didn't follow post-operative procedure and ended up with an infection so was readmitted via A&E. He was also given a psychiatric evaluation and spent a night in Landley.' She pauses. 'Somehow, the next morning, probably at staff swap-over, he got himself out of Landley without anyone noticing. Even though he was in a wheelchair.' Robyn shoots her a look. 'Non-motorised at that. But he got himself onto a bus and back home before anyone realised. That night he took his own life.'

Liv reads over Robyn's shoulder, as she slowly scrolls down through the inquiry statements by the various members of staff and management, their excuses and explanations for gross incompetency and lack of care.

'Did anyone lose their job?'

'No. But people got written warnings. The union argues that these members weren't given appropriate training, resources and supervision. The ward the patient was on that night didn't have a nursing unit manager on call or any primaries. Most of the staff were temps. Supervision had been signed over to the unit manager for floor two and four who only checked in on the floor the patient was on – floor three – once at around 11 p.m. There was no one on reception overnight and just one member of security covering the whole of the eastern part of the campus.'

Robyn raises her eyebrows, waiting as Liv takes in the significance of what this means.

'Of course, hospital management refuse to accept any responsibility even though understaffing is the main issue. And they've made it clear, if there's another security breach, if another patient gets out, the unit managers and head of security for the hospital will probably lose their jobs.'

Liv's heartbeat quickens. 'So it's in everyone's interests to remain very quiet about any other breaches.'

Robyn gives a grim nod.

When Liv is alone in the living room later that night, she composes another anonymous email to DI Mitchell giving him all this information.

That evening after work, Liv finds herself standing next to Meredith in the queue at their local supermarket. They acknowledge each other with polite, slightly embarrassed smiles.

'How are you?' Liv says softly, conscious the shop is probably filled with Northern employees. Meredith gives an awkward shrug. An automated voice announces the availability of a free checkout. Meredith begins to move but then glances back to Liv. 'I've got my car if you need a lift back?'

'Oh thanks,' Liv responds after a beat, feeling a lurch of guilt at the woman's kindness. 'That's really kind of you.'

Liv's whole body feels rigid as she settles inside Meredith's car.

'I'm really sorry about what's going on. About the suspension and everything. I hope everything gets sorted out soon.'

'I'm not holding my breath.' Meredith's window glides down and she puts her parking ticket into the slot, waiting for the boom gate to rise. 'Assaulting someone at a hospital social event isn't a good look for anyone. Especially when it's a consultant.'

'Gracie told me that Richard was harassing you, practically stalking you before what happened,' Liv says as Meredith pulls out onto the main road. 'Have you told management or the police what he was like? What a shit he was?'

'How I had a motive to want him dead?' Meredith's eyes remain on the road. 'No, not yet.'

'I'm sure he's got a massive file of complaints against him from other women at the hospital.'

She doesn't reply and they drive in silence.

'For the record I had nothing to do with his death,' Meredith says as they come to a red light. 'Not that I can say I'm particularly devastated that he's gone.'

'There was nothing going on between you both? No … relationship?'

Meredith gives Liv a look that makes her feel a curl of shame.

'I would never go near a man like Richard Wellington in a million years, even if I was straight,' Meredith says. 'But he was the kind of man who wouldn't take no for an answer.'

An image of a terrified Gracie and a predatory Richard in the Gully that morning flashes into Liv's vision.

'And because he was the way he is and thought every woman in the world would be falling over themselves to be with him, he assumed the same of me.' She lets out a long exhalation. 'And because I turned him down, everyone thinks I killed him.'

The lights change and the car accelerates.

'What have the police said to you?'

'They've told me to instruct a solicitor, which I've done, and this morning my solicitor told me the police now consider me a person of interest and want to interview me again. So I'm going back in tomorrow morning.'

Liv glances at Meredith. 'But they don't have anything on you, right? It's all just circumstantial? You were there at the park, you had some kind of past situation with Richard, but that's not evidence. That's not enough evidence,' she corrects herself.

They are on their street and Meredith pulls into a parking spot near Liv's house. She pulls up the handbrake but keeps the engine running.

'I guess they want to put as much pressure on me or any other suspect as possible. I suppose that's how they think they'll flush out the real killer.'

Liv's mind is racing. How much has Meredith said about Gracie being at the park last Thursday? She remembers her daughter's puffy eyes that morning. Would Meredith have seen how upset she was, and will she mention this to the police tomorrow? Will she speculate to the police that Gracie may have seen Richard that morning?

'I think I have proof that Martin Finch killed Richard,' she says suddenly.

She needs to plant the seed in Meredith's mind too. She needs this idea to grow and germinate and move from being a whisper of a possibility and rumour to being something solid and absolute.

Meredith turns to her, quizzical. 'I thought the police had ruled him out?'

Liv pauses. 'If I tell you what I know then do you think you can work out a way to tell it to the police? Don't say you know for sure obviously, but just say this is one of the rumours doing the rounds at the hospital.' Meredith looks confused but Liv continues. 'Just promise me that you'll try to keep Gracie out of everything. That you won't mention her to the police again except that you briefly saw and said hi to her that morning. You don't comment on her appearance, how she seemed that morning, her mood, any of it.'

Another frown. 'Okay.'

Liv tells Meredith everything she knows and has learnt about Martin Finch and his possible flit from the hospital, its lax security and how its workers might have kept his escape quiet. She explains how it would have been easy for Martin to have learnt about Richard's running routine thanks to the vain idiot posting updates about his new regime on Instagram and reposting his times and pace.

The killer, Liv tells Meredith, could have worked out when he'd be at the Gully park thanks to all of these posts and then that Thursday, lay in wait for him.

Meredith is silent for a few moments.

'I don't know. It seems pretty far-fetched. How would he have got to the Gully?'

'He would have driven. His car would be parked up near the hospital.'

'He wouldn't have been allowed to keep his keys,' she says, echoing Liv's thoughts.

'Maybe he tucked them on top of the wheel or hid them somewhere along the way?'

Meredith looks dubious. 'It doesn't seem very likely.'

'I don't know but it's doable,' Liv says, her frustration rising. Why doesn't Meredith think this is the perfect solution? It will clear her. It will clear Gracie. 'Just tell them this is what you've heard people saying at work. You don't have to work out the logistics of it.'

'But you want me to tell the police all of this?'

Liv nods and Meredith is silent, presumably thinking it over, trying to work out whether the police will think she's crazy or this will give them a bit of a push to go down this line of enquiry.

'Okay,' she says finally. 'I'll try.'

Liv puts her hand on the car door.

'There's something else.' She averts her gaze from Meredith. 'I would prefer you to stay away from Gracie. I don't think you should message her anymore and if you see her out, I don't want you to stop to say hello.'

'Why?'

'Because I think it's for the best if you stay away from each other while this investigation is going on.' Liv opens the car door, her gaze travelling along the road to the tall building where Meredith lives. The sun will set in the next half an hour but for now the summer sky is the palest of pinks. 'I don't want people to hear that you were at the park that morning and that Gracie was also at the park that morning and turn this into something it's not.'

She gets out of the car and with her hand resting on the top of the door, ready to close it, adds more softly, 'I'm sorry, but I'm just doing what I need to do to protect my daughter.'

There is a beat before Meredith speaks and in that split second, Liv sees hurt pass across the other woman's face.

'You should know that I wasn't going to mention Gracie to the

144

police at all. I would never say anything to anyone that might make them think Gracie was involved in what happened to Richard. Honestly? I'd rather the police think I did it. I really would. I'd rather the police thought I killed Richard.'

Meredith looks at Liv with such intensity burning in her eyes that Liv has to look away. It is uncomfortable. Too much. Too … Meredith.

Andy is on a call, facing the other way when Liv drops the shopping bags onto the floor and heads straight for the cupboard so she can pour herself a glass from the wine bottle on the counter next to him. He doesn't turn to look her way until he ends the call with a soft 'thank you' and 'we'll be there very soon'.

He turns and Liv's stomach gives a lurch as she sees his grave expression. Whatever it is that's happened is bad.

Gracie? Has something happened to Gracie?

'That was your dad. He's been trying to call you.' Andy looks visibly shaken. 'It's your mum. She's expected to recover but she's in hospital. She's had another stroke. A big one this time.'

Chapter 27

MEREDITH

January 2025

Later the day Meredith met Sandra, Gracie texted her.

How's the running/New Year resolution going – see you at the oval tomorrow – 6.30?

Meredith had told Gracie that it was her new year's resolution to run four times a week, if not five. So the next day Meredith set her alarm and forced herself up and out by six, attempting a few laps around the oval before heading over to the grass by the water to find Gracie.

'I only had a week off and I feel like I've gone back to the beginning,' Meredith groaned as she lifted one leg to the back of the bench next to Gracie.

Gracie laughed. 'It'll only take a few sessions and you'll pick up where you left off.'

They did their various stretches as they caught up on the vague outlines of what they'd both been doing over the festive period. The presents, the nights out with friends, the New Year's Eve fireworks.

They were halfway up the hill to home when Gracie asked if Meredith knew of a doctor at Northern called Richard Wellington.

Meredith glanced at Gracie before replying that she did.

'He lives opposite us,' Gracie began and then stopped as a man stepped from the house they were passing, dragging a very brown and dead-looking Christmas tree from his house and depositing it on the grass verge.

'So you were saying about Richard Wellington?' Meredith prompted when the man was out of earshot but Gracie didn't immediately reply so she added, 'He's not a friend of mine if that's what you're worried about. In fact, I think he's a pompous idiot.'

But Gracie still didn't say anything.

'Has he done something?' Meredith asked, now concerned.

They were walking up a steep stretch of road, both of them panting with the effort. When they got to the top, they stopped to catch their breath.

'So on Christmas Eve my friend was dropping me home and as I got out I saw Richard was standing outside his house, having a cigarette.' Gracie paused a moment. 'He waved but I just ignored him because, you know, he's a bit creepy. But I'd been dropped on the corner so I had to walk like four houses down to mine and by the time I was by our gate, he'd crossed the road. He said something like "you look like someone looking for trouble" or some crap like that.' She made a face. 'Then as I was about to pull shut the gate, he kind of lurched at me and tried to hug me. He was saying "merry Christmas, sweetheart" and he was really drunk so I pushed him away, but in a kind of jokey way.'

They began to walk again, this time at a slower pace, enjoying the cool of the shady side of the street.

'He stepped back a bit and apologised but then he followed me to the front door. It was really late, like 1 a.m. and my parents' room was right there and I knew they'd be sleeping and he was

147

being really loud so I pointed to our front windows and said, "My parents are just there", and then when he wouldn't move I just said, "Piss off home, Richard." But he laughed and kind of grabbed at my arm and started saying how I should come and celebrate Christmas with him. *Come and have a glass of champagne.* She gave a small shudder as she said the words in a sing-song voice.

'I said no, I was going to sleep but he kept on at me and being loud. I was really annoyed but I didn't feel like, threatened or anything. I knew Mum and Dad were right there if I needed them, so I decided to guide him back onto the road, and then once I got him there, I told him to be quiet and go home because everyone was asleep.

'I was holding my keys like this' – she motioned with her hand – 'thinking if he tried anything I could stab him with them, but I knew he probably wouldn't. He was just being an old drunk idiot. But he refused to go inside, even when I said I'd knock on his door and get his wife. Then he kind of nudged at me and I dropped my keys.'

She let out an irritated sigh. 'He picked them up before I could and did that thing where he kept holding them out of my reach. I was really, really pissed off by then and told him to stop being a fucking dick and give them to me and then he kept telling me I was uptight and boring. I told him I'd start shouting for help if he didn't shut up and he looked a bit put out. Anyway, I eventually managed to snatch back the keys and I told him I'd call the police if he didn't fuck right off.'

Gracie checked Meredith's expression.

'There's more,' she said grimly. 'He eventually went and sat down on the steps by his front garden and I got into my house, but then a bit later, after I'd had a shower and I was in bed just looking at my phone, there was this tapping on my window.' Her eyes widened. 'I swear I nearly had a fucking heart attack. It was him, obviously. And he was saying my name, over and over.'

'What did you do?'

'Nothing. I ignored him. Thank god my window was locked and my blind down.'

'Did you tell your mum and dad?'

She shook her head. A sharp, defensive shake. 'I handled it. They don't need to know.'

'Why?'

'I dealt with it. Anyway, they'd just tell Sandra and she's really nice and I don't want to upset her. She has enough to put up with being married to an arsehole like him.

'Anyway, he finally left. But then it's happened a few more times last week, between Christmas and New Year.' Gracie swallowed. 'Sometimes he kind of whispers my name in this weird voice, mostly he just taps on the window.'

'Jesus, Gracie. What do you do?'

'Nothing, I don't want to give him the satisfaction of even knowing I'm there.'

'When did it last happen?'

'A few days ago. I think he went away the morning of New Year's Eve. His car's been gone.'

'Would you consider reporting him? I could go with you to the police.'

Gracie gave a sharp shake of her head. 'No, I can handle it. And please don't tell my parents.'

'Why? They'll be angry at him not you. This is about his behaviour.'

'I know, but they're overprotective and I don't want them to worry,' she said.

'You're their daughter. They just want to keep you safe.'

She made a face. 'Listen, he's just a creep. I can handle it. But I wanted to tell you because I overheard something at the café this morning. About you and him.'

She glanced at Meredith.

'I heard these two women talking. I guess they work at the hospital because they were wearing scrubs.' She paused. 'They

149

were saying how you were together. And that you'd had this fight, a physical fight at some hospital event?'

Meredith let out a sigh.

'Obviously that's not the whole story or even true but after what happened … what he did to me …' She trailed off. 'Well, I figured there was more to whatever happened with you.'

'Men like Richard Wellington are nothing if not predictable.'

'You obviously don't have to tell me,' Gracie said. 'But I'm here if you want to talk about it.'

And that was the beginning of it all. Meredith told Gracie about Richard and what had happened at the Christmas party, and the lead-up, the messages and his obvious interest in her that she most definitely didn't reciprocate or have any interest in. How that had morphed into something darker. How Richard had taken her rejection badly and then turned the tables on her and tried to make it appear as though she was drunk.

Then, once they were at the top of the stairs that led to the cul-de-sac reserve, Meredith told Gracie her suspicions that Richard had ended her father's career and how she was now concerned he would try to end hers.

'What a fucking bastard,' Gracie said when Meredith finally finished explaining and they were standing in the shade of a tree by the reserve. 'I can't believe he's been getting away with this shit for so long.'

'Men like him always do.'

'Well, not anymore,' Gracie said and Meredith smiled as she saw the glint in the young woman's eyes.

'What are you going to do?'

Gracie appeared to consider this for a moment, her gaze travelling across the reserve and down the street towards Richard Wellington's house.

'Find a way to stop him,' she said, her voice full of the kind of self-righteous youthful determination that only a nineteen-year-old possesses. 'For good.'

Chapter 28

LIV

Tuesday, 11 February 2025

Angela looks peaceful as she sleeps, the only sign of the stroke, a slight droop to the right side of her mouth.

Earlier, the doctor warned Liv that the effects of the stroke would become more obvious when her mum woke. She'd had a left hemisphere cerebrum stroke so may have right-sided weakness or paralysis and problems with speech and understanding language. It was a big enough bleed, Liv is told, that Angela will likely not make a full recovery but could one day, with luck and rehab, be able to regain some of her mobility.

If she is one of the lucky ones and doesn't swiftly have another stroke within the next few days, Liv thinks to herself. This is Angela's second major stroke in six months and Liv knows that means the stats aren't in her mum's favour.

Pete is sitting in a chair in the corner of Angela's private room; Andy somewhere in the hospital corridors, tracking down a coffee machine. They are in a hospital on the other side of the city; one of the best for stroke care, she's heard.

'She'll be okay, Dad,' Liv says, just as she had done about half a dozen times over the past few hours. 'I'll take time off work, do all her rehab. Be her own personal physio.'

Pete makes an affirmative noise from the corner and Liv feels a wave of sadness wash over her. He looks so exhausted and confused and Liv knows he is struggling to process what is going on.

'Dad, I think Andy should take you home,' Liv says when Andy returns with three cups of coffee in a tray. 'It'd be good for you to get a few hours of sleep.'

'I really should have picked milk up on the way,' he says, getting up from the chair.

He's been repeating this phrase over and over again since Liv and Andy arrived, stuck in some kind of loop.

After they leave, amid more confusion and some protests from Pete, reassurance from Andy and an unspoken agreement that passes between him and Liv that Pete should not be left alone for the remainder of the night, Liv finally sinks back into the chair beside Angela's bed. She is exhausted although she knows she won't sleep a wink tonight.

Liv pulls the chair a little closer to the bed so she can rest her hand on Angela's arm, careful to stay clear of all the monitoring equipment that trails tubes from various parts of her mum. She traces circles across Angela's hand and wrist. She says the occasional reassuring and pointless murmur as if Angela is a baby that needs soothing.

At some point Liv must fall asleep because she wakes suddenly with a jolt, her phone buzzing in her back pocket. She fumbles as she tries to retrieve it.

'How's Gran?' Gracie asks as soon as Liv accepts the call, seeing that it's just past midnight.

'Good. Well, okay. Resting. I'm here with her now.'

'Can we switch to FaceTime so I can see her?'

'Sure. But don't be too loud.'

Liv turns on the video and angles her camera towards Angela. The video is grainy in the dim light but Liv keeps it in place so Gracie can watch her grandmother. After half a minute or so she switches back to call mode.

'She looks peaceful. The same,' Gracie says but Liv can hear the obvious fear in her daughter's voice.

'The doctors say she's got some paralysis and her speech will be affected but with rehab she should regain some of that. But it'll be a hard slog.'

'Can I come and see her tomorrow?'

'Course. Try and get some sleep and come in the morning.' Liv looks towards the window and sees the inky black and remembers suddenly that Gracie is alone in their house. 'Are you okay, on your own?'

'Fine. I'm an adult, Mum.'

'I know, but, you know, with everything. Make sure the doors and windows are all locked.'

'I know. I already have.'

Liv wonders if Gracie really is as fine as she says she is. 'Okay, I better go. My battery's about to die. Bring my charger when you come tomorrow? Or get Dad to?'

Gracie agrees and then promises to double-check the front door and sleep with Sophie beside her. Liv knows she's probably making Gracie even more fearful with her worrying but she'd rather that than have something happen to her daughter in the night.

After ending the call, Liv checks other messages but as she's about to email work and explain that she won't be in tomorrow, her phone dies.

She retrieves her mum's handbag which her dad had, bless him, known to bring when his neighbour drove him to the hospital after the ambulance left with Angela. No matter what state Angela is in when she wakes, Pete knows from years of being told, that his wife will want her powder and lipstick, even if she's unable to apply the make-up herself.

Angela's phone is a newer model than Liv's and has a bejewelled purple cover. Liv correctly guesses the passcode, the same four digits both Angela and Pete use for everything – 8888.

There are a comical number of selfies in the photo folder, Liv sees, many of which appear to have been taken by accident when Angela was applying lipstick but not much else. Few apps and even fewer text messages. Liv taps out one to Andy and Gracie, explaining that her phone has died and to contact her on Angela's and asking Andy to bring a charger in tomorrow morning.

Then she checks the news to see if there's been any developments with Richard's murder, which there haven't, and then googles 'second stroke in six months recovery time' then closes the page before reading any of the results. She knows them all anyway.

Then because there's nothing else to do she checks the settings on the phone are all up to date and goes through the handful of apps Angela has downloaded until she is left with just the voice recorder app to check. She is surprised to see there is a long list of recordings, the most recent from the day before yesterday.

Liv plays the first, from last year which is just eighteen seconds long. There is white noise and rustling and then a voice says, loudly, 'Bloody hell' and Liv smiles at the sound of her mum's familiar voice. The next one is longer and made less than a minute after the first. Her mum's voice has the same tone of impatience in it, presumably from trying to figure out how to use the recorder.

'I don't really understand why I'm doing this,' Angela begins. A long, exasperated sigh. 'So today is a Wednesday.' Another pause. 'I only know this because I'm looking at the newspaper in front of me on the kitchen table. It's very possible the newspaper was bought yesterday of course. So it could be Thursday today, I suppose. Anyway …' Another pause. 'Who cares. Not me.' The recording ends.

Liv plays the next one, recorded four days later.

'Onions, garlic, soften, low heat, add mince, brown, add herbs and spices, a slug of red wine, turn up heat for a few minutes, then add a tin of tomatoes, put down to a simmer for an hour with the lid on.' Angela clears her throat. 'See? I remember it perfectly.'

The recording ends and Liv listens to the next one.

'This morning I must get dressed, brush teeth, wash face, make-up, brush hair and then have breakfast with Livvie.'

Liv feels a thickening in the very back of her throat. Mercifully, Angela's voice is jauntier in the next one.

'Livvie came and brought me the most delicious biscuit. Cookie she called it. It was like a little party in my mouth. Full of all spice and dried fruit and other things. It was quite delicious. Not too sugary either. We went for a walk. Tonight ...' Angela's voice trails off. 'Well, I'm not quite sure. But I do know I'm looking forward to it because my black silk skirt is hanging up ready to go!'

The recording ends.

Liv lowers the phone to her lap and looks at Angela. Her poor mum. She'd been diagnosed with vascular dementia two months after her stroke, just a few weeks after Pete had been told about his Alzheimer's.

Since then Angela had been part of a seniors support group organised by her GP, which meant she attended a weekly meeting where she was given what was called memory support, chair-based exercise classes and other workshops and events Angela could barely disguise her contempt for, but still attended. The voice note idea must have come from that.

Liv clicks on another recording but just a few seconds in, a nurse comes in to check on Angela and Liv pauses it, excuses herself and heads to the twenty-four-hour ground-floor café. She buys a sticky pastry and a cup of tea and then sits down at one of the tables, waiting for her name to be called.

A few minutes later she takes the paper cup and bag containing her pastry outside to a nearby empty bench, breathing in the muggy night air which is a relief after the institutionalised scent of the hospital. She opens up her mum's phone again and brings up the voice note she was about to listen to, holding the speaker end of the phone to her ear.

Her mother's voice is markedly different from last year's. There is still Angela's distinct and rich actress's timbre that infuses each word with depth and character, but there is also a hesitance. A stop start. But not, Liv realises immediately, just from confusion and the aftermath of the strokes.

'I don't know why I'm recording this. Well, I suppose I do. Because Alison tells me I must.' A sigh. 'Alison is very … insistent. So here we are. Talking about my past. After all, if Peter gets to talk about his and we all know how he'll probably conveniently forget so many things, then I suppose I should talk about mine.' A pause. 'But where to start? There are so many memories. So many years … And yes, yes, I know I sound dramatic and goodness knows I'm always being accused of being dramatic, but really when you're my age and you're talking about your past, it's hard to know where to begin. There *are* so many memories. So many secrets.' A note of hesitation creeps into Angela's voice. 'But that's what I want to record. The secrets. Because when those memories are gone, so are those secrets and one day … well, I suppose Livvie should know about them, shouldn't she? So here we are. The family's story. Her family's story.' A long pause. 'From the very beginning.' There is a longer pause. 'Oh bugger.' A rustling follows and then another sigh. 'Is this stupid thing even recording? Oh for goodness sake.'

And then, nothing. The recording ends.

Chapter 29

LIV

Wednesday, 12 February 2025

After Liv has spoken with the doctor, it becomes clear that Angela will remain in hospital for a while. She sits with Angela, holding her hand, willing her mum to gently slip away if she is ready to but not saying the words out loud. She can't bear to.

Gracie arrives just before midday and then half an hour later they are joined by Andy and Pete. Both Gracie and Andy are solemn faced and, in Gracie's case, pale and strained and Liv wonders if her worries about safety kept her daughter awake last night.

But before she can ask, they get told off by one of the nurses who explains that even though Angela is sleeping, there can only be one visitor with her at a time. They all dutifully rise and file out of the room.

It is decided that they will all take a break for a while. Gracie goes off to a university lecture while Liv takes Pete home and Andy returns to theirs, Liv leaving clear instructions with the nurses to call if anything changes.

Liv imagined Pete would be distressed and confused but he seems happy enough that afternoon, pottering in his studio, watching TV or sitting in the kitchen, reading the paper, as she cooks up some chicken soup even though this seems the most ridiculous thing to make in 30-degree heat. But it is what her family always cooks in a crisis.

Andy arrives after a few hours so Liv can go home and shower and change her clothes before returning to the hospital. When she's back on the ward another nurse tells her that Angela had been awake for a few minutes earlier, although she was unable to talk. Liv once again sits by her mum's bedside, willing Angela to be okay and be herself again. Just for a little longer, please, please, please.

Then around six in the evening, Angela wakes and greets Liv, not with a smile, but a sort of crooked grimace due to the palsy on her face from the stroke. Then, to the astonishment of the nurses, she motions that she is hungry with her good hand and soon after eats a pot of yoghurt that Liv feeds to her slowly, murmuring encouragement with every spoonful.

Liv gently squeezes her mum's hand when she is done. 'Well done,' she says softly and her mum gives a lopsided smile.

That night, buoyed by her mum's progress, Liv stays over with her dad and is woken by him around three in the morning.

'She's left me, she's gone,' he is muttering over and over when Liv finds him standing in the sitting room in his pyjamas, trying to find the car keys.

'It's okay, Dad, she's not left. Mum's in hospital, but she'll be home soon,' Liv says, her voice soothing as she attempts to guide him up the narrow stairs and back to his bedroom. It takes some time but Pete finally calms and after Liv gives him the sleeping pill she'd stupidly decided he didn't need earlier, she locks all the doors and makes sure the keys are hidden away.

The next morning, Andy arrives with coffee before Liv is even dressed and she takes it from him gratefully, places it on the side table then draws him in for a hug.

As she breathes in his familiar scent, the calm she instantly feels at being next to him swiftly morphs into something else: an awful realisation that this might be their life for the foreseeable future. Seeing each other briefly in between shifts looking after her parents; exchanging worn clothes for new ones. Gratefully and desperately accepting strong cups of takeaway coffee from whoever's managed to stop by a café, the elixir of survival after another disturbed night.

'I can't do this,' she says into his chest, panic needling at her. 'I really, really can't do this.'

Andy hugs her a little tighter. 'You can.' And then, 'We can.'

Later, when the new carer arrives to be with Pete and Andy is driving Liv to the hospital, she finally remembers the voice note and that she keeps forgetting to tell Andy about it.

'Listen to this,' she says, and opens the recording she now has a copy of on her own phone.

As her mother says the words – 'I suppose Livvie should know about them, shouldn't she? So here we are. The family's story. Her family's story' – she watches her husband for his reaction.

'So? What do you think it's about?' she says. 'What secrets is she talking about?'

Andy frowns. 'I have literally no idea.' He glances at her for a split second. 'Have you?'

'No, not a clue. Could there be some kind of dark secret in the family?' Liv asks.

'Possibly,' Andy says, a smile crossing his face. 'But I think it's probably just Angela being dramatic? Maybe she has a random memory about her time working with Sam Neill that she's never told you about.'

Liv laughs. 'Oh my god, yes, it's probably exactly that.'

Later, when Liv is sitting by Angela who is sleeping, her phone beeps and she goes into the corridor to take it.

'Stan just called me,' Andy says down the line and there's something about his tone that makes Liv's blood turn cold. 'There's been some more chatter about Martin Finch being arrested, but the police are apparently waiting on some forensic results first.'

'What kind?'

'Richard had markings around his wrist indicating some kind of struggle. The pathologist apparently believes the attacker pulled at Richard's arm at some point. They've found DNA at the site that belongs to persons unknown.'

Liv knows they are both thinking the same thing.

'What if it's Gracie's?' she whispers. 'From when Richard made a grab for her? We need to ask Gracie if she dug her fingernails into him.'

'I did already,' Andy says. 'She says she can't remember.'

There is a long pause.

'Look, it's probably not even Gracie's DNA,' Liv says, trying to reassure herself. 'We're worrying unnecessarily.'

'But what if it is hers?' Andy says, and Liv can hear his usually calm tone has a note of panic setting in. 'Maybe she should come clean and tell the police what happened – that she was assaulted by Richard and during that, she fought him off. It doesn't mean she had anything to do with his death. If anything, it'll mean the police will have reason to accept her version of what happened.'

'But if it is Gracie's DNA, and it all comes out that Richard assaulted her, the police will know she's been hiding things,' Liv says. 'Won't that make things worse for her?'

There's another long silence.

'We should have told her to be honest from the start,' Andy says eventually, this time his voice matter of fact. 'We should have pushed her to be honest. She should never have lied to the police in the first place.'

Liv frowns. 'We were trying to protect her, Andy. We're still trying to protect her.'

Andy doesn't respond but Liv knows instantly that he's thinking: *yeah and now look what's happened.*

Chapter 30

MEREDITH

January 2025

The Friday after they first met, Meredith received a message from Sandra, asking if she wanted to come and meet the kittens.

No pressure, but they are adorable. Guaranteed to turn anyone into a cat lover. My husband is away – stay for a glass of wine after?

It was a balmy evening and the sky was darkening into an indigo blue. On their street, most of the Christmas lights that had been strung up on front walls and the blow-up Santas and reindeers that had sat on verandas a few days before had been packed away.

As Sandra took Meredith out to the garage where she kept the enclosures, she explained how Richard was down the coast at their holiday home and she was taking advantage of that by looking after a second litter of kittens and their mum.

The first trio – Smudge, Smoky and Sausage – had been found

abandoned in a nearby car park. They were ridiculously adorable and fluffy, around twelve weeks old and Meredith immediately decided the black-and-white one, Smoky, was her favourite.

Over in the far corner was another larger enclosure which was half covered with a blanket and contained the recently rescued mum and her four tiny kittens, tucked into a corner. The mum eyed them warily as Sandra and Meredith crouched down to look at her.

'She's starting to relax and trust me but I leave her alone most of the time,' Sandra explained. 'Her kittens will stay with her for another month and then we'll start readying them for adoption and get her spayed. But the others are ready to go to new homes now.' She gave Meredith an expectant smile. 'No pressure, though.'

They sat on the deck and Sandra kept Meredith's glass topped up with wine and brought out a platter of cheese and crackers. 'Richard always goes overboard buying too much for Christmas,' she said, waving away Meredith's protest that she didn't need feeding.

As they ate and drank, Sandra asked about Meredith's work and what had brought her back to Sydney and Sandra explained how she got into volunteering for the local animal charity during the pandemic and was now considering getting a qualification in animal care.

Meredith asked if Richard was also an animal lover. He wasn't, but had learnt to love their dogs and grudgingly put up with the rescues. She asked if Meredith and Richard's paths crossed much at the hospital and Meredith kept her expression neutral as she explained how they'd met at various hospital events but that was all. Meredith couldn't tell if Sandra knew the truth or had heard the rumours. She hoped not.

Sandra swiftly redirected the conversation after that and asked Meredith what she was enjoying about Sydney. They talked about their mutual love of sea pools and bush walks and how Meredith had been getting back into running but was finding it hard going in the heat of summer. Soon they'd finished the bottle of wine and most of the cheese, and Sandra was heating a pizza in the oven for them to share and opening a second bottle although Meredith had already said she shouldn't have anymore.

'You don't have work tomorrow, do you? It's Saturday.'

'No, but I have a lot on,' Meredith said, although she really didn't, accepting another glass of wine regardless.

Sandra didn't mention Richard again that evening and Meredith thought how strange that was and wondered if they were one of those couples she occasionally encountered who only stayed together because separating would be too complicated.

She'd seen it before, especially in couples who were older and richer, as Sandra and Richard were. Perhaps this was the perfect set-up: together on paper, separate in all other ways, leaving Richard free to behave badly, have affairs and harass women with the smokescreen of remaining respectably married.

But what did Sandra get out of the arrangement? Meredith couldn't work it out. She didn't strike her as the kind of woman to be placated with a big house, healthy bank balance and a double garage big enough to fit multiple rescue animals. But maybe she was too set in her ways to start over. Or too scared?

As the cicadas began their evening roar and the garden cooled in the darkness, Meredith felt fuzzy with the wine and utterly content in Sandra's company. That this interesting and funny woman was Richard's wife was unfathomable to her, so, when she'd had more than enough wine to ensure she didn't feel the need to censor herself, she asked her outright.

'Your husband,' Meredith began, then hesitated at Sandra's expression. The other woman was looking at her with interest. 'Sorry but I've heard some things about him and now I've met you, I can't help thinking, well, if he's the way he is and you're the way you are, why on earth are you still together?'

Sandra let out a surprised bark of laughter. 'Well, that's quite a question.'

'Sorry, I probably shouldn't pry. I don't drink usually and people always tell me I'm too blunt when I do.'

'That's okay. It's refreshing. More people should be as honest.' She lifted her wine glass to her lips as she considered the question. 'So, you want to know why I put up with him?'

'I suppose so.'

'Well, our marriage wasn't always like this. Richard wasn't always like this. He was a good man when we met. We were very happy.'

'And now?'

Meredith saw the other woman's smile falter slightly.

'Now we are much older and we've been through decades worth of life.' A small shrug. 'People change. People put up with things they might not put up with at the beginning of relationships.'

'Are you still happy together?' Meredith saw she'd pushed too far and began to apologise.

'No, it's okay,' Sandra said, shaking her head. 'I look at it this way: there are parts of my life that make me very happy. There are others that I try not to concentrate on. Does that explain it?'

Sandra gave her a polite smile and they sat in silence for a moment, the cicadas whipping into a crescendo of noise around them.

'When did you meet?' Meredith asked eventually.

'At university. I was doing an arts degree, and I wasn't keen at first. Medics didn't have a great reputation.' She smiled knowingly. 'Arrogant and entitled. Well, the men, anyway. And Richard certainly had that in spades but he was also charming. He won me over.'

Meredith wondered if Sandra knew Richard at the time her father taught him.

'Where did you study?' Sandra asked Meredith.

'Sydney. But a few years later than Richard.'

'Quite a few, I'd say. But I bet the men were as arrogant then as they were in our day.'

Meredith smiled. 'Probably.' This was the moment she should say something, she realised. 'When I was there I heard some rumours about a group of students who must have been there around the same time as Richard. They played a prank on one of the professors and it all went horribly wrong?' She attempted to relax her face and try and look as though she found the idea of this amusing. 'Apparently the professor was removed from his position over it or something. I think he got very upset and lashed out at one of the pranksters.'

'How unfortunate,' Sandra said, mildly. 'Sounds typical of medical students. Most of them were incredibly clever but totally inept socially.'

Meredith felt a sting of recognition.

'They're probably now some of the country's most successful doctors,' she said.

'No doubt,' Sandra said, draining her glass of the last half-inch of wine in it and eyeing her momentarily. 'And I expect you work alongside a few of them, don't you?'

The next morning Meredith left a message for one of the few former colleagues of her father who was still working at the university and had been there in the late Eighties when Stephen was teaching.

Alexander True called back a few hours later, surprised to hear from her but after she told him a little about her life, how she was back in Sydney and how Meredith's return had prompted reflection on her father's career and the circumstances around him leaving teaching, he was quick to offer his own thoughts.

He told Meredith, hesitantly at first, clearly uncertain about how frank he could be, that Stephen hadn't been a natural teacher.

When Meredith laughed, saying that was probably an under-statement, he sounded relieved and after that spoke more freely.

He explained how Meredith's father had found the youth and immaturity of many of his students baffling and irritating; how

Stephen would complain that their paths had been greased with privilege and money and that meant none of them had developed the grit needed to be a focused student or a talented physician.

'Your dad didn't understand why they weren't more serious about their future careers,' he said. 'But I'd always remind him that he'd been a scholarship boy from the western suburbs. He'd had to overcome so many odds to get to where he was.'

Alexander explained how Stephen would get frustrated that he was sending the student doctors out onto the wards to interact with patients they clearly thought little of and were often patronising towards.

'They were pretty awful, that year in particular,' he added. 'You get that sometimes.'

Meredith asked if her father had mentioned any names in particular or if Alexander could recall any of the cohort involved in the complaint made against her father and there was a lengthy pause.

'I think it would probably be a little unfair for me to share their names with you,' he said.

They had, he added, presumably outgrown their immaturity and made up for their youthful mistakes.

'But I think it's possible I work with one of them,' Meredith blurted out. 'And I just need to know for certain.'

Meredith continued, saying how this particular person worked in plastics but was also known in other, more public-facing arenas unrelated to the hospital. She didn't outright say he worked in television but it was obvious, she hoped.

Alexander didn't say anything for a moment, then in a tone that was a little sharper than before said, 'I suspect, of course, that not everyone your father taught had the benefit of learning from their youthful mistakes.'

That's when Meredith knew her hunch was correct.

Richard Wellington had been among the cohort of students who had ended her father's teaching career and caused him to have a breakdown. A breakdown from which he never truly recovered.

Chapter 31

LIV

Thursday, 13 February 2025

The next few hours are agonising as they wait for the police's next move. Liv returns home from the hospital, assured that her mum is doing well and fine to be left for increasingly lengthy periods and Andy arranges for a neighbour to check in on Pete. As the afternoon ticks by, Andy messages Stan to find out whether anything more has happened, hoping this doesn't raise his friend's suspicions, but there are apparently no updates.

The wheels of the forensic side of the investigation apparently move slowly and there doesn't appear to be enough evidence for the police to charge Martin yet. And not enough other evidence that anyone else might have been involved.

The only thing giving Liv any reassurance is that she hadn't seen any markings or scratches on Gracie's arms, or anywhere visible, that would indicate a struggle or transference of DNA from her to Richard. So perhaps there is no need to panic.

They are in their bedroom talking in hushed tones having agreed they won't tell Gracie any of this, when Andy's expression changes and Liv turns to see Gracie standing in the doorway. She has a bag on her shoulder and is holding her pink Frank Green water bottle Liv got her for Christmas the previous year.

'What's happened?' she says. 'Is Gran okay?'

'She's fine. Doing well.' Liv sees the relief briefly flood her daughter's face, only to be replaced with one of concern again.

'What is it then?'

Andy glances at Liv. Liv looks at Gracie and tries to calculate the cost of telling their daughter what is going on. Gracie is clearly not doing well. She has dark shadows under her eyes which confirm she's not sleeping well; she is sulky and quick to anger and her room is tidier than ever.

But in this moment of considering what to say, Gracie goes from looking worried to clear panic.

'What is it? What's happened? Tell me.'

Andy explains and as he speaks Gracie goes rigid, her fear palpable.

'But it'll be okay,' Andy says when he's finished. 'The DNA probably has nothing to do with you. It probably belongs to the real killer and the police will arrest him soon and then this will all be over.'

They both watch for their daughter's reaction. Andy, Liv knows, for confirmation from Gracie that he is right, that of course it's not her DNA; Liv for something else. A flicker of doubt across her daughter's face, an obvious sign of worry or guilt. Something that will reveal what really happened early that Thursday morning at the Gully because right now Liv isn't sure of anything except she has the distinct impression Gracie is keeping something from them.

'It will be okay, Gracie. We'll make sure it is,' Liv says, although she doesn't believe her own words.

Gracie gives a stiff nod and then mutters, 'I'm going out' and a moment later, she is gone and the front door clicks shut behind her.

Later, when Andy is back across the city with Pete, and Liv has returned from briefly visiting Angela at hospital and is in the kitchen making dinner, she hears the front door open and then close shut. Gracie appears in the doorway. Her cheeks are flushed and she looks better. Happier? Not really, but certainly more relaxed than earlier.

'Where've you been?' Liv asks, returning to the chicken she is dicing.

Gracie shrugs. 'What's for dinner?'

'Thai curry,' Liv says, returning to the stove where the onions are browning.

'Can I eat something now or is it ready soon?' Gracie's hand is on the handle to the pantry cupboard.

'Yeah, course.' Liv smiles. 'This will be a while.'

Gracie takes crackers and hummus over to the other side of the kitchen counter and sits on a stool, eating and watching Liv as she cooks, just like she used to do every day after school when she was younger. Liv adds curry paste and coconut milk to the chicken and then turns back towards Gracie, reaching into the fruit bowl next to her for a lime.

Liv watches her as she eats. She isn't scrolling on her phone, as she would be usually.

'Your gran's doing much better,' Liv says. 'She was sitting up in bed this afternoon. She's not speaking but she's letting me know what she thinks about things.' Liv lets out a laugh. 'She was able to let me know she doesn't like one of the nurses and needed her make-up done.'

'When will she be able to go home?'

'The doctors think she's stabilised but they're suggesting rehab first.' Liv turns away to stir the curry. 'I'm not sure Mum will agree to that but I don't see how she'll cope at home without it.'

'You could move in and do it.'

'Well, I don't really want to be away from home at the moment.'

'Because of me?' There is an edge to Gracie's voice.

'In part, yes, but also because one of our neighbours was killed. I know we're not at risk but still. I just want to be here.'

'I'm fine. Gran should be your priority.'

Liv looks back at her daughter and sees Gracie's phone is out and she is looking at it intently, her shoulders hunched.

'Gracie, you know it's going to be okay, don't you?' Liv waits a moment but when Gracie doesn't respond, she continues, 'If anything's found, if they discover it's your DNA then we'll make sure you have a lawyer and you can make a full statement to the police telling them exactly what happened. They'll believe you. You'll be okay. You haven't done anything wrong.'

Gracie says nothing. Instead she slides off the stool, puts the lid on the hummus and returns it and the crackers to the fridge. Her face gives nothing away.

'But I do think it's a good idea to wait until then. Until the police make a move, which they might not.'

Gracie closes the fridge door and goes to the sink, taking a cloth and then going back to where she'd been sitting. Wiping at the smear of hummus on the counter; brushing crumbs into the palm of her hand.

'I promise everything will be okay,' Liv says, her voice soft. 'You're not going to be in trouble for what that man did to you.'

Gracie doesn't respond.

'I know it's scary, not knowing what's going to happen. But I'm sure the police will figure it all out soon. Everyone's saying it'll be just a matter of days before Martin Finch is arrested. I guess they're just gathering all the evidence they need first.'

A flicker of something crosses Gracie's face.

There it is, Liv realises, the tell she's been looking out for.

'If you need to tell me something. Anything at all, you know you can, right? I won't even tell Dad if you don't want me to.'

Another irritated sigh. 'God, Mum, I'm fine. There's nothing to tell.'

She starts pulling knives and forks from the drawer and sets the table. Liv watches Gracie place them carefully on the dining table, adjusting and readjusting their positions, tearing off kitchen roll and folding the squares neatly before placing them next to the knives.

'So you're okay? You're not too worried?' Liv can't help herself.

'Mum, I'm fine, really. Stop stressing. I know it'll all be okay.'

How? Liv wants to ask. She doesn't even believe the things she's saying to reassure Gracie.

'Where did you say you were this afternoon?'

'I didn't.'

Gracie takes three glasses from the cupboard, her expression not giving anything away.

'Did you see Meredith?'

Gracie briefly glances across the room towards Liv then begins putting the glasses on the table.

There it is, a momentarily flustered look, Liv is sure of it.

'Gracie.'

'What? Just because you aren't friends with her, doesn't mean I can't be.' Gracie rolls her eyes. 'Honestly, why are you so weird about her?'

'I told you to stay away from her.'

A small laugh as Gracie looks across the room at her mum. 'Excuse me, what am I, nine? I can be friends with whoever I want to be.'

And with that she leaves the room and a moment later Liv hears her bedroom door shut with a bang.

That night, Gracie has another night terror but wakes as Liv is sitting on the edge of her bed, soothing her.

'Go away,' she says, her voice thick with sleep as she rolls over. 'I'm fine.'

Liv withdraws her hand, but remains sitting there a moment. She listens as her daughter's breaths lengthen and when it is clear Gracie has returned to a deep sleep, she goes back to her own bed.

Chapter 32

LIV

Friday, 14 February 2025

It is just over two weeks since Richard Wellington died and the homepage of the *Daily News* leads with a full-screen headline screaming: SANDRA'S GRIEF FOR RICHARD alongside an old picture of Richard on the *Morning!* sofa, his rictus grin in stark contrast to the accompanying inset of Sandra walking down their street, her exhausted expression haunted, eyes cast down.

A police report detailing how Richard died had been leaked to one of the papers the night before and Liv and Andy had been shocked to learn that Richard hadn't died from drowning, nor the blunt force trauma to his head as the newspapers and gossip had speculated but from a ruptured cerebral aneurysm.

He had, reportedly, been in the care of a neurologist at the time of his death and had been aware of his condition although he had told no one about it, not his colleagues, nor his wife. The postmortem added that being hit so forcefully on the head had likely caused pressure in the brain which led to the pre-existing aneurysm to bleed.

'So he might have survived it if he didn't have an aneurysm,' Liv had said to Andy. 'Does that mean the death was accidental, so not manslaughter or murder?'

'It could still be both. Manslaughter if the court found the perpetrator acted recklessly or negligently. Murder if there was clear intent to cause death or harm.'

Liv feels Andy's words ringing in her ears as Sandra greets her at the front door with a weak smile. She is wearing rubber gloves and holding a dishcloth; her hair scraped off her bare face as she glances out to the road, presumably checking there are no photographers lying in wait.

'How are you doing?' Liv asks as they pull apart from a hug.

'I felt better before I saw myself looking like an old hag in the newspaper this morning.'

'I can't believe they photographed you like that,' Liv says as she follows Sandra into the garden and out to the garage at the back of it. 'Bastards.'

'I suppose they're just doing their jobs. But I still hate them.'

'I hate them too,' Liv says and Sandra smiles thankfully.

She motions for Liv to follow her as she heads to the back of the house. 'I've had a nightmare with the possum I'm looking after. He's got a stomach upset and I'm having to clean out his enclosure again.'

They go through to the garage and Liv watches as Sandra picks up a hose from the concrete floor and directs the trigger at a large, upended metal enclosure.

'Nearly done,' she says.

After a little more rinsing, Sandra turns off the hose and removes her gloves. She goes over to another enclosure in the garage, presumably the one housing the unwell possum. Lifting the large blanket shrouding it she crouches down.

'Poor thing's had a terrible time of it.'

Liv sees two tiny fearful eyes looking out at her.

'What happened?'

'We think he got attacked by a cat or a fox but then he had a bad reaction to the antibiotics. Doesn't agree with his tummy.' She drops the blanket. 'I'll move him into the clean enclosure later. So, how are you? Do you want a drink? Cup of tea?'

'Thanks but I've got to get to work,' Liv says, following Sandra back into the house. 'I just thought I'd swing by quickly and see how you're doing.'

'I'm okay.' Sandra forces a smile as she opens the fridge and takes out a bottle of water. 'Surprisingly okay actually.'

Liv isn't sure that can be true. As she watches Sandra pour two glasses of water, she can see the exhaustion and strain etched onto her neighbour's face. She's never been the kind of woman who ever seems to be at rest, but now her nervous, fluttery energy seems almost manic.

'I hope the police have apologised for the breach.'

She gives a small shrug. 'I think they probably did it on purpose. Maybe they think it'll flush out the killer? Or perhaps they're just fed up with being criticised for not having arrested anyone yet.'

'Was this the first time you heard about Richard having an aneurysm?'

'I saw the coroner's report a few days ago but before that I had no idea.'

Liv watches her friend. 'I'm so sorry, Sandra. I can't believe he didn't tell you.'

She give a small shrug. 'He didn't like reminding people he was mortal. Or himself. But I wish he had. I'd have been far stricter about things. Him looking after himself. Not exercising, not drinking or smoking.' She shook her head. 'Not taking up running. Not that he'd have listened.'

'And I heard a rumour about some DNA being found?'

'Apparently. Although they've not told me anything official.' She gives a small shrug. 'They never seem to tell me anything so I've got no idea whose it might be.'

Liv feels the dull thud of disappointment. 'I'm sorry. It must be so hard being in the dark like this.'

'And now the coroner won't release the body while there's an active investigation,' Sandra says as she opens the dishwasher and begins emptying it. 'So I can't even organise the funeral.'

'Have they said how much longer it might be?'

'No idea.' Sandra puts knives and forks in a drawer. 'They keep telling me they're following leads but they never seem to get anywhere.'

'Have they mentioned any possible suspects? The newspapers keep mentioning that Martin Finch.'

Sandra lets out a small sigh. 'As far as I know the police talked to him but ruled him out. Has a rock-solid alibi, apparently.'

Liv hesitates only momentarily. 'Sandra, I know this sounds totally mad and I wouldn't usually listen to hospital gossip, but you know what it's like – people find stuff out and then before you know it everyone's got a theory and people get talking. I mean, it might be nothing, but it could be … something.' She pauses, her heart is hammering and she feels a little breathless. 'Look, I don't know if it was a police leak or gossip from someone in security at the hospital, but Martin Finch was admitted to Northern the day before Richard was killed. He went there to … well, it looks like he wanted to make some kind of last protest and throw himself off the car park roof, because of, you know, what happened with the court case and Richard and his wife.'

Sandra is holding a fork in mid-air. 'Oh my goodness.'

'Anyway, apparently he was intercepted by security and eventually put into involuntary hold at Landley, the high-security psych ward. But it turns out, it's not that high security.' Liv grimaces. 'There have been quite a few security breaches there in the past few years. High-risk patients getting out, people not being accounted for. A few staff members lost their jobs and others were given red warnings which means if it happens again, they're out.'

Liv swallows hard. She feels more confident now; less like she is reading from a script.

'I think it's possible, very likely even, that Martin could have got himself out of Landley for a few hours in the early hours of the morning Richard died and got himself down to the Gully and … well, you know the rest.'

Sandra stares at Liv for a few moments until she puts the fork in the drawer.

'Do you think the police know about this?' she asks finally.

'I don't know. And the problem is Landley nursing staff and security will probably stick to their original stories that Finch was locked up securely, so I'm not sure how the police would go about disproving what they've already been told.'

'CCTV footage?'

'Probably,' Liv says, because she is aware she needs to tread a careful line here. 'The whole place has them but they're often faulty.'

Sandra nods, clearly absorbing everything Liv is saying.

'He had the motive and opportunity,' Liv adds. 'So I think it's worth the police looking into this a bit more.'

There is a long, stretched-out silence while Sandra appears to digest this information. Liv is briefly worried that she's spoken out of turn or caused the woman to be even more upset than she already is, but Liv isn't sure she can count on Meredith to pass on this information to police. And who knows if they've read her anonymous email.

'And he'd been threatening Richard for months, hadn't he? Wasn't there a restraining order out against him?'

'An apprehended violence order, yes. Richard was convinced Finch was going to hurt him.'

Sandra's gaze travels across the room and then stops. Liv sees she is staring at a photo in a large silver frame on the sideboard. It's a new one Liv hasn't seen in that spot before, recently taken from the looks of it, of Sandra and Richard standing side by side in evening wear. Richard is holding what looks like an award of some kind and looks very pleased with himself.

'It's probably worth the police having another look into him again, I think,' Liv says, but she's not sure if Sandra is even listening.

'You know, Richard never understood why people got so upset with him,' she says, still looking at the old photo across the room. 'He was always so … delighted with himself, he just couldn't fathom why other people didn't feel the same way.'

She gives a slight shake of her head as if dislodging the thought as she takes items from the dishwasher and places them on the kitchen counter.

'Can you imagine being that confident? Not believing you're capable of making any mistakes? I loved my husband dearly and I'm devastated that he's gone, but I will never understand why he couldn't have just told Martin Finch how sorry he was that his wife died.' Sandra lets out a soft exhale. 'I think that's all he wanted. For Richard to say he was sorry.'

Sandra reaches into the dishwasher again and this time takes out a water bottle and begins to dry it with a tea towel. Liv feels a jolt. It is a pink Frank Green one, just like Gracie's. She watches as Sandra dries the lid with a tea towel and then screws it onto the base and puts it away in a cupboard.

'It's a terrible thing to say, but I'm quite angry at him,' Sandra says. 'That probably shocks you, doesn't it?'

'Of course not. Grief is strange. You're allowed to be angry.'

'I just can't believe he didn't tell me about the aneurysm.' Sandra's eyes narrow. 'He knew about it for six months and he kept it to himself.' She shakes her head. 'I just can't understand why he would do that.'

'Maybe he didn't want to worry you.' Liv pauses. 'He loved you,' she says automatically.

Sandra's eyes fill with tears. 'Then why did he do this to us?'

Chapter 33

MEREDITH

January 2025

The Sunday morning after Meredith spent the evening at Sandra's, her neighbour messaged to ask if she wanted her spare ticket to a film at the open-air cinema at the Botanic Gardens.

It's French. No idea what it's about – something about refugees? If you're keen, we can meet at the gates around 7.30?

Meredith felt a jolt of relief course through her. She'd replayed everything she'd said to Sandra the night before over and over, hyperfixating on certain things, cringing inwardly at missteps she was sure she'd made. But now, here was proof that it hadn't been a total disaster: Sandra wanted to see her again.

The large cinema screen rose up high above the water and settled into its picture-perfect position with the twinkling bridge and city behind it. As the American tourists in the row behind marvelled at the stupidly photogenic harbour in front of them, Meredith felt a glow of pride for her beautiful hometown.

After the film, which was depressing but beautiful, Sandra and Meredith strolled through the city streets, vaguely heading in the direction of the bus stop that would take them home to the north side of the city. It was, at least to Meredith who rarely went into the city at night, surprisingly busy considering it was late on a Sunday.

'Shall we get a drink?' Sandra suggested as they were about to turn onto the street where the bus would pick them up.

Meredith's eyes had begun to droop by the end of the film but she also wanted to get to know Sandra and not only find out more about Richard, but enjoy this new friendship. So she suppressed a yawn and said, 'Sure, why not,' and Sandra beamed at her with approval.

They found a bar on a cobbled laneway, took a free table outside and ordered drinks, a tea for Meredith and a brandy for Sandra, plus a bowl of hot chips to share.

'I usually avoid films about children dying,' Sandra said as the waiter placed their drinks on the table. She waited until he left and said, 'I lost my daughter when she was eleven months old.'

Meredith looked at the other woman, shocked. 'Oh Sandra, I'm so sorry.'

'She'd be twenty-eight now. SIDS.' Sandra lifted the brandy to her lips. 'Her name was Annabel.'

'That's a beautiful name.'

She nodded. 'She was a beautiful baby.'

The waiter reappeared and placed the chips between them and Sandra ordered a second brandy.

'We decided not to try again,' she said as she picked a chip from the bowl.

Meredith understood immediately that Sandra felt this statement was necessary – people probably always asked why she hadn't had another child, as if that would make up for her loss.

'Actually that's not true. We did, but it didn't happen.' She glanced at Meredith briefly. 'I don't usually tell people any of this but I feel like you probably understand.'

The statement was open-ended and Meredith realised it was

180

really a question. Sandra wanted to know her situation, why she didn't have any children; whether she had tried.

'I wanted kids but my partner didn't,' Meredith replied. 'She's stepmum to her ex's two and pretty much helped raise them from birth and when we got together, she didn't want to do it again. You know, nappies and sleepless nights.'

'Were you okay with that?'

Meredith hesitated. 'Not really, no. I think it's probably one of the reasons we split up, not that I am going to have children now. I'm too old. But I think it meant there was always this … division between us. She felt a bit guilty; I felt a bit resentful.'

'How long were you together?'

'Ten years.'

The waiter reappeared and put a fresh glass of brandy in front of Sandra and she smiled her thanks.

'And you broke up?'

'Last winter.' Meredith took a chip from the bowl. 'But that was because of a lot of other things. We were both having our own mid-life crises. I needed a change. She needed a twenty-five-year-old girlfriend, it turned out.'

Sandra laughed at that.

'But you and Richard have made it work and stayed together. That must have been incredibly hard after losing Annabel.'

Sandra took a sip of her brandy before answering.

'I never imagined we would, but yes, here we are, still together after all these years. Thirty years in fact.' She made a face at that. 'Three decades. God, how is that possible?'

'You must love him very much,' Meredith said and she nodded.

'I do,' she said softly.

And Meredith's heart sank a little. She hadn't, or couldn't, imagine that Sandra still loved a man like Richard.

181

Chapter 34

LIV

Friday, 14 February 2025

Angela is in bed, watching a show on the iPad when Liv enters the room.

'Hey, Mum,' she says, reaching down to kiss Angela on the cheek. 'How are you doing today?'

Angela doesn't respond of course – her speech hasn't returned yet although she can make some noises – so Liv does what she always does; chatters nonsense, telling her about the food she's brought for her today so she doesn't have to eat the hospital offerings, how Gracie is busy with a uni assignment and Andy is with Pete. She tidies her mum's room although there is not much to tidy, filling up her mum's water glass and then retrieving the fresh flannel she's brought in to give her mum a little freshen up.

The sweet, smiley nurse announces herself as Liv is gently dabbing the warm flannel to Angela's face and gets to work immediately, checking charts and Angela's blood pressure, adjusting the bed so Angela is sitting more upright. Liv has removed herself from Angela's bedside and stands stiffly by the window, out of the way.

'She's doing really well,' the nurse says as Liv follows her from the room. 'She's much more alert and she seems pretty mobile on her good side.'

'I'm trying to do some physio with her but she gets tired easily.'

'That's understandable. She's still got a long way to go.' The other woman smiles kindly. 'She'll get there. I can tell – she's one of the tough ones.'

'She's really nice,' Liv says, when she's back in Angela's room. 'Not like the blonde one. God, she's terrifying. Told me off for bringing you that lemonade the other day. Bit of moisturiser?'

Angela doesn't respond so Liv finds the pot of Elizabeth Arden and applies some gently, first to her mum's face and then hands.

'How about some make-up?'

At this Angela shifts slightly and Liv takes this as a yes.

Liv finds her make-up bag and begins applying a little powder and rouge to Angela's face, then some lipstick. Then she dabs some of her mum's favourite perfume, Joy by Jean Patou, which does a good job of blocking out that specific hospital tang that fills Liv's nose every time she steps foot inside this building and lingers on her clothes for hours after she's left.

'I hope that helps you feel more like yourself,' she says when she's finished, stepping back to admire her work.

Angela makes a small noise Liv thinks might be 'thank you'.

'Any time,' Liv says, then turns quickly away, feeling a sudden surge of emotion as she looks for her bag which she originally placed at the foot of Angela's bed. 'I brought you a new charger today, a longer one, so you can keep watching even when the battery runs out.'

Liv retrieves the cable and takes it from its wrapping. Her mum's eyes flicker with a vague acknowledgement of understanding as Liv unravels the lead and plugs it into the iPad and then places it on Angela's lap, propping it up with a small cushion. Angela swipes the screen with surprising deftness with her left hand and changes to Netflix. When she is absorbed in whatever it is she is watching, Liv places a small foam ball in Angela's weak hand and then puts her own over it and begins to gently squeeze.

Liv is making it her mission, through sheer force of will, to ensure her mother recovers some level of independence. Every day she arrives with new objects to help Angela's recovery: today this soft ball for her mum to clench to build up strength in her grip; yesterday it was therabands for holding and to pull at. Liv has also brought hand-held electric massagers, which she plugs in and places on her mum's arms and legs, and downloaded games onto the iPad specially designed for stroke patients: ones that promise to enhance cognitive function, memory and recall; others that are simple puzzles, word searches and crossword apps.

Generally, however, Angela refuses to try any of these, preferring to watch endless TV shows.

Yesterday Liv found her watching a particularly gruesome scene in *Squid Game*. Later today Gracie is planning on visiting and after hearing about her grandmother's new viewing habits and apparent taste for horror, has told Liv she's planning on them watching some terrifying-sounding Japanese film about child-eating zombies. It is not the kind of rehab that will help Angela get out of bed and get moving, but Liv supposes it's some kind of start. Perhaps it'll help get her synapses firing.

After an hour of TV-watching and feeding Angela from the selection of morsels she's bought from Paco's, Liv manages to cajole Angela into a wheelchair for an outing. She rolls her down the corridor, into the lift and to the ground floor, to a small courtyard where patients can sit in the open air.

She parks her mum in a spot out of the direct sun, then retrieves a book from her bag which she has been reading out loud to Angela, *My Life So Far* by Jane Fonda.

But before she begins to read, she turns to her mum and puts her hand over Angela's.

'Mum, I heard a recording on your phone the other day.

Something about a big family secret you needed to tell me. Do you remember?'

Her mum looks steadily at Liv, giving nothing away.

'Do you remember doing the voice note, Mum? You said there were so many secrets and that I should know them. You said you wanted to let me know about our family's story.' She pauses, giving her mum time to digest her words. 'Do you remember that? Our family story,' she repeats.

But Angela doesn't give any indication of understanding or even hearing what Liv has said. Liv squeezes her mum's hands and opens the book in her own lap.

'Okay, let's have a read. Hopefully we'll get to the Hanoi Jane bit today and things will start getting really interesting,' Liv says.

She reads the first page and then glances at Angela to see if she's keeping up. But her eyes have already closed.

That evening, Liv is making dinner for her father when Sandra messages that she has spoken to her police liaison officer and been told that they already know about the security breaches at Landley.

CCTV requested but won't give me any more detail. They also won't tell me if Finch is being reinterviewed but they have confirmed they've spoken to Landley staff to corroborate his movements.

Then, as Liv is readying herself for bed, she receives another message from Sandra.

Apparently 'technical issues' means no recordings available for main external hospital CCTV feed for the 24-hour period around Richard's death. And the Landley internal one has been defective for three months. Unbelievable!

Although it is frustrating to not have any proof that Finch

left the unit, the ambiguity might be good, Liv decides. It will leave questions around what happened and put more pressure on Finch to prove he wasn't there at the Gully. It will take any possible focus away from Gracie, and Meredith.

The next morning comes the news Liv has been waiting for, relayed in a late-night message from Andy.

She clicks on the link and feels her stomach flip when she reads the *Daily News* headline: FINCH QUESTIONED OVER TV DR DEATH!

The accompanying article is brief but fills Liv with hope.

> *The hunt for Richard Wellington's killer took another turn late last night when Martin Finch, who last year lost his court case against the TV surgeon, was taken to North Sydney police station and interviewed under caution. While no arrests have been made and there is no suggestion Finch has anything to do with the former high-profile plastic surgeon's death last month on January 30, it is a significant step by investigators.*
> *'We can confirm a 54-year-old man from South Sydney is helping with our enquiries but have no other comments to add at this time,' a statement from the police media unit confirmed this morning.*

Of course, Liv doesn't want Martin Finch to be accused if he really had nothing to do with Richard's death. But surely everything points to him being the most likely suspect. He had the motive, he had threatened Richard's life, he'd been in the location, the timing was tight but possible.

She calls Andy and her first words to him are 'Surely this means it's all over?'

Chapter 35

MEREDITH

January 2025

Meredith once read a book about a former cult member who only broke free from her extreme beliefs when she made a friend online who began asking her seemingly benign questions about the group and how she felt about it. The friend didn't challenge the woman's beliefs or tell her they were ridiculous or dangerous. He didn't try and get into a debate or an argument; the questions were simple and when the woman answered them, her friend would respond, 'Thanks, that's an interesting perspective' or 'I appreciate you explaining that'.

Over the course of many months, the woman began to realise how absurd her answers sounded and soon found herself unable to answer many of the questions without hesitating or backtracking or tangling herself up in knots. Late at night, she'd turn her friend's questions and her own answers over and over in her thoughts and after a while this led her to begin picking apart everything she believed in. After a year of questions from her friend, the woman made the decision to leave the cult.

Meredith decides to try the same idea out on Sandra. Her first question came the Friday after their trip to the cinema when they had crossed paths when Meredith had arrived home late after work and Sandra was in the reserve with her dogs. Sandra had called out a greeting and Meredith waved and then went to join her. They sat on the bench as an incredible sunset – a psyche-delic blaze of pink and orange – swirled above them and both women talked about their weeks, their highs and lows, how lovely Wednesday had been with its brief respite from the intense heat.

A young family appeared at the top of the stone stairs and the man had a tiny baby strapped to his chest and as they passed, Sandra said softly, 'So tiny.' Meredith nodded. 'Must be a newborn,' and as she spoke she saw it in Sandra's eyes: the grief and longing.

'How did Richard cope after losing Annabel?'

There was a pause. 'Not well,' she said. 'Typical man. Never wanted to talk about her or how he felt. Still doesn't.'

'How do you cope?'

'I let myself have half an hour a day to think about her and remember certain things.' She fell silent for a few moments. 'This morning's memory was her first bath after we took her back from the hospital. God, it was terrifying. She was so little and slippery. I made Richard do it, I was so scared I'd drop her.'

There was another long silence as both women became lost in their thoughts.

'You know, we couldn't even look at each other after she died,' Sandra said finally. 'It was just too painful to even see the other one's suffering.'

'How did you cope?'

'Not well. A few months after Annabel died, a friend offered me their place on the South Coast. I don't think I even told Richard where I was going or asked if he wanted to come because I didn't want him to. I just wanted to be alone with my grief. I wanted to think about Annabel and dream about her and even talk to her, I did that a bit – talk to her.' She glanced at Meredith. 'Is that odd?'

'I don't think there is such a thing when you're grieving.'

Sandra looked a little surprised at that.

'It felt good to be alone with her,' she said, nodding. 'It was a relief honestly. I didn't have to think about him and his needs and his sadness.' She paused a moment. 'I think it took two or three months until I stopped waking up every day wanting to die. I would go out for walks, hoping I'd be hit by a car or something. Hoping a storm would start and lightning would strike me. Lots and lots of long walks by the beach. I began swimming too. Probably hoping I'd drown at first, but then, after a while, enjoying it. I stopped eating bowls of cereal and began cooking for myself. I started checking before I crossed roads. I suppose I started to come back to life a bit. Just a little bit.'

'Did you keep in touch with Richard?'

A shrug. 'I sent him a few letters. This was way before email and neither of us had a mobile and there was no landline at the house. He never wrote back.' She exhaled. 'I think it was the middle of November when I decided I was ready to go home. But when I got back to the city, there was no sign of him.'

'Where was he?'

'I tried contacting him at the hospital but they couldn't help. I paged him – that's how I used to get in touch with him in emergencies back then. I rang a few friends, but they didn't know or said they didn't. Then, after a few days, I bumped into a work colleague of his at the supermarket.' At this point she shifted slightly in her seat.

'It was another surgeon Richard was good friends with. He looked embarrassed to see me and mumbled something about how he was very sorry to hear that I had separated from Richard.' She let out a hollow laugh. 'I think I just stared at him, baffled, and the poor man couldn't get out of there fast enough. That evening I decided to call my sister and see what she thought and if she'd been in touch with him. Eve and I don't get on, never have done, but when we're dealing with difficult issues, when neither of us has anyone else to turn to, we somehow find each other. Or at least, we did back then. Not anymore of course.'

There was another long pause.

'So anyway, I called Eve and she asked how I was, how I was feeling, did I feel stronger, all that, and I said I was better but sort of weary, like a soldier returning from battle or something and I remember she laughed and said, yes, that's what Richard says it's like. I said, "Oh, have you seen him?" and she said, "Well of course". I had no idea what she was talking about and then she had the gall to get irritated with me. She told me I was as absurdly self-involved as usual.' Sandra shook her head. 'I told her I didn't understand what she was saying and she just told me, outright. Matter of fact.' She let out a dry bark of laugh. 'She told me how Richard had moved in with her a few months before, literally a few weeks after I'd left for the South Coast, and why on earth was I pretending that I didn't know and when was I going to stop playing these silly games.'

Sandra closed her eyes. 'It turned out Richard had fooled us both, in a way. He'd told Eve that we had decided mutually to separate when I went to the South Coast and that we would be getting a divorce. He also told her that I knew all about his new relationship, with her. My sister. And apparently I was fine with it. Had even given them my blessing. I found out later that they'd been having a thing for years, on and off.'

Meredith stared at her, shocked, and Sandra gave a tight nod.

'My sister,' Sandra confirmed. 'My sister and husband had been having an affair for almost as long as we'd been married. While I was pregnant with Annabel. When we lost Annabel. The whole time.'

Chapter 36

LIV

Saturday, 15 February 2025

Early on Saturday morning Liv receives a call to say Angela has been deemed well enough to move to a rehab clinic. Andy has organised for an agency nurse to stay with Pete every night, getting him into bed and up in the morning, which is one less thing to worry about, but the situation with her parents nags at her. She needs a better solution for when her mother returns home; she is almost certain Angela will never agree to having a live-in carer.

Liv is at work heading up the Saturday morning shift when a woman called Alison leaves a message on her phone. In eager, syrupy tones, Alison explains she is calling on behalf of all the staff at the Marigold institute and having only just heard what happened, wanted to send everyone's best wishes to Angela.

Angela had been attending what was described as a 'post-stroke social group' since her first stroke. Her mother, Liv knows, hated the place with a passion but was somehow cajoled into going there every Thursday morning because it was mahjong day led by the daughter of one of the other attendees who always provided

191

a spread of homemade cakes and biscuits. The way to Angela's heart has always been sweet carbohydrates.

When the phone rings on Liv's break, this time she picks up, thinking it might be Angela's rehab clinic. Alison barely gives Liv time to explain how Angela is doing before launching into how she is a huge fan.

'My mum was such a fan of *Greener Grass*, you know. Used to watch the reruns every day before she passed.' Alison's voice is silky with reverie. 'She had a scrapbook of all her favourite soaps. *A Country Practice*, *Sons and Daughters*, some of the American ones like *General Hospital* and *The Young and the Restless*. Loved a bit of *EastEnders* too, on occasion. Oh, and that's what I also wanted to ask, if we're not going to see Angela for a while, I wondered if she might want to continue her scrapbooking at home?'

Liv frowns. 'Scrapbooking?'

'It's our way of helping with memories. The client's short-term memories might be failing but we find their long-term ones are usually pretty good and making scrapbooks that include those memories, you know, old photos, snippets of events, old letters maybe if they're available, is a really nice way of having them focus on something positive. Something … happy.'

Liv imagines her Mum's scrapbook. It's probably full of self-congratulatory tears from *TV Week* or gossip stories about her and Dad from *Woman's Day* and *New Idea*.

But then she decides seeing it would probably cheer Angela up. Apart from when she is watching her horror shows, she shows little interest in doing any rehab exercises or even getting out of bed. It might help.

'When can I pick it up?' she asks.

In the end, Andy gets the scrapbook and Liv finds it sitting on the dining table that evening when she goes to check in on Pete. It's a surprisingly lovely insight into her mother's life, full of magazine tears as expected and old photos, but also sketches by Angela.

Her mum had always been a talented artist but Liv hasn't seen her sketch for years. When Liv was little, Angela would do simple pencil line drawings of Liv and the cat or just a scribbled outline of the tree in the garden. The pictures in this scrapbook are less defined, more textured but just as lovely and evocative – sketches of children and flowers and a house, perhaps the one her mother had grown up in.

She keeps turning the pages until she gets to a section that's titled 'My family'. Here, there are actual photos, presumably taken from the family albums her parents have dozens of, stuck onto the page in a collage effect with some overlapping others, but only fixed at one edge so they can be lifted to look at the back and see the caption either her mum or dad had written in neat black ink years and years before.

There is a particularly cute one of her mum and Liv standing bare-bellied in a skirt and, randomly a top hat, grinning at the camera while Angela, kneeling next to her, kisses her cheek. She checks the back: 1983. Liv would have been around five.

Then she turns the page and sees, tucked under the edge of a photo of Pete and Angela in evening wear from the early 1980s, one of her aged about three standing next to another little girl of about the same age. They are wearing matching outfits: floral purple dresses with frilly bits around the chest and puff cap sleeves, long white skivvies underneath. They are holding hands and while Liv has her fair hair in bunches, the other girl's dark hair is cut in a slightly severe, short bob.

Heart thrumming, Liv turns the photo to see what's written on the back. Someone – possibly her father – has scribbled on the back: *The girls*.

She studies the photo, knowing without a doubt who the other little girl is: the intense stare is the same, the dark eyes, hair colour, the same slightly awkward smile.

Meredith.

14 September 1992
Dear Liv,

Thank you for your sweet note earlier. Yes, it is quite exciting. I never thought Mal Jeffreys even knew I existed until last month. He smiled at me when we went to the debating final but I was so surprised when I got that first letter.

He's so nice, Liv. I know everyone thinks he's one of 'those guys' but he's actually really sweet and sensitive. He told me about the situation with his family and I was so touched he opened up to me. He's been through a lot – his parent's separating, then divorcing, having to go and live with his mum and having to travel an hour every day to get to school and back again. Then his dad moving overseas. I think he's dealing with it really well considering.

But he's also quite shy. When I see him at the interchange he is really sweet and because he's with all his friends he doesn't say anything to me because he doesn't want them to be all silly and tease us. That's good by me.

Will keep you updated and thank you for being so lovely.
Meredith xx

PS Am I still coming to stay at yours on Saturday night? I think your Mum said it was this week.

Chapter 37

MEREDITH

January 2025

Meredith texted to check Sandra was okay the day after she'd told her about her sister and Richard's affair, and to ask if she'd like to go for a walk or a coffee soon. No reply was forthcoming and a few days later Meredith texted again. Once more, there was radio silence and as that day ticked by, Meredith realised there could be just one reason for this: Sandra had finally heard the rumours about her and Richard and wanted nothing more to do with her.

Since she'd returned to work in the new year, there had been no outward signs that people were still gossiping about what had happened at the Christmas party. Although Meredith didn't have any close work friends to tell her if there were. Still, the occasional glances her way or more obvious sudden silences when she entered the staff lounge in the days after the party had dropped off. People had moved on to other news. There was a surprise Christmas break-up between two other staff members that was preoccupying everyone.

On the Thursday night after she'd last seen Sandra, Meredith stood outside Sandra and Richard's house. Richard was back from his trip to the South Coast – his car was back in its usual spot in the driveway – but Meredith was impatient to talk to Sandra and somehow explain things in a way that didn't jeopardise their friendship. She'd tried texting again but had received no response. Perhaps she could knock on their door and explain herself?

Wanting to check whether Richard was home before she did so, she decided to go around the back laneway and look through the garage window to see if she could see him first. He might be out, having left his car and taken an Uber. God knows he drank so much he shouldn't drive when he went out.

It was after nine but as Meredith peered through the glass window, through the garage which was wide open at the garden end, and beyond, she could still feel the heat of the day coming off the structure. There was no sign of anyone inside the house but she could see the bifold doors that divided the deck from the house were pushed back. She glanced at her phone, wondering if she should try calling Sandra this time. She could just immediately apologise and try and explain everything before the other woman hung up.

But Meredith couldn't bring herself to, so instead she just stood there in the darkness, wondering why out of all the people in the world, she'd found a possible friend in the person who was married to Richard Wellington.

Then just as Meredith was about to give up, slip from the shadows and make her way home, Richard stepped onto the deck. Meredith's heart galloped and she moved back in case he could see her through the glass.

But he was oblivious. He lit a cigarette and as he exhaled, the smoke billowed into the night air and carried across the garden so that Meredith smelt its tang. He moved closer to the edge of the deck, swaying slightly. He was drunk.

Then there was a noise from inside the house and he turned, his shoulders squaring as Sandra appeared in the doorway. She was wearing a slip, the kind you might sleep in or wear under a dress, and her bare arms were crossed against her torso. She said something Meredith couldn't catch over the constant buzz of cicadas and then in swift and shocking movement, Richard rounded on her and swiftly slapped her hard across her face.

Meredith let out a gasp as Sandra caved in on herself, her torso bending while her hand lifted to cup her cheek. Then Richard stepped from the deck onto the grass and went over to the swimming pool, which was softly illuminated with underwater lighting.

He took a deep drag on his cigarette then flicked it into the water and then turned again and Meredith thought for one heart-stopping moment that he was heading for the garage. But he crossed the grass to the driveway and headed down it towards the front of the house instead.

Sandra had straightened up, her hand still on her cheek, and Meredith reached for the handle to the garage door. It was locked. She raised her hand to bang on the door, but then there was movement in the driveway and Richard reappeared and she quickly moved back into the shadows.

A few moments later she moved back to look through the glass. Richard had disappeared again and now Sandra was inside the house and the main light was on. She turned and the left side of Sandra's back was illuminated briefly, showing the livid smudge of an older bruise across her bare collarbone. Then the light was turned off and Sandra's silhouette disappeared from sight.

Chapter 38

LIV

Sunday, 16 February 2025

Somehow, Liv is not sure how, the nurses at the rehab centre have cajoled Angela out of bed. Or perhaps they didn't give her the option to remain there, but either way, when Liv visits, her mother is sitting upright at a table in an otherwise empty communal area.

The room is coloured in various shades of brown. Brown tables, tan chairs, dark brown high-backed armchairs. It is depressing despite the sunlight flooding in through the large windows and Liv can see immediately that her mum isn't happy: there is a steely fury in her eye. But Liv will take that over passive acceptance any day.

'You're up, that's wonderful,' Liv says as she kisses Angela's cheek and inhales a waft of Joy. 'This place seems okay,' she lies. 'Well, it'll be okay for a week or so anyway.'

Liv immediately sees the alarm on her mum's face and kicks herself for putting a timeframe on Angela's stay. She immediately reaches into her bag and pulls out the scrapbook.

'Look what I've got.' Liv places it on the table in front of

Angela and opens it. 'Andy picked it up at the centre the other day. They've been missing you there.'

She turns the pages slowly so Angela can take them in. She stops at one of her favourite pages, pointing to the pencil sketch of Angela as a young woman opposite the black-and-white photo it was copied from. It must have been taken in the mid-Sixties given the hairstyle and outfit.

'You're such a talented artist, Mum. And look, isn't this photo of you and Dad lovely? God, you were both gorgeous.'

She checks her mum's expression but she's looking away into the distance, clearly not in the mood to be cajoled with flattery.

'Come on, Mum. Have a look, please? Look at this one of you and Dad.'

Liv points to what looked like a candid full-length shot of Angela and Pete, both of them looking directly to the camera, her dad with his hands placed on her mum's shoulder. There's a slight smile on Pete's face while Angela's expression is more startled, her mouth slightly opened, her eyes wide as if she'd been surprised by the camera flash. Liv checks the back. *1975 premiere – Glass Towers*. The film that made stars of them both. They'd won awards in Australia and overseas and the costume design had even got an Oscar nomination. 'The film that made us,' her dad always said.

'Can you remember that night?'

Angela doesn't react so Liv turns the page.

'Look, you and Sam Neill, Mum. And you've both got your clothes on!'

But there is no sign of amusement from Angela. Liv continues on, pointing out different photos, keeping a running commentary and occasionally glancing to see if her mum is following, which she now seems to be.

Finally Liv comes to the photo of her and Meredith.

'And look at this one.' She tilts the scrapbook more towards her mum. 'That's Meredith when she was little, isn't it? She must have been, what, around four? I suppose I was about three.' Angela's expression gives nothing away. 'Mum, look carefully. This little girl is Meredith, isn't it? Meredith Edwards.' She lifts the photo which is only taped along the top edge. 'On the back it says *The girls*.'

But Angela doesn't react or give any impression that she's registered what she is seeing so Liv tries again.

'Were we good friends when we were little? Because I don't remember her at all. I do remember meeting her years later at the school fair that time before I moved to St Mary's, but that's it. Did we know each other from nursery or something?'

Liv stares at her mum, willing her to respond. Even just a flicker of her eyes would do. Something to suggest she is hearing what Liv is saying.

'Remember how I told you Meredith recently moved to my street and got a job at the hospital where I work?' She waits a moment. 'Well, thing is, I reckon she came back for a reason and I'm trying to find out what that reason could be. I thought maybe it was something to do with the big secret you mentioned in that recording you made.'

But Angela's face remains a blank mask.

'Do you remember how Meredith used to come over and look after me, Mum? I didn't like that much. She wasn't that much older than me and I thought she was a bit odd to be honest. I remember seeing her trying on your clothes and jewellery once when she thought I was asleep and being quite annoyed at her.'

Liv pauses for a moment and then continues.

'She was always asking questions about you. Maybe she was just interested because you were famous, I don't know. Maybe it was because her mum was dead?' Liv witters on, knowing her mum probably isn't taking any of it in.

'She was always a bit of a target at school – most of the other girls thought she was a bit odd too and were really mean to her. They called her Buggy Mole.' Liv pauses. Her mum's eyes are beginning to droop. 'When I was in year nine, I started joining in with the bullying. When the other girls called her names or did mean stuff, I … Well, I suppose I helped them. We did some awful things. I did awful things,' she corrects herself. 'Lots of icing her out and pretending she was invisible but saying horrible things about her when she was in earshot.'

Liv looks down at the picture in the scrapbook. The two little girls, holding hands.

Little Liv looks so proud to be friends with a big girl; those eighteen months between them a reason on its own for her to be delighted at a friendship with a slightly older one. Fast forward ten years and Liv didn't want anything to do with her. Fast forward another thirty or so and Liv is shifting constantly somewhere between both feelings.

And now, the guilt she feels at what a monster she was as a teenager has expanded to add in the guilt at, if not framing Meredith, then at least putting her firmly within the police investigation's line of sight.

Except of course, her concern might be warranted. Meredith could be the killer, couldn't she?

Liv looks back to Angela and sees her mum's eyes have closed and her head's tipped back a little against the armchair. She closes the scrapbook and takes her mum's cool hand in hers, feeling the now familiar sense of grief wash over her. Grief and guilt and fear. She goes back and forth between those three emotions almost constantly.

Grief about her mum, guilt over Meredith and fear over Gracie.

Chapter 39

LIV

Monday, 17 February 2025

It is just after seven in the morning and Liv has showered and dressed and is about to leave for work when the call comes through on the house phone.

Liv sees the blood drain from Andy's face as he puts his hand over the mouthpiece.

'It's North Sydney police, for Gracie. They need her to go in as soon as possible or they'll send a marked vehicle.'

She blinks.

'What do they want?'

'I don't know,' he says and for a moment they both stand there looking at the phone Andy is holding, frozen with the uncertainty of what to do in this moment. Liv feels a strange ballooning of her extremities. Like she could rise up in the air, untethered by the sudden sense of unreality of this moment.

It is happening. She thinks she might be sick but then Andy moves and Liv returns to earth.

Gracie is in the shower but as if moving in slow mo, Liv takes the phone to the bathroom and knocks on the door until her daughter responds with an irritated, 'I won't be much longer'.

'Gracie, it's the police on the phone. Can you come out and take it?' she says, her voice wooden.

Gracie appears a moment later, wrapped in a towel but still wet from the shower. Her face is a picture of pure terror.

'What do they want?' she whispers.

'Take it. They need you to go in or something.'

'Hello,' she says cautiously, the phone at her ear, then, 'Yeah, Grace Logan.'

Liv watches as Gracie listens to whatever it is the person at the other end is saying, then nods and says, 'Yeah, okay,' then there's a pause and she says, 'So, as soon as possible?' and again, 'Yeah, okay. Bye.'

The call ends and Gracie hands the phone back to Liv.

'She needs a solicitor,' Andy says as Gracie gets dressed and Liv nods even though she wonders if instructing legal counsel might make it seem as though Gracie is trying to hide something. 'Because if for some reason the police know about the assault, she needs someone in her corner making sure the police don't take one and one and make three,' he says as if reading her thoughts. She nods and he looks relieved. 'I'll call Simon Hollis. He's good.'

Liv and Andy sit on the plastic chairs in the waiting area of the police station, two rows forward from where they sat last time. It is almost midday when Simon appears through the double doors doors, but without Gracie.

'Where is she?' Andy asks, sounding panicked.

'She's okay,' Simon says, immediately. 'She's having a bit of a break and we'll be starting up again in a few minutes but I thought I'd come out and bring you up to date.'

'What's happening?' Liv asks. 'Why is it taking so long?'

Simon motions for them to move to the other side of the room, where there are no other people nearby then he drops his voice as he explains.

'It appears that there is some discrepancy on timings the morning of his death. Another witness has come forward saying they saw your daughter emerge from the Gully pathway at 6.45 the morning of Richard Wellington's death which is roughly half an hour later than Gracie's original statement. This witness says they recognised Gracie from her distinctive pink running shorts.' He pauses a moment. 'As a result of this Gracie has spoken in more detail about what happened the morning of the incident. She has explained how she was in fact assaulted by Richard Wilkinson and involved in a sort of … tussle. Because of this and because some unknown DNA was found under Richard's fingernails, the police are now requesting Gracie supply a DNA sample to see if it matches. It won't make much of a difference to things as Gracie has already explained how she struggled to get away from her attacker, but of course this admission also opens up other possibilities and areas of enquiry.'

Liv feels icy dread creep across her body. The police will think Gracie did it. Of course they will.

'Like what?' Andy asks, his voice tight.

'Gracie's explained how she was on the Gully track when she crossed paths with Richard. She's told how they stopped and briefly chatted and then Richard made several lewd comments and lunged at her. That there was a brief scuffle and Gracie pushed Richard away. She has explained how Richard apparently staggered slightly, causing him to fall to the ground, landing on his arm, but not, Gracie insists, causing him to hit his head which remained off the ground.'

Simon looks from Liv to Andy as if checking they are following what he's saying and then, apparently satisfied, continues.

'At that point Gracie says she turned and ran along the footpath until she was in the open space beside the playing fields and confirms that's when she then saw and briefly spoke to Meredith Edwards, a friend and neighbour.

'You should know that Gracie's denied hitting Richard with the item that eventually caused the aneurysm to bleed in the way that ultimately killed him. She denies hitting him anywhere. She's also confirmed he didn't hit his head while in her presence.

'She confirmed Richard got to his feet by the time she was moving away from him and was unaffected by that fall.' He looks directly at Liv. 'And there's another thing which we've learnt today which corroborates this version of events. The pathologist report confirms Richard's injury suggests he was likely hit with a rock. The angle suggests the perpetrator was right-handed and was behind him when Richard was struck.'

Liv feels a sudden woosh of giddy-making relief. 'Gracie's left-handed,' she says quietly.

Simon nods. 'That will certainly help cast doubt on her hitting him with the rock.'

'Have they got enough to charge Gracie?' Andy asks immediately.

Simon hesitates for just a split second.

'Because Gracie insists she pushed him and watched him as he fell and that Richard didn't hit his head when he was with her, the police believe she could be omitting what happened next – that the interaction lasted longer than she's saying and led to her delivering what was ultimately the fatal blow to Richard's head. I imagine they'll start focusing on the gap between the assault on her and Richard being struck.' A pause. 'And if that delay can be proved, or if there's any question of doubt over timings, there's a possibility they'll change Gracie's moves from initially acting in self-defence into acting with unreasonable and excessive force.'

'Oh god, would she be charged with murder then?'

Simon looks at Liv. 'Likely no, but she could be charged with manslaughter. They could argue that she struck Richard in a way that was reckless or negligent and that this trauma caused the rupture of the aneurysm, leading to death.'

'But Richard was attacking Gracie. Wasn't she justified in

defending herself?' Andy asks.

'In general, as you know, the use of deadly force is only justifiable in situations where a person believes they, or someone else, is in immediate danger of death or serious bodily harm.' Simon gives a brief smile. 'Sorry, I know I sound like a textbook but what this means is, the police believe Richard was no longer posing an immediate threat after being pushed onto the ground. So if they can prove Gracie struck him at that point, then she could be charged.'

'That's ridiculous. How can she go from being a victim to an assailant like that?' Liv asks, her voice high with panic. 'It doesn't make sense.'

Simon keeps his expression neutral. 'That's the way the system works. But either way the police have enough to hold Gracie for more questioning and are justified in requesting a DNA sample. They've also taken her phone and will have grounds to search your house and possibly question you both.'

Andy still has Liv's hand in his and he squeezes it. One, two, three times and Liv understands.

This is their code. Their code for everything is okay, don't worry, I'm here. But today it feels meaningless. This isn't them against the world; this is them against the police. Liv drops her hand from his.

'She's being interviewed under caution which is standard,' Simon is saying when Liv tunes back in. 'My hunch is they won't charge her and she'll be out before the end of the day unless the search of your home brings up something. But I've spoken to Gracie privately and she's assured me that what she's told the police is all that happened.' He gives a nod and shifts, making to leave. 'Hang in there. This could all be over in a matter of hours.'

Chapter 40

LIV

Monday, 17 February 2025

Seven very long hours later, Liv, Andy and Gracie are walking from the police station towards the car. Gracie remains silent on their short drive home and neither Liv nor Andy push her to explain what happened although Liv is desperate to ask, to find out what Gracie said, what the police, if anything, have divulged about the case and what will happen now. Whether they have made any hints about charging her. Whether their lives are about to change irrevocably.

Andy suggests they remain outside the house while he goes in to see what kind of state the place is in after the police search. Sophie comes and sits next to them on the tiles, apparently unaffected by having her home invaded by strangers, and after a few minutes Andy reappears in the doorway.

'It looks fine. You can come in,' he says.

And he is right, incredibly. Everything appears relatively undisturbed. The occasional cupboard door has been left ajar and Liv can see that the folded clothes in her walk-in wardrobe have been pushed aside and then back into place again, that food in the pantry has been moved a little from their original positions and that some of the books on the bookshelf have been taken out and put back again, less neatly than before.

She had imagined fingerprint powder or whatever it is forensic investigators use left in dusty piles and floors strewn with their personal items, the kind of chaos you see on TV shows, but there is none of that. Her home still feels like her home.

Gracie goes straight to her bedroom and closes the door while Liv hovers outside for a moment, checking to hear if she's crying. But there is silence. She imagines Gracie will probably get into bed and go to straight sleep – her default response to the aftermath of a stressful situation. When the bullying was at its worst, she would come home from school and sleep for hours.

Andy's hand appears on her shoulder and Liv gives a start of surprise.

'Leave her to rest,' he says.

She nods and sees the strain on his face as he kisses her forehead. He looks wretched and exhausted and every one of his forty-eight years. She supposes she looks the same.

Andy's phone buzzes and he pulls it from his pocket.

'What is it?' Liv says, heart thumping. He tilts the phone so she can read the message. It's from Simon and she feels another lurch of dread at what is written.

Been confirmed they want you both to come in for questioning too. Wednesday at 9.30.

Gracie emerges from her bedroom at seven and settles on the sofa. The TV is already on and Gracie switches to Netflix and puts on an episode of *Friends*. Liv is helping Andy in the kitchen, making a salad while he prepares Gracie's favourite dinner of spaghetti bolognese although she can't imagine how any of them will eat.

'When do you think I'll get my phone back?' Gracie asks. Her tone is sullen and Liv steels herself for what might be coming.

'I don't know. But probably a while,' Andy replies. 'We could get you a cheap pre-pay tomorrow or maybe ask one of your friends if they've got a spare?'

Gracie doesn't respond, just pulls Sophie in a little closer to her, curling her body around the dog.

'You can use mine for now,' Liv says. She picks up her phone from the table and takes it over to her daughter. 'You can add whatever apps you want and log me out.'

Gracie's eyes narrow. 'What will you do?'

'Use my work one.'

'Thanks.' Gracie takes the phone and swipes it awake, tapping in Liv's passcode. 'When's dinner?'

'Not long,' Liv says and reaches down to kiss Gracie's forehead. She feels her daughter stiffen and tries not to take it personally. Gracie is scared and when she is scared she is prickly. Closed off. Hostile.

They eat dinner in front of the TV, none of them in the mood for a family meal around the table. Gracie and Liv watch another episode of *Friends* while Andy watches some stand-up show on the laptop. Gracie barely touches her food while Liv only manages a little of hers. Andy, of course, finishes his plate and has seconds.

Later, he looks up suddenly from the laptop screen. 'I forgot to tell you. I think I found the letters you were looking for.' He stands up and goes over to the pile of bags he brought back from her parents; bags of paperwork and photos he's collating for the documentary. He holds up a large manila envelope like the other one she'd found in her bedroom. 'The ones from Meredith?'

'You're kidding. Where did you find them?'

'Your parents' bedroom. They've got boxes in the top of the corner cupboard – it's like Narnia in there, practically a whole little antechamber.'

'The coat cupboard?'

'That's what it looks like but there's a sliding section and behind that a whole kind of recessed bit.'

'What else did you find in there?' Liv begins sifting through the envelopes. There must be at least two dozen or more.

'Mostly old scripts, production notes, a few old family photo albums.'

Liv begins to open the envelopes and pull out the letters inside and organise them into a semblance of chronological order. They are all dated but she can also tell immediately the rough age Meredith was when she sent the notes thanks to the designs on the paper. She'd dreamed of having Meredith's seemingly vast stationery collection – Hollie Hobby, Hello Kitty, Strawberry Shortcake, Pierrot. She remembers Meredith saying how her dad always bought them for her birthday. She had only switched to faintly lined file paper and regular white envelopes by the time their shared high school experience came to an abrupt and premature end.

'What are those?' Gracie is hovering by Liv's side.

Liv hesitates. 'Letters Meredith sent me when we were kids.'

'Why?'

'Because that's what we did back in the olden days,' she says wryly. 'Phone calls were expensive.'

'Can I read them?' Gracie asks and is reaching for one before Liv can tell her not to.

Liv watches her daughter's face as she reads the first one. When she's finished, Gracie hands it back to Liv and takes another. Liv feels a momentary pang of worry then begins to read them herself, glancing up only occasionally to check on Gracie, concern growing as her daughter continues to work her way through all the letters.

When Gracie has finished reading and has placed the last letter back on the pile next to Liv, she regards her mum through narrowed eyes.

'So what happened at the café?'

Liv feels her cheeks warm under her daughter's steady gaze.

'Oh, there was just some boy, someone she had a crush on.' Liv waves away the rest of the explanation but Gracie isn't satisfied.

'Yeah and what did you do?'

'He was one of the popular boys from a nearby school and some of the girls in Meredith's year thought it would be funny to have her think he liked her. To set up a fake date and then turn up to watch her arrive …'

'And be humiliated,' Gracie finishes the sentence. Liv nods. 'You were involved in that?'

Liv swallows. 'Not exactly, but I was there.'

There's a beat of silence and then Gracie gives a nod of understanding. 'So you bullied her.'

'She wasn't a bully,' Andy interjects quickly. 'It was just normal teenage stuff.'

'That was the line Mr Jameson used on me, remember?'

Liv remains silent for a few moments, not knowing what to say. She does remember. Mr Jameson, the deputy at Gracie's high school, had repeated the same line to her and Andy during the meeting they had insisted on having to get the school to take some kind of responsibility for their daughter being bullied by her fellow students. 'It's normal teenage behaviour. Gracie would do well to ignore it and just get on with things,' he'd told them.

Liv feels a pang of shame at her own teenage self.

'I know it's no excuse but I was desperate to fit in. To be like everyone else.'

But Gracie is unswayed. 'You know, you could have just ignored Meredith if you didn't like her.'

'I did, mostly.' Liv pauses, trying to grasp for an explanation of what it was like for her in secondary school. The daughter of two celebrities. The interested gazes whenever her mum was on the cover of one of the gossip mags that week. The nudges in the corridors the year her dad's film was protested by that hardline religious group and made the news.

'I was a target too. My parents were well known. My mum

was really famous. And when I was at high school she was most famous for being in a movie where she rode topless into Broken Hill on a bloody horse and had sex with Sam Neill.' But Liv's joke falls flat and she starts again. 'Look, Meredith was an oddball but she always gave the impression she didn't care what people thought about her. Except she was also my babysitter so I was terrified everyone would find out about our connection and tease me. It would have been …'

'Social death,' Andy offers and Liv shoots him a look.

'It would have been harder for me to keep flying under the radar if that happened. And I just wanted to be invisible. To fit in. Blend in with the pack.'

'And how do you think Meredith felt? Being a target? Being bullied?'

'Awful. I know, and I feel terrible about it now. I felt terrible about it then but in my defence Meredith never seemed affected by any of it. She didn't even seem to notice what people did or said about her most of the time.'

'Well, she obviously was aware. She said so in the letters.'

'I know. But at the time …'

Gracie eyebrows rise as she waits for Liv's response.

'I don't know,' Liv says eventually, hating the pathetic whine of her voice. 'I honestly don't know what I was thinking at the time. And obviously with hindsight and seeing what you went through, I hate myself for doing it. But I was also …' Liv searches for the word to explain how Meredith made her feel. 'Well, I was also a little scared of Meredith, I suppose.'

Gracie's eyes narrow. 'Scared?'

'She was … I don't know, unsettling.'

'How?' Gracie asks, scorn heavy in her voice.

'Before she started babysitting me, before I started at St Mary's, there was this time, the summer before, when she used to stand outside our place, just watching the house for hours and hours. It was odd. *She* was odd.'

'What do you mean she watched your house?'

Liv lets out a long exhale. 'Gran and I bumped into her at my primary school's summer fair. She knew Gran from when she'd been at school there and then she and I got talking and I explained how I was going to St Mary's after the summer and she was really pleased because she was already there and offered to tell me all about it. The next day she began dropping off these letters and said we should be pen pals. You've seen them, she was very sweet and I was excited at first.' Liv pauses. 'But then I would also see her standing outside our house – opposite under that big fig tree. She'd just stand there, watching, night after night.'

Gracie is looking at Liv as though she's an idiot. 'Well, she obviously just wanted to be friends.'

'Maybe, but it was a creepy way to go about it and she would never mention doing it in her letters. It was weird. And then, a few months later, Gran announced that this odd girl who stood outside our house all the time, watching us, was coming to babysit me. This girl who had just appeared in our lives randomly and would write to me almost every day and was only a few years older than me.' Liv shrugs. 'I don't know. It was unsettling and by then I knew Meredith's reputation at school. How everyone thought she was weird, so that just played into it all.'

Liv pictures Meredith, aged thirteen, fourteen, then fifteen and sixteen, always with her little brown attaché case in her hand and a slightly glazed smile on her face. Her severe bobbed haircut. Those dark all-seeing eyes.

'Did you tell Gran about the letters or her standing outside?'

'No.'

'Why not?'

Liv shrugs. 'I have no idea. I just kept it to myself.' She has a sudden, very clear memory of Meredith leaving one day with one of her mother's bracelets on her wrist. Liv had seen it and immediately said so, in front of Angela and Meredith, all but accusing Meredith of stealing it. Her mother had waved away

Liv's concerns and then ushered Meredith away with a smile and a 'see you soon, thank you,' while Liv stared at her confused and wrong-footed.

Why had her mother given the babysitter a piece of her precious jewellery? Why wasn't Angela angry?

'Darling, it was my way of saying thank you,' Angela had explained later. 'It was just an old bit of junk, some costume jewellery. It's not worth a penny but she seemed to like it and it might make up for you being such a little madam to her all weekend.'

But Liv knew her mum was lying. The bracelet was a pretty art nouveau piece with small delicate flowers that Angela once told Liv her mother had passed down to her. It might not have been worth much, monetarily, but Liv knew that it had a lot of sentimental value.

'I nearly forgot, I brought back something else.'

Andy is crouching down over the bags again and pulls out a small cardboard box, holding it up for Liv to see.

'I didn't open it in case it was special but it's got your name on it.'

He brings the small purple box to Liv. It's an old Dairy Milk chocolate box but 'For Olivia Elliot' had been written across the top in White-Out and it is fastened with a thick black ribbon that is double knotted. Liv uses scissors to cut the ribbon and lifts the lid carefully. The scent of old burnt paper immediately lifts from inside and Liv stares at the contents, bewildered.

'What is it?' Gracie says.

'Burnt paper,' Liv replies, but as she says the words she sees it's actually burnt letters. Or rather, letters that have been partially burnt and then seemingly torn into many tiny pieces.

She picks up a piece and tries to make out the handwriting on it and Andy does the same.

'This is your writing,' he says finally, looking up at her.

Liv takes the piece from him, holding it carefully between her finger and thumb and studies it.

She can see from the roundness of an 'a' and 'e' that he's correct.

Then there is a space and an 'M'.

Her stomach drops. 'These are the letters I sent to Meredith. The ones I wrote back to her.'

'Why did you burn them?' Gracie asks.

Liv shrugs. 'I have no idea.' She looks towards her husband for an explanation, although he of course won't know either.

'Maybe you didn't burn them. The box says "for Olivia Elliot",' he points out. 'Maybe Meredith burnt them and delivered them back to you like this?'

When Liv is in bed later that night, she remembers back to that day at the café; the most shameful and awful memory she has from her teenage years.

Liv had been sitting in a corner seat, surrounded by school friends and can still recall clearly the rush of adrenaline and fear and delight and horror she'd felt as Meredith pushed open the café door. She'd worn a bright red, off-the-shoulder dress with a full skirt, the kind of evening outfit you'd wear to a school prom in the 1950s. The poor girl had stood in the doorway, looking utterly mortified after they'd all gasped and then burst into peals of laughter.

Liv can remember how she'd immediately looked to her right, to check this response was Marie Hadley–approved. When she saw Marie was laughing so hard she actually had tears in her eyes, Liv upped hers too.

Marie Hadley was queen bee of year nine and the main reason Liv was there that day.

Meredith had stood frozen for a moment, eyes scanning the café, travelling to the back where they were all sitting in a booth, watching her, waiting for her reaction when she realised the boy she liked wasn't there. That it had all been a set-up. Locking eyes with Liv, her face had flushed a deep red, as red as her stupid dress they'd all said later, then she'd turned a little shakily on her heels and scuttled back onto the street as they cackled and whooped triumphantly behind her.

'You're not the only sad cow who likes Mal Jeffreys, Buggy Mole,' Marie Hadley had called out after her.

Liv feels a surge of pure shame remembering how it had all stemmed from her, this awful, cruel, public practical joke.

She'd offered up the idea of writing a pretend love letter to Meredith from the best-looking guy at one of the nearby boys' schools, requesting she 'meet' him at the café one Saturday afternoon for a date.

She can still picture Marie looking at her with surprise and then approval.

'Amazing idea, Livvie,' she said. 'Let's do it. And afterwards, if you're free, come over to mine – I'm having a pool party.'

3 October 1992

Liv,

Please don't contact me again. What you and your friends have been doing is incredibly cruel. I don't even care that you all laughed at me last Saturday – I'm glad my humiliation amused you and your friends.

And in reply to your last question, no, I won't make up an excuse about not staying with you next weekend. If Angela asks me outright why I'm refusing to come from now on I will tell her the truth and she can live with the disappointment of knowing how unkind her daughter is.

Regards, Meredith Edwards

12 January 1993

Dear Liv,

I wanted you to know that I won't be coming back to St Mary's this year. I'm moving to Glendale College in the Southern Highlands and will do my HSC there. I'm sure I'll see you around the neighbourhood in the holidays.

Because of that, I was hoping I could ask you a favour. Would you mind mentioning to Angela and Pete that I'm going to boarding school and asking if they wouldn't mind occasionally dropping by and seeing my father? They are old friends and I'm worried Dad might be lonely without me at home. It would do him good to see a friendly face on occasion. I've written your mum a note too, but just in case she hasn't seen it.

Thank you.

All the best, Meredith Edwards.

Chapter 41

MEREDITH

January 2025

Sandra messaged Meredith the day after she'd seen Richard slap her. She wrote that she'd been unwell with a summer flu and apologised for not being in touch, to which Meredith replied immediately, asking if she needed anything. Just a few more days of rest! she replied.

Two days later, around eight on the Sunday evening, Sandra messaged again, explaining Richard was away and she was taking the dogs for a walk – did Meredith want to meet down the steps at the reserve?

When Meredith joined her on the bench, there was no sign of bruising or swelling on Sandra's face. But the sun had set and the streetlights barely lit the area directly beneath them and, besides, Meredith assumed Sandra was adept at covering the signs of Richard's abuse under thick foundation and long-sleeved shirts like the one she was wearing tonight. She wanted to tell the woman that she knew what her husband did to her. To offer help and a roof over Sandra's head if she left him. But for now she remained silent.

Instead they chatted about a new Netflix drama they'd both been watching about a man on the run and then, quite abruptly, Sandra said, 'It's Richard's daughter's birthday today.' She saw the look on Meredith's face and gave a watery smile. 'My niece.'

'Eve?'

Sandra nodded. 'They live in New York. Moved there years ago. It's okay. I've had a long time to get used to it.'

'How did you find out?'

A sharp laugh. 'Oh, she made sure I did.'

'So you stayed with Richard when you found out about him and your sister, but she also continued seeing him?'

'It's a long and complicated story but yes, effectively. When I found out about Eve and Richard and she found out that Richard had lied about telling me and that we weren't divorcing, she kicked him out. Richard and I decided to try and make things work.' There was a pause. 'And I wanted to have another baby.'

She frowned. 'I had six miscarriages before we stopped trying. Then around four years after we lost Annabel, I happened to be in a supermarket near Eve's office. I saw her standing at the deli counter and it took me a moment to realise it really was her because of her big belly and I hadn't seen her in person for years by then. I refused to. Anyway, she turned and saw me and she looked … relieved. And I just knew. I knew it was Richard's baby.'

'What did you do?'

'I left my trolley and walked out.' She bent down to stroke one of her dogs who was asleep at her feet. 'It all made perfect sense. Richard had been in a better mood; he'd been more attentive, more considerate. Lighter, somehow. Now I knew it was nothing to do with me, nothing to do with his career. He was happy because Eve was pregnant and unlike me seemed to be able to hang on to her baby.' There was a long pause. 'And no, I still didn't leave him. Even though I knew he was having a baby with my sister.'

'Did you confront him?'

'No.'

'Did you ever see her again? Your sister?'

'She phoned me about six months after I'd seen her in the supermarket. She said she was leaving the country, that she'd been offered a position in New York and hoped it would be a new start for her and her daughter and for me and Richard. I didn't say a word. I didn't wish her good luck, I didn't congratulate her on having the baby or ask about her. Our parents died years ago, we didn't have any other family, so I was very aware that once she was gone, that would be it.'

'But you knew for sure he was the father?'

She nodded.

'Did he know you knew?'

'Oh yes. He would leave out birthday cards to post over the years, and presents, so I worked out her birthday.' There was another pause. 'After she left, things between me and Richard got worse. He blamed me, I suppose.'

'For what?'

'For Eve leaving.'

'How? It wasn't your fault.'

'Because if I didn't exist, he could be with Eve. He could be with the baby.'

Meredith looked at her confused. 'But why couldn't you separate?'

'Ah, well, he decided he didn't believe in divorce.'

Meredith frowned. 'Decided? Is he religious?'

Sandra chuckled. 'No, but his TV career had started to take off. He needed a wife to parade to events. He needed to look respectable.'

Meredith tried not to look appalled.

'Sometimes he's lovely,' Sandra said finally. 'The Richard I fell in love with all those years ago. Funny, charming, caring.'

'And when he's not?'

She gave a defensive shrug. 'It's the little jibes which I hate the most,' she said eventually. 'Little things that pick away at you. You start to believe them. Pick, pick, pick. The way I wore a certain dress when we went out for dinner, the way I did my hair or drove home, how I asked the waiter for tap water not bottled, how I shouldn't ask for well-cooked steak, it's ridiculous. Why I forgot to take his shirts to the dry-cleaners. That was just last weekend. It all just chips away at you after a while.'

'I imagine it does,' Meredith said softly.

'And when those criticisms get really bad, I know we're leading up to one of our big bust-ups. Except I used to be able to ride those out and then things would be fine for a while.' She paused. 'But nowadays, ever since all those patients came out of the woodwork making complaints, it's been an almost constant cycle of having to ride things out. Since then, it's just all been very difficult. He's gets very … stressed.'

This was Meredith's opening.

'Sandra.' She paused. 'Does Richard hurt you?'

There was a long silence.

'I don't want to make you feel uncomfortable,' Meredith said. 'I know it's very hard to talk about, but I also want you to know that whatever you tell me, I'll keep it to myself, if that's what you want.'

They walked for a little longer, and then finally, she began to speak.

'The first time he hit me was on my fiftieth birthday.' She let out a long exhale. 'I understood why. I got really drunk and I was a bitch to him. He'd bought me this bracelet from Pandora. It was sweet but it was the kind of thing you'd buy a teenager and I told him that, without thinking. And he slapped me.' She shrugged. 'I'm not saying I deserved it but I understand why he did it.'

'It's not okay for anyone to hit their partner.'

'I know.'

But she said it in a resigned way, as though this was something she'd said many times to herself but didn't quite believe.

'Have there been other times?'

221

She hesitated. 'It's become quite bad again since the court case. He won but there have been other pressures. He's lost a lot of patients, a journalist's been threatening some kind of exposé.'

'But none of that is an acceptable excuse for him hurting you.'

'No, it's not. But at least I know how to handle him. I know how to calm him down when he … when things are bad.'

Meredith looked at her quizzically.

'I overheard him on the phone the other day talking to his secretary.' She shook her head. 'He'll be lucky if she doesn't report him. He was so rude to her and she was only helping him plan his schedule for next month. It was very unlike him. He's not usually so externally aggressive and … Oh, I don't know.'

Sandra gave a slight shake of her head and Meredith saw something in her expression. A hesitance to expand.

'Is there something else?' she asked.

The other woman made a face.

Meredith pictured herself standing in front of Richard by the lifts, his lunging, her pushing him away. God, he'd probably tried that move with a hundred other women over the years. Had Sandra heard about another of his victims?

'On Christmas Eve he got very drunk,' Sandra says, her voice low. 'I think he might have even taken something too. Cocaine? I don't know. He'd been out earlier with friends and something seemed off. He was really belligerent and unpleasant so I went to bed. But I couldn't sleep and so I started watching a film on the iPad but I must have nodded off because I suddenly woke with a start at the sound of the front door closing. I was worried the dogs might have got out so I went to check but they were fast asleep in the living room. Anyway, I went back to the front of the house and had a look out of the window there and saw Richard was standing outside our house, drinking a bottle of beer and smoking a cigarette and he was talking to our neighbour's daughter.'

Meredith nodded, already knowing what was coming next.

'Gracie.'

She nodded. 'Sweet girl. I knew he was probably saying something inappropriate but I just hoped she could handle him because if I went out there I knew it'd become this whole big thing. So I watched them and tried to listen. After a while she went into her house, opposite ours, and he came and sat on our steps. I went back upstairs but after about twenty minutes he still hadn't come back – well, I hadn't heard the front door closing. So I went to the front of the house again, this time looking out from the spare room because I was upstairs.'

She exhaled. 'I couldn't see him at first. I assumed he'd come back in the side entrance or maybe he was in the garden. Then I saw the tip of his cigarette. He was coming out of the side passage of Gracie's house.' She glanced at Meredith, swallowing hard. 'I think he'd been watching her through the window like some kind of peeping Tom.'

'What happened next? Did you confront him?'

Sandra shook her head. 'I know I should have. The next day I expected the police to knock on our door or for Liv to come over, demanding to know what the hell Richard thought he was doing. Or Andy, fists swinging, ready to knock him out for scaring the life out of his daughter and being a disgusting old pervert. But no one came. Maybe Gracie didn't know. Maybe she did and didn't tell anyone. I just – I don't know why I didn't say anything. I just … I couldn't.' Her face crumbled momentarily before she gathered herself again. 'Silly really.'

'It's okay,' Meredith said. 'You were worried about his reaction. That's understandable.'

'But I need to say something or do something,' she said. 'I really must. This can't go on.'

Meredith looked at her quizzically. 'Has something else happened?'

Sandra let out a long, shaky exhalation. 'Richard's new year resolution is to start running again. There's a 10k coming up he wants to do.' She paused. 'He goes down to the park and does a few laps around the oval every morning since he got back from the beach house.'

Meredith thought of Gracie and her morning runs and how she'd been less diligent about her own training since the new year. It was too humid. She couldn't drag herself up. There always seemed to be an easy excuse to reach for.

'I was wondering …' Sandra paused. 'I was wondering if he knows Gracie runs down there and perhaps he's going on the off chance he'll see her and get her on her own. So I've started following him. Every morning he goes out for his run, I go along too,' she said. 'Just far enough behind him that he can't see me.' A pause. 'Just in case.'

'Just in case what?'

She dropped her gaze. 'Just in case he … does something really stupid,' she said. 'Something that will get him into even more trouble. Something that could hurt Gracie.'

Chapter 42

LIV

Tuesday, 18 February 2025

It is late morning and Liv stands in front of 36 Abbey Street, St Peters, staring at the large block of flats. A warm breeze has picked up and the sky is heavy with dark clouds, promising a cleansing shower before the day ends.

Liv got the address via Robyn, the clinic receptionist who has somehow maintained her access to the many online systems for the various departments she's worked for over the years at the hospital. Liv didn't ask how she kept her access and Robyn didn't ask why Liv wanted the address. But she is pretty sure Robyn will be using this as fodder for the gossip mill.

Now, standing in front of the bleak structure in front of her, Liv feels dismay that she has only managed to unlock one very small part of a larger puzzle. The address in the hospital system had specified a building number but how will she find Martin Finch's flat among what must be several dozens of others?

The enclosed gate is flanked by a wall of post boxes on each side, stuffed full of junk mail and telling her there are thirty apartments in all. Liv tries pushing open the security gate but it's locked. She could ring every one of the doorbells until she finds Martin, or more likely until someone buzzes her in just to get rid of her. At first glance this doesn't look like the kind of place where people would be too concerned about strangers roaming corridors but she is aware she's probably being prejudiced. Being poor doesn't mean you don't want to protect what is yours.

As if to make a point, an elderly woman appears on the other side of the security door, and after pushing the door open, and ensuring her wheeled shopping trolley has followed her, makes a point of securely closing it behind her. She gives Liv a steely glance before shuffling away.

Liv returns to her car and with her eyes fixed on the entrance, waits there, in the hope that Martin Finch will eventually appear. But she manages only half an hour before her need for a pee overtakes her desire to remain in place.

Google Maps takes her to the nearest McDonald's, just one block over from Martin Finch's place.

After using the bathroom, her attention is caught by one of the self-serve computers and she orders herself a burger, small chips and iced coffee. She eats at a table by the entrance, staring into space, not even tasting the food as it passes from her hand to mouth, her thoughts absorbed with the constant puzzle of trying to work out what she can do to save Gracie from the threatening sceptre looming over her.

'What will we do if she's charged?' she'd asked Andy earlier.

'The truth will come out eventually.'

'Eventually?'

'Well, she didn't kill him, did she? So something will come out, some piece of evidence maybe. I don't know. Something.'

Liv looked at him with disbelief. How could he be so naive?

'People go to prison for things they didn't do all the time. Miscarriages of justice happen every day.'

'Not to Gracie. It just ... won't. We won't let it.'

'But what if we can't stop it? What if there's nothing we can do?'

'There's always something. The truth will come out, I know it will. We'll find a way.'

We'll find a way.

And that's why Liv is here, finding that way, picking away at a possibility. And if that possibility proves to be another dead end, she'll keep going until she finds another one and another one and another one.

As she chews, Liv pictures herself older, greyer, more desperate, more broken, still searching, still hoping, still desperate to help free her innocent child. The idea that this might just be the beginning, that a solution, a possibility and explanation and the real killer could be just around the corner could be a mirage and that Gracie could actually go to prison and Liv and Andy could spend the rest of their lives trying to prove her innocence. It is like being trapped in a horror film. An endless jump-scare of a life on a continuous loop.

Suddenly nauseated by the idea of putting one more item of food into her mouth, Liv stuffs the remaining burger and half a packet of chips into the paper bag it came in and picks up her coffee. But as she turns to leave she slams straight into another customer.

'Sorry,' she mutters as the man, a scruffy-looking guy in his fifties shifts to the side and keeps going towards the counter. There is a tang of alcohol coming off the man and this makes her pause and look at him again. And she knows it's him instantly. Martin Finch.

Liv stands there frozen, observing as he says something to the young worker at the counter distributing food to other customers, and watches as he is directed to the self-serve screens. But he doesn't move and instead asks the server something else and this time the teenager turns away, busying himself with orders. A few moments pass, a quiet rage crosses the features of the man who Liv is certain is Martin Finch, then he suddenly looks defeated, his shoulders slump a little and he goes over to a free screen to tap in his order.

Liv stuffs the bag and her coffee into a nearby bin and then positions herself just outside the exit. She scrolls on her phone, googling Martin and then checks his image online with the one through the glass doors and decides that yes, this is undoubtedly him, although he now looks far older than his fifty-six years. It's obvious he's a heavy drinker, and not just from the smell of alcohol. His face is flushed and when he takes his wrapped-up burger from inside the bag, his hands are trembling so much he struggles to remove the food from its paper wrapping. Liv looks away and lets the man eat his McDonald's without being observed.

When Martin Finch has finished his meal, he steps outside into the hot humid morning. Liv watches as he crosses the road and goes into an off-licence, coming out with several bottles in a plain plastic bag. Liv gets back into her car, watching as he turns off the main road and heads back to Abbey Street. By the time Liv has negotiated the one-way system and finally returned to her previous car spot, he is crossing the road opposite, his pace quicker now, likely keen to get home and crack open one of those bottles.

Liv crosses the road, calling out as the security door shuts behind Martin.

'Martin, please wait a sec,' she calls after him. 'My name's Liv Elliot, I'm Richard Wellington's neighbour. I need to talk to you.'

He glances over his shoulder but keeps walking.

'Please, Martin, wait. I need your help. I'm not a journalist,' she adds, desperately. And finally he stops walking and turns around.

'What do you want?' he says, more grumpy than aggressive but Liv sees she has mere moments to keep his attention. To convince him.

'My daughter's being investigated for Richard Wellington's death but she's innocent.' The words tumble out and Liv sees a brief flicker of comprehension pass his ruddy features. 'I hoped … I hoped you might be able to help me. I hoped you could talk to me and help me. Maybe help work out who really did it?'

As she says the words she realised what a futile exercise this is. What does she expect this man to do? Take pity on her and agree to somehow take the blame. Pretend he killed Richard so Gracie is off the hook?

Martin Finch blinks. 'I didn't fucking kill him,' he says in a low voice. 'Someone else got there before me.'

He resumes his slow walk down the pathway.

'Please, Martin, I really need your help,' she calls after him. Her face presses against the cool metal of the gate, her hands grasping at it. 'You're the only person who can help me.'

Then she thinks of something.

'Why don't I go to the bottle shop and get you something really nice? What's your favourite, vodka? Or maybe a really nice whiskey?'

He stops in his tracks and turns back towards her, his interest finally piqued.

'Whiskey?' she tries again, disgusted with herself as she says the word. 'How about a nice Scotch?'

His eyes narrow.

'Johnnie Walker?'

A hesitation then he gives a stiff nod.

'Johnnie Walker.' She nods. 'What's your apartment number? I'll go get it and come straight back.'

He regards her suspiciously for a moment, then presumably deciding the whiskey is worth the risk, replies, 'Fourteen.'

Liv nods again. 'Fourteen. Okay. Won't be long.'

'Red.'

She frowns. 'What?'

'Make it Johnnie Red,' he says.

'Red it is,' she says, feeling ashamed at what she is doing as she turns to walk away.

Chapter 43

LIV
Tuesday, 18 February 2025

The flat is small and sparsely furnished, smelling of mould and cigarettes but it is neat and clean. A casement window is open a fraction but none of the air outside has found its way in. Martin is sitting on a brown armchair opposite a TV that rests on a chest of drawers while Liv is perched on the only other seat in the room, a wooden chair next to a small table over in the kitchen area.

The most striking thing about the place is how little clutter or signs of life there are anywhere. There is no mess, no bowl with keys and small change, no piles of paperwork or junk mail. There are no pictures on the wall, no food on the counters, no unwashed plates, no drying rack by the sink, no plumber magnets tacked to the fridge.

Liv watches as Martin downs his first glass of whiskey almost in one go, his second in two mouthfuls and then as he sinks back into his chair with his third, which he appears happy to savour.

'So what did Richard Wellington do to you, then?' he asks finally. 'He fuck you over too? Kill someone you loved?'

'No, but he assaulted my daughter.'

Martin sucks in his breath. 'When did that happen?'

'The same morning he died.'

Martin's eyebrows rise.

'And at the same park where he died. And now it's possible the police think she could be the one who killed him.'

'Could be?'

'I suppose they need more evidence. They haven't charged her.'

'Why can't she say it was self-defence if he attacked her?'

'Because she didn't do it.'

He shrugs. 'But if the police decide she did, she can just say that, can't she?' Martin raises the glass to his lips, drinks a mouthful, then rests the glass on the arm of the chair. 'Then she'll be cleared.'

'She can't admit to something she didn't do. The police need to find the real killer. Besides, Gracie shouldn't be caught up in any of this; she had nothing to do with it.'

'You know that for sure?'

'Of course. She's my daughter. She's also a nineteen-year-old girl. She's not … capable.'

'If that arsehole attacked her, she'd be well within her rights to fight back. To do whatever it took.' He sips at his drink. 'How did he die again?'

'He was hit on the back of his head. Probably with a rock, the newspapers say. Then somehow he slipped down the embankment of the Gully and suffered an aneurysm in the creek.'

'That'd do it.' A grimace of a smile crosses Martin's face. 'Well, I'd like to thank whoever it was who did the deed because they did the world a big favour giving that bastard what he deserved.'

Another slug of whiskey and the glass is empty. Martin rises, surprisingly steady on his feet, and crosses the room to the fridge where he pulls out a can of beer. He offers one to Liv but she shakes her head.

'I thought you might have done it,' Liv says as he cracks it open. 'You sent enough threats saying you wanted to.'

He takes a sip of his beer. 'Yeah, can't deny that. Got a few restraining orders put in place off the back of them threats.' He is leaning back against the kitchen counter. 'Not that those would've stopped me given the chance.'

'You did have the chance though. I worked it out. You were only a few minutes' drive away when it happened, in Northern, in Landley Clinic right? That's just a kilometre or so away from the Gully park.'

Liv waits for a response but he just lifts the can to his lips and takes a long mouthful.

'I've been so convinced it was you, or wanted it to be you, I actually timed it.' She shakes her head at how desperate she's been. 'I parked my car a few streets away from the hospital, then went to Landley, put the timer on my phone and went back to my car, drove to Ashley Crescent at the top of the fire trail and then walked down through the bush to the Gully. To the spot where Richard was killed. Then I worked out how long it would have taken for you to hit him, push him into the water and then go back the other way.' She lets out a small laugh. 'You could have done it. Easily. Well, if you had access to a car.'

He frowns. 'You timed it?'

'I timed it.'

He nods, clearly impressed.

'And you reckon I could have got myself out of a secure unit by …' His eyebrows rise as he waits for her to complete the sentence.

'Climbing up one of the walls?' she offers.

He appears to consider this. 'I reckon it's more likely I'd just walk out the front door. The security in that place is pretty crap. Or maybe I'd have gone out through the back kitchen door? That's what most of the patients do. Except most of them just want to nip across to the nearest bottle shop to get a six pack and some smokes.'

Liv nods. 'Sounds doable.'

'And then I'd probably manage to get out by the staff car park entrance.' His eyes narrow. 'Yeah, that'd work. Okay so what next? Find my car? Well, I s'pose I drove myself over the day before and parked up on a side street.' He nods. 'Lucky.'

'You'd have had to have stashed your car keys somewhere along the way. Or near the car.'

'No need for that. Personal effects are all left in the nurses' station by the kitchen so we can all help ourselves to our ciggies. We all have our own plastic tubs and my car keys were in there along with my smokes.'

'That's convenient,' Liv says.

'Talking of which.' He pulls a packet of cigarettes from his pocket and lights up, blowing the plume of smoke up to the ceiling. 'So I've driven down to the park for my walk through the woods.'

'First you'd have parked up on Ashley Crescent and then gone into the Gully from there. The one you went along the time you visited with your wife's gardening group? Via the old fire trail.'

He looks at her a moment. 'You've done your research. Okay, so down through the fire trail. A few minutes to wallop old Dickie-boy, hope I've managed to murder him or maybe I help him along by pushing him in the water and then what, back the way I came?'

'Then back the way you came,' Liv agrees. 'Back to Landley and in through the kitchen door.'

He shakes his head, as if both impressed and amused by this plan. 'Back into the unit and into my usual spot for brekkie, right?' He drains his can and suppresses a burp. 'A round trip of what, an hour, hour and a half?'

'Give or take.'

There's a long pause as Martin appears to consider all of this. 'Okay, let me get this straight. An hour and a half where I drive myself to a park, scope out the dickhead, bash him and leave him for dead, then return and slip back into Landley without being seen.' He glances at her to check he's got it right and she just smiles. 'Fuck me. You must think I'm Superman.' He shakes his head, letting out a low chuckle. 'Look, that unit, Landley, is a fucking shitshow. Half the time we weren't even checked on until mid-morning after the early shift change but I reckon even those idiots might have noticed if I went missing for an hour and a half.'

Liv nods. She knew it was a ridiculous theory. 'Yeah, you're probably right.'

'Love, I don't know if you noticed, but I'm not in great shape. I'm not sure if I could even walk up a bloody hill anymore let alone pick up a rock and hit someone with it.'

She smiles. 'I was just speculating. It doesn't matter anyway, you've been cleared, haven't you? The police know you didn't do it.'

'Yeah,' he says, lifting his cigarette to his mouth. 'Shame for you. I reckon I'm the obvious suspect, aren't I? And it'd be a pretty perfect ending to everything that's happened.'

He takes a long inhale and then drops his cigarette into the empty beer can, stands and heads over to the fridge for a fresh can.

'I'm so sorry for what happened to your wife,' Liv says after he's returned to his chair.

He nods and doesn't speak for a while, just cracks open the can but this time lets it sit there, not drinking from it. 'I told her not to have the bloody operation,' he says eventually. 'She was perfect as she was. But I understood. I knew she didn't feel like herself, that she wanted to feel … womanly again – her words, not mine. She was always all woman to me.'

'Did you try and talk her out of it?'

'Not my place. But I said, well, if you're going to do it, get these implants, then you'll have the best. The best of the best. She'd been through all the cancer treatment in the public system and don't get me wrong, it was great. The doctors … the nurses … they were solid. No reason to complain.' He sips his beer. 'But I wanted her to feel like this next step was something else. Something that had nothing to do with the cancer, so in a different hospital with you know, nice private bedrooms, her own bathroom, that kind of thing. I wanted her to feel like a queen. So we found the best

234

surgeon in the country. And, yeah, well …' He trails off. 'You know how that went.'

Liv remains silent as Martin lifts the beer can to his lips. It is his second beer and he's also had three whiskeys. She doesn't know how he still appears sober although of course she does: he is a chronic alcoholic. And she just provided him with a bottle of poison that will make him sicker.

'You know you're killing yourself with all that booze,' she blurts out.

'That's the plan.' He raises the can and gives her a small sad smile. 'Not long to go now, I reckon.'

'You could get help,' she says. 'I could get you help. I can make some calls, get you into detox, then rehab.'

'God, no, none of that for me, thanks.' He shakes his head at the thought and then sees her expression. 'It's okay, really. I know what I'm doing and I'm ready.' He fingers the necklace around his neck and Liv sees that it's a St Christopher's cross. 'I'll be seeing her soon and that's all I want.'

'But what about your children? Don't you want to stay around for them? Get healthy for them?'

'Ah, they don't want anything to do with me anymore and I don't blame them. They're better off without me and they'll be even better off when I'm not around for them to worry and feel guilty about.'

'You dying won't stop their guilt.'

He shrugs.

'I've learnt the hard way that you can't keep trying to protect your kids from all the shit that life throws their way.' His fingers tap at the side of his can. 'Doesn't stop us trying but eventually you realise it's pointless.'

Liv instantly pictures Gracie and the fear in her eyes when she was taken in for more police questioning. The same expression she wore every time Liv insisted she go to school. That hunted look of pure terror. 'I can't do it, Mum. I can't go in.' And how

Liv had finally, for that three-month period when Gracie's anxiety was at its most debilitating, given up the fight and agreed that she could stay home. She'd never gone back and they'd moved her to a smaller, co-ed school away from the bullies and slowly she'd regained her confidence. She found a lovely group of friends. She'd learnt how to manage her anxiety. But the after-effects of that time still lingered.

Martin's low voice breaks through Liv's thoughts. 'Bad things happen to us and bad things happen to our kids,' he says, his voice slurring a little now, she notices. 'Better to let go and let them learn that, then they'll figure out how to save themselves if they have to. Then' – he pauses a moment – 'they won't have to rely on us anymore.'

Chapter 44

MEREDITH

January 2025

After that conversation with Sandra about Richard possibly stalking Gracie, Meredith resumed her runs, now going every day and coinciding them with Gracie's. She set her alarm to make sure; getting dressed before the sun rose and watching from the building doorway until she saw Gracie run past and down the steps by the reserve, usually just before or after six.

Meredith would wait a few moments and then slip from her hiding spot and follow a little way behind. She didn't want to raise Gracie's suspicions or admit her and Sandra's concerns over Richard until they had to. Gracie didn't need to be scared unnecessarily.

Most of the time she kept Gracie in her sights, because she couldn't keep up with her. When Gracie ran through the Gully, Meredith would position herself at the mouth of the path, running back and forth along the widest stretch that part of the park offered. Or doing step-ups and press-ups against the large boulders that rested there.

She would see Richard jogging his very slow loops of the oval most mornings but made sure to keep her cap low on her face, sunglasses on, so he wouldn't pick her out in the distance. He never went into the Gully as far as she knew but Meredith imagined it was just a matter of time before he attempted it. He was getting fitter every day, she could see. But then, so was she.

Gracie never asked why Meredith was now coming to the park on a daily basis when previously she'd only managed to go three or so times a week. Meredith supposed Gracie thought it was a new year's resolution. But seeing Gracie every morning started to become a way for Meredith to begin her day feeling grounded, which she hadn't felt for a very long time. Gracie was no longer just a conduit for getting closer to Liv, she became the main reason for Meredith's growing determination to win Liv over and become a part of all their lives.

Then one morning, towards the end of January, Meredith woke to find a message on her phone that Sandra had sent after she'd gone to sleep seven hours earlier.

Just received a message from Martin Finch – the man who took Richard to court. He wants to meet. What should I do?

By the time Meredith replied it was apparently too late. Sandra had driven over to his place at eleven o'clock the night before, to hear what he had to say.

'He's in an even more pathetic state than he was at the end of the court case,' Sandra told Meredith that evening when they met at the reserve bench. 'I presume he's been an alcoholic for years but he's really gone downhill since September. I don't think he's long for this world the rate he's going.' She paused. 'And I got the impression that's why he wanted to see me.'

'What did he say?'

'I think he always thought I sympathised with him during the trial. I mean I did, but not in the way he hoped. I was really very sorry his wife died but I still don't think it was because of anything Richard did. For all his faults, he's an excellent surgeon and I just can't see him being negligent in any patient's care. And nor could the court, which is why he won.

'But anyway, I think Martin wanted to see me because he knew I sympathised with him despite that. And basically he just wanted me to reassure him that his wife, Maria, wouldn't be forgotten.' Sandra frowned. 'It was very touching. He asked me to occasionally remind Richard about her, to just mention her name in passing to him and to our friends. He said that once he was gone there wouldn't be anyone else left to stand up for her, to remind people what she went through. And he was very adamant that I tell people that it wasn't about revenge, but love. He wanted me to know that everything he'd done, everything he'd been through with the court case, the restraining orders, being estranged from his children and the rest of his family, it was always all about Maria and it was always all about how much he loved her and missed her.'

'Sandra, he sounds suicidal,' Meredith said, alarmed at this. 'We should try and organise proper help for him.'

'I don't think he'd want that,' Sandra said.

'Well, we could try and convince him. We could go over together and explain that I'm a doctor and that you were concerned and asked me to check him over physically because you're worried. We can improvise.'

But Sandra looked uncomfortable at the suggestion.

'I think he's ready to go,' she said, her tone softer. 'He's been through a lot and if he's decided this is the end of the road for him then I think we should respect that and leave him be.'

'We could ask someone from the local area to check on him? Would you let me know his address and I can pass it on to someone at the community health team?'

'I don't know.'

239

'They won't force him to get help but they'll make sure he's all right. Like a welfare check.'

Sandra had shrugged. 'Maybe,' she said, non-committally.

Then came January 30. A text from Gracie had come through at 5.20 while Meredith was still asleep, to say that they might not cross paths today because she'd headed out earlier than usual. Meredith wasted no time getting into her workout gear and hurrying to head out the door. Without bothering to brush her teeth or have a glass of water, she left her apartment and sprinted down to the park, texting Sandra as she went. Is Richard at home?

As Meredith ran, briefly thankful that her fitness was so much better now, she thought how ridiculous this was, two women acting as bodyguards to keep Gracie safe from a predator. They couldn't go on like this. They had to confront Richard or put a stop to it somehow. Tell Gracie their concerns and ask her to change her routine. Maybe finally tell Liv and Andy what had been going on.

Meredith had also decided to make a formal complaint at work about Richard's behaviour before Christmas and perhaps even make a statement to the police, in case anything did happen to Gracie. She would tell them what he'd done to her and show them the texts and emails she'd kept. She would explain how Richard had practically been stalking Gracie, how he'd stood outside her window doing god knows what around Christmas time. How he was a menace. A predator.

Gracie wasn't there when Meredith got to the park. She wasn't in her usual stretching spot by the water, and she wasn't doing laps on the oval even though it was now around fifty minutes since she'd texted to say she was beginning her run.

Meredith tapped out a text on her phone: Where are you? and when there was no response she called Gracie but it went straight to voicemail.

240

Meredith jogged over to the Gully entrance and saw Gracie's distinctive pink water bottle resting next to the side of the path. She would have to go in.

Giving one last glance to the oval, in case Gracie miraculously appeared there, Meredith stepped onto the pathway, and that's when she heard the muffled scream.

Chapter 45

LIV

Wednesday, 19 February 2025

Liv gets up before six, having not slept more than a few hours, her brain circling a constant loop of worry. She is of course worried about Gracie but today's worry focuses more on her and Andy having to talk to the police later on.

She picks up her phone from the side of her bed and as she walks into the kitchen, looks to see if there's been a text from Gracie since she last checked a few hours ago. Gracie didn't come home last night and hasn't messaged to say where she is, and Liv is trying very hard, but mostly failing, to remain calm about this too.

The day before, Gracie had a frenzied air about her, clearly counting down the hours of freedom she thought she had left. She had been up early and told Liv and Andy she had a full day of activities planned as she stood in the kitchen, drinking a smoothie after returning from her morning run through the local streets.

She was meeting friends for brunch, going to the beach for a swim, to another friend's for dinner and then out for drinks later. Normally Liv would be happy that her daughter is filling her days, that she wasn't letting her worries keep her trapped within the four walls of their house. But this wasn't Gracie living her best life, she realises now, this was Gracie preparing for the end of her freedom.

Liv checks the family-tracking app and sees the last place registering Gracie's phone is still somewhere in Newtown.

She messages Gracie again asking her to please let them know she's okay. She debates calling her daughter but decides that's a step too far and instead makes herself a strong coffee and lets Sophie out into the garden, breaking her own rule about not letting the dog out unless they give her a proper walk. But today, she has too much else to worry about.

By 7.30, Liv is showered, dressed, has eaten breakfast and checked her phone for the millionth time when it buzzes with an unfamiliar number while, simultaneously, Andy appears in the doorway looking tousle-haired and bleary-eyed.

Liv puts the phone to her ear. 'Hello,' she says.

'Hi, is that Liv?' The voice is young and female and sounds uncertain.

'Yes, who's this?'

'It's Kristina. Gracie's friend.'

Liv's heart picks up pace. 'What's happened? Is Gracie okay?'

A pause at the other end. 'Is she not at home?'

'At home?' Liv looks at Andy who is watching her with a concerned expression. 'No. Her bed's not been slept in and she hasn't messaged me. Why?'

There's a moment of silence and then the words tumble down the line.

'Um, so we ended up at a party in Marrickville and it got late and we just all ended up falling asleep. I woke up about half an hour ago and Gracie wasn't there and someone, I don't know his name but he's at uni with us, well, he says he saw Gracie leave at around 2 a.m. Told him she had to go and meet someone? But it's just … well, I don't think that sounds like something Gracie would do and if she did, she'd wake me and tell me first.' She sounds panicked and that in turn makes Liv feel panicky. Liv quickly switches it to speakerphone so Andy can hear.

'And it wasn't like I was drunk or anything, I would have woken up easily. I'd have gone with her.' There's a pause. 'I've tried calling and messaging but she's not picking up and I've also tried some of our other friends and they've been asking around but no one knows where she went. She's turned off her location on Snapchat, which is how we usually know where each other is which is … Strange. And then five minutes ago she posted this weird story.'

'Story?'

'On Instagram. It's a few seconds of video of like … nothing, it's all dark, you can't see where she is but you can hear her breathing, it's heavy like she's running and then she kind of makes this surprised noise, not a scream, sort of like she's been startled and then it stops.'

'I'm going to look, hang on.' Liv motions to Andy. 'Check your phone,' she instructs him and he immediately crosses the room to the kitchen counter where his phone's charging. 'See if Gracie's messaged you and try phoning her.'

Liv opens up her Instagram app and finds Gracie's story. It's just a few seconds long and the accompanying clip is entirely pitch black as though the phone has been recording while laid flat on something or inside a bag or pocket.

Liv can vaguely hear that the soundtrack is Gracie breathing heavily, not in a panic attack kind of way, but more like she is walking very quickly or perhaps even running. Then there is an audible gasp and the clip ends. Liv listens to it again, this time with the sound up higher and she tries to work out if it is a scared gasp or a surprised-sounding one. Her heart thrums. What has happened to Gracie? Where is she?

'She's not picking up. And she's not on the tracker,' Andy says. 'Kristina, do you know if she's meant to be at uni today or has she arranged to see anyone?'

'We both have the morning free and Spanish later. I think she has a shift at the café but she wanted to get out of it because we were having a late one.'

'Call Paco,' Liv instructs Andy. 'Kristina, what was she like yesterday? Was she worried about everything that was going on with the investigation? Has she talked to you about all that?'

There is a pause.

'Yeah, a bit,' Kristina says, sounding uncertain. 'I mean I know she was interviewed and I know she's been really worried but last night she seemed kind of okay? Almost like she was pretty sure everything would work out.'

'Did she say that?'

'Not exactly but she just seemed … different. I don't know how to explain.' There's a pause at the other end. 'Will you tell the police you can't find her?'

'I don't think that's necessary at this stage. Hopefully there's a simple explanation and Gracie will turn up. Why don't you keep messaging people and keeping an eye out and we'll do the same here? Let me know if you hear anything, even if it's something tiny?'

'Okay. I will.' There's a pause. 'You don't think something bad's happened then? That the person she was meeting … I don't know. That they did something?'

Liv glances at Andy and takes in the grave expression on his face. She wants desperately for him to reassure both her and Kristina that all is okay. He must sense this because he moves closer to the phone.

'Hi, Kristina, this is Gracie's dad. I actually don't think she would go and meet anyone at two in the morning. I think she probably just said that to explain why she was leaving.'

'But then … where is she?'

'I don't know, but we'll find her,' Andy says. 'We'll find her and I'll let you know as soon as I know anything. Just try not to worry, but let's stay in touch. Let us know if you hear anything or if you hear from her.'

They end the call. Liv looks at Andy, seeing her own panic reflected back in his.

'She knew there was a chance she'd be charged today,' Andy says. 'That's why she went out with her friends, went to the beach, went to a party. She knew it might be her last chance.'

'You think she's bolted?'

'God, I hope not,' he says. 'If she has, she'll just make everything ten times worse.'

Chapter 46

LIV

Wednesday, 19 February 2025

They have just an hour and a half before they are due at the police station for their interviews. Liv suggests they call and ask to postpone but Andy shakes his head. They have to be there, no matter what is going on with Gracie. It will just be worse for their daughter if they fail to show up or make a flimsy excuse.

While Liv remains glued to her phone, looking for clues, Andy checks with Paco and learns Gracie hasn't messaged him or any of the others at the café to cancel her shift or explain her absence this morning.

Kristina texts to say she's contacted all their mutual friends but no one's heard from Gracie since she left the party. Then five minutes later she texts again with the address of where it was and Andy springs into action.

'I'll go there and try and speak to someone. You go to the police station on your own. Explain that I've had to ... I don't know, check on your dad?'

Before Liv can protest he's out the door, car keys jangling in his hand.

'But what do I tell them?' she calls out.

'You know what to say. Keep it simple. You'll be fine.'

Liv showers and dresses, her hands trembling as she buttons her top. She has no idea how to keep things simple, as Andy has instructed. She is sure she's going to mess this up and cause even more problems for them all. Then as she is pulling open her car door, her phone goes and she picks it up so hastily it nearly slips from her hands.

She listens to Simon at the other end of the line and replies in simple yeses and nos. Then she lets the car door close and leans back against the hot metal, her eyes closing, relief coursing through her.

Their police interview has been postponed until tomorrow.

Liv stands there a moment before lifting her phone again and calling Andy to let him know.

'Good,' he says, already onto other matters. More important ones. 'No one's even answering at the Marrickville address so I'm parked up calling hospitals.'

Liv's stomach gives a lurch. 'Why?'

'Just checking no one of her description's been brought in overnight.'

'Andy, where is she? What's happened?'

She finally voices the fear that's been skirting her thoughts all morning, that she hasn't allowed herself to dwell on.

'Andy. What if whoever killed Richard has done something to Gracie? What if there is someone out there? Someone who's been watching us all? What if she's been hurt?'

There's a brief pause. 'No, absolutely not,' Andy says, his tone clear and determined. 'She's got spooked and run off. Or I don't know, she did something stupid like taking off with a stranger and spending the night with them or … or she took a pill with someone and went dancing.'

'What? No, no, she hasn't. That's not Gracie. She wouldn't do something like that.' Liv makes a face at the absurdity of what Andy is suggesting. God knows at this moment she'd prefer it if Gracie was doing one of those things, but Liv knows her daughter. There's no chance.

'We'll find her. Just let's not panic. She'll turn up.' A pause. 'It's going to be okay.'

Liv goes back inside the house and sits on Gracie's bed, as if that might offer some clues. It is made neatly, the clothes Liv had taken off the line the previous day still in a folded pile on Gracie's desk, a book on politics sitting on the bedside table with an empty glass sitting on top of it.

Then a question dislodges in Liv's thoughts: Gracie's water bottle. Where is Gracie's water bottle?

Liv scans the room and then she goes over to Gracie's backpack that she uses for uni and checks inside. Nothing. She goes into the kitchen and checks in cupboards and the dishwasher even though Gracie is always reminding everyone how the stainless-steel pink water bottle is not dishwasher safe. It's not there either.

Was it the one she saw at Sandra's or is that just a coincidence and her mind is making connections where there aren't any?

Liv thinks about Sandra and wonders if her neighbour is the kind of woman who would buy a $55 limited edition ceramic bottle. Sandra is the kind of woman who wouldn't think twice about spending this amount on a bottle of wine but a water bottle? Liv isn't sure.

Her phone buzzes. It's Andy and Liv accepts the call, hungrily. 'Have you found her?'

'No, sorry.' He pauses. 'But I've been thinking about what you said earlier. About this being related to what happened to Richard.'

'And?'

'I remembered something your dad said, last week, when I was talking to him about the investigation and what was going on. I was asking him if he remembered Meredith.'

'I already asked him, he doesn't remember anything about

her,' Liv says impatiently, willing her husband to get to the point, because this is definitely not the point.

'Well, he remembered when I mentioned her. He said we needed to be very, very careful and to remember what happened with the fire.'

'The fire? What fire?'

Liv has made her way into the kitchen and sees Sophie lying on the sofa asleep and goes over to her.

'He said that Meredith set his studio on fire when she was a teenager. When she was meant to be looking after you one weekend?'

Liv frowns. 'What?'

'He couldn't remember much else but kept saying over and over that there were scald marks on the outside and they had to paint over it.' He pauses only momentarily. 'But there's more. Then the next day Meredith left a small box on the doorstep and it was full of partially burnt letters. Letters you had sent Meredith over the years. That's what that box was. She burnt your letters and then left them for you.'

Liv feels another wave of irritation. 'What's any of this got to do with Gracie going missing?'

There's a pause. 'Liv, if Meredith was some kind of … arsonist when she was a kid, then maybe she's worse now. Maybe she's the one who killed Richard.'

As her husband says the words that Liv has wondered to herself so many times over the past few weeks, she realises how preposterous an idea it is. There is no way Meredith killed Richard Wellington; she is almost certain of that, even though she is not certain of very much else in this moment.

She lets out a long exhalation. 'No, Meredith didn't kill Richard.'

'Liv, you've said it yourself. The woman is seriously weird. What if she's got Gracie? What if this was her plan all along – to get friendly with Gracie. To, I don't know, *groom* her and then do something terrible to her. To get revenge for what you were like to her all those years ago?'

Liv closes her eyes. She pictures Meredith. This woman who suddenly appeared one day at the hospital campus where Liv works; how she moved onto the cul-de-sac where Liv and Andy and Gracie live. She thinks of Meredith's hurt expression at that café, all those years ago. How she turned and ran, the skirt of her ridiculous red netted dress bobbing up and down as she went.

Could Meredith really want revenge for being bullied as a teenager, after all these years?

Chapter 47

LIV

Wednesday, 19 February 2025

Liv calls Meredith's number but it rings out so she leaves a message. She does her usual routine of checking Gracie's social media accounts, her WhatsApp and then finally the location tracker and sees, with a jolt of surprise, that it has updated.

Liv zooms in on the address, last recorded ten minutes ago. She gives a start at seeing where her daughter is, then screenshotting the image as she quickly descends the stairs, Liv texts it to Andy. Meet me here, she adds.

As she gets into her car, Liv leaves a message with reception at work telling them something's happened at home and she has to take urgent leave. She drives as quickly as is possible through Sydney mid-week traffic, changing lanes and overtaking where she can, ignoring the beeps from cars she cuts up and driving through orange lights that are perilously close to turning red. She doesn't care. All she knows is that she has to get to Gracie. And then finally, after twenty minutes of white-knuckle driving and maddening traffic jams and a near miss with a cyclist, she is there.

A double-parked ambulance and two parked-up police cars are outside Martin Finch's building and Liv feels a wave of dread.

She springs from the car and joins the small group of onlookers who are huddled around the entrance to the building, the steel gates now both wedged open. A male paramedic emerges from the back of the ambulance, holding something under his arm, something dark in a plastic casing and Liv and the other spectators watch him walk purposefully towards the building's main door where a uniformed police officer is standing.

'What's happened?' Liv says in the hope that someone will enlighten her.

A bearded man immediately responds. 'They found a body. Suicide.'

Liv's heart thumps. 'Man or woman?'

'Man,' says an elderly woman, pulling a shopping trolley to Liv's left. The same one Liv recognises from the last time she was here.

Liv feels almost giddy with relief. She moves a little closer, scanning the gathered crowd and road, searching for Gracie. She checks her phone but her daughter's location hasn't been updated now in forty minutes. She can see that Andy is moving slowly along King Street, probably caught up in the same traffic she had to get through.

She extracts herself from the small crowd and moves past the onlookers, keeping a wide berth from the police cars and ambulance, and walks a little up the road in case Gracie is, inexplicably, somewhere nearby, perhaps watching from a distance. But there is no sign of her so Liv backtracks, this time positioning herself a little way back, so she can watch the whole scene and Martin Finch's building from afar.

Finally, after ten minutes, two other paramedics, one male and one female, emerge from the building laden with bags and guiding a wheeled stretcher on which there is a body bag, possibly containing the body of Martin Finch or some other poor soul.

A ripple of shocked reactions carries through the crowd. Liv feels a flutter of intense sadness mixed with heavy guilt, remembering the deeply troubled, obviously unwell man she'd met just yesterday.

If it was him, how had he done it? Had he finally drunk himself to death or had he decided to take a quicker route from this world?

And had Liv helped him make the decision to end things by buying him that bottle of Johnnie Red? She feels disgust and shame settle over her.

The onlookers take several steps back, the bearded man Liv had been standing next to, removing his cap as the paramedics move past, others variously dropping their heads respectfully or just continuing to stare, apparently unaffected, at the sight of a body bag in their midst. The back of the ambulance is opened and the body is lifted in by some kind of hydraulic system that makes a loud whirring noise.

Liv does another scan of the area but there is still no sign of her daughter. The elderly woman pulling the shopping cart is now over by one of the young officers, presumably trying to convince him to let her back into the building. He nods and goes over to another, more senior officer, who shakes his head firmly. The younger one returns to the woman, an apologetic look ready on his face, but Liv's attention is distracted by a group of people over by the building's main entrance.

A group of uniformed officers and others in smart regular clothes are making their way along the path to the gate and behind them is Detective Inspector Mitchell. Liv squints to see the woman walking next to him, being almost guided by him, and gives a start when she realises who it is: Sandra.

Liv immediately takes a few steps back so she is shielded by the thick trunk of a plane tree and watches as her grave-faced neighbour is guided towards one of the marked police cars and it drives away.

Liv is opening her driver's door when Andy's car pulls up alongside her, his passenger window lowered. She explains what's happened and how Sandra was here. She will tell him about visiting Martin Finch another time. She can't do it now, while everything is all jumbled up and uncertain.

'What do we do now?'

Liv shrugs. 'I don't think Gracie's here anymore so, home? Wait for Sandra to get back? Maybe you should stay here and keep watch, in case she shows up or something.'

He nods, his expression grim. 'What the hell is going on? What's our daughter caught up in?'

Chapter 48

LIV

Wednesday, 19 February 2025

There are two police cars and at least six news vans lining Liv's road. The world, it appears, has heard about Martin Finch's death. News crews mill around the pavement outside her neighbour's house, scruffy-looking cameramen alongside their smarter on-screen colleagues who are poised to go live as soon as something happens, flushed and sweaty in their shirts and ties. Then there's suddenly a flurry of activity. Sandra's front door opens and the news crews rush forward as DI Mitchell and another suited man, followed by a uniformed female officer Liv recognises from the morning Richard died, walk down the steps and onto the pavement. Liv moves to join the throng and hears the reporters' questions.

'Can you comment on reports that Martin Finch has been found dead?'

'There are reports he took his own life. Is this an admission of guilt for Richard Wellington's death?'

'No comment,' responds the younger detective and a moment

later they are inside their cars while journalists continue firing questions and the cameramen keep filming.

Liv tries calling Sandra but after one ring it diverts to voicemail so she taps out a message:

Are you okay? Outside your house. Where is Gracie?

A response comes back immediately.

Can you meet me in the laneway with your car? Text me when you're outside.

It takes another ten minutes for Liv to get her car out of its parking spot and then another five to get out of the street and into the laneway behind Sandra's. Finally, when her neighbour is inside her car, wearing dark glasses and a hat, she says immediately, 'Meredith and Gracie are meeting us at the Gully park. At the car park.'

'Is she okay? Where's she been? We've been looking everywhere for her.' The questions tumble out.

'She's fine, she's absolutely fine.' Sandra gives a tight, business-like smile. 'I'll explain everything, but can we please just get out of here before the vultures descend?'

Liv stares at her neighbour for a beat. She has a million more questions for her. Why has Gracie been AWOL, why was she and Sandra at Martin Finch's building? What is Meredith's involvement? Is she dangerous?

'Please, Liv,' Sandra says again, a sharpness to her tone.

'Sure, sorry,' she says, automatically, and puts the car into drive, calling Andy through the car system as she pulls out on the main street and leaving a message to explain what's happening.

'Where is she?' Liv asks as she pulls into the car park, her eyes scanning the area. She is itchy with impatience to see her daughter. To check she is okay.

257

'Over by the water. Past the picnic tables.'

It's late afternoon and the sun is low, momentarily blinding Liv as she half-jogs to the picnic tables. Then she sees her.

Gracie. Intact. Completely fine. As beautiful as always.

Her girl.

'Thank god,' she says, running and pulling Gracie into a hug. 'We've been so worried.'

'I'm fine, Mum.' Resistant at first, Gracie finally sinks into the physical contact, hugging her mum back. 'I'm fine,' she repeats, this time in a softer tone. 'Stop stressing.'

Liv breathes in her daughter's scent, enjoying every visceral moment of being able to touch her and see her and smell her, and then, pulling back but still holding Gracie's wrists, she searches her face for answers. Then the frustration and fear of the past few hours tumbles out.

'Where the bloody hell have you been? You scared the shit out of us.'

Liv sees Gracie glance at Meredith who is watching them with her usual, unreadable expression.

'Did she do this? Did she … do something?'

'No, course not.' Gracie looks affronted at the suggestion, but there is a strange, charged energy among the three of them. Liv's relief at seeing Gracie has been replaced with an uneasy sense that she is about to learn something bad. She looks from Meredith back to Gracie and then to Sandra, who has hung back a little and isn't meeting Liv's gaze.

'Please can someone just tell me what the hell is going on?'

'Martin Finch is dead,' Sandra says. 'He took his own life last night.'

'I know that already. And I saw you at his building. Why were you there?'

An older couple pass with their dog and they all fall silent until they're out of earshot.

Gracie speaks first. 'What were you doing at Martin Finch's

place?'

'I was trying to find you,' Liv says. 'But why were you there?' She directs her comment to Sandra. 'And where were you? The tracker said you were there,' she asks Gracie.

But instead of Sandra and Gracie explaining, Meredith begins to speak.

'Martin emailed Sandra yesterday saying he was going to commit suicide,' she says, her voice low and matter of fact. 'He wrote that by the time she received the email, he'd be dead. He explained that he was leaving a note and in it he would explain how he killed Richard. He hoped this would give her peace of mind and be enough to convince the police of his guilt.' She pauses. 'He also said that the evidence was clear.'

'No, he wrote that the evidence was clearly *there*,' Gracie says.

Liv frowns, still not understanding.

'He was speaking in code,' Gracie explains. 'In case the police read his email later. Sandra didn't understand but Meredith knew straight away what he was getting at.'

'Knew what?' Liv asks, still baffled.

'That he was telling Sandra that he'd be taking the blame for Richard's death in his suicide note. But he knew if the police were going to accept that he did it, that he killed Richard, there needed to be physical evidence too,' Meredith says. 'He was telling Sandra she needed to place it at the scene of his death.'

'What physical evidence?'

Liv sees Meredith and Gracie exchange a look.

'We needed to take the rock that Sandra hit Richard with and put it in Martin's apartment,' Gracie says.

Liv stares at her daughter. 'Sandra hit Richard?' she says finally, then turns to Sandra who gives the faintest of nods. 'It was you all along? *You* hit Richard?'

Sandra's face crumples and her hand flies up to cover her mouth. Gracie is immediately by her side, a comforting arm around their neighbour.

'You did what you had to do. It wasn't your fault,' Gracie says, then glances at Liv. 'She saved me, Mum. She hit Richard to save me. And Meredith helped us.'

Meredith has moved over to join them and rests her hand on the small of Sandra's back. 'And it was the aneurysm that killed him. Don't forget that.'

Liv stares at the three of them, still trying to process what she's being told. She tries to picture it, recalibrating everything she's thought until this moment, all the various scenarios: Gracie, Meredith, Martin Finch. The possibility of each of them landing the fatal blow to Richard Wellington's skull that led to the aneurysm bleed.

'So Sandra hit Richard with a rock when he was assaulting Gracie,' Liv says, still not sure if she's got it correct. 'And that stopped him and then what, he collapsed and died? But wasn't he found in the water? Or near it?'

But the other women remain silent, apparently too focused on Sandra, who is now silently weeping, to address Liv's questions. She turns to Meredith. 'So Sandra planted the rock she used at Martin's, after he died? To make it look as though he'd killed Richard?'

Meredith nods. 'We offered to plant it. Me and Gracie.'

'We didn't want Sandra going to his flat,' Gracie says. 'We were worried someone might recognise her.'

'But they couldn't get into the building. They nearly got caught,' Sandra says, voice wavering. Her face is streaked with tears, her cheeks pink. 'And besides, this wasn't anything to do with them and I didn't want either of them involved. I was very clear about that.'

'It would have worked,' Meredith says, gently. 'We could have got in there, left the rock and got out before anyone noticed.'

'That's not true,' Sandra says, sniffing. 'Your fingerprints would have been everywhere. How would you have explained that? Anyway, we don't even know if it's worked.'

260

Liv's stomach drops. Fingerprints. Will the police find her fingerprints at Martin's flat?

'It has. It will,' Gracie says. 'It's going to be fine.' She gives Sandra's arm a squeeze. 'The police have got the letter and they've got the rock.'

'I can't get the image of Martin out of my mind,' Sandra says, fresh tears sliding down her cheeks at this. 'I don't think I'll ever forget what he looked like. Just sitting there.'

Liv's mind races, trying to work out exactly what happened. Had she touched anything? Had Gracie touched the exterior of the building anywhere?

'So you both tried to get into Martin's place in the middle of the night?' She looks from Gracie to Meredith for clarification. They both nod and she feels queasy. 'But then when you couldn't get in, Sandra went back there, what, just earlier today and she planted this rock and then what?'

'Someone had to report Martin's death. He might have been left for days otherwise.'

Liv looks at Sandra. 'How did you get in?'

'I got the neighbour to let me in.' Seeing Liv's expression she elaborates. 'I banged on Martin's door and finally a woman came out of one of the other flats, I ... well, I explained how concerned I was and that I'd received a worrying message from him. I said we should probably call the police but this woman said they'd be ages, that they always were when things happened in their block. Then thankfully this woman thought one of the other neighbours might have a key from when the previous tenant lived there. Anyway, luckily the locks hadn't been changed and we went inside. Well, they didn't. As soon as the door was open they hung back.' She pauses. 'And that's exactly what I told the police when they came.'

'Was it you called who the police?'

'I think one of the neighbours did.'

'But you had time to plant the rock before they came?'

Sandra nods.

'And you got the email from Martin last night?'

'Yes, as I said, late last night.'

'When?'

'Around midnight.'

'And your first thought at that point, at midnight, was to plant the rock?' Liv asks. 'Not to check on Martin or call an ambulance or the police to try and save him?'

Sandra stiffens a little.

'God, Mum, give her a break. Sandra called Meredith straight away. Then Meredith called me. We got to Martin's place as soon as we could.'

Liv remembers what Kristina had told her. Gracie had left at 2 a.m. Two hours after Sandra received the email from Martin.

'But you couldn't get into his building,' Liv points out. 'You had no way of knowing if Martin was actually dead. I just don't understand why your first instinct wasn't to call an ambulance or the police?'

Gracie frowns and the other women look at her, blankly.

Then, after a beat, Sandra speaks. 'When the paramedics arrived on the scene I overheard one of them saying that Martin had probably died early in the evening, around six hours before I got his email.'

'We think he wrote the email earlier but scheduled it to send at midnight,' Meredith adds.

'He had it all planned,' Gracie says. 'He knew what he was doing, Mum. He didn't want to be saved.'

Liv continues to watch Sandra. 'You're sure of that?'

'Absolutely,' Sandra says, her tone brittle. 'There was no chance of him surviving.'

'No chance at all,' adds Meredith.

'It's true, Mum. He wanted to go.'

'And you agree with that, Sandra?' Liv asks.

Her neighbour gives a firm nod but still doesn't, Liv notices, meet her gaze.

Chapter 49

LIV

Wednesday, 19 February 2025

Andy is standing outside their gate when Liv pulls into a parking spot a few doors down. She remains in the car as Gracie gets out and turns to watch through the windscreen as her daughter and husband embrace. The TV vans are still parked along the street, presumably hoping Sandra might appear although Liv knows she has taken refuge at Meredith's.

'Gracie's been cleared of any involvement' are the first words Andy whispers to her as she joins them, conscious of the many journalists nearby. 'DI Mitchell just called. He's been trying to get hold of her. She's not a person of interest anymore.' He pulls Liv into his other side and the three of them hug. 'It's over.'

Liv feels the weighty comfort of his arms as her own reaches out for Gracie. She knows her daughter is still irritated by the way Liv questioned them and Sandra in particular. On their solo drive home – Meredith had driven Sandra back to hers – Liv had tried to explain her concern but Gracie had given her the silent treatment.

'I just need to know exactly what happened,' Liv had said repeatedly, not adding how she wanted to check and recheck that Gracie hadn't somehow implicated herself in another person's death. That the police wouldn't check for fingerprints and find hers inside Martin's flat and Gracie's somewhere on the outside. How would they explain that?

'Mum, seriously. Leave it. Leave me alone. We've told you everything,' Gracie had said, a warning tone in her voice.

Gracie has a shower and afterwards she sits with a towel wrapped around her as she eats a plate of eggs and toast that Andy makes with surprising gusto. When she's finished she announces that she is going to sleep.

She waits a few minutes to be safe, then Liv tells Andy everything she has been told. She still doesn't mention her visit to Martin's place.

'I can't believe it was Sandra all along,' he says, finally. 'I never even suspected her.'

'And the one person we thought probably did it, wasn't involved but has taken the blame anyway.'

'And the police have bought it.' He shakes his head. 'Incredible.'

'Do you think they really have? It seems too convenient, doesn't it? They won't check his place for fingerprints and find Gracie's outside?' Liv searches his face for reassurance.

He frowns. 'Nah. It's pretty clear cut that he killed himself.'

Liv nods. She feels a little better now. Andy always makes her feel better.

'I still don't understand how Richard died,' she says after a while. 'Sandra hit him and then what, they just left? How did he end up in the water? What did Sandra and Meredith and Gracie do next? Did they leave him there, unconscious?'

Andy goes over to the kitchen and opens the fridge.

'They'll tell us when they're ready. The most important thing is Gracie is in the clear with the police. It's over, thank god.' He takes out the cheese and bread followed by pickles and mayonnaise.

'And there isn't a serial killer lurking in the shadows of our street after all.'

When Gracie emerges from her room, Liv can tell from her body language that although she is still not ready to talk, she appears less frosty and closed off.

She curls up on the sofa and switches on the TV. Liv joins her and they watch the first episode in the new season of *MAFS* while Andy orders pizza.

Around seven, Liv remembers with a start to call the rehab centre and check in on her mum, feeling a pang of guilt that she hasn't thought of either of her parents once in the past twenty-four hours.

She is told that Angela is doing well and will be discharged in the morning and Liv says she will be there early. Then she calls the new night-time carer, Darren, to check her dad is also okay and learns that he is fine. Happily working in his studio, the young man tells her, and before she asks, he adds that he has been sitting in the courtyard so he's able to check on Pete constantly. They're planning on watching an old DVD of one of Pete's films.

The next morning, Liv, Andy and Gracie drive to the rehab clinic and discharge Angela and take her back to her home. She is able to walk normally now, the only sign of the stroke a slight palsy in her arm and her continued inability to talk.

They have been told there is no way to know whether Angela will recover more of her speech in the coming weeks but that continued work with a speech pathologist and physio will all contribute to her possibly having a better outcome. It's the line Liv recognises as she always trots it out to the family members of her stroke patients. Be patient. Explore other methods of communication in the meantime. Focus on the gains Angela has already made. Liv knows she needs to stay positive but she is also realistic. Her mum is never going to be the same again.

Liv and Andy watch as Gracie puts her grandmother's arm

through hers and slowly guides her along the pavement, towards the house. They hear Pete's delighted greeting and then, as they follow Gracie and Angela, his wide beam of happiness as he opens his arms to hug his wife.

Liv feels a swell of gratitude. Focus on this, she thinks, focus on small moments of happiness.

Later, Liv sits on the edge of the sofa, watching Angela in the chair opposite as she attempts to squeeze the small foam ball. She manages eight.

'Well done. Now tongue out and wiggle it side to side. Slow then fast.'

Angela's tongue darts out but the action of moving side to side is harder. She stops and arches an eyebrow, clearly unimpressed by what she's being forced to do.

'You can do it, Gran,' Gracie says from her position next to Angela on the floor. 'I'll do it with you.'

Angela smiles as she watches Gracie stick out her tongue, widening her eyes dramatically.

'Okay, this time up down,' Liv instructs. 'Ten times, then we'll pause and go again.'

Angela and Gracie exchange a look and Gracie nods.

'Yeah, I know. She's always bossy like this with me too.'

They leave in the late afternoon when Darren arrives. Liv hasn't met him before; Andy has dealt with all of the logistics of interviewing candidates but she immediately understands why her husband gave him the job.

He is in his early twenties and has a soft, smiling face and gentle manner that Liv immediately warms to. Her mum brightens as soon as Darren greets her with a cheery, 'Angie, how's my favourite girl doing today?' and even Pete seems pleased to see the young man who immediately gets to work making gin and tonics for both of them – 'It's cocktail hour, people!' – which are light on the gin, Liv sees, shooting Darren a grateful glance.

Later, Liv puts her head around Gracie's bedroom door and sees her daughter lying on her bed, scrolling on her phone.

'I'm taking Sophie to the reserve. Want to come?'

Gracie looks up, considers this and then nods.

It is cooler tonight than it's been in a while and there's a delicious fresh edge to the air. Even Sophie seems more energetic as they walk towards the reserve, not needing her usual cajoling or treats to move along the pavement.

'You okay?' Liv finally asks Gracie when they are seated on the bench, looking out at the houses which are shadowy silhouettes against the darkening sky.

'I'm good,' Gracie says, slapping at her ankle. 'Bloody mosquitoes.' She pulls her legs into her chest and pulls down her long cotton skirt, tucking it under her bare feet.

'You've been through a lot over the past few weeks,' Liv says. 'It's okay if you're feeling exhausted and overwhelmed.'

'I'm fine.'

Liv nods. 'Well, I'm here, you know, if you want to talk about it.' A pause. 'Or if you prefer, you could make an appointment with Ally.'

There's a long pause. 'Yeah, I probably should,' Gracie says. 'I'll call the clinic tomorrow.'

This would usually be Liv's cue to say that she would call on Gracie's behalf but this time she doesn't.

'I can tell you everything that happened if you want? With Richard. At the Gully that morning.'

Liv glances at her daughter, surprised. 'Only if you want. I don't want you to have to relive it all if it's upsetting.'

Gracie lets out a small laugh. 'I can tell you've never had therapy.' She turns a little towards the building next to the reserve. 'Although I think Meredith should probably be here for this. Let me text her.'

Ten minutes later, they are sitting in Meredith's living room. Andy has also joined them and Sophie has taken up residence by

Meredith's closed bedroom door where she is apparently standing guard. On the other side of the door is Meredith's new kitten, Smoky, who hasn't yet got the full run of the apartment.

'Do you want to go first?' Meredith says. 'Or I can if you want?'

Gracie smiles. 'I'll go.'

Liv sees the connection and friendship between the two women and once again feels a pang of guilt for having attempted to frame her neighbour for Richard Wellington's death. She glances at Andy, wondering if he still thinks Meredith has somehow arrived in their lives, intent on a kind of revenge.

And then their daughter begins to speak.

Chapter 50

GRACIE

Thursday, 30 January 2025

Since her last year at school, Gracie had a rule that she went out in the morning, first thing. For a run or a walk, but either way it was non-negotiable. Not in an unhealthy obsessive way like the various rituals she had when she was fifteen. Nothing bad would happen if she didn't do it, but if the day started off like this, well, it promised the start of something good. It helped her headspace get off to the right start. There was something about breathing in the fresh air, seeing the sky, seeing the water. It became almost sacred. Gracie's special morning thing. Grounding, like all those cringe posts her mum loved on Instagram.

So when she began noticing Richard Wellington down at the park, puffing his way around the oval like he was going to have a stroke, she was angry.

Since what happened on Christmas Eve and the nights that followed, Richard had made Gracie scared of going to bed at night. Now it seemed he was doing his best to ensure her morning ritual turned into something she also feared. Something that was no longer special and sacred.

But Gracie refused to change her routine. The Gully and its park by the water were her favourite places in the world.

So, instead, Gracie made the decision to pretend Richard didn't exist. If she caught a glimpse of him in her peripheral vision, she wouldn't allow her brain to acknowledge it with a 'that's Richard Wellington' and would instead list five other things she could see in the vicinity. The massive white house that gripped the side of the tree-covered hill. The red brick toilet block on the far side of the park. The boat ramp where the pelicans hung out waiting for fishing scraps. The overhanging rocks that provided a brief respite of shade when you travelled along the path towards the Gully. The dogs and their owners who gathered in the same groups every morning. Sometimes it worked, sometimes it didn't.

But one thing Richard couldn't take away from her, and was too old and unfit to do himself, was running the trail through the Gully. And no matter how fit he got, he'd never be nimble enough to negotiate the slippery path and steep rocks and catch up to her. That route was all Gracie's. Her own private crazy video game, jumping from boulder to dirt track, over bracken and tree branches. It was always a buzz.

Then the night before the morning everything happened, there'd been a big storm. Yeah, agreed, it was probably not the best idea to run the trail, but Gracie wanted to test out the new trainers she'd bought with her Christmas money. They had all the high-tech grip stuff and she was hoping they'd help her run more easily along the slip-slidey mud paths like the guy in the running shop promised. She was excited at the thought and that's probably why she woke at five, half an hour earlier than usual.

There was another upside: Gracie had started to suspect that Richard was watching her leaving and that's why he was always at the park when she was. Today he might think she hadn't gone. She might finally get the place completely to herself.

She stood with the front door open, as Sophie did a pee out

the front, keeping her eyes on his house opposite. There weren't any lights on or signs that anyone was awake and Gracie hadn't put any lights on in her house either. When Sophie was finished, she went back inside and Gracie closed the door softly behind her, looping her finger through the lid of her water bottle.

The air smelt of freshly damp earth and the heady vanilla jasmine scent of the murraya buds that were now scattered like a bed of snow along the pavement thanks to the heavy rain. It was forecast to rain again later but with luck Gracie would be in and out of the park by then.

As she passed Meredith's building, she pulled her phone from the side of her running shorts and tapped out a text letting her new friend know she was going for an early run.

At the park, Gracie warmed up with a loop around the oval, keeping at a slow, steady pace, letting her muscles ease into the movement, enjoying the sensation of the softer-than-usual ground, thanks to the rain as well as the new shoes. Then she jogged onto the Gully path. It wasn't as dark as she'd feared and she quickly fell into a comfortable pace, the shoes making a big difference to her grip. She slowed down and used the torch on her phone to guide her way through the really dark parts and hoped her phone's already low battery would hold out until she'd finished.

She was careful and steady and as a result it took longer than usual for Gracie to get to the top of the trail. Once there, she decided to run a little farther, following the path as it opened up onto a more traditional tarmacked route that ran alongside the netball courts and car park. The sun had almost risen and the difference between the cool, dankness of the Gully path and here was stark. But Gracie didn't like it half as much. The tarmac felt wrong under her feet. Too easy. It felt like cheating.

She turned and retraced her steps, taking the less steep, down-ward-sloping path this time and walking when the path was too slippery to navigate safely, her hands reaching out to grasp onto tree branches or rocks when she needed to. Her heart rate had slowed to normal by the time she got to the bottom, so for the last stretch, the flat section, she sped up, sprinting to reach the edge of the creek where she knew she'd have to slow down to carefully step her way across the five strategically placed rocks that acted as a bridge. Then as she stepped from the last rock onto the path, she tripped over a tree root and slammed to the ground.

It was like a comedic fall, her face fell in a shallow puddle and her arms and legs splayed out across the damp leaves that carpeted the ground.

'Fuck's sake,' Gracie muttered to herself as she straightened up and brushed muddy water and leaves from her. It took a moment for her to realise she'd lost an earbud and Gracie began searching the area for it, using her phone's torch.

A male voice called out suddenly, startling her. 'Gracie, you okay? What have you lost?'

Richard stepped from the path and Gracie stiffened, automatically taking a step backwards.

'There it is,' he said, gesturing to her left. 'By that rock.'

She didn't move and he gave her a questioning look before retrieving the earbud himself.

It was an effort, she could see, for him to bend down and reach for it in the undergrowth but she remained motionless. No way was she bending down for him to cop a look.

When he finally straightened up and held out his hand, the earbud resting in his palm, he gave an encouraging smile.

'Go on,' he said, when she didn't move. 'These things cost a lot of money.'

'Thanks,' she muttered, taking it before he did that stupid thing of holding it above his head like he'd done with the door keys on Christmas Eve.

As Gracie made to move, he stepped across her path. A jolt of fear passed through her.

'I've been wanting to apologise about that business on Christmas Eve,' he said, with an expression that was almost contrite. 'It was inexcusable and I'm really very sorry. I probably scared you and I want you to know that was never my intention.'

It was an oddly formal apology, and yet, there was still a vague trace of droll amusement on his features.

'I honestly have no idea what my intention was,' he said, giving a slight shake of his head. 'I was … well, drunk obviously and I can be careless when I have too much to drink, as my wife's always telling me. Anyway, I'm very sorry.'

'Okay, thanks,' Gracie said and then added, 'I need to go. See you,' as she slipped her earbud in, eager to get away from Richard.

She picked up her pace, returning to the main path and heading towards the Gully entrance, checking he hadn't followed her. But instead of going right and taking the path back to the park and the oval, she stopped in her tracks and took a left, which took her back into the thick of the Gully.

It would be a really stupid split-second decision. But she needed to rid herself of the icky feeling that Richard's presence had left. She needed one more turn through the darkness of the Gully. That buzz of springing from track to rock to track that would help push away the strange feeling this interaction with Richard had left her with.

After climbing the first small set of steps, she looked back along the dim pathway once again to check Richard wasn't following her. The woodland here wasn't as thick and the early morning sunlight was starting to get through and light up the area. There was a flash of movement and Gracie saw Richard's figure, jogging slowly along the flat path that she would be running along if she hadn't taken this detour.

Now grateful for her decision, she watched him for a few moments until he disappeared within the thick of the trees and then turned and set off in the opposite direction.

Running, jumping, climbing.

This time she didn't go all the way to the top and around but simply turned halfway and came back the same way. Both her

273

phone and earbuds had run out of battery but she estimated from the light that it was now probably around 6.45. Meredith would probably be at the park by now.

Gracie paused at the bottom of the path, where she had fallen just ten minutes before, and stretched her cramping calf muscle. As she did so, she thought about all those other times she'd heard Richard tap on her window.

He hadn't apologised for those; hadn't acknowledged that it wasn't just that one time on Christmas Eve that he'd stood in the narrow path along her house, his occasional, creepy crooning, 'Gracie,' making its way through her firmly shut and locked window and blinds. Terrifying her with the possibility of what he might do if she made a mistake one night and left her window ajar. Causing her to check and recheck it wasn't and then go and do the same to all the other windows and doors in the house. Waiting until Mum and Dad were asleep so she could check the ones in their room too.

It had been like being plunged back through the years to a time when her life was full of exhausting little rituals and days spent off school lying in her bed staring at the ceiling and crying, too anxious to leave the house. She felt a burning fury rise up in her.

As she began walking back along the path towards the entrance, Gracie decided she would confront him. She'd tell him exactly what she thought of him and how he had affected her and that he needed to really understand what he'd done and promise to never do it again to any other women. She would demand he get help. And if he refused or laughed then she would go to his wife and maybe even the newspapers.

A thrum of adrenaline coursed through Gracie as she picked up her pace; her attention focused on the pathway in front of her and the entrance which was almost within view. She would talk to Meredith. Maybe they could join forces. Confront Richard together.

Then she felt a hand on her shoulder.

Chapter 51

GRACIE

Thursday, 30 January 2025

Richard had his hands raised in mock surrender. That grin was in place. That horrible, creepy smirky grin.

'Sorry, sorry!' he said, not sounding sorry at all. 'Didn't mean to startle you.'

Gracie had stepped back as far as she could without falling into the large shrub she was next to.

'What do you want?'

'I'm sorry,' he repeated. 'I didn't mean to frighten you.'

'You keep saying that, but that's all you do. You scared the shit out of me when you tapped on my window all those times and you're frightening me now. Why? Why do you keep doing this?'

He blinked. 'I just want you to understand where I'm coming from.'

'You want me to understand where you're coming from?' Gracie looked at him. Was he for real? Was he really this dense? 'You need to stay away from me. Stop harassing me. Stop scaring me. Stop creeping up on me. It's not that complicated.'

'Oh, come on, Gracie. Don't you think you're overreacting? Just a bit?'

She began to walk away and this time, even though he was standing in the middle of the path, she shoved hard past him.

'Oh, for goodness sake,' he said, suddenly pompous and outraged at her aggression. 'There's no need to behave like this. Look, I've known you since you were a little girl, I'd never do anything to hurt you. You know that. I'm friends with your parents for god's sake,' he said after her.

She turned and looked at him, hoping her scorn and disgust were obvious.

'That's what makes all this even creepier,' she said. 'Do you not see that? The way you look at me, the way you watch me, the way you're suddenly coming down here every morning? You're a dirty old man and you need to leave me alone.'

He looked outraged at this, his mouth a wide 'o'.

'I'm trying to get some bloody exercise!' he said, his voice rising. 'It's the new year and like most people in the new year, I'm trying to get a bit fitter.' He shook his head. 'My god, your generation! Not everything is about you.'

Gracie took several steps closer to him, no longer scared.

'You've been coming to my house, tapping on my window, freaking me out and then you start coming here every morning, at the same time I come, no matter if I come early or late. Tell me you haven't been watching my house, waiting for me to leave so you can get down here at the same time?' She paused. 'Go on, tell me.'

He looked at her with undisguised disdain.

'Goodness, you really do have a high opinion of yourself, don't you?' he said, giving a slight shake of his head. 'Gracie, love, I was drunk on Christmas Eve. I came and knocked on your window because you were the only person who I knew was still awake at whatever ridiculous time it was and stupidly, really stupidly, I thought you might want to come out and have a drink with me and, I don't know, continue the party. I didn't want to do anything to you. No offence, you're not my type. I just didn't want to go home or go to sleep. I wanted a bit of company.'

He cocked his head, watching Gracie through narrowed eyes.

'I thought we could maybe sit on a bench and I could smoke a cigarette before we both went back to our homes and I passed out and woke up the next day with a raging hangover and a determination to stop treating my body like shit and maybe, I don't know, start running.' He gave an exaggerated shrug. 'Maybe you were my inspiration because I'd see you going off for your morning runs when I was half dead with a hangover. Maybe I thought, hey, I might be nearly four decades older than that girl but maybe I can do what she does. Maybe I can run a few kilometres every morning and feel a bit better.'

His gaze narrowed.

'I've said I'm sorry and I am. I'm sorry I'm inappropriate and I'm an idiot and as my wife would also undoubtedly tell you, I don't read signals very well. I don't read women very well. I made a mistake and I'm really sorry. It was inappropriate and I understand you might have been scared.' He held up his hands. 'But I was pissed.'

Gracie stared at him, disbelieving.

'But it wasn't just the once,' she said finally, her tone calmer now, like his. 'You did it again and again and again.'

He frowned. 'I did no such thing.'

'Yes, you did. I was there. In my bedroom. I heard you.'

He looked confused. 'I promise you I didn't. I'll own up to Christmas Eve, but I never did it again. I promise you, Gracie.'

He smiled, and then, in that smile which Gracie could see was the sort of smile that was meant to convince her that he was just a nice, easy-going guy who meant no harm, she could also see he'd convinced himself that he was telling the truth.

'You're pathetic,' she said, turning away. 'And the world should know that.'

'Gracie, come on. Wait a minute.'

She felt his footsteps behind her and then felt his hand land on her upper arm.

'Gracie, wait.'

'Fuck off, leave me alone,' she said, pulling away. He reached for her again and this time she could feel his nails digging into her bare shoulder and gave a yelp of pain. 'What the hell? You've scratched me,' she said, examining her shoulder which now had a livid streak where he'd scraped his nails.

'Oh, it's nothing, don't overreact,' he said, but she could hear a note of panic in his voice. And then she looked at him and saw it in his eyes too. 'It's fine, you're fine,' he said again, sounding far less certain.

'I'm not fine. That's assault. And I'm going to show people and then I'm going to explain what you did. I'm going to tell everyone how you creep around outside girls' windows in the middle of the night and follow them on their morning runs and how you grab at them and assault them in the middle of the woods.'

'Oh, for fuck's sake.' He shook his head, dismayed. 'I expected better from you, Gracie, I really did.'

She turned away, not bothering to respond, and a split second later, she felt the force between her shoulder blades. A heavy push that tipped her a little, but combined with another raised tree root across the pathway, caused her to trip and fall to the ground. Then there was an additional pain as Gracie felt Richard's hands grabbing at her, pushing her over, onto her back, a hand suddenly clamped over her mouth.

'I just want to bloody talk to you,' he said, his words almost spat out.

Gracie thrashed and squirmed and tried to cry out but he had his leg jammed between hers, his other arm across her torso. He was like a leaden weight. The arm moved from her chest and there was a sudden, sharp pain between her legs.

Her eyes instantly closed with the brute force and shock of it.

Then she heard a dull, reverberating thwack and a new heaviness as he slumped on top of her. Gracie's eyes opened and she saw that Richard's head had slumped into the small of her shoulder. She screamed and then looked up and saw Sandra's face where Richard's had been just seconds before.

Sandra was standing above both of them, her arm raised, a rock in her hand.

Gracie was momentarily confused and then realising she still had Richard on top of her, give a cry of panic and pushed at him and somehow got out from under his heft. She straightened up, the pain between her legs duller but still making itself known.

Once upright, she looked around, trying to make sense of what had happened. Why Richard was lying prone on the ground and Sandra was standing, frozen, above him.

Then there was a crack of a twig breaking and Gracie spun around, heart hammering.

Meredith.

Chapter 52

MEREDITH

Thursday, 30 January 2025

Meredith crouched down and gently rolled Richard onto his back, checking his airway and pulse. It was steady and he was likely just knocked out, but it was possible he had internal bleeding.

'We should call an ambulance,' she said, but when no one replied, she looked up.

Sandra and Gracie were both standing there, apparently too stunned to move or respond.

'Sandra,' Meredith prompted. 'Call triple zero.'

But Sandra didn't move. She was staring at her husband, her face filled with horror and disbelief and shock.

'Whatever's happened, we need to call an ambulance and make sure he's okay. Then we can talk to the police and explain everything. You can explain what happened.' She pulled out her own phone and then saw the look on Gracie. 'Did he hurt you?' A small nod and Meredith understood immediately. She addressed Sandra. 'You saw it happen and stepped in to protect her?'

Again, there was no response.

'Is he … dead?' Gracie asked, staring at Richard.

Her face was streaked with mud and her hands and legs too. Her whole body was trembling.

'No,' Meredith said. 'He's probably just concussed but he needs checking over. And the longer we wait, the worse it might be. He needs medical attention and I don't have anything with me.'

She looked at her phone, but she didn't want to move her hand from Richard's pulse, just in case. Meredith held it out to Gracie.

'Call triple zero, Gracie. Quickly.'

But Gracie didn't take the phone.

'Why can't we just leave him?' she said. 'Leave him here and just … go home. Someone else can find him.'

She looked at Meredith who saw a glint of steeliness in Gracie's eyes.

'Why not?' Gracie said. 'He doesn't deserve any help.'

For a few moments, there was silence, only punctuated by the birdsong and faint sound of traffic in the far distance. It wasn't even seven but most Sydney-siders liked to get to work early in the summer months. Arriving at work well before eight, leaving before five so they could enjoy those extra precious hours of late afternoon sunshine.

Gracie turned to Sandra. 'What do you think?'

'Gracie, seriously, just call triple zero,' Meredith instructed. She held out her hand a little further but Gracie didn't take it when Meredith thought she was going to and the phone slipped from her fingers and fell to the ground.

Then Richard made a moaning noise and Meredith swivelled back to him, checking his pulse and gratified his heartbeat was strong. She was worried there was still the chance he was suffering an internal bleed.

'The police will get involved, won't they?' Sandra said finally, her voice reedy.

'Yes.'

'What if they find out it was me?'

281

'They'll understand. You were stopping him from hurting Gracie.'

'What if they don't believe me?' She let out a sob. 'I can't go to prison.'

'It won't come to that.'

Meredith bent down again to check Richard who was still giving the occasional groan but hadn't opened his eyes. The colour on his cheeks wasn't too bad. He had a bad gash to the back of his head but the blood had already begun to clot.

'He was facing away from me. They'll twist it, they'll make it into something it wasn't. They won't believe me.' Sandra was on the verge of hysteria.

'It will be okay. We'll back you up. We'll explain what he's like. Gracie and I will tell the police what he was like with us. Won't we?'

Sandra was shivering; clearly going into shock. She sat down suddenly as if she were about to faint but Gracie got to her in time and took her arm and kept her upright.

'Put her head between—'

But she was cut off by a louder groan. Richard. He gave a whimpering noise, halfway between a moan and a cry.

'Try not to move too much, you've had a knock to the head,' Meredith said as Richard's hand reached to the back of his scalp.

'Fuck,' he said, seeing the blood that came away on his hand. 'What happened?'

'You took a hit to the head and got knocked out for a while so try and stay still. You've probably got a mild concussion.'

He groaned again and pressed his hand to his forehead. 'It bloody hurts.'

'Can I run through some checks?'

Meredith didn't wait for a response, lifting Richard's wrist and checking his pulse again, which was now a little fast but steady and then guiding his head so that his eyes met hers, checking his pupils.

She ran through the usual questions. Did he have double

vision? Dizziness? No. Yes. Any other pain apart from the back of his head? No. Tingling anywhere? No. Headache? Nausea? Yes. Actually no. Did he know where he was? The park. Do you know what you are doing here? A pause. Running? What day of the week is it? Thursday. No, Wednesday. No, Thursday. What month is it? January. And so on.

He needed to be properly checked out but Meredith felt more confident that he wasn't about to drop dead on them. Richard began to sit up and Meredith was about to tell him not to, but actually, it would be good to see if he was okay upright. In another patient she might be less cavalier.

'Take it easy and stay seated,' she told him as she turned her attention to his wife. 'We should still get him to hospital. He was out for a while and I'm worried about internal bleeding.' Meredith studied the woman. 'Sandra, when you feel better maybe you could go and get your car and we could drive him to Northern? We can walk him slowly over to the car park.'

But Richard interrupted as he slowly got to his feet. 'I want to know what the hell happened? Did someone hit me?' He reached out to steady himself on a nearby tree.

He looked from his wife to Gracie and then back to his wife. Sandra's guilty expression gave her away.

'You did this?' He regarded her with disbelief. 'You bloody hit me?' Sandra flinched. 'Why? Why would you do that?' He loomed over her and Sandra scrambled to her feet while Meredith stepped in between them.

'Come on, Richard, we need to get you to hospital. I think we'll just walk you over to the car park and get one of the dog walkers to drive you. It'll be quicker.'

But he ignored her.

'You hit me on the head? Why?' He felt for the back of his scalp again. 'What the hell were you thinking? Were you trying to kill me?'

'I'm sorry, Richard,' Sandra stammered. 'I'm so sorry, Richard.

I didn't mean—'

'So why would you hurt me?'

Sandra kept stepping backwards and Richard kept moving closer.

Meredith held out her hand and pulled at Richard's T-shirt. 'Stop it,' she ordered and he finally did so, looking around, outrage across his features. 'Enough, Richard.' She motioned to Gracie. 'Take Sandra home. Use the fire trail. Go back to her house and I'll call you later. I'll deal with this.'

But as they walked away, Richard staggered across the clearing to follow them.

'You're a bloody menace. You should be locked up.' He made an attempt to lurch for her and Meredith darted to hold him back.

'Stop it,' Meredith said, with such authority that Richard did exactly that, surprise at that or over him being hit by his wife, writ across his face. 'Leave her alone, Richard, for god's sake.'

'She hurt me.' He spoke almost petulantly. 'She could have killed me.'

'And what are you going to do? Hurt her back? Talk to her later. Right now you need to remain calm. We don't want your blood pressure going up.'

Gracie and Sandra were hovering a little way along the path.

'Go,' Meredith instructed them again. 'I'll call you later.'

Gracie nodded, taking Sandra by the arm and guiding her away.

'Stupid bloody bitch,' Richard called after her and Meredith heard Sandra's small sob in response. When they'd disappeared into the thick of the trees, Meredith looked at Richard who was a pitiful sight, muddy and dishevelled and red-faced.

'Have you calmed down?'

Richard made a dismissive grunt.

'Do you feel okay to walk over to the car park and I'll call an Uber from there? Got your phone?'

He patted at his pockets then scanned the area. 'Must have dropped it. Let me have a look around.'

'You've got a significant head injury, Richard, and you need to go to the hospital. Leave your phone, it doesn't matter.'

But he waved her away. 'Just go. I'll get an Uber when I find it.'

Meredith felt a fresh surge of anger for this arrogant, unpleasant man.

'Just … sit and rest for a moment.' She motioned to a boulder. 'I'll look for your phone. But if I can't find it in five minutes, we're going. You need to get to the hospital.'

Chapter 53

GRACIE

Thursday, 30 January 2025

Gracie and Sandra walked along the fire trail and then took the back way home and parted at the entrance to Sandra's garage at the laneway. It was around 7.30 by then and the clouds were heavy and darkening in the sky, the earlier sunshine lost underneath them, rain threatening again.

'She will make sure he gets to the hospital, won't she?' Sandra said for what felt like the millionth time and Gracie reassured her that yes, of course, Meredith was a doctor. She'd make sure everything was okay. But still she looked doubtful.

'Stay here until you hear from Meredith. She'll come and be with you when she's sorted Richard out. You won't be alone for long.'

'He was so angry,' she said. 'Will it be okay?'

'He's not going to do anything to you. We won't let him.'

Sandra nodded but still made no move to go in through the garage door. She looked down at her hand and Gracie saw she was still holding the rock she'd used to hit Richard.

'You need to get rid of that,' Gracie said. 'Hide it in your garden somewhere, maybe?'

The other woman nodded but Gracie wasn't sure she had even heard what she'd said.

'You have to hide it, Sandra. Promise me.'

This time Sandra looked up and nodded.

'You know you saved me,' Gracie said. 'Just keep reminding yourself of that. You saved me from Richard and for that I'll always be grateful. And if Richard goes to the police or something, that's what I'll tell them because it's the truth. He was hurting me. You stopped him. Simple.'

Sandra nodded and then finally turned away. Gracie watched her push open the door next to the wide garage roller and then after it was closed behind her, heard the sound of a bolt being put in place. Gracie wondered if she would go straight to the front door and do the same. Deadbolt herself into her house so that Richard couldn't get in. Even though Sandra was still apparently concerned about her husband. Concerned and yet frightened. Gracie couldn't understand.

In hindsight Gracie knew she should have stayed with her or at least gone straight home. But it was nagging at her. What if Richard was hurting Meredith? What if she was fighting him off but had no one to save her? The fear and not knowing felt like a tight knot in her stomach and Gracie knew she had to go back to the Gully. To check. To make sure Meredith was okay.

Chapter 54

MEREDITH

Thursday, 30 January 2025

There was no sign of Richard's phone anywhere. Meredith stood up and looked along the pathway.

'You definitely had it with you?'

'Yeah,' he said.

'Well, you can check your Find My Phone when you're home. Or Sandra can.'

He gave a grunt that was neither a yes nor a no.

'Let me check your pulse again,' Meredith said when she'd returned to the clearing.

His arm rose and she took it, checked it. It was fine. Normal and steady.

'It's just a bad bump. I'll be okay. Go. I'll get myself home.'

'I don't think that's a good idea. Let's walk to the car park. Just look up again, into the light.'

He waved her away irritably. 'Stop it. I'm fine. Look, just piss off would you, Meredith. None of this involves you.' He frowned. 'Why are you even here?'

'I'm here because I care about your wife and Gracie. Because apparently you can't be trusted not to hurt either of them. And now I want to make sure you don't hurt yourself.'

He shot her an icy glare. 'Says the woman who assaulted me.'

Meredith gave a dry laugh. 'I didn't assault you. As you well know.'

He studied her. 'What exactly do you want from me, Dr Edwards? Because for someone who apparently wants nothing to do with me, you always seem to be on the periphery of my life somewhere. Here at the park, having late-night chats with my wife, hovering around.' He paused. 'Making yourself known.'

'We're neighbours, I'm friends with your wife. It's coincidental.'

'It's funny you never actually told me you lived on our street.' He straightened a little. 'I wonder what the board would make of that. First you become fixated, you move onto my street, befriend my wife, and then you assault me.' There was a slight smirk on his face. 'And now this. Perhaps you assaulted me here. Perhaps you were the one who thumped me on the back of my head.'

Meredith held his stare a moment. 'I'm here because you've been harassing Gracie and I wanted to make sure she was okay. I know about the visits to her window at night; how you've been coming down here, following her.'

'Following her?' He almost laughed the words out. 'Christ, she's a bloody child. I have no interest in young girls.'

'She's nineteen.'

'Exactly.' He shook his head. 'I don't like girls. I like women. Straight women,' he clarified pointedly, his tone haughty.

'You assaulted Gracie today.'

He looked predictably outraged at that. 'A misunderstanding. You people,' he muttered. 'So quick to make assumptions.'

Meredith walked to the edge of the creek and looked down the bank.

'You must have dropped your phone somewhere else.'

He made a grunting noise. 'I'll buy another one.'

Meredith looked across the dank-looking water, churned up by the storm the night before. She knew she should go home. Let him sort out the mess he'd made. She would be there for Sandra later and ensure Gracie spoke to her parents about what happened and encourage her to go to the police about the assault. They would explain what happened to Richard this morning and the circumstances which led to it. Everyone would be fine and Richard would hopefully move on with his life – elsewhere. Meredith might still see him in the Northern corridors but they would look straight through each other. Pretend neither one existed.

She began to walk towards the path and then stopped and turned, remembering what she wanted to ask him. If she didn't now, there might not be another chance.

'Can I ask you something, Richard? About my father.'

He regarded her, only momentarily confused. 'Go on.'

'Were you the student who put in a complaint against him after the prank went wrong?'

There was a moment's pause. 'The student he assaulted? No, that was Harrison Parker. He's over in New York now, at Mount Sinai's cardiology unit. So presumably no lasting damage from your father's assault.'

Meredith bristled. 'It wasn't an assault. He provoked my father.'

'You think a student deserves to be punched by a teacher?'

'It wasn't a punch. My father was defending himself. I know what those students did to him. The jibes and complaints and undermining. How they cheated. And pressured him into adjusting their assessment results.'

'Did you know he broke into their rooms and tried to find evidence?' A low chuckle. 'He really was his own worst enemy.'

'You were one of them, though, weren't you? One of the students involved?'

'Your father had some very serious allegations laid at him. I don't think you can compare that to any youthful exuberance by his students. He should never have been teaching.'

290

'Well, thanks to you and your friends, he wasn't able to anymore, so well done for that.'

'That had nothing to do with us,' Richard said, dismissively. 'Your father made the choice to step out on to that train track. He was the one who tried to kill himself. The university couldn't have someone like that on staff.'

Meredith stared at Richard, confused.

'Oh dear,' Richard said and pursed his lips. 'You didn't know about that?'

'It was an accident. Dad fainted. His blood pressure was low from the medication he was on. He was too close to the edge.'

Richard made a scoffing noise. 'I'm sure that's what he told you at the time to protect you. But you're not a child anymore. I'm sure you can handle the truth.'

Meredith recalled everything she had been told about her father's accident. That her father had fainted onto the train track at Bondi Junction and was pulled to safety by a pregnant woman. It had made the newspapers. The woman feted for her heroism.

'It was an accident. He would never have tried to … kill himself.'

Richard looked across towards the water. Meredith saw it then. Sympathy. A brief moment of something other than his usual brittle, arrogant shell. A tiny glimmer of humanity.

'Were you there? Did you see something?'

His expression hardened again. His humanity extinguished.

'Richard.' She almost barked his name. 'Were you there?'

He let out a long sigh. 'Yes, I was there,' he said finally.

'And?'

'I'd seen your father in line for a ticket but I ignored him. Then when I was waiting for the train he came up to me and started saying what a disappointment I was.' Richard rolled his eyes. 'He gave me a big lecture about expecting more from me and how I needed to distance myself from the group of other students who'd been causing all the trouble that year.'

He paused and Meredith waited for the rest. 'Go on,' she said.

'What else?'

'That was all. He said that I had a bright future ahead of me and I was doing myself a disservice associating with them.' He paused. 'And then he turned and went to the other end of the platform.'

'That's it?'

Richard nodded. 'That's it.'

'And then?'

He shrugged. 'He fell on the tracks. I mean, I didn't know it was him in that moment but there was a commotion down the end and screaming and people rushing over.' Richard shook his head. 'A terrible commotion. Someone called out for a doctor and, well, I wasn't a doctor yet, but I knew enough so I went over. I didn't even realise it was him at first. But then I saw. He was lying on the ground. A woman had dragged him from the tracks onto the platform and he was sort of lying there, moaning. He'd broken his wrist. The woman was heavily pregnant, I don't know how she managed it. She must have climbed down onto the tracks herself, pulled him up by sheer force.

'I checked him over. Then checked her. People seemed to think he'd possibly had a heart attack, but he didn't give any indication of that. He was fine, apart from the wrist. She was too. The station attendant got everyone else to step away so I could listen to his pulse and do my checks.' Richard paused. 'I don't think anyone else heard what he said to me.'

'What did he say?'

'A train had arrived in the station by that point. The train your father would have been hit by if he hadn't been pulled from the tracks.' A pause. 'He told me he wished it had hit him.'

'No, he didn't.'

'I'm afraid he did. Then the ambulance arrived. They asked him what had happened and he confirmed that he'd felt faint, that he'd been feeling unwell all day. One of the paramedics looked to me for confirmation and I said, yes, that was right and then he was put on a stretcher and taken away. I didn't see him again.'

'Why didn't you tell anyone?'

'It wasn't my place.'

'He might have got help if you had. Proper help.'

'Psychiatric?' Richard made a scoffing noise. 'He'd have been held involuntarily on a horrific secure ward. It wouldn't have helped him. He'd have been tarnished.'

'Tarnished?' Meredith frowned. 'Because he was ill?'

'This was the late Eighties, Meredith. It wasn't like today. People didn't talk about mental illness in the same way as we do now. Not even doctors. It was taboo. Utterly taboo.'

Meredith thought back to the November it happened. She could still remember the date: 15 November 1988. She had been eleven years old and it had been just a few weeks until the official start of summer. A few weekends later her old school had held its end-of-year fete and that's when she'd found Angela and Olivia.

'That would have been better than what happened,' she replied. 'After that day my father never went out again.'

Richard looked confused. 'What do you mean?'

'He never went out again,' she repeated. 'He stayed at home.'

'He was agoraphobic?'

She nodded. 'You were the last person to see him out in the world.'

Richard was still sitting on the rock, his arms folded across his chest. He looked better than he had done even five minutes ago; his pallor good, his gaze steady. She began to walk down the path back towards the oval and then stopped and turned back.

'You really should get checked out.'

'I'm fine,' he said, waving her away with his hand. 'I'll go to the medical centre later.'

'I really shouldn't leave you alone.'

He slowly got to his feet and began to scan the clearing again, still searching for his phone.

'I'll have another look for my phone and then I'll head home.' He looked across at her and then, his tone sharp and imperious

293

again, said, 'For god's sake, woman, leave me be, I'm fine.'

Meredith watched Richard for a few moments as he began poking around in the undergrowth with a stick, then, only a little reluctantly, turned away.

As she stepped from the cool of the Gully path into the open air of the park, she grabbed Gracie's water bottle and headed across the grass towards the car park and the main road.

Chapter 55

GRACIE

Thursday, 30 January 2025

Returning the way she'd come, Gracie ran quickly down the back streets, crossing the road at the turn and entering the fire trail and keeping her pace brisk as she travelled back down the hill.

When she got to the bottom and as she began walking the little way to the other path, she slowed down, ensuring she remained hidden by the shrubs and bushes.

Richard was sitting on a rock and Meredith stood opposite him, talking quietly about something Gracie couldn't quite catch. Having some kind of weirdly normal conversation from the looks of it. A tiny fairy wren sat on a spindly branch a few metres away and Gracie willed it not to move and cause either of them to turn and see her.

She moved sideways through the scrub to where it was thicker coverage and then closer, until she could pick up on their words. Something about Meredith's father, something Richard had seen. Gracie strained to hear but only caught every second or third word. Meredith moved closer and bent down, checking Richard over again, vitals, pulse, asking him to tip his head so she could check the wound. Gracie bristled as Meredith stepped closer to see. She wanted to call out, 'Stay away, get away,' but instead she kept watching, poised to leap from her hiding spot if Meredith needed her.

There was discussion about his injury. Meredith wanted Richard to go with her and get checked out but he didn't want to. He wanted to have another look for his phone. Meredith looked irritated but eventually gave up trying to convince him and left, passing just a few centimetres from Gracie's hiding spot. Gracie wanted to call out and say, 'Hey, I'm here' and walk back home with her, but then something caught her eye. A flash of metal in her peripheral vision. A phone. Richard's phone, presumably. Halfway down the slope to the water's edge. He'd never see it from where he was standing.

Richard had stood up and was now slowly walking down the path, head down, scanning for the device, poking at the ground with a stick. His head was sticky with dried blood and Gracie gave a shiver, remembering the heft of him, the fear, and then the confusion she'd felt when he'd fallen, a dead weight, onto her. Knocked out just before …

What would he have done?

That's when she felt the bubble of panic and knew she needed to get out of there. She had to be away from him. Away from the trees and the shrubs and the dark and the Gully. Away from Richard Wellington.

Gracie was about fifty metres up the fire trail when she heard the desperate cry of pain and spun around. It came again, a plaintive, 'Help me!'

She froze. Then there was another one, even more pitiful, like a wounded animal. 'Please help!'

Gracie didn't move. It could be a trap. It could be a terrible mistake.

'Help me! Help please,' Richard called out again. 'Someone!'

This time Gracie found herself turning, against all her better instincts. She took a few steps then listened but there was no more sound.

She should go back and check. She didn't want to but she should. He might be dying.

She didn't want that on her conscience.

Gracie began walking back along the now familiar path, all senses alert to the possibility that she could be walking into a set-up. Then there was a splash; the sound of something or someone in the creek. She moved from the thick of the forest to the clearing and then over to the edge of the slope that fell down towards the water. That's when she saw him.

It was kind of comical, kind of sad.

An old man floundering in deep water, trying to get himself upright after presumably slipping down the slick muddy drop. He must have seen his phone and tried to reach it, but stumbled and fallen. And now Richard Wellington was stuck and couldn't get out of the water.

'Gracie,' he called out, seeing her. His face was desperate and panicked. 'Help me, Gracie, I'm stuck. I've done something to my ankle and I can't move. I can't pull my foot from the mud. It's drawing me down and I'm getting out of my depth. I can't stay upright.'

Gracie studied her neighbour for a few moments, wondering briefly whether there was any way she could help him without going near him. And then the random thought: she'd never seen the creek this deep.

'Oh, come on,' he said. 'Bloody help me, would you? The mud's too thick, I need help. I think it's a fracture and the mud's literally sucked both my fucking legs in.'

Gracie knew she would help him but she decided there was no rush. She could afford to play with him, to make him suffer a little first.

'Why should I?' she said.

A series of emotions crossed his features one after another: confusion, embarrassment, then a sort of recognition and understanding amid the obvious pain he was in.

'Give me one good reason why I should help you.'

'I'm sorry,' he almost shouted. 'I'm really, very sorry for everything.' He winced, the pain obviously intense. 'But Gracie, please. Can you pull me out? Or, I don't know, get some help, call someone. Please. I'm begging you. This water is getting higher and I'm sinking down. It's going to cover me soon.'

Gracie stared at Richard for a beat and then rolled her eyes and began to carefully manoeuvre herself to the very edge of the slope. It was even slicker than it looked from a distance. The slope had eroded badly with the storm and she needed to be careful in case she also slipped and injured herself. Her new trainers might not be up to the job.

Richard made a sort of huffing noise and began trying to extricate himself again before giving another groan of pain and briefly slipping under the water. He gave a cry as he came up for air, gasping with panic.

'Please, Gracie, help me, I'm sinking more, every time I move.'

'Okay, hang on. Let me think.' By that stage she wasn't being sadistic; she honestly couldn't work out how to get him out.

'Use your phone. Call someone. Triple zero,' he said, his voice more urgent now.

'I can't. It's run out of battery.'

'Go into the park, find someone. Please – just ask anyone.'

'I don't think you've got time. Hang on. I'll try and get you out first.'

She scanned her surroundings looking to see if there was a stick or tree branch she could pass down to him.

'I need to find a branch,' she called. 'I'll be back in a sec.'

'No, don't leave.' His tone was urgent. 'Just pull me. Reach out. Please.'

'I can't get close enough. I'll just fall in and get stuck too. Sorry,' she added automatically. 'But I'll be back.'

'Don't go, Gracie, please. Just come to the edge, reach for my hand.'

Ignoring him, she searched the vicinity but there was nothing heavy or large enough nearby, so she retraced her steps back along the fire trail path which was strewn with fallen branches. But every one of them seemed to crumble under her touch, all of them too rotten or wet or too flimsy to be of use.

There was a fork in the path and she went left, where the trees weren't too dense but here there was nothing so she went in the other direction, going along a path she'd never been down before that ran parallel to the Gully. Her breath was coming quick and fast now; she was starting to panic that she wouldn't find anything in time and even if she did, she might not figure her way out. Then she spotted one. Finally. A branch that looked sturdy enough to work, but not so heavy she couldn't drag it back to the creek.

But as she lifted it, it broke in two. It had been softened by rain or whatever creature eats wood. Termites, most likely.

'Shit,' she muttered.

She backtracked and found the main path again, feeling a surge of relief that she wasn't lost, and then tried along a different stretch. She finally found a branch that was still half hanging from the lower part of the trunk and let out a satisfied murmur. It only needed a little pulling and pushing for the last part of it to splinter off and come loose. Then she half ran as she dragged the maybe three-metre-long branch behind her, back towards the water.

When she finally got to the clearing and the edge of the Gully beyond it, she stopped in her tracks and let out a cry of shock. Richard was face-down in the shallows, his hands floating on the surface of the water.

He'd freed his feet and made it to the water's edge but then somehow collapsed. Dropping the branch Gracie scrambled down the bank but as she crouched to drop down, there was a sharp grip of a hand on her shoulder for the third time that morning.

Another hand on her left side pulled her back up the embankment.

'Don't,' Meredith said. 'Leave him. He's gone.'

'What? We need to get him out.'

Gracie made another attempt but Meredith yanked at her this time, her expression pained. Apologetic.

'Gracie. There aren't any bubbles.'

'I've got a branch.' She gestured to it. 'We can use it and get him out. You can do CPR.'

'I already checked.'

That's when Gracie saw the mud smeared across every bit of Meredith. Grey streaks of it, watery and streaking down her legs, thicker around her bare feet.

'I tried but I was too late.' Her words were gentle and low as if that would better help Gracie understand. 'Richard's dead.'

'He was just looking for his phone.' Gracie's eyes returned to Richard's prone body, which looked horrific now, the way his T-shirt billowed from him with the water. 'I should have just told him where it was when I saw it. I should have got it for him.'

'It's not your fault. It's an awful accident.'

'But he was fine. I was just talking to him.' Gracie took a step closer to the edge and Meredith's hands went to her again, then dropped when she saw Gracie wasn't going anywhere. 'He hurt his ankle. He'd hurt it so he couldn't pull his leg out and I went to get something to help get him out.' Her brain couldn't compute what had happened. How someone could be there one minute, gone the next. 'I don't understand.'

'It could have been the head trauma. It could have caused a blood clot.'

'Was he like this when you got here?'

She nodded.

'Not breathing?' Gracie's eyes searched Meredith's. 'And you checked?'

'I checked. I tried to get him out but I couldn't so I … well, I checked everything but there was no sign of life and I couldn't pull him out and up the embankment. He's too heavy.'

'But I was only gone a few minutes.' Had it been longer? Gracie tried to work it out, replaying her movements, searching for a branch and then finally finding one. She couldn't have been longer than five minutes, surely. Six at the most.

Meredith reached out to grab her hand.

'I'm sorry, but he's gone and we need to go.' Her voice was steady but insistent. 'We have to get out of here.'

'What?'

'No one can see us here, Gracie.'

'But we need to call an ambulance. We need to … we need to tell someone. Get him out. Just … check.'

'If we do that then the police will want to know why we're here and then we'll have to explain everything. We'll have to explain Sandra, what she did. What happened. He probably died from being struck by her. A delayed bleed on the brain.'

'No. We can just say we found him like this. They don't need to know anything else.'

Meredith shakes her head. 'We can't.'

'But we can't leave him here, in the water.'

But she just nodded. *We can. We have to*, her eyes seemed to say.

'Please, Gracie, we have to go. Now.'

The creek was flat and a dull brown. Gracie tried to imagine what it would be like to float in it. This boggy, awful grave.

'This is wrong. It's all wrong. We can't do this.'

'I know, but there's nothing we can do to help. It'll be okay.' Meredith reached out her hand to guide Gracie. 'Come on, let's go.' She paused. 'It's going to be okay.'

Gracie finally nodded. Meredith picked up her trainers and gave them to Gracie to hold and then lifted the branch with her other hand and pulled it beside her as they moved from the clearing. She dropped it after a few metres.

'How long until someone finds him?' Gracie asked when they were halfway up the fire trail.

'Not long. It's quieter than usual this morning. The rain's kept a lot of people at home. But they'll be out again soon.'

When they got to the top of the trail, Meredith stopped abruptly. 'I can't go out like this.' She gestured to her muddy legs and feet and then scanned the area as if something might miraculously appear to help her clean herself. 'I put your water bottle down somewhere.'

She walked a few steps and then went around the back of a scrubby-looking shrub and emerged with the pink bottle in her hand. Gracie watched as Meredith used it sparingly to sluice the mud from her arms and legs. There wasn't enough to thoroughly clean her but there was maybe just enough so that she didn't look like some creature from a lagoon. So that people passing wouldn't notice and wonder what had happened to them.

Gracie's stomach gave a small lurch.

What had happened to them?

They were both involved in Richard's death. From now on, everything Gracie did, every day she lived through would be tarnished by the memory of knowing she had been involved in what happened here today.

A faint buzzing rang in her ears. An adrenaline-fuelled panic that had been bubbling away since she first crossed paths with Richard.

How would she live with this?

Meredith caught Gracie's eye. She must have sensed her panic because something shifted in her expression.

'It's going to be okay, Gracie. This was just a terrible accident but it's nothing to do with you. This was between Sandra and Richard. You were only peripherally involved and there was nothing you could have done to change what happened. He had a head injury and it would likely have killed him even if the ambulance had got here in time.'

Gracie nodded although she didn't believe what Meredith was saying.

'You should go home now. I'll sort this. Take a right at the top, start running again. Go straight home. Try not to be seen. I'll go to Sandra. Explain. Make sure she's okay.'

'No, I'll stay with you. I'll help. It's fine,' Gracie said automatically.

'I'll be okay. Please, just go.' Another reassuring half smile. 'Go. It's going to be okay.'

And then, as if some kind of celestial force heard their predicament and wanted to help, it began to rain. At first it was that lazy summer rain, just a few fat drops here and there, then in a sudden, violent woosh that often seems to happen in a Sydney summer, it turned into a downpour. Water beat at the tops of the tree canopy and Gracie's nose filled with the earthy scent of wet vegetation.

Meredith stepped from the relative shelter of where they were standing, into an open clearing. She tipped her head back, spreading out her hands as the rain pummelled down on her and in seconds the mud streaking her limbs and workout clothes and trainers had run clear.

Gracie wasn't muddy like Meredith, but she still placed her running belt containing her dead phone and earbuds on a rock where they would remain dry and stepped into the clearing.

Any other time Gracie might have laughed and whooped with joy but instead she began to shiver. It wasn't even cold.

'You need to get home. Have a shower, something sweet to eat for the shock,' Meredith instructed as she picked up the water bottle and Gracie picked up her belt. 'If you need to talk, send me a WhatsApp.'

Gracie nodded, understanding immediately. WhatsApp was encrypted.

'Go on,' she said. A brief, reassuring nod. 'You go first. I'll be fine.'

Gracie took a few steps and then looked back at her neighbour.

'There was definitely no chance,' she said, searching Meredith's face. 'For Richard?'

Meredith gave a small shake of her head. 'No chance. He was already gone.'

Gracie nodded and then began to walk. She glanced back and saw Meredith was still holding her drink bottle. Never mind. Gracie didn't want to see it again after today. It would only remind her of this terrible morning.

Chapter 56

LIV

Thursday, 20 February 2025

Gracie is looking at her mum, her eyes filled with tears.

'It's not your fault,' Liv says, pulling Gracie to her. 'It's not your fault. It's not either of your faults.'

Meredith is standing over by the sliding glass doors that lead out to the balcony.

'There was nothing either of you could have done. It was a terrible, awful accident.'

'We should have called the ambulance as soon as it happened. As soon as Sandra hit him,' Meredith says, flatly.

'The outcome would have likely been the same. You know that,' Liv says.

Meredith shrugs. 'He'd have had a dignified death. Not the ugly one he ended up with.'

Liv doesn't understand how Meredith can have any sympathy for Richard Wellington after all he put her through and all he did to Gracie.

'He doesn't deserve any of your guilt.' Liv squeezes Gracie a little tighter. 'Or any of our sympathy. He was an awful man and he died the way he lived.'

Andy reaches to put his hand on Gracie's arm. 'This wasn't your fault. Richard didn't deserve to die but he didn't do anything to help himself. He was a monster.' He looks towards Meredith. 'And you all did what you needed to survive him.'

The next morning, Liv finds Andy already in the kitchen, on his laptop, and kisses him good morning before going to make a coffee.

'Did you sleep?' he asks.

She nods. 'Is Gracie up?'

'Still sleeping.' He glances up. 'She'll be okay. She just needs to process everything and rest.'

She slots a capsule into the machine. 'What are you doing?'

'Working on your dad's film. Going through old archival material.'

The coffee machine whirrs for a few seconds and Liv adds a little milk before taking it over to the dining table. Andy quickly snaps shuts the laptop and Liv pretends not to notice.

'Shall we go out for an early swim?' he says, his tone bright. 'Head over to Balmoral and get some brekkie? It's a beautiful morning.'

She looks at him confused. 'It's Friday, Andy. I've got work.'

'Oh yeah.' He laughs. 'Sorry. I've lost track of time.'

She stares at her husband a moment. 'You okay?'

He shifts slightly and Liv notices the way his hand rests on his laptop and her stomach lilts.

'What is it? Has something happened with the investigation?'

'No, no, nothing like that.'

But his expression tells her otherwise.

'Andy. What? You're worrying me.'

'It's okay, it's got nothing to do with what's happened.' He is watching her with a strange expression on his face. 'But I just

306

came across a couple of recordings I hadn't seen before, from your dad's archives.' Andy opens up the laptop and brings it to life. The screen is filled with a black-and-white clip that's paused mid-movement. 'I'm not sure you should see this. I'm not even sure what it is.'

'Don't be silly. Let me see.'

Liv reaches over Andy and taps at the laptop and the clip starts up again.

Pete is in what looks like a public park. It's shot in colour cine film – Liv recognises that immediately because Pete used his cinecamera to record family clips throughout her childhood.

There's a flicker of darkness and her dad moves towards the camera as if adjusting something and then he's back in shot, laughing and beckoning for someone at the side to come into camera range. His hand reaches out and a moment later, a young, dark-haired, very beautiful and very pregnant woman appears, smiling shyly, glancing every so often at the camera as she stands there, clearly not sure what to do with herself.

Then Pete lifts her arm and twirls her around and they begin to dance, the woman smiling shyly as she laughs. Then Pete moves in and kisses the woman on the lips and she is clearly embarrassed, her eyes darting towards the camera. They kiss again, longer this time and then the clip ends.

Liv blinks at computer screen.

'It's marked as being filmed in September 1976.'

Liv does the sums. Eighteen months before she was born. And this woman is absolutely not her own mother.

'There's something else.' Andy's hands move across the keyboard and another image, in freeze frame, fills the laptop screen: her parents looking to camera. He looks at her, his expression apprehensive. 'I found this at the same time but I haven't watched it. The file title is 'For Liv' so I didn't think I should. It was recorded about eight months ago.'

She frowns. 'What it is?'

'I've no idea.' He stands and motions for her to sit, passing her his earphones. 'I think you should watch it first, whatever it is.'

Liv looks at him alarmed. 'No, I don't want to.'

The possibilities of what this recording could be appear in her mind's eye: some kind of living will or a recorded explanation of what they want their funerals to be or their end-of-life care? Or will it be something more tender – a message for Liv to watch when they are gone? Something that will have her weeping in the first minutes?

Andy is watching her with concern. 'Do you want me to look at it first?' he asks.

'Yes,' she says automatically, then, 'no, no, it's fine. I'll watch it.'

Liv stares at the image on the laptop screen. Her mum is wearing her emerald green top and her hair is freshly done, a soft wave framing her face and carefully applied lipstick. Her father looks as he always does – a collared blue shirt, his white hair trimmed neatly. They are sitting side by side in the living room on the sofa by the window. The file's date is 5 June, so around eight months ago, near the time of her dad's Alzheimer's diagnosis and she can tell: her father has that slightly dazed look which has become so familiar over the past year.

'I'll leave you to it,' Andy says and leaves, closing the door softly behind him.

Liv takes a deep breath and presses play.

'Hello, darling,' her mother says to camera, the kind of smile on her face that Liv has seen many times before on camera, when she is greeting an interviewer or the viewers of *Play School*. Professional, glossy, delighted to be here with you. Her father's crooked smile is a bit less certain and Liv has the urge to somehow reach through the screen and give her sweet old dad a hug.

'This probably seems a bit over the top and dramatic,' her mum begins. 'So perfectly in keeping with something we'd do.' She lets out a small laugh. 'But really, we wanted to make this recording so it was all official and here for you when we're unable to tell you ourselves. Before we're totally gaga.' She glances at Pete. 'And we've talked about doing this a lot over the years, haven't we?'

'We have,' her dad says, shifting slightly, clearly far less at home than Angela in front of the camera's lens rather than behind it.

'But we wanted to set the record straight. We wanted you to know everything just in case we ever get to the stage where we couldn't tell you in person.' A brief pause. 'And this seemed like as good a time as any, didn't it?'

There is a small grunt of agreement from Pete.

'Livvie, sweetheart, we wanted to talk to you about something we really ought to have spoken to you about years ago.' Angela has a slightly pained smile on her face now.

There's a long pause. Liv's dad's gaze remains looking down, as if he's found a spot on the floor just in front of him to focus on.

'I really hope that what we're going to tell you won't upset you too much and that you find it in your heart to forgive us and understand,' she says, glancing once again to Pete. 'We just want you to know that we had reasons for doing what we did.' She nudges Pete gently and he looks up towards the camera. 'We had reasons, didn't we, darling?'

'Yes,' he says, vaguely. 'Reasons, yes.'

Chapter 57

LIV
Friday, 21 February 2025

Angela draws in a deep breath and takes a moment to compose herself.

'The decisions your father and I made years ago aren't necessarily the ones we'd choose now. And that's not to excuse any of them but to perhaps help you understand that it was a … different time.' Another glance at Pete. 'People weren't as open about their feelings. We weren't as … open as your generation is to different types of families, you know … what's the word?' She looks at Pete who doesn't respond and there is a moment of silence as she tries to remember before recognition suddenly lights up her face. 'Blended,' she says, triumphantly.

'Blended,' he repeats, nodding.

'It wasn't a thing, having these blended families, darling. We thought we were so much more liberated than our parents but there were still certain things that we didn't know how to handle.'

Liv's mum falls silent for a moment, clearly finding it difficult to say whatever it is they're wanting to.

'We had a difficult time in our marriage in the mid-Seventies,' she says finally. 'Well, not difficult.' She turns to Pete. 'How would you describe that time? The mid-Seventies?'

'Well, we were very busy. We travelled a lot and worked a lot.'

'We were apart a lot too.'

Pete nods.

'And there was … bad behaviour on both sides,' her mum says.

'Affairs,' Pete says bluntly.

Angela nods. 'Affairs. Indeed. But we were very young. Only nineteen and twenty-four when we got married. Probably far too young. And Livvie, darling, you hadn't come along yet and we were very, very bohemian. We didn't want to be like other boring married couples.' Her hand gives a theatrical gesture. 'Darling, we were … artists.'

Pete gives a grunt of acknowledgement.

'Anyway, your father had an affair with a local woman,' Angela says in a quick flurry of words. 'Zara Edwards.'

Liv sits up suddenly.

'I think half the attraction was that Zara Edwards wasn't at all your usual kind of woman,' her mum says. 'She was quiet and sweet and had nothing to do with show business.'

'She was your best friend,' Pete says.

'Yes, she was.' Angela gives a sharp nod. 'At least you had good taste.' She shoots a knowing look to the camera. 'So your affair lasted … How long was it?'

'Not very long. A year?'

'Zara felt very guilty,' Angela explains to the camera. 'Her husband, Stephen, was a difficult man. An odd fish. But she loved him very much.' She pauses. 'I sometimes wonder if half the reason she had the affair was to get pregnant. They had been trying for a baby for a long time but it never happened. Zara assumed it was her fault.' Her lips purse. 'Women always assume it's their fault, don't they?'

There's a long pause and his gaze still firmly fixed on the floor ahead of him, Pete grabs Angela's hand and squeezes it tight. Later, Liv will wonder why it was only in this moment, when she saw her father clearly overcome with emotion – that the penny finally dropped.

Meredith. Of course, Meredith.

'So, Zara got pregnant with your father's baby,' Angela says, matter of fact. 'And we were all very grown-up about it, weren't we?'

Liv can see, for all her mum's acting training, Angela is finding it hard to suppress her emotions.

'Go on, Pete. You tell Livvie about what happened with the baby. This is your story to tell.'

Pete straightens a little but struggles to find the words.

'You wanted to end things with Zara when she found out she was pregnant,' Angela prompts. 'And she came to talk to you.'

'She said she would raise the baby with Stephen as their own,' Pete says finally. 'He knew I was the father but said he would be on the birth certificate. The baby would be his.'

'Meredith would be his,' Angela says.

'That Meredith would be his,' Pete agrees.

'So, darling, you see, you have a half-sister,' Angela says, looking back to the camera. She blinks rapidly and Liv can see that for once they're not what Angela called her actress tears. 'She's eighteen months older than you.'

'Eighteen months,' Pete echoes Angela.

'You got to meet her a few times after she was born, didn't you?' Angela asks and Pete nods. 'But after a bit, we understood they wanted to keep their distance. Then I got pregnant with you, darling, and life got so busy we just … well, we didn't forget but I suppose we all moved on.' She pauses. 'But then when you got older and I took you to the church playgroup, Zara and Meredith were there and although it was a bit awkward at first, you two just … found each other.' Angela smiles. 'Meredith loved you. Loved playing with you – bossing you around a bit, pretending she was your mother, you know, those sweet games little girls play. And you adored Meredith. Stuck to her like glue. It was very charming.'

'What was it Livvie called her?'

'Meddy.'

'That's right.' Pete nods. 'Meddy.'

'We continued like that for some time. Zara and I weren't exactly good friends but we would communicate. We wouldn't avoid each other. Then a year or so on, you joined the preschool attached to the playgroup. Meredith was already there but in an older group. I don't think she played with you quite as much but you were certainly aware of each other and Zara and I would sort of give each other this look when we'd see you together.'

'You weren't angry at her?' Pete says suddenly.

'Zara? For the affair?'

He nods.

'No, not by then. And I was never angry with the woman.' She gives her husband a wry look. 'Besides I got my own back, didn't I?'

Pete lets out a grunt.

'Alexander Masson.' Angela says the name with relish, then to the camera, with a more circumspect expression adds, 'Sorry, darling, I know you don't want to hear these things but I really was quite divine when I was younger and with your father behaving the way he behaved, it was only fair that I got to have the occasional dalliance with my leading men.'

'There wasn't any more funny business after Livvie was born,' Pete says.

But Angela's expression made it clear to Liv that this wasn't necessarily true.

'And then Zara became unwell,' Angela says. There is a brief pause. 'She was just thirty-two when she died. No age at all.'

Pete frowns. 'How old was Meredith?'

'Five. Poor child. No one should lose a parent that young. It does untold damage.' Angela clears her throat. 'Then you and Meredith continued to be at the same school until Meredith was

313

about eight or nine, and she went to St Mary's but we didn't see much of her even before then. I think there was a nanny for a while and Stephen was never around.' Angela gives the camera a brief smile. 'But then of course, she found us at the summer fair that year.

'That's when we decided to try again and see if Stephen would be open to you getting to know Meredith a bit.' Angela glances at Pete. 'But he wouldn't agree. We kept calling and even wrote him a letter. Do you remember you went round to talk to him and he wouldn't even answer the door?'

Pete nods. 'He wasn't an easy man.'

'He wasn't a well man. He'd been through a lot. He'd lost his wife and I think he lost his job at some point? Thank goodness Zara's inheritance meant they had enough money, but I still don't think Meredith should have remained there with him. He wasn't well. God knows what it was like for her.'

'Darling, he wouldn't allow it. You know that. We talked about it. Endlessly.'

Angela makes a dismissive sound. 'We should have pushed harder.'

'We did what we could. We tried.'

Angela looks into the camera again. 'So that's why Meredith began babysitting. We wanted to have a … connection to her. We wanted you girls to know each other and we also wanted to make sure she was … okay, I suppose. We explained a certain amount to Meredith – not everything obviously. Not the truth. But I told Meredith that Zara had been a very good friend of mine and that we had all spent time together when she and you were little. I told her that Zara had requested I keep an eye on her, which was the truth. And I explained that it would be better if we didn't tell her father – that he didn't much like me and she agreed to keep it a secret.'

'We should never have asked her to keep it a secret. Children can't be expected to keep secrets,' Pete says.

'Well, she did, for years. And besides, she wasn't a child. She was a teenager.'

'Yes, but she still told her father eventually.'

Angela gives a contrite shrug. 'Well, I don't regret it. You got to see your daughter and Livvie got to know her sister. Even if it did all go a little wrong at the end.' Angela glances at the camera, an almost guilty expression on her face. 'At least we tried.'

'At least we tried,' Pete agrees.

'We should have been more gentle after that whole fire business.'

Pete frowns. 'She nearly set fire to the studio. I think I was more than fair.'

'You were far too stern. You frightened the poor girl away!'

'I did nothing of the sort. I just told her she couldn't go around behaving like that. All my work was there.'

'It's true, the whole place was a tinder box because you never tidy up.'

'She left the fire drum unattended. In summer! This is Australia, for goodness sake. She could have set the whole house on fire.'

'Okay, calm down.' Angela rests her hand on Pete. 'I'm not sure we ever got the whole story in regard to that.' She glances to camera. 'Perhaps you'll fill us in one day, Livvie?

'Anyway, the point is, things came to a head when that happened. Meredith got very upset, perhaps rightly so, and when she went home it all came out. She told her father what had been going on, how she had been spending time at ours and presumably the various dramas between Livvie and her.' She cocks an eyebrow. 'And the next thing we knew, Stephen had issued us with a cease and desist!'

Pete shakes his head. 'It was absurd and legally totally unenforceable.'

'That wasn't the point. He wanted to send us a strong message—'

'Well, he managed that,' Pete mumbles.

'I think he wanted to show Meredith just how strongly he felt.'

'He managed that, too.'

Angela nods. 'Yes, he did.'

Both look defeated and sad.

'We tried reaching out over the years. We tried to check on him when Meredith went to boarding school.'

Pete nods.

'And we kept an eye on her from afar. We knew that she'd gone to Sydney University to study medicine. We followed her career as she got older. And you went to see Stephen a few times over the years, didn't you? To offer support and help.'

'But he always refused. Too proud.'

They lapse into silence again for a few moments, then Angela looks directly into the camera lens, her gaze watery.

'Livvie, I'm so sorry we never told you any of this.' Angela pauses. 'Please don't judge us too harshly. Don't judge your father too harshly.'

Once again, Angela reaches out for her husband's hand and he gives her a grateful nod.

'But I know his biggest regret is not getting to know Meredith properly. We should have tried harder to assure Stephen we had no intention of replacing him.' She glances at Pete. 'I know you think that too.'

'If I had my time again, I would have fought harder for her.'

'We both would have,' Angela says softly.

Chapter 58

LIV
Friday, 21 February 2025

That day Liv goes through the motions at work, barely conscious of what she is doing or who she is speaking to. The various pieces of the puzzle which have been scattered and not quite within her grasp until now have finally come together but she still has so many questions. So many feelings. So much grief and emotion.

Had Meredith known all this time that she was Liv's half-sister? Despite what her parents believe, did she know back in 1988 when she first approached Liv and her mum at the school fete?

After work Liv crosses the hospital campus to the main building and then takes the lift to the Orthopaedics floor. She is still in her physio clinic uniform so when she approaches the nurses' station and asks where she can find Dr Edwards, a nurse doesn't even hesitate before saying, 'She's been off. Back Monday, apparently.'

Liv had forgotten about Meredith's suspension, which she supposes has now been lifted in light of Richard Wellington's death being solved. The familiar pang of regret and guilt swirls in her guts.

Liv is not sure she will ever be able to admit to having sent those anonymous emails to the police but she will do her best to make amends to Meredith in other ways. She sends her a text:

We need to talk. Are you free tomorrow morning?

Andy and Gracie pick Liv up from the corner outside the clinic and they drive over to Angela and Pete's. When Andy is busy in the kitchen making pasta for them all, Liv sits with Gracie in the courtyard and explains what she has learnt about Meredith.

She is nervous to tell Gracie; aware that her daughter has been through so much over the past month and may not be ready for another seismic change in their lives. But Gracie takes the news with surprising maturity and understanding. She asks to see the video and Liv opens the file she now has saved on her phone and then passes it to Gracie. Then she leaves her daughter to watch it in private and goes inside to talk to Angela and Pete.

Liv has weighed up whether to talk to her parents about seeing the recording but she is aware now, more than ever, of time being finite. There may not be other opportunities.

Angela understands immediately what Liv is saying and while she is unable to verbally express this, Liv can see from her expression that she is relieved. Glad that the truth has been revealed.

She beckons for Liv to move closer and grasps her hand, smiling and cupping her daughter's cheek and nodding. Through teary vision, Liv turns to Pete who is sitting across from them and whose reaction is far harder to read. He is looking at her blankly, like he might not have understood anything she said, so she repeats it, more simply.

'Dad, I know Meredith is my sister and I'm really happy about it.'

A look of confusion and then his face visibly softens.

Liv gets up and crouches down in front of him and takes his hand and says, 'Would you like to see Meredith, Dad? Would you like to see your daughter?'

A little while later, they are sitting at the dining table by the window, eating. Liv looks out of the large window to where Meredith stood and watched them that summer nearly forty years ago.

'It's probably time I admitted that it was me who nearly set the studio on fire, Dad. Not Meredith.' She glances towards her father who is concentrating on spooning mouthfuls of spaghetti carbonara into his mouth and shows no sign of hearing her. 'I'd completely forgotten until I saw the recording you did.'

Angela's eyes widen.

'Was that also part of your bullying campaign?' Gracie asks tartly, then glances towards her grandmother. 'Did you know about that? How Mum and her friends basically bullied Meredith? They pretended to write her letters from a boy and set up a fake date to humiliate her.'

'In my defence—'

'Mum, there's no defence.'

'I was a stupid teenager and I was desperate to fit in,' Liv says, although she is aware this continues to be a flimsy argument. 'Having famous parents is really no fun when you're in high school, believe me.'

'Yeah, yeah, we know. Gran got her tits out in Broken Hill. Everyone thought Sam Neill was her actual lover. Most people would be proud of having such legendary parents, not use it as an excuse to be a bully.'

Liv sees her mum's expression, the twitch of amusement on Angela's lips.

'I know that doesn't excuse my behaviour, but that's the back-drop of me being so awful.' She gives a pained smile and sees Andy's faint nod of encouragement. 'Okay, let me explain.' She sighs. 'So one weekend after the incident with the fake date, you were both away in Melbourne and Meredith was staying over. I don't think she wanted to. Not after what I'd done. But you must have begged her. Anyway, I snuck out and the next morning when

I came back, Meredith threatened, quite rightly, to tell you guys. I knew you'd ground me if you found out and stop me from going to Jessica Colby's sixteenth birthday party the next weekend so I threw a fit and told Meredith all this horrible stuff about what I really thought of her. What everyone at school thought of her.' She swallows. 'Anyway, she went home and got all the letters I'd written to her over the years. You know, from back when we were pen pals after the fair? Anyway, she threw them at me and said I was a spoilt little madam and didn't know how lucky I was. She said she wanted nothing more to do with me and was going to tell that to you two.

'I threw a fit, of course. I got all her letters and being the ridiculous, dramatic fifteen-year-old I was, I tore them up into little bits and put them in the steel drum out in the courtyard and chucked in some lighter fuel and set them on fire. Except it was one of those blustery, hot days and the embers jumped to the studio.' She makes a face. 'I was such an idiot. Anyway, thank god, Meredith was still there and helped me put it out, otherwise the whole house might have burnt down.

'When you guys got home, she presumably took the blame for the scorch marks. I don't know why. I think I had disappeared to a friend's house by then. I never knew what happened to the half-burnt letters though. She must have taken them with her or maybe you guys picked them out of the drum and put them in a box?' She glances at Andy. 'That bit's weird, isn't it?'

Her husband shrugs, mild amusement still across his face. Angela is gesturing to Gracie with her good hand and Gracie automatically reaches for the iPad and brings up the app Angela is now occasionally using for communication.

They wait for Angela to tap the words onto the screen and then the disembodied voice, set to Australian English Female, speaks the words:

'Olivia Elliot you should be bloody ashamed of yourself.'

Chapter 59

LIV

Saturday, 22 February 2025

Meredith stares at the photo of her and Liv as little girls.

'When did you find out?' she asks finally.

'Two days ago.'

'And you had no idea before then?'

'None.'

There is a moment of silence and then Meredith puts the photo down on the table and looks across at Gracie.

'I'm sorry I lied to you,' she says and Gracie gives a slight shake of her head to protest this but doesn't speak. Instead she reaches across the table and her fingertips rest on Meredith's.

'I think I knew for sure when I was thirteen,' Meredith says finally, looking at Liv.

'How?'

'My dad gave hints over the years. Then the year after I met you at the fair, I found letters from your father to my mother from years before. Just little scraps of notes really, but they were dated so I eventually worked it out.'

'You didn't know at the time of the fair?'

'No, although I must have sensed there was some kind of connection. I knew our mothers had been friends and I vaguely remembered you from preschool. Then of course, I knew you'd been at my primary school and by then I was aware of who your parents were. Everyone knew them.'

'So when you started babysitting me, you had no idea that my dad was your biological father?'

Meredith shakes her head. 'To be honest I think I was more desperate for your mum to notice me than Pete.' She gives a shy smile. 'Because my mum had died, I suppose. I would fantasise about Angela adopting me.'

'Did your father know when you started babysitting?'

'Not at first. He wasn't very well at the time. I don't think he had much awareness of anything that was going on. That was when he had the breakdown.' There's another long pause. 'Things had happened at his work and he attempted to end his life, although I didn't know that at the time. But I knew he was unwell. He'd always struggled with depression but by the summer I met you at the school fair, things were bad. Very bad.'

'Did he get help?'

She shook her head. 'I don't think anyone really knew except me and I didn't really understand what was going on. I just knew that suddenly he was at home all the time and never went out. His whole life had been his work and the university and now that was … gone. He just withdrew. He'd spend days and days in his office at home. He told me he was doing research but I'm not sure he was at that stage.

'He didn't seem to sleep. He lost so much weight that summer I remember asking him if I should call the doctor back. I thought he might have cancer and was dying. I knew that was how my mother had died and I remembered how weak she'd been at the end. I was terrified he would die.'

'Did you ever tell anyone what was going on?'

'No. We'd had a housekeeper, a lovely woman called Elsie who would cook and clean for us but when Dad stopped going into the university, she stopped coming too. She would still come and check on me occasionally but I made sure she never actually came into the house and saw what a mess it was in. I'd tell her everything was okay.' She gives an awkward shrug. 'I knew how to cook the basics so I kept us fed. We ate a lot of eggs on toast. We had food deliveries from the deli. I paid the bills. We always had enough money, thank goodness.'

Understanding finally dawns on Liv.

'Is that why you came to our house that summer? Were you trying to let us know what was going on? That you needed our help because your dad was sick?'

Meredith gives a weak smile. 'The day of the fete I'd gone up to Angela because I thought she might be able to help. My father didn't have many friends but I knew that Angela and my mum had this connection so I decided she would be someone good to tell. But I just ... couldn't. So I decided to make friends with you. I thought that maybe if I told you, you would tell your parents.'

Tears prick in Liv's eyes. 'Oh Meredith, I'm so sorry.'

'It's okay. You weren't to know.' Meredith straightens in her seat. 'Dad began getting a bit better that autumn when I went back to school. He still had times when things became too much and he withdrew into his bedroom but for the most part he was ... okay. He had his quirks and things he could and couldn't do but he began working again – an old colleague asked him to co-author a paper and that sort of brought him back to life. He was never quite the same but he was never as bad as he had been that summer. He was still agoraphobic but he had good days as well as bad ones.'

'It must have been so difficult for you,' Gracie says softly, her hand still gripping Meredith's across the table.

'I managed.' Meredith smiles. 'Other children survive far worse.'

'I can't believe no one knew. Didn't your teachers realise

something was very wrong? Or your dad's colleagues?'

Meredith makes a face. 'My dad was intensely private. Pathologically. We never had people at the house, I was never allowed to bring friends over. Actually that's not true, he never said that explicitly, but I knew. I knew there were boundaries I could never cross. But he was a good dad.' Her face softens. 'Very gentle and very kind.'

'I'm glad,' Liv says, thinking back to how Stephen had been described by her parents in the recording and how they painted quite a different picture of him.

'He was terrified someone would decide that he wasn't capable of looking after me,' Meredith says, as if reading Liv's thoughts. 'I always got the feeling he was looking over his shoulder, that one day he'd be told he had to give me up. And I presume the person he was most scared of losing me to was your father. My biological father.'

'How did you explain being away from home, when you were at our house?'

'I told him I was with friends and he never asked for more details.'

'Did my parents ever tell you the truth? About my dad being your biological father?'

A sharp shake of her head. 'No, definitely not. Looking back I presume the whole babysitting thing was their way of reaching out and somehow including me or getting to know me?'

'I think so.'

Meredith smiles. 'I'm glad. I always loved the time I spent at yours.'

'Even though I was a monster?'

'You were just a kid.'

Liv feels the sting of guilt once more. She was a kid then, but what was her excuse a few weeks ago when she was doing all she could to push the police investigation towards Meredith?

'I found your old letters,' Liv says finally. 'I had forgotten what we did to you with that boy. Pretending to be him and sending you letters; setting you up to be humiliated at the café. It was an awful, spiteful thing to do. I'm so sorry.'

Meredith smiles. 'Believe me, that wasn't the worst thing that happened to me in high school. Do you remember Marie Hadley?'

'Vaguely.'

'She was my real tormentor. The reason I eventually left St Mary's for the last year.'

'What did she do?'

'What didn't she do.' Meredith lets out a sigh. 'It's a long story. Anyway, I eventually told Dad and that's why he moved me for year twelve.'

'I thought you left because of what happened with the fire.'

'Oh god, the fire.' Meredith lets out a laugh.

'You should never have taken the blame for that. God, I was such a brat.' Liv makes a face at the memory.

'She really was,' Gracie says, eyes narrowed. 'I'm actually ashamed of her.'

'I'm so sorry. Again. For everything,' Liv says, not adding, although she should, that she has other things to apologise for as well.

Meredith shakes her head. 'Your dad was furious with me about that fire. Did he ever tell you what he did?' she asks and Liv shakes her head. 'He put all the half-burnt letters in a plastic bag and left them outside our house with a leaflet about bushfire safety.'

'What?'

'It worked. Ever since then, I've been very responsible about fires,' Meredith says wryly. Gracie and Liv exchange a look, which Meredith catches. 'What is it?' she asks, looking from Liv to Gracie.

'Do you remember what you did with those letters – the burnt ones?' Gracie asks.

Meredith thinks for a moment and then understanding spreads across her features.

'Oh god, I think I gave them back to you, didn't I?' she says to Liv who just smiles.

'You put them in a chocolate box,' Gracie says. 'Such a brilliant gothic touch. The perfect response to a bully.'

But Meredith just shakes her head while Liv lets out an embarrassed laugh.

'Your generation was so messed up,' Gracie says.

Later, when Andy calls to say he is on his way with the coffee and pastries Liv asked him to get, she looks at her daughter and sister and says, 'Shall we meet him down at the park?'

Gracie is with Sophie by the water, encouraging her to have a swim by throwing endless sticks she ignores. Andy stands next to her, drinking his coffee while Liv and Meredith are sitting on a nearby bench.

'Why did you come back now?' Liv asks.

'Dad died two years ago and then last winter, I found out Pete had Alzheimer's from that newspaper report. Dad and I stayed close after I left Sydney but I only visited him a couple of times a year. We spoke on the phone most weeks, but I'll always regret not making more of an effort to be with him in the last few years of his life.'

'I'm sorry,' Liv offers.

Meredith takes a sip of her coffee. 'There was so much I wanted to ask him. About himself, about Mum. I did try but he found it very difficult to talk about her and I didn't want to force it. He never recovered from her dying so young and whenever I brought her up, he would get upset. When he died, I knew I didn't want to waste any time and that I needed to find a way to talk to Pete and your mum.' She glances at Liv. 'I don't want any formal recognition. I don't need any big reunion – the long-lost daughter. None of that. I'd just like to meet him as an adult and, I don't know, have a cup of tea with them.'

'I think they'd like that,' Liv says quietly.

'More than anything though, I'd like to talk to them about my mum. I've got so many questions. So many things I'd like to know. I know Angela's not been well either, but do you think she might be able to tell me a little bit about her? I'd love to hear anything she can remember. Even the tiniest thing.'

Meredith looks so hopeful that Liv can't bring herself to explain the reality of the situation with Angela so instead she nods. They'll figure out a way, Liv will make sure of it.

Chapter 60

LIV

Sunday, 4 May 2025

The barbecue takes place on the first weekend of May. It is autumn but you wouldn't know it with the daytime temperatures still hovering in the mid-twenties. But at least this afternoon there is a light breeze that ripples across Andy and Liv's garden, even though this occasionally causes smoke from the barbecuing sausages to billow around alarmingly. None of the guests seem to mind, everyone is just happy to be here. Happy to celebrate Andy and Pete's documentary.

This rough cut is only thirty-five minutes long – more of an extended trailer or introduction than a full-length film.

'Any longer and everyone will fall asleep,' Andy had said earlier.

As it is, when the clip ends, there is a round of applause that's truly enthusiastic rather than just polite. There are pats on the back for Andy and a cheer for Pete, who gives a small but pleased wave of acknowledgement from his seat, and then another for Angela, who does as she always seems to now: smile beatifically without saying anything or giving any indication that she understands what's going on.

'It's obviously really early days,' her husband says when the chatter dies down. 'And there are many more aspects of Pete and Angela's incredible life and work to cover in the full film. But I hope this has given you a glimpse of one of our country's finest and most important filmmaking duos.'

He raises his flute of champagne towards his parents-in-law.

'The most important thing for me to say today is thank you, to my father-in-law, Pete, and my mother-in-law, Angela. Thanks to you both. For the legacy of your careers, for the wonderful films you made, for letting me help tell the story of your lives and taking a chance on a very, very inexperienced would-be filmmaker.' There is a ripple of laughter and Andy gives an embarrassed nod of acknowledgement, before gathering himself. 'To Pete and Angela,' he says, looking at them both. 'Thank you for trusting me with your memories.'

'To Pete and Angela,' the rest of the party-goers agree in unison.

Meredith is sitting next to Angela, holding a paper plate in between them. It is covered with the tiny cakes Liv had Paco make especially and Angela is steadily making her way through a selection of them. Her sweet tooth is as strong as ever and Liv is taking that as a good sign despite Angela losing a significant amount of weight since her stroke.

'How are you two going?' Liv asks as she sits down next to Meredith.

Angela takes a tiny chocolate tartlet from the plate with her good hand and deposits it quickly into her mouth as if Liv is about to snatch it from her.

'Very good, thank you,' Meredith replies. 'I think we've decided all these cakes are equally delicious but my absolute favourite is the lemon tart.' She raises her eyebrows at Angela. 'And Angela's is the berry mousse?'

Angela doesn't respond, just chews silently, and Liv feels a tug of sadness. Angela suffered another mild TIA a few days before and is now having difficulty with her balance and any small communication gains she'd been making seem to have been lost.

'The film looks amazing. You must be so proud.'

Liv nods. 'Very. We all are, aren't we, Mum?'

Angela doesn't respond, just continues to chew. Liv can see her mum is less able to understand what is going on around her than before, but as everyone keeps saying – she, Meredith, Gracie and Andy – that despite this she seems content. Perhaps even happier than usual. Much of this, Liv suspects, is down to Meredith.

In the past few weeks Meredith and Liv have fallen into an easy rhythm of keeping a joint eye on Pete and Angela when their carers aren't there or even when they are. Along with Andy and Gracie, they make sure one of them visits daily. They keep encouraging Angela to do her verbal and tongue exercises although, privately, Liv thinks it's pointless. Meredith in particular is painstaking about Angela's rehab and the pair seem to really enjoy their sessions. Although Pete is her biological father, Meredith's connection to Angela is far stronger and they truly enjoy each other's company.

Meredith was hesitant at first, asking Angela about Zara. She was conscious that it might upset her or bring back bad memories, but on the contrary, Angela seems to love answering questions about her old friend. They occasionally use the text-to-speech app on the iPad although that seems to tire Angela out more quickly these days so often Meredith resorts to simpler methods. She'll ask a question and Angela will respond accordingly. One squeeze for yes, Zara loved the beach, and two squeezes for no, Zara did not like shopping unlike Angela. Simple answers but they are painting an increasingly clear picture of Zara, and Liv can see how much that means to Meredith.

At any other time in Liv's life, this relationship between Angela and Meredith might have made her feel a little envious, but now it feels like a gift. That her mum can, at this point in her life, have and enjoy a new friendship or whatever you call this relationship with the long-lost daughter of her husband, when she is unable to do much more than share smiles and nods and eye contact and hand squeezes, is a happy and welcome surprise to treasure.

Meredith and Pete's relationship is a little harder to gauge. Meredith made it firmly, but kindly, clear to Liv that she isn't looking for another father. Pete understands who Meredith is and appears quietly pleased to have his long-lost daughter in his life but doesn't say much about it. Mercifully, he doesn't get confused and mistake her for Zara, not yet at least.

At first Liv had wondered if Meredith had residual anger towards Pete but now she wonders if Meredith's slight stand-offishness towards Pete is her way of showing loyalty towards Stephen.

'How does Sandra seem to you?' Meredith asks, when the crowd of people around them has begun to spread out. 'Have you spoken to her today?'

'Did you see the piece today in the *Daily News*?' Liv makes a face. 'Brutal.'

'Brutal but truthful. Celebrity surgeons have been getting away with poor patient care for too long. Richard was a talented surgeon but he was sloppy.' Meredith offers the last cake, a small butter-scotch tart topped with a round marshmallow dome, to Angela who takes it and pops it into her mouth with relish. 'Do you think she'll really sell up and move down the coast?'

'I think I would if I were her.'

Gracie appears in front of them, proffering a bottle of champagne. Liv holds up a glass for a refill but Meredith shakes her head.

'You okay?' Liv asks as Gracie fills her glass. She is still tiptoeing lightly around her daughter, conscious of all Gracie's been through.

'Great,' Gracie says brightly. 'You guys good?'

'We are,' Meredith replies, then, glancing at Liv, says, 'We're great.'

Liv watches as Gracie crouches down so she's on the same level as Angela and only half listens as her daughter begins to talk about an old friend of Pete and Angela's who just told Gracie a very funny, very rude story about Sam Neill. Angela's smile grows wider and Gracie's hand reaches out to Angela's knee as she recounts it and Liv gets a flash of her daughter's new tattoo.

She thinks back to this morning when they both presented themselves in front of Liv, Gracie excitable and giggling, Meredith more muted but smiling, a little guiltily.

'Look what we did,' Gracie said, proffering the underside of her arm.

It was a simple black tattoo covered with some kind of protective plastic but Liv could see it was a sort of pleasing geometric squiggle. Not too big, thank goodness.

'It's a symbol of family. A never-ending cycle. Meredith got one on her stomach.'

'More easy to cover up for work,' Meredith says, briefly lifting the side of her shirt to show off hers.

'Oh wow. Very pretty,' Liv said, and then seeing the slight awkwardness on Meredith's face, added, 'Maybe I should get one.'

'I thought you said you'd never get a tattoo in a million years,' Gracie said.

Liv shrugged. 'I don't know. Now I've seen yours I've kind of got fomo.'

Gracie cringed. 'Don't say that.'

'Hey, be nice to your mother,' Meredith joked, then, glancing at Liv, said, 'If you decide you want one, I'll go with you. Maybe I'll get a second.'

'Oh god, I said you'd get addicted,' Gracie said. 'It's literally impossible to just have one tattoo.'

'No more, Gracie, please, no more,' Liv said, half-joking, half-pleading. 'If I get one you've got to promise me, no more for you. Okay?'

They all laughed and Gracie began talking about a

complicated-sounding colour one she really wanted on her back and then Andy appeared in the doorway and he began telling them the longwinded story about his own failed attempt at having a tattoo.

'Yeah, we know, Dad. You fainted and as a result you've only got one tiny dot on your arm where an actual tattoo should be.'

Andy had grinned, already pushing up the sleeve of his T-shirt and beckoning to Meredith to come and look.

Liv thinks about how she has noticed a change in Gracie over the past few weeks. A shifting in the way they interact, in how Gracie seems different, seems older and more assured and spends less time at home. Gracie often disables her location from their shared tracking app and Liv is trying to accept that her daughter wants a little more privacy, but it does bother her, not being able to keep an eye on her daughter's movements.

Andy keeps telling her it is normal. It is right. Neither of them had their parents watching their movements when they were nineteen, he reminds her.

'Not so long ago, Gracie was too anxious to go out on her own. Now look at her,' he said the other night and Liv had nodded and agreed and made all the right noises.

And she is trying to be more relaxed. Really she is. She's even being relaxed about the fact that her sister and Gracie appear to have become surprisingly close.

Sister.

Liv keeps rolling the word around in her mouth, trying to make it fit.

She hasn't found herself able to say the word out loud just yet. It still feels a little unnatural. A bit odd. But it won't be long now before it slips out, and that's good. It'll happen when the time is right.

Similarly, she will tell Andy about her meeting with Martin Finch the morning of his death when the time is right.

She looks at Meredith and sees that her sister is glancing at her quizzically.

Okay? she mouths and Liv nods, aware her throat is suddenly dry and her vision blurry.

Meredith smiles and then turns back to Angela and Gracie, her expression a little shy now.

Chapter 61

LIV

Sunday, 4 May 2025

Liv finds Sandra sitting on the bench on the front veranda. She has a glass of wine in her hand and is wearing large sunglasses and a straw hat and Liv realises she's probably wearing both to disguise herself in case there are any photographers lurking nearby.

'Sandra,' Liv says from the doorway. 'Are you okay?'

Sandra gives a jolt as she turns and sees Liv. She gives a limp smile. 'Sorry, Liv. I'm not much good at parties. But that film was wonderful. Andy's very clever. You must be so proud.'

There is a loud crash from down the corridor, a plate or pan being dropped, and both women give a start and then acknowledge each other's reaction with wry smiles.

They are still jumpy and on edge. Liv still half expects to see the police on her doorstep most mornings, announcing that it's all been a big mistake and how they now know Martin Finch had nothing to do with Richard's death. And that fingerprints have been found inside and outside his home that could suggest foul play was involved with Martin's death, too.

'Richard would have loved this party,' Sandra says after a while. 'Stupid old fool.'

Liv smiles. 'You know, it's okay to miss him.'

Sandra gives a stiff nod and takes a sip of her wine.

'I spent so many years wishing that he'd just leave me, wishing that he'd make a decision for both of us and set us both free. And now he's gone ... I don't know what's wrong with me. Ever since the funeral I've just felt so ... adrift.'

'I think that's probably very normal.'

'Should we have told the truth to the police?' Sandra says after a while.

'No, definitely not,' Liv says, firmly. 'If you told the police what really happened, Meredith and Gracie would have been implicated too. What you all decided on was the right thing. The best thing. For everyone.'

But Liv can see it in Sandra's eyes. She's not convinced and Liv suspects she will be spending a lot of time in the coming weeks and months, if not years, convincing her neighbour they did the right thing. Convincing her to remain silent.

'You were very close to figuring it all out, weren't you?' Sandra glances at Liv. 'Clever you.'

'Well, I was just trying my best to figure out a way to keep Gracie safe, that's all.'

Sandra nods. 'Meredith and I worked hard to predict the police investigation. To keep ahead of it all and keep ourselves and Gracie safe from suspicion. But we didn't count on having our very own Miss Marple living on the street.'

Liv laughs. 'Well, it all worked out in the end.' She crouches down and rests her hand on the other woman's linen-clad leg. 'It's time to think about your future, Sandra. It's time to start planning what happens next.'

The other woman lets out a long exhale and Liv follows her gaze, which she sees is now almost steely, through the front garden and across the road to her house.

336

'You're finally free and now you get to do whatever you want with your life.'

Sandra gives the briefest of nods. 'I suppose I just need to work out what that is,' she says.

Chapter 62

MEREDITH

Thursday, 30 January 2025

Doctors in Australia don't pledge the Hippocratic oath anymore, although at Meredith's graduation they did a version of it. As she stood with her peers, they promised to do no harm and to put the interests of their patients first. And ensuring patient safety and good outcomes wherever possible has been at the centre of all the work Meredith has done since graduating nearly twenty-five years ago.

So when Meredith got to the top of the street that ran parallel to the Gully and was about to walk past the entrance to the old fire trail Sandra had pointed out to her, she stopped in her tracks. She knew immediately that she'd done the wrong thing. She needed to go back and check Richard was okay.

But for the first time in Meredith's life, when she got there and saw Richard suffer what she assumed at the time to be a catastrophic bleed – a hematoma caused by the rock Sandra had hit him with – she didn't do anything.

She didn't move. She didn't rush into the shallow water to help him, to pull him out and attempt resuscitation.

She did not rush to ensure the possibility of a good outcome.

Richard had been kneeling in the shallows of the water when she returned to him, a defeated, bewildered expression on his face.

'Meredith, help me,' Richard had said through ragged breaths when he saw her. 'Please.'

'What happened? Can't you get out?'

He had gestured around him, to the murky water. 'I nearly drowned. I was in the deep bit and I'm pretty sure I've got a fractured Lateral malleolus.' He winced. 'Rolled it when I was reaching for my phone, stumbled and … just please help. I can't move anymore. I can't get up.'

'I'll go and get help. We need to get you to the hospital.'

'Gracie's here,' he said as she began to walk. 'She went off to get a branch to help pull me out but I pulled myself from the mud and now I can't go any further. Please, don't go – pull me up.'

'Gracie's here?'

'You might have to dig around my feet, they're wedged in again. This mud is incredible. It's like quicksand.'

She looked at him briefly. 'Just let me call for help. I don't think I can pull you out without hurting you more. You're in the shallows; you're safe. Just – just hang in there. I'll get some help.'

'Don't leave me,' he snapped. Then seeing her expression he said in a more circumspect tone, 'Sorry! Sorry. Please, Meredith. Come down here. Please.'

She looked down at him and then sighed and crouched down to undo her shoes. 'Hang on. Let me take my shoes off.'

Meredith had pointedly taken her time pulling off both shoes and then her socks, slowly balling them and placing them into her trainers. Then she scanned the clearing in case there was a stick or something she could use to help dig out Richard's feet from the mud. Finally spotting one that was about the length of a ruler, she retrieved it and only then, turned back to the water.

It took a few moments for her to realise what she was looking at.

Richard's head was face-down, half in the shallows, half in the mud, his arms out at his side in some kind of grotesque parody of a bow.

'Richard, you okay?' she called out.

No response and she repeated herself, which was pointless as it was now obvious to her that he was dead.

Later, Meredith told herself that she only hesitated for a few seconds before wading into the water but really it was probably many more.

Ten, twelve, maybe fifteen, twenty at the most?

Too many. Five is too many. Twenty, an appalling number.

Far too many for a doctor when a person is dying, or has just died.

Then she finally moved, stumbling down the creek bank and feeling her bare feet sink into the thick, soft mud and the surprisingly warm water, her fingers sinking into the soft, oozing mud. All those seconds before she gently lifted Richard's head and saw his eyes were wide open, his mouth gaping, and she fumbled for the pulse she knew wouldn't be there.

Too many seconds.

But forgiving herself would have to wait. For now she had other things to do.

Chapter 63

SANDRA

Sunday, 15 June 2025

Sandra didn't make a habit of going into her husband's study and looking through his paperwork. But in April 2024, she'd noticed a marked change in him and was curious as to what was going on.

Richard had always suffered from migraines, but they'd been getting worse over the previous few months. He'd been more distracted and bad-tempered than usual and was sleeping so badly he'd suggested separate bedrooms. Sandra suspected they'd never go back to sharing one again and, privately, this didn't bother her too much.

But something, she decided, was definitely going on. Perhaps to do with that legal case his solicitors were now advising him to settle.

It turned out to be something else entirely.

The letter sat at the top of the pile on his desk among the bills and bank statements. It came from the offices of Professor Jonathan Ackerman, a neurologist Sandra recalled was an old friend and colleague of Richard's.

She skimmed the letter quickly, taking in the words, *chronic migraine thought to be caused by high blood pressure ... unruptured intracranial aneurysm ... confirmed by cerebral imaging.*

Then she started again, from the beginning, reading more slowly this time, taking in the words and digesting the Professor's advice – *surgical options are not advised at this stage. A 3mm aneurysm ... Lifestyle changes should be immediately implemented and Dr Wellington is strongly advised not to smoke, take recreational drugs or drink alcohol ... he has to take steps to control his blood pressure, eat a healthy diet and do only gentle exercise and avoid stress.*

It all sounded rather serious.

Over the coming days, Sandra became an expert on brain aneurysms and began to keep a close eye on Richard. His behaviour, as far as she could see, hadn't changed. He still drank most days, had the occasional cigarette and his high colour suggested he probably hadn't taken his neurologist's advice on starting medication to reduce his blood pressure. So far it was typical, arrogant Richard to ignore the advice of other doctors.

A few weeks later, Sandra considered raising the topic with her husband; perhaps coming clean about how she had seen the letter in his study. But something always stopped her. A sharp word from him that made her baulk. An unkind comment in front of friends at a dinner party. A dismissive wave of his hand when Sandra moved to offer him some salad.

The small voice inside her which she'd always done a good job of ignoring, or at least quelling, became a little more insistent around this time. Probably not helped by the legal case.

Sandra had always been very interested in medical malpractice cases, probably because having lived with a medic for so many years she'd always been concerned about Richard being sued.

His private patients were demanding and had very deep pockets. Not a good combination. She worried endlessly about one of them complaining and causing him to face a disciplinary hearing, losing his registration or, worse, being forced to pay huge sums of compensation if the insurance companies found a loophole that meant Richard was personally liable.

She was always astounded – as a lay person – that he hadn't been sued more often because of this, but in their decades together, Richard had only faced two serious complaints from his spoilt, rich private patients. And both had been settled confidentially between the parties' legal representatives.

But the Martin Finch case was different. Maria Finch wasn't like his usual patients and, of course, she had died.

Sandra had read the hundreds of pages of submissions and could see that Richard had possibly been negligent in some ways and, if worst came to worst, would be lucky to walk away from the case with his medical licence intact. She lay in bed at night imagining they might lose the house. Lose Richard's healthy bank balance. Lose the garage and her ability to rescue the animals. Lose her whole life.

But as the weeks ticked by, and Richard's stress levels rose, so did his unpleasantness. The occasional slap became a regular, almost weekly occurrence and unlike with previous times, the aftermath was rarely filled with regret and profuse apologies.

Sandra found herself becoming less and less concerned that Richard had an aneurysm ticking away under his skull. When she saw that his consumption of all the things that he was meant to avoid was increasing rather than reducing, she also found she didn't much care.

By the end of the year, Sandra had started to add cigarettes and several bottles of whiskey, Richard's favourite tipple, to her weekly shop. She added a little more salt than usual to their home-cooked meals.

It was nothing too terrible and she didn't imagine any of these things would cause him much harm in the scheme of things. Richard was doing enough damage to himself, with every glass of booze he threw back, every cigarette he smoked out in their garden, every snort of cocaine she supposed he indulged in whenever he had a late night out with his ghastly friends.

She would have left it at that except for what happened on Christmas Eve when she witnessed Richard's fumbling and embarrassing attempt at chatting up Gracie.

After that, she knew she'd finally hit a wall.

She'd put up with Richard's affair with Eve; his flirtations with other women over the years; how he'd even occasionally bring them home like the one she'd seen him kissing outside their house a few months back before sending the stupid woman off in a taxi. There were the occasional blind items in the social pages about his inappropriate behaviour and then, just recently, his infatuation with Meredith Edwards who was – how the stupid idiot couldn't even see – a lesbian. Now Richard was apparently unable to stop himself from pestering their teenage neighbour.

It was mortifying and it had to stop.

Sandra had already laid much of the groundwork, befriending Meredith, and then slowly, carefully, revealing what Richard was like to the other woman. His dreadful behaviour over the years, the coercion and abuse.

She had exaggerated only a little where necessary – Richard had never, thank goodness, had a child with her sister for example and Sandra had never birthed a baby, although she'd miscarried several times.

Sandra worried she was over-egging it, but it worked out well in the end.

The other woman, who was easily persuaded, had reacted just as Sandra had hoped.

Sandra had wondered if tapping on Gracie's window was taking things too far. Sandra could have quite easily been caught out and if she had, how on earth would she have explained that away? Tapping on the outside of a teenager's bedroom in the middle of the night? Crooning at her in that ridiculous attempt at sounding like Richard.

But it had been a master stroke in the end.

Then when Sandra had explained how she believed Richard's new year's resolution to get fit was actually a way for him to stalk Gracie at the Gully park, she had seen Meredith's alarm. The cogs had been set in motion.

It helped that Richard was so predictable. Of course he would take up vigorous exercise when he should be taking it easy; of course he'd try and talk to Gracie at some point. Of course he would frighten her.

He wasn't half as charming as he liked to think he was.

Sandra and Meredith would be there to rescue Gracie. One of them would have to hit Richard on the head to stop him from attacking the young, vulnerable girl. That would do it, surely. Bang. The aneurysm would go pop.

Except it didn't quite go according to plan.

Sandra would have much preferred Meredith to have been the person who thumped Richard, although in the end it didn't matter. She got the job done, in a roundabout way.

It took a while for everything to fall into place. Sandra imagined at one point that they would have to come clean about what had happened when it looked as though first Meredith, then Gracie might be implicated. But then, like a small miracle, Martin Finch had appeared stage left and saved the day, thanks to Liv's sleuthing and abundance of imagination.

Sandra couldn't believe her luck. Their luck, really.

Of course Sandra feels sadness that Martin was never able to find peace in this life, but she finds comfort in knowing he would have approved of what she has done. And understood her reasons for doing it.

Because, ultimately, he saved them. By sacrificing himself, by 'killing himself', he saved Gracie, Meredith and Sandra. And by hastening both Martin and Richard's departures from this life, Sandra likes to think she not only saved Martin from the burden of grief but also avenged the death of his wife, Maria.

It all tied up quite neatly in the end.

And now, as she sits on the deck, as the last of the day's sun slips below the paper gum tree at the bottom of the garden, Sandra feels a sense of calm settle over her that she hasn't felt in years.

She smiles at her three friends. Her three neighbours and co-conspirators, Liv, Meredith and Gracie.

'I brought you here today, because I wanted to thank you all so much for what you've done.' She allows an edge of hesitation to creep into her voice. 'I honestly don't know how I would have got through the past few months without you.'

Her gaze travels to the women, lingering a few moments at each.

'Thank you for looking after me and thank you for all you've done. Keeping this secret among us isn't easy, I know that. But the fact that you've done so, without question, means the world to me.'

Sandra feels a stirring of emotion deep in the pit of her stomach as she looks at Liv and reaches out to take her friend's hand.

'I never imagined I'd survive on my own, but you have helped me realise that I can. And that life without Richard might be a blessing.'

She blinks and then Gracie, sensing the moment has come, lifts her glass of champagne in toast.

'To four strong women,' Gracie says, smiling.

'To strong women,' Liv agrees and Sandra sees the other women's eyes are watery.

Meredith gently taps her glass against Sandra's and the others do the same. 'To neighbours who become friends and family,' she adds.

Sandra gives a small shiver, not from the slight cooling in the air which has become more present now it is officially winter, but because she realises she is in possession of something she never imagined she'd have.

Freedom and absolution.

This time her smile is broad as she raises her glass a little higher.

'To friends and family keeping each other safe.'

Acknowledgements

The setting for the Gully in this novel is a fictionalised reimagining of Flat Rock Gully which leads from Tunks Park in Sydney's Middle Harbour, near where I live. It's a special and beautiful place and, as for the characters in this book, it's somewhere I regularly visit for walks and picnics and bench sitting and daydreaming out across the water.

It is also the unceded home of the original custodians of the land on which this book was written, the Cammeraygal people, who I would like to acknowledge and honour.

Thank you so much to team HQ. To Georgina Green, for acquiring The Neighbours and all your enthusiasm and patience with my endless questions. Sophia Allistone, Sarah Bauer, Lou Nyuar, Georgia Hester and Emily Scorer – it's so exciting to be working with you.

To Sue Brockhoff, Jo Munroe, Stuart Henshall and Francesca Roberts-Thomson in Australia – you've made me feel so at home across the road. Louisa Maggio, for the beautiful cover and the swimming pool – I'll never have one in real life so this is the next best thing.

Thank you also to Eloise Plant, Karen-Maree Griffiths, Robyn Fritchley, Katrina Batten, Karen Ferns and Sandra Noakes for your hard work.

Thank you to my agent Nicky Lovick at WGM Atlantic for all your hard work and patience with my writerly neurosis.

To my gorgeous colleagues at team WD for all the fun and enduring my constant book chatter, especially Erin, Laura, Liv, Katherine and Wade and team real life: Brigid, Maisy and Harry.

To Liz, Jude, Susannah and all my friends who have listened patiently and encouragingly for the years and years I've been at this.

To my author pals who understand the delight and pain of writing and trying to get published, especially the Solitary Scribes and 2025 Debut Crew.

To my family above all else: Amelia and Ella – love you both so very much. Tiggy – favourite child? Who could say.

To Mum and Dad. Dad – you named me Emma Jane Wright because you thought it made an excellent by-line. Sorry I switched, but thank you for the writing genes. Mum – thank you for liter-ally everything and more.

And, to John-Paul. Because you've never once said, 'Do you think you should rethink this seemingly impossible ambition', or 'how about you get a better paying job than journalism/writing'. Instead, you gave me encouragement, support and love – since 1996, baby. Love you the most.

Dear Reader,

We hope you enjoyed reading this book. If you did, we'd be so appreciative if you left a review. It really helps us and the author to bring more books like this to you.

Here at HQ Digital we are dedicated to publishing fiction that will keep you turning the pages into the early hours. Don't want to miss a thing? To find out more about our books, promotions, discover exclusive content and enter competitions you can keep in touch in the following ways:

JOIN OUR COMMUNITY:
Sign up to our new email newsletter: http://smarturl.it/SignUpHQ
Read our new blog www.hqstories.co.uk

𝕏 https://twitter.com/HQStories
f www.facebook.com/HQStories

BUDDING WRITER?
We're also looking for authors to join the HQ Digital family!
Find out more here:

https://www.hqstories.co.uk/want-to-write-for-us/

Thanks for reading, from the HQ Digital team